... the critics ...

'An excellent page turner that positively hurtles along, brimming with menace and plot twists'
Daily Telegraph

'A brisk, event-filled fantasy'
Sci-Fi Online

'An impressive debut ... that brings magic, fantasy and science together'
The Big Issue

'Very well written and consistently gripping'
Carousel

'Exciting and pacy, but with a great deal of thought and thematic depth'
thebookbag.com

'An exciting read with lots of action'
Teen Titles

'Fast-paced inventive writing with original plot involving strange creatures and weird science, it's guaranteed to satisfy the hunger of voracious readers everywhere'
Julia Eccleshare, lovereading.com

'Older readers will be gripped by this gritty, urban, fantasy adventure'

D0599771

Also in this series . . .

1: *Twisted Symmetry*

2: *Strange Energy*

3: *Blood Alchemy*

4: *The Nonsuch King*

5: *A Crystal Horseman*

THE BAD TUESDAYS:

THE SPIRAL HORIZON

Benjamin J. Myers

Orion
Children's Books

First published in Great Britain in 2012
by Orion Children's Books
a division of the Orion Publishing Group Ltd
Orion House
5 Upper St Martin's Lane
London WC2H 9EA
An Hachette UK company

1 3 5 7 9 10 8 6 4 2

Copyright © Benjamin J. Myers 2012

The right of Benjamin J. Myers to be identified as the
author of this work has been asserted.

All rights reserved. No part of this publication may be
reproduced, stored in a retrieval system, or transmitted,
in any form or by any means, electronic, mechanical,
photocopying, recording or otherwise, without the prior
permission of Orion Children's Books.

A catalogue record for this book
is available from the British Library.

ISBN 978 1 84255 644 3

Typeset by Input Data Services Ltd
Bridgwater, Somerset

Printed in Great Britain by
Clays Ltd, St Ives plc

The Orion Publishing Group's policy is to use papers that
are natural, renewable and recyclable products made from
wood grown in sustainable forests. The logging and
manufacturing processes are expected to conform to
the environmental regulations of the country of origin.

To Juliet

PROLOGUE

Splinter is dead.

Chess held the words in her mind, turning them over, weighing each of them as she might have weighed stones in her palm: heavy, blank, cold as tombs.

Splinter is dead.

The winter wind flicked chestnut curls across her face. She brushed them away with the backs of her fingers before pushing her fists into the pockets of her leather jacket. Her brown eyes were wet from the raw air and she blinked tiny droplets of moisture from the thick lashes. Then she shut her eyes and felt the plunge of space from where her trainers were planted at the edge of the tower to the depths of the drains which twisted in dripping darkness through the roots of the city.

But the plunge was not only downwards. For Chess, space plunged forwards and backwards until it was lost in a vanishing point as distant as time, as distant as she could think. But however far she thought, however deep, no matter how she searched, Splinter was nowhere to be found. Chess didn't know where he was.

There was so much she didn't know, didn't understand. She knew that across the universes, war was raging; she knew that a roiling hatred was heading towards her world, her city; she knew that in a matter of days, maybe only hours, time itself would hang in the balance; and she knew that she could end everything as easily as thinking. That was what she was here for: that was how she had been made. And with their machines and warp technology, the enemy, the Twisted Symmetry, had filled every shred of her spirit with the dark energy they had reaped from aeons of pain and suffering. So Chess had seen all the pain, she had seen all the suffering, she had actually felt it. And now the Symmetry were waiting, waiting for her to explode, to use the Eternal to destroy everything, to destroy time itself and leave only them.

'No,' Chess whispered to a wind that snatched the words from her lips. She didn't want what the Symmetry wanted. But when the time came and the universes were in her grasp, Chess didn't know what she would do.

CHAPTER 1

The winter light of late afternoon died in the filthy glass of the dome. Only a pale glow leaked through, illuminating the concrete floor in dim patches. The thud of the girl's boots reverberated as she entered the gloomy entrance hall of the old bus depot. There was a stirring of bodies in the half light, the scrape of a wooden stick, a cough and then there were shapes in the murk. The shapes surfaced from the shadows like phantoms: phantoms that smelt of beer and sweat. The tramps guarded this part of the depot. They didn't challenge the girl with the jet black hair and the sapphire eyes because they knew her. They knew that she worked for the Committee, and they knew that she could wield the sword she carried in the bag across her back quicker than light.

'They're waiting for you, Anna,' drawled a bearded man in a greasy raincoat.

'They want my blood,' replied Anna. It was meant to sound lighthearted but her voice was swallowed by the gloom. The tramps remained silent as she crossed the barren chamber, eyes watching her all the way. Only once she had passed through the door on the far side of the entrance hall did they return to the deep shadows and their half-drunk bottles.

Anna entered a long, low-ceilinged room. It was almost the size of a car park and the grimy windows were caged in mesh. The last time Anna had been here, it had been set out partly as a hospital ward and partly as an old lady's parlour. Now it was packed with racks of weapons and chests of ammunition and crates stamped with the words 'EXPLOSIVE – HANDLE WITH CARE'. Men and women in combat uniform worked in silent busyness.

'Miss Ledward?'

Anna turned to face a uniformed man with a clipboard in his hands. She nodded. 'Looks like you guys mean business.' She was used to seeing guards inside the old bus depot which functioned as Committee Headquarters, but not this many and not with so much weaponry.

The guard chewed harder on his wedge of tobacco. 'The Twisted Symmetry are headed this way,' he said. 'We don't have long. We're expecting reinforcements.' He jerked his head towards the nearest rack of weapons. 'Reckon we can put up a good fight,' he said, proudly.

'I reckon you can,' agreed Anna, more enthusiastically than she felt. She knew the enemy better than any of the guards in here. She knew that it would take more than soldiers and gunfire to survive an onslaught by the Twisted Symmetry. But she knew that the man standing in front of her now didn't need to hear that.

'Are you ready? For the operation?' The guard shifted his stance, uncomfortably.

'Can't wait,' muttered Anna, with a stomach that felt as if a litre of glue had been poured into it.

'They asked me to check that you'd taken the pre-op medication they'd sent.'

'Yeah, I've taken it.' The medication had arrived a couple of days ago at the house in Mendoza Row where she'd been living: a parcel containing a syringe with instructions to inject the contents two hours before the operation.

Anna could still feel the sting inside her elbow where she had pushed the needle into her vein after tying a tourniquet around her upper arm. The injection had numbed her arm and then her whole body. But her heart was in the grip of a cat's claws at the thought of what was about to happen.

Anna cast her piercing gaze about the room, eyes bright beneath her sharp straight fringe. 'The Committee are meant to be the good guys but it's hard to believe it when I feel like this,' she muttered.

'Of course they're the good guys. And the Twisted Symmetry are the bad guys: they want all of us dead. They want *everyone* dead, apart from the Twisted Symmetry.'

'I know, I know,' sighed Anna. But she knew more about fighting the bad guys than the guard did, and she knew that the closer you got to the darkness, the closer the darkness got to you. Just look at Chess. Chess was only fourteen but she was the most powerful being in the universes. But that power had put her so close to the darkness that now she was fighting just to keep her grip on the light.

'The Committee know what they're doing,' the guard assured her. 'You'll be OK, miss.'

Yeah, thought Anna, just like *you'll* be OK when the

Symmetry show up. But she just smiled, straightening the ponytail into which she had fastened her long black hair.

'You'll make a great Blood Sentinel,' added the guard, as if that might make her feel better.

Blood Sentinel. Anna repeated the words to herself. The Committee's greatest warriors: humans whose blood was mixed with blood from the immortal warrior, Julius, his DNA grafted onto theirs, an echo of his power shared with them. That was why she was here: to undergo the operation that would turn her from human to Sentinel. Deep in the vaults of Committee HQ, the operating theatre was waiting for her. The glue in her stomach turned to lead.

The guard was still talking and Anna realized that he was looking about as if he were preparing to divulge a confidence. 'Me and the others have been placing bets on which of the Sentinels will kill the most enemy,' he whispered. 'The smart money's on you: assuming you survive the operation.'

'Great,' said Anna. 'That's really confidence-boosting. Thanks.'

He nodded sagely. 'You'd best go down now, miss. They're waiting to start,' and he spat a treacle-coloured jet of saliva into a nearby mug.

Anna followed the corridors and the stairs which led down, noting the extra patrols clunking along the subterranean passageways, their faces pale, muscles taut. And as she went deeper into the complex that had been cut out of the earth beneath the decrepit brickwork of the old bus depot, she felt the distance between where she was now and her old life stretch to vanishing point.

Ever since she had met Chess and been caught up in

the universal war between the Committee and the Twisted Symmetry, Anna had slipped further and further away from her real life, her family, her other friends. But she had discovered that she had been slipping into a place where she was meant to be, a place where she fitted perfectly: but it was a place of danger and violence, a place which had cut her off from her old life completely. And now, descending into this vault of damp stone, bare cables and flickering safety lights, Anna knew that she was about to slip out of her old life altogether. The final clash between the Committee and the Twisted Symmetry was about to erupt and when it did so, she would be fighting with the blood of immortals in her veins.

So long as her body survived the procedure. There were no guarantees.

That was why she had been sent the pre-op medication. There was always a risk when Julius's blood was mixed with a mortal's blood: a danger of system shock when mortal blood was exposed to eternity. The pre-op medication was designed to reduce this risk. But it could only *reduce* the risk. And it would do nothing about the pain.

Anna came to the door that led into the operating theatre. She didn't *want* to go through with this: she *had* to go through with this. She took a deep breath, pushed the door open and entered.

The chamber was illuminated by a harsh, white light which speared off steel cabinets and instruments. Under a bank of merciless spotlights, there were two operating tables. Between the tables there was a bank of monitors and consoles from which there trailed hundreds of tubes, narrow as wire.

'Hello, dear,' said an old lady in a tatty sage cardigan, a blouse that was waxy yellow, and an ill-fitting orange and white skirt. She sat on a high metal stool beside one of the operating tables, liver-spotted hands clenched between knobbly, ladder-stockinged knees.

'Hello, Ethel,' said Anna.

Ethel pushed her greasy, grey hair away from her smudged spectacle lenses. 'Have you injected?' she enquired. Anna nodded and Ethel clapped her hands as if with delight. 'Splendid!'

'As one of the brains behind the Committee and one of the most powerful beings in the universe,' observed Anna, 'you are very easily pleased.'

'As one of the brains behind the Committee and one of the most powerful beings in the universes,' observed Ethel, 'I have to be satisfied with whatever victories come my way, however *small*,' and she gave a long-suffering smile.

'There's nothing *small* about injections,' remarked Anna, looking across a steel table to one of the other two occupants of the room. 'Hello, Lemuel,' she said, noting how the person she called Lemuel was inspecting a scalpel so sharp its blade was like a gleam of light.

Wearing a black gown, high-collared and criss-crossed with fine silver hatching, Lemuel Sprazkin gave a courtly bow. 'Miss Ledward,' he crooned, slanting eyes smiling up at her sidelong. His chalk-white face was like a crescent moon, the curve of his long chin suggesting a reflection of the thin fin of a nose. The harsh spotlights were reflected in a perfect dazzle in the glass panel on the top of his bald head. A tiny aperture in the panel allowed a drill to be inserted into his brain as a means of controlling his behaviour.

Lemuel was a warp, one of the Twisted Symmetry's genetically engineered scientists. And he wasn't just *any* warp: he had once been the Symmetry's primary warp. But he had switched sides to the Committee years ago. The Committee had relied upon his technological knowledge for centuries, but Anna knew that he had to be handled with as much care as the boxes of explosive upstairs. He stood erect and blew Anna a kiss.

The third occupant of the room was Julius. His back was towards her and he had already removed his coat and shirt and had hung them over a chair in one corner of the chamber, together with his belt and machine pistols. His long yellow hair straggled loose over his shoulders and down his lean, strong back. His skin was almost as pale as Lemuel's.

'Ready?' he asked, turning towards her.

Anna shrugged. 'As much as I can be.' She knew Julius well enough not to be startled by his face, which was composed half of the same pale flesh as his body and half of silver metal as soft and contoured as the flesh itself. A red eye burnt in the flesh; an eye of icy blue in the silver. And his hands gleamed in the bright light, silver as his face, the metal merging with the skin of his forearms in tendon-thick strands. Even a demi-god needed repairing when he had battled against the Symmetry for as long as Julius had.

Anna un-slung the hockey bag in which she carried her sheathed sword and dropped it by a second chair. She began to undress, shaking off her loose leather jacket, pulling her shirt over her head. She and Julius moved mechanically.

Anna felt as if she was watching herself preparing for the operation.

'Your physical condition,' trilled Lemuel, in his high-pitched voice, 'is perfect.'

Ethel cast him a suspicious glance but Anna just muttered, 'I bet you say that to all the girls,' and she sat on the chair to kick off her boots. She preferred not to look towards the trolley at the head of one of the steel tables on which there was arranged a variety of needles, probes and scalpels: all gleaming, all perfect for slitting skin and paring muscle.

'Have you seen Chess?' asked Ethel.

'Not today,' replied Anna.

Ethel sighed. 'It's nearly time.'

Anna looked up as she pulled off the remaining boot. 'For?'

'For the end of time, my love.'

'You make it sound so ordinary,' commented Anna, standing, talking automatically whilst she tried to keep her eyes and mind off the way Lemuel was caressing his surgical instruments.

Ethel's scrawny shoulders rose and dropped. 'It is all too desperate to talk about in any other way.'

Anna noticed how Julius glanced darkly at Ethel, clenched his jaw but maintained his silence. It was evident that the Committee's commanders were not in perfect agreement about the situation, however desperate it was.

'When the time spiral reaches the fifth node, its final point,' continued Ethel, 'everything will depend on Chess. If she gives in to the Symmetry, everything is over.'

'And if she doesn't?' enquired Anna.

'Then the enemy will be in for a big surprise.' Ethel smiled, hopeful as a child. 'Only Chess will decide.'

Anna looked at Ethel as if she had just spoken with as much sense as a barking bullfrog. 'Are you joking? Chess is in such a state she can't even decide what to have for breakfast. How's she meant to decide what to do with the universe, Ethel?'

'*Universes*,' smiled the old lady.

Anna glared back, unable to hide her irritation at Ethel's smugness and angry at the way Ethel expected her friend to carry the fate of the universes when Anna knew how Chess's spirit was breaking under the burden.

'Mevrad chooses uncertainty,' murmured Julius.

Ethel's other name reminded Anna that there was a lot more to the old lady than met the eye, but she continued to regard her hotly.

'I want to defeat the Symmetry, Julius. *Forever*,' snapped Ethel.

Julius was holding out a sheathed sword, a Samurai sword like Anna's but longer and broader. 'I prefer certainty,' he stated, his smooth, deep voice calm but hard. 'Tonight the Symmetry will attack this city, as they will launch their final attack across the universes. Whilst Mevrad waits to see what Chess will do, *we* will fight to protect the city, to protect its people. *That* is certain.'

Ethel pursed her thin lips but said nothing.

'By "we", you mean the Blood Sentinels?' Anna hesitated, on the brink of taking the sword from Julius, last of the race of heroes: the last of the Nephilim.

'It is what we are here for, Anna.' He nodded and thrust the sheathed sword towards her.

Anna took hold of the smooth, curved scabbard and as she did so, Julius clasped her forearm and his eyes blazed into hers. In that moment her mind filled with a vision of fire, and the clash of blades and the roar of creatures: huge, obese, sweating pus and wielding rough-bladed axes.

Julius released Anna from his gaze and his grip, and her mind cleared. 'The Plague Breed is coming to the city,' he said. 'And tonight, we will stop them.'

Anna weighed the weapon in her hand. 'What kind of sword is this?'

'A Muspell blade,' replied Julius. 'Phosphorous coated. It burns. Fire is the most effective means of destroying plague beasts.' He nodded towards the sword. 'You will need it tonight.'

'I won't go out without it,' she promised and she propped the sword against the chair she'd been using. Then she removed the rest of her clothes and, naked, slipped beneath the thin sheet that was draped over one of the tables. Julius did the same.

Lying on the cold steel like this, the room seemed to press down upon her. She could feel the throb of her pulse in her neck and she realized that her breathing was so shallow she hardly seemed to be drawing breath at all.

Slow down. Control. That was what she had been taught.

Anna breathed deeply, slowly, sought to steady her thumping heart. It wasn't easy. She had faced danger many times, was quickened by its electric touch, but that had been when she was fighting, when her life had been in her own hands. Now, her body was in someone else's hands and even the light in here seemed sharp enough to cut. Without raising her head, she watched Lemuel as he moved between the operating tables with balletic grace. When he came close she looked upwards, preferring not to watch how his fingers worked with the fine tubes, inserting them into her right arm and her body, working them beneath the skin so that they tickled and then stung.

'Your right hand, it's silver,' said Anna, hoarsely, noticing the shining skin for the first time, wanting to take her mind off what was about to happen.

'I cut the original off to make a trap,' he tittered, and then, bending down so that his dark lips brushed her cheek, he added, 'It's a long story.'

'We don't have long, Lemuel,' warned Julius from where he lay on the adjacent table, tubes already strung between his arm and body and the central units. 'We have work to do.'

'Time to start, time to start,' twittered Lemuel. 'Nothing needs so much time as an immortal in a hurry. But we mustn't rush, Julius, we mustn't rush.' His smile peeled up to his slanting eyes. 'We mustn't make this even *more* dangerous than it already is.'

'Thanks for that,' muttered Anna, closing her blue eyes tight as if that might relieve the dull pains in her arm and side. When she next opened them, Lemuel was out of sight but she sensed him close by. He was moving about the little trolley that was positioned inches above her head: the trolley that carried the instruments. There was the shearing scrape of metal blades as Lemuel selected the tool he required.

How much would this hurt?

A needle came into view, a long needle, longer than any Anna had ever seen. Lemuel walked around the table and took hold of her right arm.

'Don't wiggle,' he giggled as he pressed the tip of the needle into Anna's wrist. Delicately, he rotated the needle between the metal fingers of his right hand and pushed: pushed until half its length had vanished into the girl's forearm. Anna closed her eyes and breathed in deeply through her nose.

'Just making sure we have everything where it should be,' whispered Lemuel, still manipulating the needle minutely. 'We don't want anything coming unstuck. We need the interface in exactly the right cells. It's no good ending up with no more than an immortal fingernail,' he tittered, and he wiggled the fingers of his left hand, with their long, black nails. 'Imagine if you cracked it, or bit it off in a moment of anxiety? We need an immortal *you*, from fingers to toes and every bit in between.'

He closed his grey eyes and smiled a dreamy half-moon smile to himself, lips wine dark in his chalk-white face. His eyes opened and slid to Julius. 'The blood of the ancients, the last of the Nephilim, mixing with the blood of ... a child.' His voice was tremulous. The purple tip of his tongue wetted the corner of his mouth before vanishing back within.

'Lemuel,' cautioned Ethel, sternly, grimy spectacle lenses flashing a warning gleam of reflected surgical lights.

'Sixteen is hardly a child.' Anna spoke through clenched teeth, eyes still shut.

'Nearly seventeen,' added Ethel.

Lemuel let go of the needle and clasped his hands, the metal fingers of the right interweaving with the pallid skin of the left. 'But still, so young, so strong. Such ... blood.'

'Lemuel,' warned Ethel.

'It is not as rare as Chess's, not as deliriously *irresistible*,' he continued to rhapsodize, shivering as he looked down at Anna, 'but nevertheless, it is *delicious*.'

'Lemuel!' snapped Ethel.

'Could you remove *this*?' enquired Anna, gritting her teeth and directing her glare at the needle protruding from her wrist. But she reserved some of her glare for Lemuel Sprazkin. Chess might have understood how Lemuel struggled with the appetites he had been created with, but *she* didn't. She knew that without Lemuel's cunning mind, none of them could have come this far against the Symmetry. But she knew also that it was his slippery, cunning brain that made him unpredictable: that made him dangerous.

'Please, Anna,' complained Lemuel, 'don't look at me like that.' His voice was intense as the sting of the needle. 'I might have been the Symmetry's primary warp, but these days I try only to do *good* science.'

He took hold of the needle and Anna tried not to wince as he plucked it free. Then Lemuel waltzed across to the central console where he flicked a series of switches. The room darkened to a lunar luminescence and inside her flesh, Anna felt the wire-tubes stirring like threadworms.

'It's dark,' complained Ethel, snatching off her spectacles, spitting on the lenses, rubbing them on the cuff of her sage cardigan and shoving them back into place.

'You have no artistry, Mevrad,' accused Lemuel. He shut

his eyes and heaved in a breath, high nostrils aquiver. 'Blood is my art, and an art such as this requires a sense of moment: the sanctity of the moment is the very pulse, and at my *will*, time is compressed into a moment.' He flicked the needle in an arc, conducting his own symphonic proclamations. 'I can change the beat of time in the flash of an eye.'

Lemuel's fingers fluttered down to a small console and he placed them there as if he was about to play a piano. 'Evolution,' he announced, 'is for molluscs. Only *I* can create gods.'

'*Demi-gods*,' Anna heard Ethel mutter, but plainly Lemuel was too transported by his own genius to register the correction. He raised a long, black-nailed finger high and then struck a button on the unit.

Anna was aware of the cascade of tubes flushing crimson as blood began to pump from Julius's body into hers. She braced herself for pain. But there was no pain, at first, and she let out a thin hiss of breath. *Then* the pain struck and it was hot as white coals, searing through her, blinding her. She clenched her teeth to stop herself from crying out, but she couldn't stop her body from stiffening and her back from arching so abruptly that her head banged against the steel table top.

She heard Ethel gasp and hurry to her side.

Lemuel gasped too, but with pleasure. 'Poetry.'

Anna's tall, lithe body convulsed again, as if it wasn't her own.

'See how the blood of immortals burns,' she heard Lemuel say, voice husky with excitement.

'Lemuel?' Ethel's voice was tense.

Lemuel's flesh hand was cold as putty upon Anna's forehead. 'She is so human,' he whispered, almost tenderly. She heard his voice but with her eyes shut tight, she couldn't see the way he looked over her prone body at Ethel, eyes like darts. '*This* is why she will be strong. Immortal blood is nothing compared with the passion of humans.' She didn't like the way that his hand stoked the side of her face but there was nothing she could do about that. Then the pain drowned out the sensation in searing waves but Lemuel's voice remained as gentle as his touch. 'She has such passion. Such strength.'

And then, as her DNA bonded with Julius's, her mind began to flood with thoughts and sensations Anna had never encountered before. She felt space fall open around her like collapsing drapes and she sensed the sound and movement of bodies throughout Committee HQ as if they cast shadows into her mind, sensations that broke the normal rules of time and place, sensations that only immortal blood could divine. And she felt a new sensation accompany the pain: a strength in her limbs, a surge in her spasming heart, a feeling that she would burst out of her own body. The heat and the overwhelming explosion of sensation seemed to be burning her out of existence. As her mind finally disconnected her body from the impact of Julius's blood mixing with her own, Anna reached for the person who she carried in her spirit, as if that was the only place of safety. Her lips moved, silently repeating his name, before she passed into unconsciousness.

Lemuel lifted his ear from Anna's lips. 'Box, she says.' He smiled to Ethel, whose grey face had become more drawn and grey than usual.

'Box and Anna have become close,' said Ethel, resting a hand as wrinkled as wet chicken skin on the hot forehead of the unconscious girl. As she did so, she looked about the chamber as if distracted by something.

'And *you* separated them, Mevrad?' Lemuel shook his head and tutted. 'How mean.' He began to work at the switches on the consoles, a smile peeping from the corners of his lips.

Julius sat up suddenly and tugged the clutches of minute wires from his arm and side. Pin pricks of blood spotted the flesh in which they had been embedded. Ethel looked away as he began to pull his clothes back on. When she looked back, he was dressed and was buckling on his belt with its holstered machine pistols. Then he threw on his black leather trench coat and tugged his yellow hair free of the collar.

'If you are right, we need her tonight.' Not asking: telling.

'Of course I'm right. But will she be ready?' Ethel's wrinkled brow wrinkled even more deeply. 'So soon after the process?'

'The process is complete,' said Lemuel.

'She is needed,' stated Julius. 'She will have to be ready.' He pointed a silver finger at Ethel. 'You had better not be mistaken, Mevrad.'

At that, Ethel stood, her scruffy grey fringe inches from Julius's chest, and she folded her arms.

'I *ain't* mistaken.' Her voice grated like stone on stone. 'I know what's coming and I know where it's coming from. Tonight, the fighting will start.'

Julius paused to look down at Anna, and maybe his eyes

softened. 'My Sentinels fight so hard and live so short.' He laughed but it was a bitter laugh. 'You see the irony, Mevrad?' He looked up at the little old lady. 'We touch them with immortality and in so doing, we give them death.' He motioned to the sword that he had given Anna. 'She will need that. Make sure she takes it with her.'

Then he vanished.

Lemuel sniffed, as if seeking any last trace of Julius. 'Remarkable,' he observed. 'I never cease to be impressed by the science of it. There is so much that we cannot see.' He tittered to himself. 'I always remind myself before I go to bed: just because we don't see something, that doesn't mean it isn't there.'

He paused in plucking a wire from Anna's arm. 'What's the matter?'

Ethel frowned, head on one side like a sparrow. 'Something that we can't see,' she murmured. 'But something that's there all the same.' Then she shook her head and shivered. 'Somebody's been watching us, Lemuel. And I don't know who.'

CHAPTER 2

Chess jerked back as if Ethel's eyes had burnt her.

'She can sense me,' she said, closing the dimensions through which she had been watching the events in Committee HQ.

'Did she see you?' asked Balthazar Broom. Chess was standing and he sat beside her, cross-legged, in dinner jacket and trousers, with his heavy wooden staff over his lap.

Chess shook her head. 'I don't think so.' Night was falling over the city. Up on this high place where she liked to come when she wanted to look out across the metropolis, out through the dimensions, the winter wind was bitter.

'And was Anna all right?'

Chess sniffed. The cold air made her nose run. 'It looked bad, but she's sleeping now.' But she had hated watching her friend suffer. And she hated knowing that Anna had suffered like that because she *had* to become a Blood Sentinel. Because she *had* to fight for the Committee. Because that was what she was there for.

'If I had my way,' said Chess, huskily, 'people wouldn't

have to do things just because the universes decide that they have to.'

Her fingers felt the smooth features of the carved gaming piece she kept in her pocket: the horse's head she had found beneath the fireplace in the old flat in Knott Street, left by Ethel so many years ago for her to find. Her other hand slipped from her jacket and found Balthazar's shoulder, broad and solid, even though the swathes of silver through his once raven hair, and the grey embroidering his long plait and thick moustache, showed that time was catching up with five hundred years of living. Balthazar's large, olive-skinned hand found hers and patted it. His skin had been roughened by age but it was warm.

Chess released her breath slowly. Balthazar Broom, mathematician, philosopher and pugilist. Ethel may have called him a fool but he was kind.

'Trust no one,' was what Ethel always said.

But sometimes Ethel got things wrong. Ethel was wrong about Balthazar. Chess knew that she could trust Balthazar.

'It's nearly time,' said Chess, shaking a thick strand of chestnut hair away from her face.

'Time for time to end.' Balthazar's base voice tolled in the dreary wind of this high place.

Chess looked down, at the vertiginous spread of the city. From where they stood on the pinnacle of the deserted CREX tower in the north, to the heaving hulks of the factory sector in the south, there was a neon-studded, smoking, cliff-dense matrix of skyscrapers, highways and office blocks. There were precincts and parks like shreds of green baize beneath looping, thundering overpasses; there was the mouldering waste of the old city which the street rats called the Graveyard; there were the cascading hovels of the Pit; there were the wrecked remains of the wharf where she had once lived with Box and Splinter and their gang of street rats. And through it all there was the great, brown, lazy sweep of the river.

A billion pieces of sense data streamed through Chess and she processed it all: the stench of diesel, the blare of sirens, crowded streets, pickpockets, arguments, a kiss, a flower dropped.

Chess heard voices, caught shapes; sensed everything.

A pavement bursting with jacks. A man in a rush. A little girl holding his hand. The touch of fingers and the fingers slipping away as the little girl's attention was caught by the flash of a silver wrapper at the edge of the road.

And a man opening a packet of gum as he drove. The grime streaked bumper of his car. Travelling too fast.

'Far too fast,' murmured Chess.

The little girl; the speeding car. Coming closer. Just a fraction of the data that swarmed through Chess's mind as she opened it to the city. But there was more. Deep within the lights and the noises and the smells, something dark was creeping into the light.

'They are here, Balthazar. The enemy: the Symmetry. They are here, in the city.' She didn't have to look at Balthazar to know how fear and fascination would both struggle for mastery of his dark face. Once you had come close to the Twisted Symmetry it entered your spirit, changed you from the inside so that it never really left you, whatever you did. She *knew*; she felt the same as Balthazar, the same as Lemuel. And she knew that part of her belonged to the Symmetry because of her father, whoever he was: he had left her with a little piece of darkness that was all her own. Once you had come close, part of you belonged to the Symmetry forever.

Chess closed her eyes and let her mind probe the spaces of the city, its hidden dimensions. 'I can feel it, Balthazar. I can feel the enemy. And one of *them* is here.' Them: the Inquisitors; the masters of the Twisted Symmetry.

'Now?' Balthazar was breathless. Expectant.

'Now,' whispered Chess, the wind snatching the word from her lips and tossing it across the city.

Balthazar stared into the darkness as if he could see what Chess could sense. 'Wouldn't you like to see it?' he asked.

'See what?'

'Their world? Their crystal world?'

Amarantium: crystal. A substance that existed in all times and all places and which the Inquisitors had used to build a dimension in which they alone would survive the crash of the universes: if Chess destroyed time and space as they wanted. A dimension in which they and their servants would continue to live forever.

'It must be very beautiful,' murmured Balthazar. 'It must be very perfect.'

This was why the Symmetry was so dangerous. 'You must go, Balthazar. Both of us must. It's late.' It was early evening, but Chess wasn't talking about the time of day.

Balthazar didn't want to leave at once. Maybe it was because he wanted to stay close to his thoughts of the terrible beauty that the Symmetry offered for a little longer, or maybe it was because he understood that after tonight, there would be no coming back to this place. He was silent for a while and then asked, 'And your brothers? Have you found any sign of your brothers?'

'My *brothers*?' For years, Chess had lived in the drains and harbours of the city, a street rat like thousands of others. And all that time she had believed that Box and Splinter were her brothers. But she had been wrong. 'I don't have *brothers*, Balthazar,' said Chess. 'I've got *one* brother, and he's not to be trusted.' That was what the shade of her dead mother had told her when she had travelled back in time to be with her, in Knott Street.

And however much mystery shrouded Splinter, Chess knew this: she knew that Splinter was the brother. 'Splinter isn't to be trusted. He betrayed me.' Her voice was wrested by the wind and her large brown eyes were bright and wet with the cold. 'He gave me to the Symmetry.'

'He wanted power.' Balthazar sounded as if he was making an excuse for Splinter. Balthazar knew how well the Symmetry could use a human who wanted power.

'He gave me to the Inquisitors and they gave me to the warps.' Chess didn't say any more. The memories were bad. The Inquisitors might have been the masters of the Twisted Symmetry, but it was the devious technology of the warps that had been used to fuse her mind with the dark energy that the Symmetry had extracted from their billions of victims: the dark energy that now surged and screamed within her, wanting to be released. And Chess knew that if she allowed that to happen, there might be no stopping it.

But did it matter? There was so much pain in the universes,

so much suffering that sometimes Chess felt ready to end it all. And that was what the Inquisitors wanted: for Chess to blast the universes back to their first point of nothingness, so that only the Twisted Symmetry would survive, cocooned within the alternative world that they had constructed out of crystal, preserving them for eternity.

'Splinter betrayed you,' pondered Balthazar, 'and now, it seems that the enemy has disposed of Splinter.'

'I have looked everywhere, and I can't find him.' Chess's voice was hoarse. She felt the shrug of Balthazar's shoulders beneath the ill-fitting tuxedo jacket. 'But that doesn't mean he's dead,' she insisted.

'And if he is alive,' murmured Balthazar, 'wherever that may be, why concern yourself with him? After all that he has done. Why?'

'He's my brother.' Balthazar looked up at her and she cleared her throat. 'Even if he is a bad one.' Sometimes it felt as if her old life in the city, when she had thought that Box and Splinter were her brothers, was the only certainty she had. And what she wanted, what she craved, was certainty, so even the thought of Splinter was a haven against the tempest that howled within her spirit.

'And Box?' asked Balthazar. But Chess noticed how his large eyes gazed out at the spread of the city as if they might see what she knew was out there.

I can feel you, she thought. And something thought back at her. A quiet laughter, cruel, hungry. One piece of sense data within the blaring chaos of the city.

Chess's mind split. Still sensing the approach of the Symmetry, still sensing the speeding car, the little girl, the space between the two shrinking, she reached for Box. This was no effort; Chess could think a thousand thoughts at once, touch as many realities as she could find. It was focusing on any *one* thing that had become difficult. It felt as if her mind could slip away from her at any moment and, if it did, she wasn't sure what would happen. Sometimes she felt so unhappy, so angry, that she knew she couldn't trust herself.

They say I can control the universes, thought Chess. But I don't think I can control me. She laughed quietly, failing to notice the frown that cast itself over Balthazar's face as he watched her.

She searched for Box. Her mind forged a channel through the universes to where a giant rock belt spiralled out of the Alpha-3-Varion supernova. Then she moved inwards: heat, the whump of plasma-fire intensifying, light flashing as explosive ordinance burst over the groaning hulls of battle cruisers, the boom of heavy guns and the relentless machinery of Dog Troopers, the Twisted Symmetry's war machine, preparing for battle.

'Too fast,' whispered Chess, sensing the closing metres between chrome bumper and the child's cranium, simultaneously and effortlessly observing the tidal wave that was the Symmetry's battle fleet as it prepared to break upon its target.

Within one of the huge, deep-vortex battle cruisers, Chess found the Fourteenth Storm, part of the Dog Troopers' cybernetic, heavy cavalry: the Dreadbolts. And amongst the Fourteenth, commanding a cohort of a thousand battle-hardened, solarion-toughened, armour-clad snouts, was Box.

He was mounted on a bolt, a colossal, bio-engineered

horse, just like the rest of his cohort. Its metal flanks were black and so were its eyes. It drew back its lips to roar and stamped a killing hoof upon the iron run. Box pulled down his visor and a hiss of gas smoked over his armour-plated shoulders as the compression pipe was unlocked from the back of his helmet. The gas trails parted to reveal the snarling dog heads of the Fourteenth Storm engraved on his armour, black amidst whorls of gold.

The interior lights dimmed to red. Box gave a command over the radio, speaking the same throat-grazing tongue as the rest of the Dog Troopers. Chess didn't understand it but she knew what it meant. It was nearly time for contact. In two minutes' time, ten thousand metal-shearing, body-pulping dreadbolts would ride out to smash their enemy.

Chess sensed Box's iron strength and cool determination. But destruction was not his only purpose. Box wanted to be somewhere else, *with* someone else. This was what drove him on, just as he had driven himself through every obstacle until he had saved *her* from the Twisted Symmetry.

Box wanted to be with Anna. Chess knew this. And she knew that he was only fighting with the enemy because Ethel had said that he must: that it was part of a plan agreed between her and General Saxmun Vane, the brutal commander of the Dog Troopers. And so, almost as soon as Box had returned to the city together with Anna and the rest of them, after he had brought her back from the warp station where the Symmetry had kept her, he had been sent back to the war zone he thought he'd left behind. That had been nearly two months ago: two months during which Chess had sensed time speeding and speeding towards its end.

—[27]—

'Box is with the enemy,' said Chess, vaguely.

'It makes no sense to me,' responded Balthazar, his voice competing with the wind which droned above the city.

'It doesn't make much sense to me either.' Chess blinked tails of hair from her eyes. 'It's part of Ethel's grand plan.'

The silence which followed was their joint verdict on Ethel's grand plans.

Chess's thoughts stayed with Box a little longer. 'Who *are* you?' she whispered. For most of her life, she had believed that Box was Splinter's twin brother. Now she knew he couldn't be. But in her heart, he remained her brother.

Sensory data from the city streamed back: tyres squealing, the dead thump of a head on a car bumper, a small body cast up and thudding back onto the road, slack as rags. A scream. A crowd. Tears. One knife through a life in a city that lacerated itself a thousand times every day.

Chess's pain flashed into anger and the anger was hard to contain. It was this anger that made her want to end everything. The winter sky cracked and electricity burst white over the city.

'No, Chess.' Balthazar looked up, worried and puzzled at the same time, not knowing what had happened but sensing Chess's sudden rage. 'Not this way, Chess. This is what they want. This is all it takes.'

And this *was* all it took. One burst of rage and the sky broke. If she let go. If she dared to unleash the cataclysm of dark energy that wanted to be unleashed ...

'Too much pain,' was all that Chess could say. Her veins burnt with fury and she tried to control it. During those months in the warp station, the Symmetry had pumped her so full of raw energy, energy from pain, energy from suffering, that sometimes she was left clutching at sanity with her bare nails.

Then she felt a brawny arm, warm and heavy, across her shoulders, and Balthazar was standing beside her. 'Life is neither fair nor simple,' he intoned, his voice a sonorous buzz, soothing the inside of her head. 'Understanding that is the beginning of understanding the universe.'

'Universes,' muttered Chess, and Behrens's words returned to her, words uttered minutes before she had destroyed him. *The universe is broken.*

Behrens might have been an Inquisitor, one of the five masters of the Twisted Symmetry, but he had been right about that. This was why the Symmetry wanted her: to restore the universes to a state of perfect nothingness. And now, after all that she had seen, all that she had absorbed, Chess understood. It might mean the end of everything, for everyone, apart from the Symmetry, but it would be so simple. So painless.

And if she didn't do what the Symmetry wanted?

A crowd was gathering: paramedics, tubes, a stretcher. But the little girl's body was in a place beyond the power of paramedics.

'So much is broken.' Chess shrugged away Balthazar's arm, even though it had felt firm; safe. 'What am I meant to do? I mean, if I can do *anything*, what do I actually *do*?'

'You do what you can,' replied Balthazar Broom. 'That is all that any of us can do.'

Chess nodded. 'Nice theory,' she murmured. Then she

heard him sigh, his broad chest expanding and falling inside the ill-fitting dinner jacket.

'For my part, it is enough that you are my friend.' He leant on his staff. 'You have already saved *me*.' She saw how he glanced at the back of the hand which grasped the staff, and she saw how the skin was wrinkled and spotted with age. 'This may be inevitable,' he muttered, studying the swift assault of time upon his body, 'but it was you who gave me back a life.'

For a moment there was a warm closeness between them. But moments like this were only moments. Bursts of sound and flashes of movement from across the city flickered through her mind and then Chess's mind fixed on what it had been searching for: a broiling hatred, festering within the city.

Hello, Chess.

Out there, in the crowded, rushing, diesel-smogged soul of the city, a beggar-man swathed in pus-sodden bandages giggled into a pool of his own suppuration. She saw him. *Only* Chess saw him. And he looked back and saw her. He giggled and stuck out a tongue that crawled with maggots.

I could destroy you, thought Chess.

Go on then, sneered the Inquisitor, Snargis. *Destroy me. And what will you save? A world full of* this.

A mortuary. A sheet over cold stone, draping a body so small it barely made an impression.

See? Snargis chuckled. *And what have* you *done to stop this? Nothing. And you do nothing because you know. You know the great* pointlessness *of it all.* Yellow bubbles of sputum popped across his lips as the Inquisitor slurped out laughter.

Destroying me saves nothing. *This universe is sick. The universe is broken. Only we offer an eternity of peace. You and us, Chess. Peace forever. No more pain. No more suffering. How can that be wrong?*

How *could* that be wrong?

She felt Balthazar's arm tight about her shoulders.

'We should go. Now,' he said. He didn't know what was happening but he knew that the darkness was clutching at Chess. 'I have kept you up here too long.'

'I can't even fight them, Balthazar.' Chess clenched her fists, digging her nails into her palms until the pain cleared her thoughts. 'If I did fight, if I let go, I don't think I'd ever stop, and that's what they want. Whatever I do, they win.' She shivered. It was cold, standing on the top of the CREX tower, staring into space. She rubbed her eyes. 'You go, please. Just leave me for a bit. I want to think before everything starts.'

Balthazar glanced over to the radio mast which needled high from the roof of the tower.

'Thanks for being here, Balthazar.' Chess smiled, eyes half shut against the wind. 'Sometimes I feel as if I'm on my own.'

'You're not on your own, Chess.' Balthazar shivered. 'I feel the cold more, now I'm becoming an old man.'

'You're not an old man. Well, not quite yet. But I am as good as on my own. Being stuck with Captain Riley ...' Chess sighed. 'He's OK, but ...'

'He's one of the Committee's top agents.'

Balthazar was right about that. Captain Riley was meant to be a police officer, a crasher, but actually he was a commander of the Charitable Operations Executive, an elite force who carried out high-level military operations for the Committee. But Balthazar had made it sound as if it was a privilege for Chess to be secured under the same roof as Captain Riley and his family.

'Come on, Balthazar. Ethel's only stuck me with him for the Committee's benefit. So an eye can be kept on me.'

'Captain Riley's a good man, Chess. He's risked his life for you more than once.'

Chess sighed hopelessly. 'I know that.' Now she felt bad for not saying the right things about him. How could she do anything when she couldn't even use words properly?

'No, listen,' said Balthazar, more insistent than usual. 'Ever since the Symmetry gave the Endgame order, Captain Riley has been a prime target. But we can't afford to lose him, so I imagine that Mevrad is relying upon *you* to keep an eye on *him*.'

Even if he was a crasher, Captain Riley and his family had been kind to her, not treated her like a street rat or a ticking bomb.

'*Me* look out for *him*?' She bit her lip. She was meant to be with him now. She had broken away from Captain Riley and his family and Trick, who had come along to be near to Chess, once they had started shopping. She had come here to spend time with Balthazar, away from everything else. It had never occurred to her that she had a job to do.

And right now, the Symmetry were entering the city.

How can I get things so wrong? She dug her nails into her palms as she remembered how Splinter had always told her that she got things wrong.

'You had better find the Captain and his family.' Balthazar

was at the foot of the radio mast. Chess knew that at its top there was a gap, a dimensional hole hundreds of metres wide, that no human could see. But to those who knew of its existence, it was a simple way of entering the vortex.

Balthazar began to climb. Halfway up, staff in hand, he looked down at her and shouted, 'I trust you, Chess. I believe in you.' The wind spun his words away.

She watched him go; vanish, not into the darkness but into space.

'Don't,' she whispered into the night.

It was time to find Captain Riley. But before that, she had to make time for something else.

You do what you can, Balthazar had said.

Chess stepped back into the time-space the city had occupied twenty minutes before. Messing with time was dangerous; it unravelled the fabric of certainty. But if the universes were on the verge of ending, who cared about twenty minutes?

She was in the street. A man and a little girl were walking towards her. Already, the little girl was pulling away, eyes caught by something which glinted at her in the road. Chess could hear the car approaching: too fast.

'Look.' Chess stopped the little girl, squatted, and held open her hand. Big eyes looked and blinked seriously at the light which sparkled around Chess's fingers: a trick, a silly piece of rogue physics. It was nothing.

I could as easily raze this city, thought Chess.

'Hey,' shouted the man, stamping back to where his daughter had been distracted by the girl in the leather jacket and jeans. His hand closed on his daughter's shoulder and he pulled her close, eyes hard on Chess: accusing.

'Don't go talking to strangers.' The advice might have been for the little girl, but he glared at Chess.

Out in the road, a car with a dirty bumper sped by, too fast.

Chess stood and raked the wild curls from her face.

'The city's a dangerous place, baby,' said the man to the little girl, and he chaperoned her away from Chess and into the crowds.

Chess closed her eyes and saw the putrid-fleshed bodies oozing into the city-sphere.

'You have no idea,' she whispered.

CHAPTER 3

For the second time that evening, Trick thought she saw the floor ripple. She squatted to inspect it more closely: linoleum tiles smudged with the wheel tracks of supermarket trolleys. One of the fluorescent ceiling lights flickered, so maybe that was why she had thought there was movement. And anyway, floors didn't move: not unless there was an earthquake. She closed her eyes and concentrated on where her feet were planted. No tremors. So, no earthquake.

'Trick? Are you OK?'

Trick remained squatting with her eyes closed for long enough to let Mrs Riley know that she wasn't in charge of her. Even though Captain Riley and Mrs Riley had let her live with them, and even though they had bought her trainers and a new pair of tracksuit bottoms, and even though they didn't treat her like a scummy little street rat, it was important not to let them think they were in charge of her.

'What?' grunted Trick, standing slowly and looking up the aisle under knitted brows.

'Come on,' shouted Jasper, who was eight. Trick ignored him.

'Come *on*, Trick,' insisted Oliver and he grinned at her. He was eleven, a year older than she was. Even though he was a jack, just like his brother and his mum and dad, just like most other people in the city, she liked him. But she didn't want him to know that, so she followed the Rileys very slowly, trailing some distance behind.

Half watching for any movement from the floor, Trick's eyes followed Mrs Riley. Mrs Riley was kind but not soft and her hair was browny-red, so it was a bit like Trick's hair.

'You've got beautiful hair,' Mrs Riley had told her when she'd made Trick have the first bath of her life. And the first hair-wash. She had said her hair was as beautiful as burnished copper. Trick wasn't sure what 'burnished' meant but she liked the sound of the words.

'Beautiful as burnished copper,' she repeated to herself, enjoying the pop of the letters from her lips.

But no amount of washing could scrub away the barbed-wire tattoo down her cheek. Trick touched it now, idly. It was the only thing her parents had left her. She kicked the sole of her trainer into the floor to see if it would make a mark. It would have been better if they'd left her with nothing.

'White or brown?'

Trick looked up the aisle to Mrs Riley and shrugged.

'White,' decided Jasper.

'Brown,' countered Oliver. Mrs Riley took a loaf and dropped it into her shopping trolley between two baguettes and a row of bean tins. 'Brown is better.' She did her nice, practical smile.

Nobody else is shopping.

The thought made Trick look about to see if what her senses told her was right. Her senses were good at this. You couldn't survive in the press and slum of the city if you couldn't smell crowds, feel the heat of eyes, hear the beat of silence.

Nobody else *was* shopping.

She scratched her head and meandered to the central aisle and then walked down it quite quickly, scanning the lanes which branched off. Her footsteps were loud. The cash tills were unmanned. On the outside of the huge front windows where the night was thick, the lattice metal shutters were down.

We've been shut in.

Trick cleared her throat. 'We've been shut in,' she croaked, turning on the spot to look for Captain Riley. Captain Riley was a crasher, a police officer: well, in everyday life he was, but Trick knew that he was actually one of the Committee's top agents. She guessed that was why she'd been sent to live with him. The Twisted Symmetry had given something called the Endgame order, which meant that they were going to assassinate people who got in their way. Ethel had said that Trick was in danger too, so Captain Riley had been looking after her. And Chess had been staying with them as well, although Chess didn't need any looking after. But Captain Riley wasn't here now and neither was Chess.

Trick swallowed and her throat was so dry it made her ears ache. The strip lights hummed and flickered.

'Trick?'

There was a raw edge to Mrs Riley's voice. Trick's breathing quickened.

—[37]—

Then louder: 'Trick?'

Trick's fingers hooked into the hole-riddled jumper she wore. They had made her wear shoes and new trousers but she had clung onto her old jumper, and she clung onto it now.

'Don't cry,' she snapped at herself, as she blinked her hot eyes. Chess wouldn't cry. Thinking of Chess made her feel better.

'Trick!' Mrs Riley's voice was followed by the stamp of swiftly moving shoes and then she emerged two or three aisles away, still pushing the trolley. Oliver and Jasper were close behind. Trick saw that Jasper was holding his mother's hand.

'Trick, we need to get ... to leave.'

When people spoke slowly, as if nothing was wrong, you knew that things were really bad.

'What's wrong?' asked Trick.

'I think we've been locked in. By mistake, I'm sure.' Mrs Riley did a bright smile that made Trick feel worse.

'It's not a mistake,' stated Trick.

Mrs Riley cast a glance back the way she'd come. But Trick knew that even though he had come shopping with them, Captain Riley had vanished.

'Where is he?' she asked.

Jasper knew who Trick was talking about at once because he wailed, 'What's happened to Daddy?'

'We just have to look for him,' said Mrs Riley, calmly. She turned the trolley in the opposite direction and hurried towards the far end of the store where the big polythene doors to the cold meat storage hung at a slovenly angle.

Trick saw that where her hand grasped Jasper's, the skin was white. Oliver looked back at Trick, eyes like plates.

'It's OK,' mouthed Trick, before setting off after the Rileys.

It's OK? *It's OK?*

It was *not* OK.

The floor. Watch the floor.

Trick stopped as soon as she had started to walk and looked at the floor a metre or so in front of where she stood.

It moved. It definitely moved. A hump, straining up and then dropping back, flat.

It moved again, harder this time, as if something was pushing up. As if something was trying to push through.

Only a couple of inches from her foot, another lump jerked into life. Trick yelped and jumped left as if hit by a stun stick.

All around her the floor began to buckle and stretch, and then she realized what the shapes were. They were faces: faces pushing up from the floor, mouths gaping, sinews taut, screaming upwards silently. The linoleum stretched like thin rubber, and now it began to reveal the shapes of body parts: arms, legs, hands, writhing, pushing, trying to get out.

Trick skittered through the surging, groping shapes and her voice burst, part warning, mostly terror. 'Mrs Riley!'

Then, ahead of her, something came out of the floor. It rose up, a figure the size and shape of a man but grey and blurred, apart from what he had in his hand. Trick's eyes fastened on the long, black hook and she knew it was time to run.

Figures began to appear rapidly, heaving up through the floor: unfolding. And there were more slipping out of the dark spaces within the shelves and crawling free of the ceiling, slithering across the tiles above Trick's head.

Trick sprinted towards where Mrs Riley and Jasper and Oliver were staring back. She could sense the wraith-wave sweeping after her and when she snatched a glance back, she saw a mass of blurred, grey bodies seethe forwards in a wedge which filled the aisle from floor to ceiling. The bodies bristled with hooks so black they looked as if they had ripped away light itself.

'Get down!'

Captain Riley burst through the polythene doors, a bloody gash over his left cheek and a pistol in each hand.

'Get down.'

Trick threw herself onto the floor, skidding on her belly to where the rest of the Rileys had flung themselves. There was a blazing volley of shots and the smell of gun smoke. Cartridge cases rained over her, bouncing off her back and tinkling hollowly on the floor. When she looked up, she saw that the nearest wave of figures had vanished. But in their wake came even more.

'Get up,' shouted Riley, wiping the blood from his face with the back of his hand. The front of his denim shirt was streaked with dark-rust stains.

'That way?' Mrs Riley pointed at the doors through which her husband had burst.

He shook his head. 'Hunters. What's left of them.' He hurled one pistol at the approaching spectres, then the other. Trick saw how the figures struck by the weapons vanished immediately, and so did the weapons. It was as if they had cancelled each other out. But there were so many shapes following that the terror sucked the marrow from her bones.

'Hold them back,' shouted Captain Riley.

'How?' shouted Mrs Riley.

Captain Riley grabbed a tin of beans from the shopping trolley. 'With anything. They can't stand impact with matter: not in our world.' He hurled the bean tin at a grey shape that came swooping down from the ceiling, hook raised.

'It's burning the air,' gasped Trick. She was sure that she had glimpsed the air flicker flame-red around the borders of the shadow shape. The tin hit the wraith and both vanished.

'Havoc Legionnaires,' yelled Riley, grabbing another tin, this time of sweetcorn. 'Shadows to us but like fire in their world.' He launched the corn tin and Mrs Riley followed with another. 'They destroy even the air they touch.' He caught Trick's eye. 'And if they get their hooks into you, they'll destroy you too. Rip you out of existence.'

'Mike!' snapped Mrs Riley, tin in hand and eyes blazing at her husband. 'Are you *trying* to frighten the boys?' But the boys were busy flinging the contents of the shopping trolley at the swarm of Havoc Legionnaires.

A cluster of man-shapes bubbled out of the surfaces of the polythene doors.

'Mrs Riley!' shouted Trick, pointing at what had appeared. She smacked away a phantom-form with a box of cereal, her hand suddenly empty.

Mrs Riley spun round in time to see the first hook coming. She ducked aside and the hook cut through the front of the shopping trolley, ripping the front mesh out of existence. The trolley split open, spilling shopping. Before another legionnaire could strike, Mrs Riley had snatched up a baguette in either hand.

'Get ... away ... from ... my ... children,' she snarled, lashing the legionnaires with the bread, battering each one out of existence until she was holding no more than stumps of crust.

Trick grasped the handle of the trolley and spun the cart round as hard as she could, then let go. It reeled across the supermarket floor until it collided amidst the legionnaires who absorbed it with a ripple of ranks.

'Too many,' shouted Mrs Riley, grabbing her children and pulling them away from the polythene doors which continued to ooze grey figures. The figures swept across the floor so that now Trick and the Rileys were encircled by the grey wraiths with their black sickles. When Trick looked up, she saw that the ceiling was covered with so many beetling shapes that the lights were no more than chipped fragments of yellow.

Captain Riley turned towards the doors and the flickering shadows which blocked them.

'I'll take them. You just get out,' he said.

'You can't.' Mrs Riley snatched his arm, pulling him back.

He shook his arm free. 'I can. You have to get the children out. Take the gap I leave.' His face was grim. 'It's me the hunters are after; you'll be OK.'

Trick knew the hunters would want her too; she was a rat. But she was more frightened about what was going to happen to Captain Riley. She saw him turn back to his wife and squeeze her hand. 'Stay close,' he said, before facing the doors.

From floor to ceiling, hundreds of legionnaires surrounded them. The Rileys were defenceless, apart from a jar of jam in Oliver's hand.

Why don't they just attack? Trick was thinking

Mrs Riley must have thought the same thing because she grabbed her husband's shirt. 'Wait.' When he stared back she said, calmly, 'Everything's stopped.'

And everything *had* stopped, or so it seemed. It was as if the Havoc Legionnaires had frozen. Oliver must have sensed the perfect opportunity because with a yell he flung the jam jar at the nearest legionnaire. But as soon as it left his hand, it slowed until it actually stopped in mid-air and remained suspended, inches from its target.

Even the hazy outlines of the legionnaires had ceased to flicker.

Mrs Riley drew her boys close and her husband's arm was about her shoulder. Trick felt his free hand take hers.

'I don't understand,' whispered Mrs Riley.

'I think I do,' said her husband, quietly enough not to fracture the frozen moment.

Trick heard the footsteps approaching from the far end of the supermarket. She recognized the tread at once.

'Chess,' she whispered, and she was angry with herself because she felt like crying.

Captain Riley nodded and heaved in a breath. 'Chess.'

Chess must have walked through the legionnaires as if she was walking through mist because suddenly she was there, appearing out of the nearest rank. Trick was surprised by the baleful burning of her eyes.

'Chess?'

But Chess ignored her. She ignored all of them. She walked up to where they were standing and then turned to face outwards, to face the figures that surrounded them.

'I know what you did.' Chess's voice was so loud and so deep that Trick backed away from her. The jar of jam dropped out of the air and hit the floor with a loud crack. Immediately the hundreds of figures were animated again: there was a bat-like shuffling across the ceiling and a silent scrambling over the floor. But although the figures edged forwards, none came close enough to use their hooks.

'I know what you did.' So loud this time that a strip light burst.

Jasper began to cry. Oliver was ashen.

'Do you remember her?' Chess stepped forwards, and all about, the shadows drew back. 'Do you? Do you remember her?'

It frightened Trick even more when Chess began to laugh. Then, very quietly, Chess whispered, 'She didn't stand a chance.' Chess bowed her head.

Trick felt the whoosh of air as the mass of Havoc Legionnaires rushed in on them. She crouched down and as she did so, she noticed Chess look up. That was all that she saw Chess do, and then her ears felt as if she'd been pushed deep under water and she felt the energy surge, flattening shelves, blasting out the huge plate windows along the front of the store, ripping apart the metal shutters and obliterating every legionnaire. Then only the six of them remained amidst the wreckage that had once been a supermarket.

A jar of gherkins rolled off a mangled rack and burst on the floor, leaving a green starfish in a pool of vinegar.

'OK. We go,' snapped Captain Riley, but before they left the demolished interior of the supermarket, Trick saw him grasp Chess by her shoulders and with a blistering intensity say, 'Thank you, Chess. Thank you.'

Chess looked back, looked through him. 'She didn't stand a chance,' she whispered.

They didn't need to find a door because the supermarket no longer had a front. They just walked out through the gaping frontage, Captain Riley leading the way, glass crunching. Chess followed and beside her walked Trick, holding her hand and saying nothing.

'What was going on back there? What was she saying to those ... those things?' Mrs Riley was trying to talk quietly, but Chess could hear her.

'They killed her grandma.' Riley barely breathed the words.

'Her *grandma?*'

Chess looked down as Mrs Riley looked towards her, and then back at her husband. 'What have *they* got to do with grandmas?'

'Esme,' murmured Captain Riley. 'That was her name. And they ripped her apart: out of existence. Almost.'

'*Almost?*'

'They left enough,' said Captain Riley, meaningfully. Both of them turned to look back at Chess, figures haloed by the lights of the car park.

'Aren't you frightened of nothing?' asked Trick, breath puffing white in the night air.

'I'm frightened of lots,' said Chess and she thought of the old photograph that she had used to track through time: track back until she had seen for herself the dark tearing of the hooks.

I made your mother out of what the Symmetry had left of hers, Lemuel had told her. But now events had come full circle. This time it was the enemy who had been torn out of existence.

'Chess?'

Chess hadn't heard Trick repeating her name. But now she woke up to it, felt the little girl squeezing her hand, and for a moment, felt Trick's strength entering her.

'Mrs Riley says I have to go with her.'

'Go with her?'

'It's just you and me from here, Chess,' said Captain Riley.

Mrs Riley kissed Chess on her cheek. 'Thank you isn't enough, Chess. What you just did . . .'

'It's OK,' said Chess.

'Can't I stay with *you?*' asked Trick, gulping at the chilly air.

Chess bent down to Trick. The girl was pale which made her copper hair redder than usual, the barbed wire on her cheek more lived.

'I think,' said Chess, 'that there are going to be people *you* have to stay and look out for.'

Trick bit her lip. 'Is it going to get bad?'

Chess nodded.

'We have to get to Committee HQ.' Riley was trying not to hurry her, but he wanted to go.

'What would you do, Trick, if you were me?' Chess kept hold of the small hand.

Trick's eyes widened and then she laughed. The laughter was like a fizz of bubbles and it made Chess laugh too.

'But I'm not you, Chess.' Then her face became serious. 'But if I was, I wouldn't ask someone like me what to do.'

'You wouldn't?'

'No.' Trick was certain. 'I'd *know* what to do.'

'*Chess*,' insisted Riley.

'Come on, Trick,' shouted Mrs Riley from where she stood with her boys by the estate car.

Trick pulled her hand from Chess's and stuck both her hands on her hips. 'Have a plan and *stick* to it, Chess Tuesday.'

Chess felt the laughter bubble again: it wasn't a bad impersonation. 'You've spent too much time with Anna.'

Trick grinned proudly.

Tyres rolled, crunched to a stop and a handbrake ratcheted like a neck breaking. Chess heard a jeep door slouch open.

'Chess. We have to go now.' Riley's patience was strained.

The engine of the jeep that had just pulled up was turning, the exhaust pumping out a fog that glowed red in the tail lights.

'OK, Boss?' The driver leant across the passenger seat, box-chested in his black combats and body armour. Chess could see his shoulder patch, the grey star in a purple circle, that was worn by agents of the Charitable Operations Executive.

'Yeah.' Riley's body was outlined crimson against the glowing exhaust fog.

'*Trick*.' Mrs Riley's voice echoed across the car park and the estate engine coughed into life.

'Stick to the plan,' grinned Trick.

Chess nodded. 'Good advice.' But she felt lonely as she watched the little girl run to the waiting car and get in.

'We can't do this without you, Chess.'

When she turned round, she saw that Captain Riley was pulling on an armoured vest, tugging the straps tight. His eyes were bright. Green eyes. You couldn't see their colour in the dark but Chess knew that they were green.

'That's what everyone keeps telling me,' she said.

A 9mm pistol was passed to Riley by the man in the jeep. Riley clicked out the magazine, glanced at where the first round was nestled, then snapped the magazine back into the grip.

'It's full,' came the voice of the driver.

'Proper drills, Caine.' Riley winked at Chess. 'Check rounds, remember?'

'You're such a rules man, Boss.'

Captain Riley pulled open the rear door. Automatically, Chess climbed in. The interior of the jeep smelt of diesel and cigarettes and leather. She sat back in the seat and the leather creaked. Her eyes shut and Trick's words ran through her head.

She did have a plan. Well, she'd once had a plan: a plan so simple, it hardly deserved to be called a plan at all. It had come to her months ago, when she had been with Anna. It had seemed a good idea then, and it wasn't any worse now. And maybe it would distract her mind from all the pain that seeped through it, from the abyss that would be an end of everything, forever, if she allowed herself to go there.

'You OK?' asked Riley, leaning on the door frame.

Chess nodded.

Riley pushed the door shut and swung into the front seat.

'Belt up, Boss,' said Caine. 'Don't want you bleeding all over the windows.' He glanced sideways at Riley before ramming the jeep into gear. 'Nice cut. I suppose you'll tell me the other guy came off worse.'

'Other *guys*,' stated Riley.

They screeched onto the street, cut through the traffic and then Chess felt the jeep swing up, onto an overpass which looped so tight round the sky-blocks that she was thrown against the door.

'There's a pedal down there,' observed Riley. 'It's called the brake.'

Caine shook his head. 'No time for that, Boss. Troops have been moving in all night and you've already missed the first command group.' He revved the engine, and slashed between two juggernauts. 'Sounds like hell's coming our way.'

They screamed along the overpass so fast that an ill-disciplined symphony of honking filled their wake.

'One day, they'll be grateful,' muttered Caine and they rollercoastered towards the old city.

The Graveyard. That was what the street rats called the old city and the name made Chess's stomach spasm. Committee HQ was located there, within the old bus depot, and so was the Elms Orphanage: narrow, cold, a rubbish bin of lost souls within the mouldering remnants of the old city. And with the Elms came memories: bad memories.

You can destroy those memories, Chess.

You can destroy whatever you like.

You can destroy *everything*.

The Inquisitors' voices were always with her now. Perhaps they were part of her. Chess knew that deep inside, there *was* something dark: a pulsing cord of hateful rage that was waiting to snap free.

'You can't tell me what to do,' she whispered to the voices.

'Are you OK?' Riley was looking round at her, forehead furrowed.

Chess nodded. 'Bad memories,' she said and she laughed hollowly. They think I can destroy universes but I can't even live with my own memories.

The tyres rolled over the broken tarmac at the front of the old bus depot. She had been here many times before but it had never looked like this.

The road which swept into the entrance bays was flanked by sand-bagged machine-gun posts. Below the cracked clock tower, its hands set perpetually at three o'clock, a row of canvas-backed trucks had been drawn up and men and women in urban combat fatigues were dismounting from the dropped tailgates, weapons rattling, boots thudding over the ground in a constant flow.

Drawn up in front of the trucks were a couple of black limousines. On the bonnet of the first hung a small pennant bearing the letters that Chess recognized as UN. She couldn't read but she knew what they were when they were printed like that. They were important. They were to do with trouble in other countries.

There was no pennant on the second limousine but Chess saw a man approach and she recognized him too. She had seen his face on the front pages of newspapers and she had seen it on the TV screens that she had watched through shop windows. The man was flanked by four suited boneheads who *had* to be bodyguards. One of them pulled open a rear door and the other three turned to face outwards, shielding the man with the famous face as he ducked inside the limo.

Then Ethel appeared at the main entrance, talking animatedly with a woman in a suit and two gentlemen. Even in the patchy darkness, Chess could tell that the woman and the men were foreign.

'She's always so messy,' muttered Chess. How could Ethel be yapping so bossily with such obviously important people when she looked like she'd stolen her clothes from the bins of a charity shop?

But Ethel and the three diplomats inclined their heads politely to one another before two black-coated figures exited from the front doors of the limousine with the pennant and opened the rear. Ethel waggled her fingers as if in a fond act of farewell and waited for both vehicles to sweep away from the depot before bustling over to the jeep.

Chess could hear the chop of rotor blades overhead but even with her nose pressed to the window, she couldn't find the helicopter. Or helicopters: there was so much noise out there that it was hard to tell.

The rear door on the other side of the jeep cranked open and Ethel's wrinkled, grey-mopped head turtled inside.

'Hello, dear.' She smiled at Chess, brisk as a party hostess. 'We have become a war zone.' She hitched up her threadworn tweed skirt and slid onto the seat beside Chess, slamming the door shut behind her. Chess couldn't help

— [51] —

noticing her knees which were bony and stuck through the holes in her stockings like giant knuckles.

'Good evening, gentlemen.'

'Good evening, Ethel,' responded both men in unison.

'The enemy are expected any time now,' announced Ethel.

Riley nodded. 'I see you've arranged a welcoming committee.'

'*I've* been *very* busy,' agreed Ethel.

'We've not exactly been having a rest,' muttered Chess.

Ethel tutted. 'I see we're quite the little cactus this evening.' She continued, 'The delegates from UNCOM didn't want to get caught up in hostilities and our premiere has gone to his bunker.'

Riley watched a tracked personnel carrier rumble by and then said, 'Wasn't expecting this much activity right now, Ethel.'

'The enemy are coming sooner than expected, and in greater numbers.' Ethel sighed. 'I'm afraid it's going to get ever so messy here.'

Out on the road fronting the depot, the machine guns hung, noses down, like storks, waiting. The trucks began to pull away and if Chess craned her neck she could see where their occupants had taken up position in the windows and doorways of the old depot.

'Who's left in there, Ethel?' asked Riley.

'Everyone's out. This is just a rearguard,' replied the old lady. 'The enemy don't know we've gone. We received intelligence of a large detachment of hunters incoming, supported by Symmetry abominates and armoured androids.'

Chess knew what that meant. These were creatures

engineered by the Twisted Symmetry's warps, designed to fight and kill: spindle rippers, whistlers, metalbacks and more, things that Chess had seen in the deepest pits of the universes. Things that could tear through the small force holding Committee HQ like a wind: a savage, mutilating wind.

'It's not fair,' grumbled Chess.

'What's not fair?' queried Ethel.

Chess jerked her head towards the depot. 'Leaving them. For what's coming.'

'How sweet of you to express your concern, my love.' Ethel shuffled into the seat to get comfortable and dolloped her hands on her lap, fingers like an arthritic nest of pink twigs. 'But since when did you start worrying about what happens to whom? I thought you were above all of this, my love. I thought, to use the common expression, you didn't give a monkey's.'

It was hard to express what she meant when Ethel was talking about monkeys, so Chess settled for glowering into space.

'Where to, Ethel?' asked Caine.

'18 Mendoza Row, dear. And careful with all this weaponry. Hit a pothole and we'll be reduced to Swiss cheese. Mind you,' she added, smiling cosily at Chess, 'I *like* Swiss cheese.'

'Where's Anna?' The last Chess had seen, Anna had been flat on an operating table inside Committee HQ, wracked by the genetic melding.

Ethel's tight, chapped lips pursed and then she said, 'Anna has been deployed.'

'Meaning?'

'Meaning she's out there, somewhere.' Ethel rapped the window with her knuckle. The jeep kicked back a shovelful of grit and roared away from the depot.

'Out there? On her own?'

'She has a job to do, my love.'

'Are you trying to get *everybody* killed?' snapped Chess.

'No, dear, that's the enemy's job.' Ethel's head cocked to one side, listening. Chess could hear it too: behind them, the outbreak of gunfire. 'And it sounds like they've started,' Ethel whispered.

CHAPTER 4

The nightclub was hot and crammed with bodies.

Pacer was sitting at a table as far away from the dance floor as possible, hood pulled up and a shotgun stare within. When Anna looked back all she could see were bodies moving with the sound: limbs working, hair swaying, slow in the flash of the lights however fast the music. Boys and girls in groups or dancing close: *together*. Crowds could make you feel lonely. Even with Pacer smouldering at the edge of the darkness, Anna felt as if she was the one person who was on her own.

The beat was so hard it made her chest thump. She pushed her way to the bar through the hot mass of bodies and wondered whether the guy next to her really had to press so close. Behind the rows of bottles filled with greens and blues and amber, there was a long mirror. Anna caught her own face looking back: fringe dead straight across her brow, long black hair tied in a high ponytail, blue eyes as vivid as the liquor-filled bottles. Then she saw a mouth close to her ear.

'Can't hear you,' she shouted, leaning forwards to shout

back in the guy's ear, but keeping her long, denim-clad legs as far away from his as she could.

'Do you want a drink?' he shouted. He had a good face, with blond hair that flopped across his forehead and brown eyes. But his wasn't the face she wanted to see.

'No. Thanks.' She smiled in a way that wasn't meant to be encouraging. The music was so loud that she couldn't hear what he said next so she shouted, 'Look, I don't even want to be here.' Which was absolutely true. She wasn't here for fun: she was here to keep a look-out for the enemy, although Anna couldn't see why the enemy would turn up in a club above the leisure complex. But Ethel had said it was necessary to stake out the place, so Julius had deployed her and five other Blood Sentinels at various locations about the complex: Jake and Vladivostok Ragg in the cinema where there was a late show, Seren and Étoile high in the superstructure of the roof, Jago Burke and the Scythian patrolling the tree-fringed perimeter of the complex and Anna in the club. Anna had brought Pacer along because she needed his help.

'You're on your own?' yelled the man, brushing his floppy blond hair away from his face.

'No,' Anna yelled back. 'I'm waiting for the enemy.'

'Waiting for *who?*' The guy looked puzzled. In a way, Anna envied him that: not having to think of the world in terms of an enemy. But it made him vulnerable too.

'It doesn't matter,' mouthed Anna, who had reached the bar at last. 'One lemonade, one beer.' She pointed so that the barman would know what she had shouted. The drinks were slammed onto the counter. Anna pulled the money from her black leather jacket and slammed it back.

The man with the blond hair was asking if she was here with her boyfriend: whether she had a boyfriend.

Did she have a boyfriend? Anna didn't want to think about Box. She wasn't even sure whether he counted as a boyfriend. He had crashed into her life, demolished everything in his way and left her with an ache in her chest she couldn't have imagined before they'd met. And now?

Now, he was out there, a million light years away, fighting someone else's battles in a war that had lasted forever.

Anna shut her eyes for a moment, her head filling with the beat of the music, sensing the heat of the dancing bodies. Space was vast, but Anna told herself that feelings were vaster. Maybe her thoughts were close to him. Maybe he thought about her.

When she opened her eyes, the blond guy was still there, smiling confidently. Your world is a million light years from mine, she thought. I hope it stays a safe world for you. She looked at him with eyes that had seen things he couldn't imagine and she saw his confidence wilt a little, so she smiled.

'Find a nice girl,' she said. 'I come with some pretty tough baggage.' She didn't wait for a reply. Feeling a piece of glass crack under her boot, she skirted the dance floor to join Pacer where the darkness was deepest.

'What kept you?' he asked, pushing back the hood. He dropped his face to the neck of the beer bottle, picked it up between his teeth, tipped back his head and took a swig without using his hands. When he had clacked the bottle back on the table, he saw Anna's blue gaze regarding him severely.

'What?' He hunched his shoulders innocently.

'Even in here,' Anna admonished him, 'you have the manners of a pig.'

Pacer started laughing. The more critically Anna stared at him, the harder he laughed, seat rocking. 'You are such a jack.' He shook his head, dropped it to the bottle and pulled another swig.

Anna ran a long finger around the rim of her lemonade glass, idly.

'Did Julius say *why* we had to come clubbing?' asked Pacer. Then the smile vanished and his face set like concrete as a couple of lads swayed towards the table.

How can a face change so much? thought Anna. But Pacer had always been like that: nice face for friends, and a face like a fist for everyone else.

The lads swayed in the opposite direction.

'We're here to see if anything happens. If it does, we report back.' But she wasn't *just* a look-out, she was a Blood Sentinel. She was here to protect. Anna put her hand around the glass but didn't lift it.

'Report back where?' Pacer turned in his seat to see where Anna was looking. 'You keep staring at stuff,' he complained.

'That's what we're here for.' Anna's eyes raked the interior of the club.

'That's what *you're* here for,' Pacer reminded her. 'I'm just here for the ride. And because you can't do without me.'

'Yeah?' Anna looked at him and raised one neat eyebrow.

'Yeah.' Pacer tried to do the same but found that he

couldn't, so he took another swig of beer. When he dropped the bottle down, the beer foamed out of the neck and up his nose. Anna rolled her eyes and he wiped his face with the sleeve of his jacket. 'You think Chess is OK?'

'You ask about Chess a lot.' Anna was still looking at Pacer when she said that.

'So?' he snapped.

Anna smiled, a soft smile. 'I think Chess is OK, at the moment.'

Pacer shook his head. '*I* don't think she is. Just 'cos she's able to do all this stuff, it don't mean things aren't lively for her.' He glared at Anna's half-smile. 'You always pull that face when I talk about Chess. She's just my friend, right. That's why I worry about her.'

Anna shrugged. 'Yeah, well there is a lot to worry about.'

Pacer used his hand to take the next drink. 'Anyway, you haven't said who we're reporting back to. *If* there's anything to report.'

'Mendoza Row. Crazy Boris's.' Anna lifted her glass but she was looking about the club again.

Pacer stuck out his chin and nodded. 'Nice one. And I like Chess 'cos she's a *friend*, right?'

Anna could tell what Pacer thought about Chess, even if he couldn't. But it was better not to say any more, so she just nodded and scanned the fringes of the club for movement that shouldn't be there.

'Boris learned me this sweet riff last week.' Pacer's fingers strummed the air then stopped. 'Stop looking round like that. It's making me twitchy, OK?' Then he saw Anna's cat's-eye stare harden. He turned round to look where she was looking, but all he could see was an empty patch on the other side of the club where there was a door marked 'FIRE EXIT' at the top of a short flight of steps. He looked back to Anna. 'What?'

Out on the dance floor, bodies moved: hot, faceless, a strobe-flashed mass.

'What's up?' Pacer rubbed the top of his shaven head.

Anna stared at him so hard he sat back in his seat. 'Have you got it?' she asked.

'Got it?' Then Pacer realized what she was talking about. 'Yeah, yeah. Course I've got it.' He reached back to pat the long bundle that was tucked behind the seat. The bundle that he had smuggled in the same way he had smuggled himself in: up the fire escape and through the toilet window.

Then he looked over to the solitary door. 'You need it? Now?'

Anna's crystal eyes were ice. 'We didn't bring it for fun, Pacer.'

Minds as broad as galaxies and as deep as the vaults of age reached out, merging, communicating with one another in the silent chasm of space.

'It is time.'

The same thought, passing from one mind to the next.

'It is time.'

Malbane, foremost amongst the Inquisitors. 'See how the time spiral bends?'

And they saw the curve of space, rushing towards them as if they were cresting the very limit of the dimensions.

'We have reached the spiral horizon, my friends. We approach the fifth node.'

Malbane's thoughts echoed across the universes, echoed through the nebula spirits of Azgor, Snargis and Veer.

The fifth node. The point at which the time spiral was most vulnerable to change. The point at which an apocalyptic blast of energy could take the universes back to that moment of perfect balance before they had expanded and taken shape. The point at which the Inquisitors and all their works would be preserved for eternity. The point at which everything else would be destroyed.

See how the suns become one, thought Snargis. Twelve suns, light chiming through the crystal symmetry as fraction by fraction their prism glares converged.

'It is time for the Eternal,' whispered the churning vastness that was Veer.

'We need Chess,' hissed Azgor. 'We need her at the Core: the heart of the universes.'

'She will come.' Malbane, as certain as the abyss. 'She will not be able to stop herself.'

'General Vane will not interfere?' questioned Azgor.

'What about our *suspicions*?' Veer, cold as the fathomless dark. 'The loyalty of the Commander of our armies of Dog Troopers is . . . unclear.'

'The escape of the girl, Chess, from the warps,' continued Snargis, as if his fellow Inquisitors needed reminding. 'Effected by a *boy*. But engineered by the General, I have heard.'

'The boy took her from us when she was on the point of breaking,' spat Veer.

'His name is Box.' Snargis, bitter as grave dust.

In a distant star cluster, so remote as to be beyond the reach of memory, green lightning raked the undertow of space.

'Azgor, Azgor.' Malbane's presence: calm, quieting. 'General Vane is fully occupied. He has no *time* to be disloyal.' His thoughts were a balm. 'The Crystal Wars have lasted for aeons and they will not stop now. Whatever his intentions, the General cannot extract his armies from the eternal battles they have been fighting. Caught between the X'ath and the Galen, they are occupied ... perpetually: occupied fighting for *us*. Is that not perfect?'

If the darkness could have smiled, it would have smiled then.

'The millions and millions of Dog Troopers are *locked* in battle. They will still be locked in battle at the end of time.' Malbane laughed drily. 'The General can do nothing to stop us, but the violence and pain wreaked by his armies will continue to feed Chess. She will be able to draw upon it, right to the end.'

'Must Chess be fed with *more* energy?' questioned Veer. 'She is so powerful already. So full of the energy we have charged her with.'

Malbane responded immediately. 'She must have more. As much as we can provide her with, right up until the end. And so there must be sufficient pain, right up until the end. The final act must be absolute.'

'The Havoc Legionnaires have been despatched.' Azgor, as cold as deep space. 'Billions of them. They shall create such a wave of suffering that the universes will weep.'

'I shall ensure the warps release the abominates, *everywhere*,' promised Veer.

'And what about the humans?' enquired Malbane. 'They are such a fruitful source of suffering.'

'I have been amongst them.' Snargis, clouds of darkness swallowing stars in their heavy folds. 'I like humans. They squeak when you hurt them, and they are frightened by mutilation.' The Inquisitor groaned and cooed in anticipation. 'Humans are so . . . soft. Even as we commune, the Plague Breed is entering their world.'

'The humans do not know?' asked Malbane.

'The point of entry was calculated a long time ago,' replied Snargis.

Azgor and Veer sighed at Snargis's cleverness. He continued. 'It is deep in their world, within its heart. And they expect nothing.'

Silence. The suns crept closer together, their brilliance cutting through the gathering dark.

Azgor broke the deep peace. 'But how will Chess be there? At the Core? At the end?'

'I have told you,' said Malbane, patiently. 'She will find her way. She will *want* to find her way.' He paused before adding, 'Which is good. All of us need Chess to be at the Core when the time comes.'

'*All* of us?' asked Veer.

'*All* of us,' repeated Malbane. 'From the Core, Chess can touch everything, every time, every place. *We* need her there to destroy it all.'

'Leaving only *our* crystal universe,' quivered Snargis.

'And Mevrad wants her at the Core so that Chess can

destroy *us*,' continued Malbane, bluntly. 'It is a question of what Chess chooses to do once she is there. In that final moment, it will all come down to her *state of mind*.'

Time turned silently.

'The way to the Core is perilous,' considered Snargis. 'It twists, it bends, it goes back and forth through time and space. It is wrapped in a fog of convolutions.' He sniggered. 'Even Chess will struggle to find the route. And so, it will be easy for *us* to find *her*. To ensure she is in the *perfect* state of mind: for our purpose.'

'Which is why,' explained Malbane, 'Mevrad made an arrangement with the Sages. An arrangement to transport Chess to the Core directly, without the peril of that final journey, without providing us with an opportunity to bend her to our will.'

'An *arrangement?*' sneered Veer.

'The Sages are meant to be neutral,' complained Snargis. 'They should not have assisted Mevrad.'

'The Sages are not to be trusted.' Azgor, like acid.

'It is no matter.' Malbane, placating his old friends again. 'Mevrad's arrangement with the Sages depends upon a key.'

'A key?' questioned Veer.

'A key,' repeated Malbane, 'which is *missing*.' He chuckled. 'We have many friends, whatever the duplicity of the Sages. When I learnt of Mevrad's arrangement, I despatched thieves, to steal the key from the Sages, only to discover that it had vanished already!'

Silence as the other Inquisitors considered this piece of information.

'I anticipate that at the crucial moment, the key's absence will come as a surprise: it will present a problem to Mevrad and her *Committee*,' continued Malbane. 'The loss of the key means that Chess cannot use the transport to the Core arranged between Mevrad and the Sages. It means that Chess will have no alternative but to travel openly and with great *vulnerability*. This will provide us with the opportunity that we need.'

The Inquisitors contemplated this happy prospect, and as they did so, a grain of darkness, blacker than the heart of the abyss itself, burnt its way into the spirit of each of them: a darkness that was denser and harder than the fabric of the Inquisitors combined, and their souls flared in dread excitement.

'Bael,' hissed Veer.

'Master,' whispered Malbane, reverent.

'My perfect servants.' Bael, effortless, capable of wielding a destruction beyond the Inquisitors' fantasy. 'Do not worry yourselves with where Chess will be. I know her, better than she knows herself. I know what she will do. With every step she takes, she will move inexorably closer to where we need her. I have seen this. Remember, my little ones, this is how it was planned, from the beginning.'

'But . . .' Snargis was hesitant, a galaxy fawning before a mustard seed of darkness, ' . . . . might Chess be too powerful . . . for *you*?'

The darkness pulsed, steadily. 'Her power and my power are indivisible.'

'And Mevrad?' enquired Malbane, cautiously. 'She can be so . . . difficult.'

'Mevrad will not interfere,' Bael was certain, 'any more than I shall interfere. Equal and opposite, my precious friends, equal and opposite. Were Mevrad and I to clash directly, *nothing* would be gained, *all* would be destroyed. *All.* The fate of the time spiral will not be settled by Mevrad or by me. It will be a matter for Chess alone.'

'But how . . . ?' began Snargis.

The darkness surged, twisted, shrank and then, standing at its heart there was an old man, an ancient man: thin, with long hands and a face like molten wax, body naked and draped in its own loose folds of flesh. A narrow man.

'Master,' acknowledged the Inquisitors.

Bael's featureless face formed a small black O of a mouth which twitched, dry and lipless, as he spoke. 'With every decision that Chess makes, she will do what I want. She cannot help herself: the darkness is such a part of her.' The little mouth twisted with dry laughter. 'When the time comes to unleash the Eternal, Chess will be precisely where we want her to be, ready to do what we require of her.'

The pan-galactic minds of the Inquisitors expanded in hungry anticipation, swallowing stars.

'However,' continued Bael, toying with an idea, 'I think that we need someone who will guide her last steps, once she discovers that Mevrad's *transport* arrangement with the Sages has failed. Someone who can ensure she is in the perfect state of mind for our purposes. Someone who will make sure that in the final moments, Chess will bend to our will. There is no room for error. *But* it must be someone whom she will trust.'

There was a pause.

'I can think,' said Malbane, 'of none amongst us whom Chess will trust.'

'Not amongst us, Malbane, no.' The withered little mouth wrinkled a smile, lips like dried apple. 'But there is, I think, someone.'

Malbane considered this before uttering the name, 'Saul?'

'I think so,' replied Bael, mouth working tightly, hungrily. 'It would suit our purposes for Saul to be there at the end. Go to him, Malbane. Make sure he understands what is expected of him: that he will take Chess to the Core, that he will loosen the moorings of her mind until she is ready to slide into violent chaos. Saul will listen to you. With me, he is . . . difficult.'

'As you wish,' replied Malbane.

The O vanished before reappearing to say the name, 'Snargis?'

'Master?'

'Your creatures have begun their work? I have a particular pleasure in the suffering of humans.'

'The first are entering their world, even as we speak,' promised Snargis.

'Good. Very good.' The aperture in Bael's empty face puckered hungrily. 'It is time for the final agony to begin.'

The heat was a fog. Bodies moved against her own but oblivious to her as Anna worked her way across the dance floor. The music was so loud that the beat and the flashes of light blurred into one numbing blast which turned a thousand bodies into one entity. But none of this distracted Anna. Her senses had been trained to operate so finely that blindfolded, she could have picked her way across the dance floor on a tightrope. And now, after what had happened earlier this evening, her mind had access to a world beyond that.

Now that Julius's blood had mixed with hers, his genetic code entwined with her own, Anna could feel space that she couldn't see, bend the space through which she moved, move through time as if it were space. The dimensions would be hers to crack open, but she knew that this would take time for her to master. And whilst the power with which Julius had infused her was only an after-beat of what Chess could wield, already she felt the fragility of time and space, and the yawning draw of the abyss-gaps behind it.

'Don't worry, Miss Ledward,' Lemuel had assured her before she had left Committee HQ, 'dancing through the dimensions will come to you as naturally as riding a bicycle,' and his black-nailed fingers had parted her long hair so that he could whisper in her ear, 'It's what you're here for. It's your *purpose*, you beautiful aberration,' and he had tittered in a way which had tickled so intensely that a whisper of an itch had plagued her earlobe for the next half an hour.

But Anna didn't want to experiment with dancing through the dimensions right now. Now was no time to experiment with anything. It would be too dangerous. Now was a time to rely upon skills that Anna had already mastered: to focus, to think as fast as light, to move as fast as thought. She would have to do this because of what was approaching. Automatically, her blood-sharpened senses had detected the heavy footfalls, heard the grunts and phlegm-bubbling snarls, felt the bow wave of air displaced by large moving bodies. Anna knew what was coming towards the door marked 'FIRE EXIT' and she knew there was no time to get this wrong.

She stood at the heart of a thousand dancing bodies, hot bodies, young bodies and she knew that the accelerated contagion of the Plague Breed would reduce them to a vomiting mass of rotting boils in seconds. One contact was all it would take. And it would be up to her to stop this.

Momentarily, Anna closed her eyes, preparing herself. Focusing.

She was a Blood Sentinel. She was here to protect. She was here to fight.

The door was smashed off its hinges and it spun into the club. Silhouetted in the white light of the corridor beyond were bodies: broad, dark, glistening. Anna counted four. One of them tilted back its tumorous head and roared, the animal bellow clear above the music.

For several seconds nothing changed. Then there were shrieks from the dance floor: shrill, brittle shrieks, and then the dancers collapsed in a crazed scramble of bodies. Limbs entangled in a bedlam knot which flailed, drowning in its own mass. There were too many people to clear the dance floor rapidly, and all about its edge, tables and chairs were upended. Bottles and glasses smashed to the floor like dominoes. The music cut out and now the air was torn apart by a cacophony of terror.

Security had gathered at the foot of the short flight of

steps: three of them in black suits, shaven-headed, log-fisted, automatically confronting the interlopers but plainly uncertain of what they should do next.

'Get back,' shouted Anna, but her voice was nothing in the chaos of the club.

The first of the plague beasts had swaggered onto the top of the steps, its swollen, virus-riddled body raw with gaping sores and streaming pus. But it was tall as an ogre and muscular, and in its hand was a long, rough hatchet, smeared with the same putrid slime as its body.

The creature turned its hairless dome of a head towards the first doorman who retreated from the foot of the steps. The creature roared, drooling thickly and opening wide its cavernous maw. As the doorman stumbled back, the plague beast began to retch violently and then to vomit onto the steps, a copious gush of yellow-green sludge that hit the metal, spattering in every direction. Some of the vomit must have splashed onto the bare skin of the man's face because Anna saw him wipe his cheek.

Within seconds, his hand returned to his face, fingers scrabbling and scratching, and as they did so, they began to gouge soft lumps out of his cheek and he began to scream. The necrosis spread swiftly, boils bursting down his neck and beneath his clothes. The other doormen backed away as he held out his hand, the bones of his fingertips poking out where the flesh had already rotted away.

The Plague Breed thudded down the steps, axes, maces and pestilence ready to rip through the mass of bodies that were fighting to escape. Only one person stood between them and their quarry.

The first beast stopped a few metres in front of Anna, looked down at her and roared.

'Anna!' yelled Pacer. He had fought his way through the panic at the perimeter of the dance floor. Now that he was at the edge, he threw something to Anna. At his shout, she looked across, saw what was coming and snatched it from the air.

'Thanks,' she mouthed and then she turned to face the enormous plague beasts, the long, slim, gently curving sword still in its scabbard.

A bursting silence filled the club.

'Go,' she said, holding the sheathed sword horizontal, across her thighs, the scabbard balanced in one hand, the long fingers of her other hand wrapped lightly round the rayskin bindings of the narrow handle. Her waist-length leather jacket was open, loose, her legs were planted shoulder width apart and her black hair hung motionless as she waited: sword, mind and body connected as one.

'How'd she get that in here?' Anna heard one doorman ask another.

She pulled the sword free and at once, the phosphorous blade burst into flame, yellow-white fire serrating the smooth edges in jagged, flickering tongues. She whipped the blade forwards in an arc and the flames *woofed* through the air. The first of the plague beasts took a step back.

'A Muspell blade,' whispered Anna, her sapphire eyes gleaming in the blaze. 'You don't like it, do you?' Fire was the most effective weapon against the Plague Breed and their contagion.

Focus.

In her mind, Anna heard the voice of her old swordmaster, Kusanagi, and she realized that for an instant she had ceased to focus.

As the foremost creature retreated, one on the flank flung his axe at Anna. She leant back, hearing the heavy blade hum past her head. Then, two of the beasts came for her, far more swiftly than she had expected. Their obese bodies covered the floor in stomping strides and as one of them spewed out an acid spray of bubbling vomit, the other drove its nail-studded mace at Anna's face.

Dropping the scabbard and using both hands to hold the sword, Anna blocked the downwards strike, bending her knees with the flaming blade above her left shoulder. But she had only moments to get out of the path of the cascading vomit. Faster than the crack of a whip, she leapt and spun full circle, driving herself away from the spewing stream and slicing out and down with the sword in an outstretched hand. The flame-tongued steel hissed into the plague beast's shoulder.

Strike and pull: draw the blade *through* the target.

Anna and sword moved at electric speed. The blade emerged from the centre of the creature's chest. Even as the flames began to spout from the blood-sludged wound, Anna had landed behind the other spewing beast. Before it could turn, the Muspell blade had kissed its neck clean, leaving a blazing stump where its gross, misshapen head had been. The head landed with a splash in a bubbling pool of green vomit.

Anna became aware of a cluster of doormen at the edge

of the dance floor and she realized that they were actually planning to come to her aid.

'Get back!' she yelled.

Focus.

There was a crack of sinews to her rear and the air moved as what she knew would be an axe blade came swinging at her head. Simultaneously, a spike-headed mace was driven towards her belly.

Too fast, thought Anna. Not enough time. I need more time.

But the rough spike was into her T-shirt already.

Not enough time. She tried to spring away.

Maybe the thought was all it took because as she leapt, Anna realized that the spike to her front and the blade at her rear had slowed. So had the plague beasts themselves. Their limbs seemed to be moving through treacle and their grunts and roars were muted as if they came from a distance, and Anna was jumping further and faster than she had ever known. She cleared the gap from the centre of the dance floor to the far wall in the time it took for a thousand jaws to drop in slow amazement.

Anna knew that she was moving fast: so fast that she had time, so fast that everything else seemed to have stopped. She leapt back at the beasts, somersaulting to avoid the doormen, and she turned the somersault as effortlessly as the thought, although she felt something strike her forehead as she did so.

The plague beasts were where she had left them. Twice the Muspell blade struck, swift, deep cuts, and before the creatures had dropped their weapons, their hulking bodies were engulfed in flame.

Anna collected the sheath from where she'd dropped it on the floor, taking care to inspect it for vomit splashes before picking it up and sliding the blade secure within. Then she touched her forehead, gauging the bleeding throb where her head had struck a low spar in the lighting rig.

Beyond the stinking smoke that rose like battlefield smog from the smouldering heaps on the dance floor, Anna could see bodies crouching, backed up along the walls. Some were embracing, shielding one another. Someone was holding up a camera-phone, recording what was happening. There was sobbing.

'It's OK,' said Anna, huskily. She wiped away blood with the back of her hand. She coughed as a trail of smoke brushed her face.

Then somebody screamed.

Anna couldn't tell what she had heard first: the scream or the heavy thump of pounding feet. But she knew at once that she had made a mistake.

There had been more than four plague beasts.

Maybe one had been shielded by the oozing mass of the others. Or maybe it had been further back, out of sight down the service corridor. Either way, it didn't matter. The fifth one was here now and was almost upon her.

Ethel had warned her about the Plague Marshalls as she had been leaving Committee HQ that evening. Ethel had said the raiding parties weren't usually accompanied by Marshalls. But she hadn't said they couldn't be.

The Plague Marshall stood a metre taller than the other beasts. In one hand he held a long goad which trailed a milk-blue cloud of electric charge. In the other he gripped a log of a club, studded with needles, strands of barbed wire, pieces of glass and rust-rough metal teeth. Before Anna could draw her sword, it had been smashed from her hand by a heft of the club. The blow nearly tore her shoulder from its socket.

The Plague Marshall roared, the festering flesh of his jowls quivering, spittle flying from his black mouth, hatred glistering his ebony, fat-pouched eyes. Then Anna saw Pacer, only a couple of metres away.

'No,' she gasped.

Pacer had something in his hand: something flaming. He drew back his arm, and as the giant beast shook his sweat-streaked dome of a head and charged, Pacer threw the firebomb onto the floor.

Glass smashed and a pool of flame streaked across the floor. The flames tumbled and then unfurled at the Plague Marshall's feet, engulfing his legs at once. The creature brayed and stamped but before he was free of the first clutch of fire, Anna had retrieved her sword, freed the blade and sent it flashing into his chest like a blazing lightning bolt. The Marshall roared once more and then his bellows were lost within the roar of the flames.

'OK, everybody,' Pacer announced, turning on the spot with arms outstretched as if taking applause. He was shouting to be heard above the blaring smoke alarm. 'Show's over. Time to go home.'

The people were slow to move and when they started, it

was in a hesitant shamble. Pacer and Anna remained on the dance floor and the bodies of the Plague Breed lay about them like beacons, great yellow smoke plumes billowing.

Anna sheathed the sword. 'Not bad,' she admitted.

'No metal, no magic.' Pacer thrust out his jaw, proudly. 'Just one hundred per cent genuine human.' He nodded at Anna. 'And good with firebombs too.' Then he inspected the tear in his black combat jacket from where he'd ripped the strip of cloth to tuck into the neck of the bottle.

'Good to see that a childhood spent committing arson didn't go to waste,' observed Anna.

Pacer mimicked Anna's clear, precise voice, and then said, 'You're such a jack.' Then he squatted, dabbed a forefinger into a liquid sheen by his feet and touched his tongue. 'Waste of vodka,' he grumbled.

'Pacer, you idiot!' snapped Anna. '*Plague*. Remember?'

'Well, he don't need it.' Pacer jerked his head at the crackling remains of the Marshall. Then he sniffed. 'Smells better than he looks.'

Anna watched him stand with his head on one side, listening.

The ceiling lights were flickering, watery through the rank smog. The alarm was still ringing, there was the clumsy scrape of furniture being shifted and there was the icicle-sharp sweep of broken glass being cleared. And from somewhere behind the pall of smoke, there was a new noise: police radios.

'Crashers!' Pacer's eyes narrowed.

'Time to go,' said Anna.

'To Crazy Boris's?'

'Yeah.'

Pacer nodded and took a last look at the smog-shrouded wreckage of the club. 'Good. Whatever's happening there, it can't be any worse than this.'

CHAPTER 5

'You said it couldn't be worse than the club,' murmured Pacer.

'*You* said it couldn't be worse than the club,' Anna corrected him. She adjusted her position on the rooftop balustrade. 'Anyway,' she added with cool precision, 'at the moment, it *isn't* worse than the club.'

They sat on the ornate parapet of a roof terrace, a block away from Mendoza Row, feet dangling over the long drop. Anna had the sheathed sword across her lap. Beside her, Pacer hunched forwards, elbows on thighs. Their silhouettes were miniscule against the mountainous backdrop of the city and the night.

'Why aren't they doing nothing?' Pacer jabbed his chin towards the army of hunters that surrounded the whole of Mendoza Row, spotlights and gun barrels trained on number 18.

'Why aren't they doing *anything*?' sighed Anna. 'It's not just grammar, Pacer. It's logic.'

'Stop jabbing me with that sword,' muttered Pacer.

'They don't know what to do,' explained Anna. 'And

I didn't jab you,' she growled. '*You* can't sit still.'

Pacer rubbed his chin, then rubbed his stubbled head. 'But there's hundreds of them?' He looked at Anna for more explanation.

'Right: ever had a fight with someone you can't beat?' she began.

'No,' was Pacer's immediate response.

Anna looked sidelong, crystal eyes unblinking.

Pacer rubbed his nose and shrugged. 'Not what I can remember,' he mumbled.

'Well,' continued Anna, '*if* you were fighting someone you couldn't beat, but you got the upper hand, for a moment, you wouldn't know what to do. Because you'd know that when that moment was over, you'd be in big trouble.' She nodded in the direction of the jack boots, the helmets, the death's-head insignia and the guns. 'That's what's happening. They've been sent to pin down the Committee, but they know Chess is in there.' Anna sucked in air through her teeth, sharply. 'One bad mood-swing from our girl and it's bye-bye hunters.'

'Well why don't she just slab 'em all?'

'Because she *don't* know what she's doing.' Anna picked a strand of fringe free of the dried blood on her forehead.

Pacer nodded to himself, resolute. 'That's what we're here for.' When Anna looked at him quizzically, he said, 'To help her.'

'Yup.' Anna heaved in a breath and looked up. 'Here to help.' She blinked at the night sky which was dark orange in the glow of the city. Starless.

Pacer watched her thoughtfully before saying, 'You miss him proper bad, don't you?'

'Yup.' Anna stayed looking up. After a pause she said, 'I don't have my family now and they don't have me. They know I've gone but they don't know why.' She looked down, eyes bright. Wet. 'And then, when I thought there was someone else, something else . . .' She shrugged.

Pacer pulled his knees away from the tip of the scabbard. 'Sorry.'

Anna heaved in another breath.

'He'll be back,' said Pacer, and he gave Anna's shoulder a gentle squeeze. 'I know Box. He wants to be with you. Nothing will stop him.'

Anna nodded, tight-lipped.

'You ain't crying?' asked Pacer. Anna glared at him. 'No. Didn't think you was. Anyway, if Box was here now, he'd want to fight his way in. Even if they was all looking the other way, he'd want to mix it. So maybe it's as well he's not with us.'

Anna laughed.

'But me? I've got a better way, even if I'm not Box. It's not a way what a jack like you would want, but I think I can get us in without a sweat.' He bit his lip. 'Hopefully.'

Anna nodded. 'Thanks, Pacer,' she said.

'That's OK. I'm smart at plans.'

'No. I mean about Box.' Anna smiled. 'Thanks.'

Pacer grunted and then said quietly, 'I know what it's like.'

Anna saw that he was staring down at 18 Mendoza Row. She cupped his chin and turned his head so that he was looking into her blue, unblinking eyes. 'We can help her, Pacer.'

Sword in hand, she slipped onto the roof.

Professor Breslaw was drumming his fingers against the wheel of his chair and from time to time he hummed to himself. His thick, ginger moustache wiggled about as he hummed and the tubes which were implanted in the loose flesh beneath his chin jerked taut as he droned. These tubes, like a web of others, curved between his corpulent body in its patchwork coat and his wheelchair.

Chess thought that even though he was plump, the Professor looked deflated. A bit sunken. Older. But despite the gloom, Professor Breslaw's good eye saw Chess looking at him and it winked at her.

'Waiting for the shoot-out to begin, no?' He cleared his phlegmy throat and wiped a hand over his bald scalp.

Chess shrugged. I'm not waiting for anything in particular, she thought. But she knew that everything was waiting for her and she hated that feeling. It made her feel as if she might slide out of herself and into a chaos that would blot her out, together with everything else.

The balance is so fine, a voice in her head kept telling her.

If it keeps telling me that, Chess thought to herself, there won't be any balance at all. I'll just explode.

She rested her forehead against the cold glass of the room-length window of the kitchen and looked through the conservatory beyond, with its huge succulents silhouetted like stooping villains. Outside, the criss-crossing beams of searchlights lanced the patio and the short rear garden with thick stripes of white. Fingers of light crept in, penetrating the gaps between the plants and dappling the kitchen which was otherwise in darkness.

'I don't want to sound unrealistic,' said Crazy Boris, whose house it was, 'but I'd much prefer it if we could avoid the shoot-out stuff.' He scratched his stubbly chin and crossed his lanky arms. 'There's enough damage being done to the carpets by feet alone.'

Everyone except Julius looked down as if they were not responsible for whatever misdemeanours their feet had committed.

'I'm not even wearing shoes,' observed Gemma brightly, sticking her legs out from the sofa where she was sitting and wiggling her toes. 'I never do.'

'In your case, I wish you would.' Crazy Boris frowned at the bare soles. 'Look at the state of your feet.'

The little blonde girl wiggled her toes some more and grinned through her uneven teeth.

'A carpet,' observed Balthazar, filling the space beside Gemma, 'is like a book, written by feet.' His staff was propped in the corner of the kitchen beyond the end of the sofa.

Crazy Boris turned his insomniac eyes on Balthazar. 'A carpet is a carpet is a *carpet*,' he recited in a plaintive brogue. 'Nothing gets written on it. And if I had my way, nothing would get stood on it. Or, with all due respect to your infirmities, Professor, wheeled on it.'

Captain Riley said nothing. Neither did Julius. They stood at either end of the long partition window which separated the kitchen from the conservatory, arms folded like shadow statues, apart from the gleam of silver down the right side of Julius's face.

'There won't be a shoot-out, my loves,' said Ethel, who had positioned herself in a fan-backed wicker chair where she could knit in comfort. 'Not yet.'

'Not yet?' Crazy Boris padded up and down the length of the kitchen. He stopped in front of the old lady. '*Not yet?*'

'I heard your rhetorical complaint the first time, dear.' The background glow from the searchlights was luminous enough for Chess to see Ethel glance over her knitting needles, reprovingly. 'They are waiting: *pinning us down*, if that's the correct expression. Is it the correct expression, Captain Riley?' she called out.

'It'll do,' replied Captain Riley, motionless.

'Good.' Ethel smiled. 'I think I'm picking up the lingo, at last,' she whispered in Chess's direction, confidentially. Then, eyeballing Crazy Boris, 'The Committee are most apologetic for commandeering your house in this fashion, Mr Sherevsky. But we are at war.'

'I'm not a big *war* man,' protested Crazy Boris.

'He's a *musician*,' insisted Chess. It was important to let Ethel know that not everyone was there to satisfy her whims. She ignored the you-should-know-better eyeball that swivelled in her direction.

'Rock star, retired,' clarified Crazy Boris.

'*They* don't care what you are, Mr Sherevsky.' Ethel jabbed a knitting needle in the direction of the searchlights.

Chess knew that out there, the house was surrounded by an army of hunters. If she wanted, she could have walked amongst them unseen, observing who was where, who was training their weapon on the house, who had drifted into sleep in the darkness. She could have destroyed them as effortlessly as thinking. She could have unleashed the power that screamed to be unleashed: the dark energy of the billions of tortured souls that the Symmetry had filled her with, a power that surged in her spirit, taking her mind almost to breaking point. And because her mind could touch every universe even as she stood here, Chess could draw upon all the pain and suffering that filled those universes right now.

But if she unleashed this power, if she let the dark energies rip free, tearing the hunters out of existence, blistering space itself with the blast ... what then? Could she stop? *Would* she stop?

Chess knew that deep within her there lurked a darkness of her own: a darkness that Lemuel had told her had come from her father. Chess didn't know who her father was, but she knew this darkness and she knew that once it broke free there would be no stopping it. It would be like a rage, a fire: unstoppable. That was why she was so frightened of losing *herself* if she unleashed the dark energy. That was why the hunters were safe from her, for the time being. And that was why Chess was waiting, like everyone else was waiting: waiting for the Blood Sentinels to return. And once the Blood Sentinels had returned, everyone would decide what to do next. But not Chess. She had decided already what she was going to do. She was waiting only for Anna.

Time is passing, she thought to herself. She could feel it in her core, the vanishing of every second into the dead end of the remaining hours. Before long, they would come to a place where all that eternity would depend upon what *she* did. That was what the Committee wanted. That was what the Twisted Symmetry wanted. But Chess knew she couldn't trust herself to make the right choice any more than she could trust herself against the hunters now. That was why she wasn't going to do what the Committee planned and that was why she wasn't going to do what the Twisted Symmetry planned. That was why she was going to do something different.

'Having driven us out of HQ,' Ethel was saying, 'the hunters have the Committee's high command surrounded, thereby making life a little more difficult for us. So far as they are able, they can see who comes and who goes. And, so far as they are able, they hope to keep us *pinned down* until the Third Wave hits the city.'

'The Third Wave?' Crazy Boris scratched his chin, loudly.

'Of the Plague Breed, dear.' Ethel huffed and untangled her wool. 'They come in waves.'

'Like headaches?' suggested Gemma.

'Like very big ones.' Ethel's needles clicked back into action.

'How can you knit in the dark?' asked Gemma.

'Practice,' replied Ethel. 'I've spent most of my life in the dark.' Then she returned to what she had been talking about before Gemma's interruption. 'The enemy don't know that *we* know the Plague Breed are coming. Everyone is waiting for someone else to make the first move. It's called a Mexican stand-off.' Silence. 'I'm right about that, aren't I, Captain Riley?' Her head remained bent over her knitting.

'I'm not sure that's the technical expression,' observed Riley.

'It doesn't matter,' muttered Ethel. 'As the Professor said, we're waiting for the shoot-out to begin.'

'Just a pity it's in my house,' grumbled Crazy Boris. 'There are plenty of derelicts where you could have holed up. Plenty of wrecks purpose-built for a shoot-out.'

'You *are* part of this, Mr Sherevsky.' Ethel looked at him, critically, over the top of her spectacles.

Chess knew that in the darkness of the attic there was a photograph of Crazy Boris and Esme, smiling: a photograph from more than forty years ago, from before the tearing of the dark hooks.

She had to get rid of that thought. 'How did you know the Plague Breed were coming?' The press of the cold glass against the skin of her forehead was a relief. Chess puffed out to fog it, then drew a large 'C' in the condensation.

Before Ethel could answer, there were gentle footfalls into the kitchen from the hallway beyond. Chess turned and saw Lemuel Sprazkin's chalk-white crescent face, lambent in the plant-filtered glow of the searchlights.

'It's happening,' he trilled. Then, in a whisper, 'It must be nearly time.'

'Time for what?' asked Gemma.

'For the fifth node, silly.' Lemuel tittered. He strode up to Gemma quickly, black-trousered legs stepping jerky as a stork's, and he put his beaming face up to hers.

'Oh!' gasped Gemma, sitting back, deep into the sofa.

'Time for the end, and the beginning. Of *something*,' and Lemuel drew in a long sniff of air and closed his eyes as if savouring an elegant claret.

'Lemuel!' snapped Ethel.

'I am trying, Mevrad,' wheedled Lemuel.

'*Very* trying,' grumbled Ethel, tucking back into her knitting.

Chess watched the ex-primary warp smile in Ethel's direction and then saw his face go blank as he realized that she was paying him no more attention. Ethel might have switched him out, but Chess knew how difficult it was for Lemuel: how difficult it was to struggle with what you were made to be when you wanted to be something else.

Ever since their return from the warp station, Lemuel had struggled. He had delayed the implanting of his virtual consciousness from Anna's Link-me computer back into his body for weeks, without any explanation. And then, once his mind was back in his body, he had been different. Chess knew that he was finding being good more difficult than before. She knew that for something that had been built to be bad, he was doing his best, but that without the brain drill he had once used to recalibrate his behaviour from bad to good, he struggled. And sometimes, she suspected that he liked being a little bit closer to badness. It was easier for him.

'What is the reading?' Julius's voice was business-like.

Chess saw Lemuel study the box he was holding. Now that he tilted it up, she could see the luminescence of the dial housing, carving his face out of light and shadow. Sensory probes extended from its top like antennae from a beetle.

'What's that?' asked Chess. 'And where's Anna? Anna should have been back by now. And Pacer.'

'It is called a metastometer.' Lemuel looked over to her, a stray spar of light from outside catching the glass panel that crowned his skull. 'It will let us know when the universes are ready.'

'Ready for what?' asked Chess.

'Ready for *you*.'

Chess stuffed her fists in her leather jacket and pursed her lips.

'The reading, Lemuel,' repeated Julius, stirring in the corner of the room. 'What is the reading?'

Lemuel put his long nose right up to the glass of the dial housing, then curved his head round, birdlike in the glow. A dark-lipped smile crept up his face. 'We have arrived,' he announced, very quietly, 'at metastasis four.'

There was a viscous cough from Professor Breslaw. 'More advanced than I imagined.'

'Goodness,' sighed Ethel, a little wistfully. 'It must be nearly three o'clock.'

'Meaning?' demanded Chess.

'Meaning,' explained Balthazar patiently, deep voice a croon, 'that we are almost at the end, just as Lemuel has said. The end *and* the beginning.'

Chess saw him inspect the back of one large, wrinkled hand before pulling his pipe and tobacco from the pocket of his tuxedo jacket.

'No way,' objected Crazy Boris. 'We may be under starter's orders for the end of the universe, but the no smoking rule still applies. Sorry, fella, but there are limits.'

Balthazar sighed, took a mighty sniff of the sweet-scented tobacco, still in its pouch, then replaced pipe and pouch in his pocket.

Meter readings, and talk about metastasis, and discussion

about the end and the beginning of things might have been science, but to Chess it might as well have been riddles. She wanted to know what it actually meant. 'How long, Ethel?' She leant against the window again. 'How long before we hit the fifth node?'

She was provided with an answer immediately. 'Eleven hours and fourteen minutes,' said Ethel. 'Give or take.'

A tall, stout man in denim dungarees stepped out of nowhere and into the centre of the room. A ginger beard curled to his chest and his orange hair was plastered flat on his head. In his hand he held a huge wooden staff. Chess could see that it was just like Balthazar's, save that this staff was shod with iron.

'It's a measure of the general level of weirdness in this room,' remarked Crazy Boris, 'that nobody was particularly surprised by that.'

Julius strode out of the shadows, boots thumping over the floor, long leather coat flapping open to reveal the heavy machine pistols at his belt. 'Ragg.' He gripped the red-bearded giant of a man by his ox shoulders. 'Have they come? Are the Breed here?'

Ragg nodded, but Chess could see that he was distracted by the tall man in the ill-fitting dinner suit who filled half of the sofa opposite. Balthazar held up a hand, palm open, and shook his head as if to tell the newcomer not to pay him attention. Not yet.

Ragg switched his rabbit-eyed gaze back to Julius. 'They are here.' He panted slightly. Damp patches stained the armpits of his rough shirt.

'Who is he?' Chess whispered to Balthazar.

'His name,' murmured Balthazar, 'is Vladivostok Ragg. He was a Guide, as I once was.' Balthazar snorted a melancholy chuckle. 'But not disgraced as I was.'

In the darkness, Chess noticed how Balthazar's bulging eyes switched to Julius for a moment: the man whom he had once been held responsible for killing; the man who was still alive because Balthazar had been sent back in time for a thousand years, thus avoiding the future in which Julius's blood would have been on his hands.

'It wasn't your fault, Balthazar,' whispered Chess.

'It will always be my fault,' sighed Balthazar. He changed the subject by returning to Chess's original question. 'For many years now, Ragg has been a Sentinel. Our paths have not crossed in centuries.'

'He looks a bit sweaty to be a Blood Sentinel,' observed Chess in a low voice.

'He is a good man,' said Balthazar.

'You are *sure* they are here?' Julius was asking.

'Metastasis four, Julius,' sang Lemuel and he turned a pirouette before sweeping past Chess, crescent-head cross-hatched by fingers of light from outside.

'They are here. I know.' Vladivostok Ragg stepped back from Julius. 'Anna has already made contact.'

'Is she alright?' asked Chess, immediately, but her question was drowned out by Professor Breslaw's long, clacking cough.

'*Contact?*' he choked.

'Joachim.' Ethel must have been worried for the Professor because she dropped her knitting to the floor and hurried to the wheelchair. She put a little hand against his bald head. 'Please, Joachim. Not so excitable.'

Joachim Breslaw growled his throat clear. He spoke to Ethel gruffly, quietly, but Chess could hear what he said. 'I am fading, Mevrad. Fading very quickly, now.'

'Not yet,' insisted the old lady. 'Not yet.'

'It was an advance party,' explained Vladivostok Ragg. 'Four beasts and a Marshall.'

'Is she alright?' repeated Chess. 'Is Anna alright?'

Ragg nodded. 'I think so.' He looked about the room. 'She isn't here yet?'

'No,' replied Chess, worried now that Ragg expected Anna to have returned already. 'And Pacer?' she asked. 'Is he OK?'

'Pacer?' Ragg shrugged his meaty shoulders. 'Who's Pacer?'

Chess shook her head hopelessly and dumped herself on the arm of the sofa by Gemma.

'So I'm the first one back?' asked Vladivostok Ragg.

Julius nodded, turned away from the carrot-headed giant and headed back to the shadows to wait.

'Call me fussy,' ventured Crazy Boris, standing in the centre of the kitchen, 'but what's with the "first one back" stuff? I mean, we're probably breaching health and safety regulations as it is. This kitchen can't hold many more.' He looked Ragg up and down. 'Not if they're all as big as ginger nuts, here. No offence.'

Ragg drew up his shoulders and smiled vacantly. 'This is where we were all told to meet, Mr Sherevsky.'

'Mr Sherevsky,' nodded Crazy Boris. 'Good. I like that. Politeness. It matters.'

'We need a bigger kitchen,' tolled Julius from the gloom.

Crazy Boris hooked his long, strong, guitar player's fingers in the belt of his jeans which hung loose about his scrawny waist. 'There's nothing wrong with my kitchen. It's a perfect kitchen, size-wise.' He looked pointedly at Julius, and then at Ethel. 'It just needs a few less people in it.'

From far away, there came the growl of a motorbike engine.

'Hunters?' Gemma's voice was small in the darkness.

'No,' said Chess. She recognized that engine, recognized the way it roared out of the depths of the vortex. 'It's Jake. It's his motorbike.'

'I told him to come straight here,' said Julius.

'*Straight* here?' choked Crazy Boris, barely audible above the screaming engine.

The wall above the sofa erupted as spinning chrome wheels, black fairings and the half-shell helmeted, Gun Toting Biker Dwarf burst into the kitchen with a strong smell of petrol and an engine-roar like a rock slide. Wheels spun through the dappled light, over the heads of Balthazar and Gemma. Balthazar threw himself over Gemma to protect her. The bike landed in the centre of the room with an uncompromising crunch.

As the last of the masonry bounced across the carpet, Balthazar uncovered Gemma. Everyone brushed the plaster and brick dust from their hair. The GTBD cut the engine. He pushed up his goggles and took the weight of the chopper on his solid, stumpy legs.

'A kitchen?' He looked about until he saw Julius. 'You didn't say these coordinates led to a *kitchen*.'

Slack-jawed, Boris Sherevsky absorbed the demolition-sized hole in the wall and the debris-strewn carpet. 'My kitchen,' he mouthed.

The GTBD dismounted, pulled a pump-action shotgun

from a holster in front of the saddle and stomped over to the windows, oil-stained boots crushing the remaining pile of the carpet.

'Not yet, Jake,' said Julius. 'The others are coming.'

'Oh yeah,' lamented Crazy Boris. 'I forgot about the *others*. Say, Julius, why don't we just knock through the entire wall? Go for a kind of open-plan battlefield look? Save the others the trouble of re-designing it?'

'That won't be necessary,' replied the commander of the Blood Sentinels. 'I hear them coming already.' He turned to look through the black pattern of plants.

Chess stood beside him, peering through the glass, trying to penetrate the crossing spars of the searchlights outside. All was still and then, in the air some way beyond the ivy-strung wall at the far end of the short garden, she saw two points moving. The points grew in size rapidly and she realized that they were coming closer.

Boris was at her side. 'I wish,' he gasped, 'that I didn't believe it.'

A pair of horsemen were galloping out of the night sky, straight towards the back of the house. The hunters must have seen them because a clutch of searchlights swung upwards, probing the darkness.

A rifle cracked, followed by another. Machine guns opened up, all along the walls about 18 Mendoza Row.

'No!' cried Crazy Boris when he saw Jake pull back the heel of the shotgun. He drove it forwards, breaking the kitchen window.

'What's wrong with the door?'

Jake elbowed out the glass, shoved his way through the

plants and then smashed the glass at the back of the conservatory where he was joined by Julius. There was a pause as the two of them assessed what was happening outside. Then Jake's shotgun blasted into action, illuminating the conservatory with firework flashes, whilst Julius's machine pistols screamed at the hunters, spitting a stream of spent cartridge cases across the conservatory floor.

'They're giving covering fire,' shouted Ethel.

'They're wrecking my house,' shouted Crazy Boris, and then he and Chess were on the floor as return fire from the hunters hammered the back of 18 Mendoza Row, shattering brick and smashing out glass.

Chess looked up in time to see the two horsemen land with a thud at the end of the garden, as if both of them had just cleared the far wall. But they showed no sign of stopping. They careered towards the conservatory in a tornado of grass, mud and bullets.

'Get out of the way!' Chess grabbed Boris's T-shirt and pulled him towards the far wall where Lemuel, Balthazar, Gemma and Vladivostok Ragg had clustered. Ethel had positioned herself and Professor Breslaw in the opposite corner and Captain Riley had joined Julius and Jake in the conservatory where he was giving covering fire.

The kitchen freeze-framed in the flash of the fire-fight. Ricocheting bullets rang across the neatly hanging pans, feather and foam jetted from a string of punctures across the backrest of the sofa, pieces of plant and charcoal streaks of earth dashed the carpet.

'*You* could stop this,' Chess heard Gemma whisper in her ear.

This is why I'd stop *everything*, thought Chess. Which is why I have to be careful: why I don't trust myself.

It was so loud, it was difficult to think at all. The noise intensified and then, as Chess looked up, she saw Riley, Julius and Jake dive to the floor as if they had been thrown there in unison. Half a nerve-jerk later, the reason for their evasive action stormed into the back of the conservatory.

The horses smashed through the remaining glass, crashed through the plants and burst out of the partition window and into the kitchen. Their legs and sweat-muscled flanks powered through the air in a hurricane of plant and glass before they landed together, a chestnut mare and a black stallion, both snorting furiously and stamping their hooves on the carpet.

Chess dropped her arm from her eyes. 'I'm sorry, Boris,' she said, when she saw him clambering up from where he'd rolled on the floor.

'Yeah, well, what the hell,' he sighed, brushing dirt from his jeans. 'I can't take it with me when I'm dead ... which, at this rate, is going to happen a lot sooner than expected.'

The horsemen wheeled their mounts about, taking stock of the occupants of the battered kitchen. Chess could smell the steaming sweat.

The rider on the stallion wore black trousers and an open-chested black tunic. His sharp face was tanned like leather with a thin black moustache and a beard tapering to a small point under his chin. His ebony hair hung loose, his eyes were like anthracite and his mouth was set in a snarl. He snapped the reins left and right, controlling his mount. On one side of his saddle hung a sword, a thick, curved bow and a quiver. On the other side hung a mighty, double-headed battle axe. The handle of a dagger stood proud of his right ankle boot, the fluid lines of an animal fashioned in gold decorating the grip which was level with Chess's face.

As the horse turned, Chess noticed the withered strips of leather that dangled from the bridle reins. But these weren't ordinary strips of leather. Once, Chess had seen dermacarts, maps made from preserved human skin. Black lipped and eyeless though they were, Chess recognized what was hanging from the dark rider's bridle reins.

'Faces,' she said to Gemma, and the rider glared down at them.

Riley and Julius were exchanging sniping shots with the hunters as they retreated from the decimated conservatory into the decimated kitchen.

Astride the massive chestnut sat a man in roll-topped riding boots and a long riding coat which Chess thought looked like the sort of coat worn by soldiers in the olden days, except that this was black and made of leather. On his head he wore a brown broad-brimmed hat and on his hands he wore gloves. Bandoliers crossed his chest, on his belt were holstered a brace of long-barrelled revolvers, at his left hip there hung a cutlass, on his right thigh a flintlock pistol. The stock of a shotgun jutted from its holster above his right shoulder. His hair was long and almost as rich a brown as his horse, his eyes were dark as moleskin and his smile was as warm as Chess imagined wine to be. He swung down from his mount, pulled off his hat.

'Captain Jago Burke. Pleased to meet you, miss,' he said to Chess. He spoke as nicely as a rich jack. But, decided

Chess, rich jacks didn't have scars like the one that gashed the left side of Captain Burke's face.

'Pleased to meet you, too.' It was weird, feeling shy like that. One moment she was ready to end the universes and the next she was acting like a tongue-tied schoolgirl, except that she had never been to school.

She caught Ethel's quizzical gaze and scowled back.

'Please,' continued Captain Jago Burke, 'forgive my comrade. The Scythian is as vicious as he looks and he has the manners of a goat, but you couldn't find a better man when there's killing to be done.'

'Unless it's pest control,' muttered Crazy Boris, 'I'm not interested.'

Jago Burke turned to Ethel and he deepened his bow. 'Madame.' He swung his hat wide and low.

'Don't act the cavalier with me, you old sea dog,' scolded Ethel with a wag of her finger. But she smiled coquettishly and Chess could have sworn that behind the grubby spectacle lenses, there was a fluttering of grey lashes.

A solitary shot cracked from outside, followed by the smack of the round into the kitchen floor. Jago Burke inspected his hat and discovered that a hole had appeared in its brim. He swept the hat back onto his head, then crunched over broken glass and through the shredded plants into the conservatory. His silhouette was stark in the wash of the spotlights.

'The hunters can't miss him,' Gemma whispered to Chess.

'He's alright; he's a Blood Sentinel,' Chess whispered back, feeling a lot less confident than she sounded.

She sucked in air sharply when the next shot came. But

Jago Burke stepped aside too quickly to be seen. He took something from a small pouch on one of the bandoliers and pulled off the paper wrapping with his teeth, whipping the flintlock free from his thigh. Then he slipped the unwrapped round into the breach and levelled the long-nosed firearm as if about to fight a duel.

A set of crosshairs sprang up in front of the hammer. A larger set sprang up from the muzzle. With a loud click, a bipod extended from the body of the gun to the floor and this was followed by more clicking and hatching until a web of stabilizers and cooling fins had cantilevered free and the flintlock had grown to the size of a small rocket-launching system.

Jago Burke pulled the trigger. There was a sound like a quarry blast and then a mountain of flame erupted into the sky where the sniper had been secreted. The flames billowed up, tiger-striping the interior of the kitchen, and debris rained onto the garden. There was a busy metallic rattling, the flintlock resumed its modest dimensions and Jago Burke returned it to its holster and marched back inside.

'I don't know when or how Miss Ledward intends to arrive,' said Captain Burke, 'but it has become increasingly dangerous out there.'

Captain Riley returned to the kitchen, having scouted through the darkness of the house. 'They have every approach covered, front and back.'

'We can't wait for very much longer,' grumbled Ethel. 'I imagine you'll want to be on your way soon, dear,' she said to Chess.

How do you know that? thought Chess but she tried not

to show how right Ethel was. 'I'm waiting for Anna,' she said.

Ethel frowned through what remained of the windows. 'I don't think we have that long,' she said.

CHAPTER 6

'You should have faith in Miss Ledward's remarkable abilities, Mevrad.' Lemuel had glided to the remains of the window from where he could look upon the back of the house. He tittered and pointed outside. 'The least dramatic arrival, I must say. But the most practical.'

Chess saw that he was pointing at a manhole cover in the flagstones of the patio. The circular lid had tilted up like the peak of a cap. It slid back. Swift as an otter, Pacer emerged. A sheathed sword was passed up to him and after the sword came Anna. The two of them ran into the battered conservatory, Anna's loose leather jacket flapping behind her.

Chess felt her chest quicken with a spark of happiness.

Anna squeezed her arm as she sauntered into the kitchen. 'Hi, Boris,' she said, assessing the wreckage. 'Nice horses. What's happened to the carpet?'

Pacer clapped Crazy Boris on the shoulder. 'At least you're OK.' He peered about the room, backing away from the chestnut mare which snuffled in his direction. 'Is it all like this?'

'No,' replied Crazy Boris. 'This is the only room with animals in it.'

Gunfire rapped the front of the house.

'Ah,' sighed Crazy Boris, 'the familiar sound of breaking glass.'

'You OK?' asked Chess. She could see the fresh gash on Anna's forehead.

Anna nodded. 'How about you?'

Chess nodded back. 'Not bad.'

'Who are you kidding?' frowned Anna. But before they could talk more, Julius was between them, questioning Anna about what had happened in the nightclub. Captain Burke and the Scythian were tending to their horses against the part-demolished rear wall of the kitchen and everybody was talking and trying to find a space where they weren't pushing up against anyone else.

I should go, thought Chess. Just go. Now.

'Hey?' It was Pacer, behind her.

Chess turned and waited for him to say something but he said nothing, so she said, 'Thanks. For getting Anna back safely.'

Pacer looked over to where Anna appeared to be arguing with Julius. 'Anna doesn't need a lot of looking after.' He smiled wryly. 'All she wanted was to get back here to check you were OK.' His dark face fell expressionless in the gloom. There was a pause and then he said, 'Me too.'

Sometimes eyes said more than words. Pacer's eyes spoke to Chess now and she didn't know what to say back.

More gunfire at the front of the house, and then a loud bang.

'*Disturbing*,' announced Crazy Boris, but in the tumult of the crammed kitchen, nobody replied.

'I have to go. Again,' Chess said to Pacer. It was too difficult to smile.

'Can I come with you, this time? I don't care what happens,' and hurriedly he added, 'to me, I mean. It don't matter about me.'

A piercing whistle. Ethel was standing in the centre of the room amidst horses, a motorbike, a wheelchair and the crush of bodies. Her cheeks ballooned as she blew on the referee's whistle again and this time everyone fell silent, apart from Jago Burke's chestnut mare, who whinnied irritably.

'Thank you,' said Ethel, without a great deal of observable gratitude. 'It has taken some doing but at last we are all here.'

'And we have created a major security risk,' observed Captain Riley, from his look-out point in one corner of the shell of a conservatory. 'Assembling the entire Committee in a place like this.'

'There's nothing wrong with a place like this,' muttered Crazy Boris. 'Leastways, there wasn't until folk started driving motorbikes through walls and showing up on horseback. And *spilling crumbs*.' This last was directed at Vladivostok Ragg who had found a packet of biscuits in one of Boris's largely empty cupboards.

'Did *you* bring those in here?' Crazy Boris quizzed Anna, *sotto voce*.

'Ages ago,' Anna *sotto voce*'d back.

'We won't be here for very much longer, Captain.' Ethel tucked the whistle inside the elasticated waist of her orange and white skirt. There was an explosion from outside which sent a tremor through the whole house. Dust and plaster pattered down from the ceiling. Ethel picked something from between her teeth, then inspected her forefinger. 'Would you believe it?' she said. 'A piece of brick.'

Nobody said that they didn't believe it.

'The most pressing business is to seal the current entry point against the Plague Breed. We must do this before the Third Wave arrives.'

'You know where the entry point is, Mevrad?' Julius faced her, arms folded.

'Obviously. How else could I have told you where you had to look for them in the first place?'

Chess found it very irritating when Ethel was so obviously pleased with herself.

'How *did* you know where to look?' asked Ragg, biscuit in hand.

Ethel's smile of self-congratulation faded. 'You of all people will recall the tragic events in the library of the CREX Research Institute.'

'And me,' growled Jake.

'Poor Samphire,' sighed Ethel.

'Who was Samphire?' whispered Gemma.

'One of us,' said Vladivostok Ragg. 'A Blood Sentinel. Killed by the Symmetry. A crystal knife, through the heart.'

Balthazar's bass voice buzzed out of the umber depths of the room. 'There can be no surviving such a wound. A crystal knife cuts through time itself.' Chess noticed how his bulging eyes flicked for an instant towards Julius.

'But still,' Ethel's voice, bell clear, 'you brought back the book that Samphire had been sent to . . . borrow.'

'She had it inside her shirt,' said Ragg. 'The Crystal Priests were so pleased with their killing that they forgot to think about why Samphire had been there in the first place.'

Ethel produced a small, grey-covered, unspectacular book from out of the waistband of her skirt.

'Why don't she use a handbag like everyone else?' muttered Pacer to Balthazar.

'Huge knickers,' Ethel muttered back, before flapping open the pages. 'People should be careful what they scribble in books. Particularly warps when they are calculating the best way to infiltrate our world. Here.' She tapped the open page. 'In the margin, calculations, idly drawn, establishing the optimum wormhole into the city by which the Plague Breed can enter.'

'There's a wormhole?' asked Anna. 'In the leisure complex?'

Ethel nodded. 'I sent your young friend, Trick, to reconnoitre it, months ago. And she found a hole with no bottom beneath the leisure complex, precisely where the calculations said it would be. Which means we are one step ahead of where the Twisted Symmetry expect *us* to be.'

'Well done, Mevrad,' chuckled Professor Breslaw with a bob of throat tubes.

'But how to hold back the Third Wave?' expostulated Jago Burke, one hand cupping his strong chin, the other resting on the pommel of his cutlass. 'There will be tens of thousands of them.'

'We start killing them now,' rumbled Jake. He cracked open the pump-action shotgun and began to feed in cartridges from a saddle bag on his motorbike.

Julius's silver hand restrained the GTBD's arm. 'We have to close the wormhole. Destroy the entry point into this world and the assault is over.'

'So, how to close a wormhole?' Professor Breslaw puffed out his cheeks, his red moustache splaying into a bristle. 'No easy thing. Perhaps, if one of us possessed a small thermo-nuclear device ...' The Professor shrugged. 'Do any of us possess a small thermo-nuclear device?'

There was a sigh of resignation from Crazy Boris. 'Funnily enough, I do.'

'*You?*' Anna couldn't believe it.

'Yes. Me. Remember the vault? The tube with the small nuclear bomb inside?' Crazy Boris's eyes tracked a line upwards. 'That small nuclear bomb is still in the attic.' He shrugged at Anna's obvious amazement. 'It's not that I thought it would come in handy. I just didn't know what to do with it.'

Ethel clapped her small hands together. 'Splendid!' A blast from the street outside rocked the house slightly. 'Yes, well, we don't have long.' Ethel straightened her sage cardigan.

'Prepare to move,' ordered Julius. 'We have to hold back the Breed for as long as it takes to close the bridge into this world.'

With a rattle of weapons and slap of riding gear, the Sentinels began to prepare themselves for departure.

Chess noticed Anna catch Julius's burning eyes.

'*We* fight the Plague Breed,' he stated. '*That* is our task.'

Anna scowled at Julius, tight lipped.

'Of course, the Plague Breed aren't the only pressing

matter,' announced Ethel. 'There is the other pressing matter. The elephant in the room, if you like.'

'An elephant,' muttered Crazy Boris, 'is about the only thing that we *don't* have in this room.'

Chess saw Ethel looking at her. 'What?' She pulled her fists from the pockets of her leather jacket and crossed her arms.

'Well, it's *you*, dear.'

Even the Sentinels paused in their preparations to stare at her. Chess stared at the floor.

'It's time for you to decide what you are going to do, my love. After all, that *is* what this is all about.'

Maybe Ethel had expected her to flounder, but Chess knew exactly what she was going to do. More defiantly than she had intended, she announced, 'I'm going to destroy the Eternal.'

There was total silence before Ethel said, 'Yes ... well ... that might not be as simple as it sounds.' Chess thought that the old lady almost sounded embarrassed.

'There *is* something called the Eternal, isn't there? The Eternal Core Decelerator. It's a weapon. *You* told me that, ages ago.' There's no need for me to sound so angry, Chess thought to herself, and she could sense how the anger made her feel as if she were slipping. Anger wasn't good. Not when she was in this state. Not at a time like this. Chess understood that her anger could have consequences far beyond a flash of rage.

'Yes, dear. I did tell you that.'

'Well, I'm going to destroy it.' Chess let everyone absorb this piece of information before adding, 'It's what everyone's fighting about. It's what the Twisted Symmetry need, to destroy time. It's what you *don't* want them to have. If I destroy the Eternal, it's over.' My voice is too loud, she thought. 'And everyone can stop fighting.'

More gunfire from the street and the sound of glass shattering in the front of the house.

Crazy Boris broke the silence inside. 'Anything that stops the fighting is fine by me.'

The Scythian was speaking softly to his horse in a language Chess didn't understand.

'This is how you wanted it, Mevrad,' said Joachim Breslaw, his guttural voice thick in the darkness. 'Right from the beginning. You took Chess out of the Symmetry's hands, chose when to ...'

'Play her?' suggested Anna, coldly.

'And now,' continued the Professor, 'now she positions herself. Just as you planned.'

'I'm doing what *I* want to do,' fired Chess. 'I'm not being *used*. I'm not being *positioned*.'

'You're doing what you *have* to do, my love.' Ethel sounded almost sympathetic.

'You're doing what you were *made* for,' Chess heard Lemuel whisper.

'Not a very helpful observation, Lemuel,' said Ethel, tersely, 'in the current circumstances.'

'This is out of your hands, Mevrad,' concluded Julius, coolly.

'Precisely.' Ethel was clipped, business-like. 'What happens next is a matter for Chess.'

'Then stop going on about it,' shouted Chess. The final

shards of glass shattered where they had been hanging like icicles from the woodwork. The Sentinels stopped loading weapons, securing blades, checking riding tack. Everyone looked at Chess.

Suddenly, Chess wanted to be away from all of this. She didn't want to be what everything else was depending upon. And she didn't want people to keep on discussing what she would or wouldn't be doing.

She breathed deeply, spoke slowly. 'I am going to where the twelve suns are one. That's where I'll find the Eternal. And then I will destroy it because that is what *I* have decided to do.'

'If you would allow me to make one tiny point, dear,' ventured Ethel, as if she was tiptoeing over gelignite, 'I don't think you know where the twelve suns are one.'

Chess resisted the desire to react with pan-universal fury. 'I don't,' she admitted. 'But I suppose you are going to tell me.'

'The Sages will be able to tell you, dear.' Ethel smiled as kindly as she ever had, although Chess suspected this had more to do with caution than kindness. 'For reasons that are rather complicated, it is better that you make your way to the Sages, rather than try to find the way to the Eternal on your own.'

Chess shrugged. 'Fine. But I don't even know where the Sages are. They're one of the things I can't find.' Like Splinter, she thought. Inside the vortex, some things were lost forever.

'The vast hall of the Sages is protected from prying eyes,

and minds,' explained Ethel. 'You can only find it if you know the way.'

'I know the way,' said Balthazar. 'I will take you.' There was a bulging silence and then he added. 'I left you once before, Chess. This time I would come with you.'

Ethel muttered crossly under her breath.

'Thank you, Balthazar,' said Chess, defiantly, her brown eyes lucent and trained on Ethel.

'Possibly, there are safer guides.' Ethel shrugged off Chess's brazen glare. 'But as I keep saying, dear, it's your choice.'

'And I'm coming too,' said Pacer. 'I don't care where it is. Or how lively it gets.'

Chess looked at Pacer. 'You sure?' she asked, but inside she realized how much she didn't want to do this next bit on her own.

Pacer was deadly serious. 'Course I'm sure.'

Chess smiled, really smiled. 'Good.'

Pacer grinned. 'Cool.'

There was a loud tut from Anna. 'You're not asking her out,' she muttered. 'The only date you're making, Pacer, is with the end of the universe.'

'Universes,' Pacer corrected her.

'I'm not going to tell you how irritating that is,' growled Anna through gritted teeth.

Chess felt Gemma's hand in her own. Gemma didn't have to say anything.

'If it's all the same,' came the ragged voice of Crazy Boris, 'I wouldn't mind making a booking for this particular trip.' He was sitting on the floor, a broken bough of greenery held loosely in his hand. It was bent, pathetically.

'You!' Anna was incredulous.

'I think,' said Boris Sherevsky, 'that it's going to be one hell of a gig. There may not be a T-shirt, but this way I get a front row seat.' Then, hesitantly, he added, 'And if time *is* about to do something weird with itself ... well ... who knows ... I might be able to slip inside and see someone I thought I'd never see again.'

Silence, and then a tinkling voice. 'And then, there's me.'

'I don't think ...' began Ethel.

'Oh, I know,' fussed Lemuel, 'there's all that primary warp nonsense, but that's so yester-millennium, Mevrad. I have been with Chess, right from the beginning. I would so like to be with her when the spiral horizon hoves into view. There would be a wonderful ...'

'*Symmetry?*' suggested Ethel.

Even in the shadows, Chess could see Lemuel purse his lips peevishly. 'I take it you *have* told her about the blood link?' he said to Ethel. 'The catalyst?'

'Blood link?' Chess knew that something that was called a blood link was bound to be unpleasant.

'It's *all* about blood, you know. It always is. Particularly *your* blood, Chess,' confided Lemuel. 'You are full of the most precious fluid. There's every chance the universe will need you to spill a little, just to get things going.'

'She ain't spilling none,' intervened Pacer.

'I won't need my blood to do anything.' Chess glowered stubbornly. 'I'm going to destroy the Eternal, not bleed all over it.' As far as Chess was concerned, that was an end of the matter.

'I don't mean to stick my nose in where it's not wanted,'

said Ethel, whose small nose was plainly preparing to stick itself into this, 'but given the delicate nature of where we are, I would have thought that Lemuel would be better placed here, with me.'

'It's not a matter . . .' began Lemuel.

Chess spoke over him. 'Lemuel's my friend,' she said. It wasn't for Ethel to decide who could and couldn't accompany her. 'If he wants to come with me, he can come with me.'

Lemuel gave Ethel a whole slice of smile.

'Are you OK, Anna?' asked Chess. Anna had been uncharacteristically mute.

'Anna has her place with us,' said Julius, before Anna could respond. His silver-flesh face glinted down at Chess in the patchwork illumination, eyes burning: one hot, one cold. 'That is what she is here for.'

Chess stared back. She knew that now she could have brushed Julius aside with a yawn. He must have known this too.

'Anna's my friend.' Chess hadn't imagined the next stage without Anna alongside her.

Julius was granite. 'Anna is a Blood Sentinel.'

Chess looked from Julius to Anna. Anna said nothing and Chess knew that no matter how unhappy she or Anna were about this, Anna would not be coming with her.

'Dawn.' Julius's voice was so powerful that it might actually have summoned the pale wash of turquoise that softened the rim of sky above the emerging rooftops.

But nobody moved: not at first.

Eventually, Ethel said, 'I wish . . . I wish I could come with you, Chess.'

She sounded so hesitant, so genuine, that Chess wasn't sure what to say back. The old lady's voice was so unexpectedly small, it was as if she were addressing Chess as an equal. No, not an equal: as something *more* than an equal. It felt so awkward, Chess tried to smile, although she didn't feel like smiling at all. 'Aren't you going to tell me that all of this has happened before?'

'You don't need me to, dear,' replied Ethel. She smoothed her hands down the indelible creases of her skirt. 'You already know it.'

'So I'll see you then?' Chess tilted her head to one side, pulling a thick swathe of hair away from where it tipped over her face.

'Oh yes, dear. You'll see me.' Ethel blinked, rheumy eyes magnified by the lenses of her spectacles.

Crazy Boris coughed politely. 'Before we set off, er ... to find these Sages, however that might be, I'll just pop upstairs.' He pointed upwards as if there might have been some confusion over where precisely upstairs was. 'There's a couple of items I'd like to be taking. And there's that small thermonuclear device you were asking about.'

Chess watched him go, and noticed Balthazar Broom and Vladivostok Ragg conversing intensely and, it seemed, comparing wooden staffs.

Anna's touch made Chess jump. But when she saw whose hand it was that had stroked her hair, she smiled.

'Be careful,' Anna said, crystal eyes solemn.

Chess raised a shoulder. 'It doesn't matter about me.' Then she found herself saying, 'But you have a real life waiting for you, so don't do anything silly. Don't get killed or anything.'

I'm starting to sound like Balthazar, Chess told herself.

'Good advice, Chess,' replied Anna with a smile, and then she embraced Chess. 'Don't you do anything silly,' Anna whispered in her ear. 'And don't lose your temper. OK?' She stepped back. 'The world isn't all bad.'

Chess nodded. 'I hope you and . . .'

'Sh.' Anna put a finger to her lips before Chess could say Box's name, and Chess realized her friend wanted to hold that particular pain at bay. 'Let's see what happens,' was all Anna said.

'OK!' Crazy Boris rushed into the room, an acoustic guitar in one hand and a small thermo-nuclear device in the other. 'Guess which one Pacer can make a worse noise with?'

'Hey, you said I was showing promise,' remonstrated Pacer.

'Just cracking a joke, Mr Touchy,' said Boris, dropping the bomb into Julius's outstretched hand. 'Trying to lighten an atmosphere which is probably setting a universal record for heaviness.' He slipped on a pair of shades and adjusted the purple scarf he'd wrapped round his narrow neck, tucking it inside the grey jacket he pulled on over his T-shirt. 'Hitting the road, one last time,' he crooned to himself.

There was a deep rumbling from outside which made the contents of the cupboards rattle.

'Tracked vehicles,' said Captain Riley.

'We go. Now,' stated Julius. Jago Burke and the Scythian readied their horses. Jake climbed onto his bike and fired the engine. He turned the throttle, then pulled down his goggles.

'Be careful, Jake,' said Chess.

She liked the GTBD, even if he had pointed a gun in her face when they'd first met. She thought he wasn't going to say anything because he stared straight ahead, but then, out of the corner of his mouth he drawled, 'It's all the same to me.' The motorbike growled. 'I'll stop when I'm killed by death.' The goggles turned to her. 'It's the best way to play, sunshine. Remember what I told you: none of us will live forever. Don't forget that. It makes things easier.'

'Thanks,' said Chess.

The bike revved so loudly she couldn't hear the rumbling from outside, or the mounting gunfire. Chess saw Anna standing on her own, sheathed sword in one hand. Then there was a whirl of motion and Captain Burke had swung into his saddle and pulled the chestnut round. He extended a gloved hand down to Anna.

'May I have the pleasure of offering you a seat, Miss Ledward?'

Anna regarded the Captain coolly before taking his hand and jumping up and onto the horse, behind him.

'I can assure you, my attentions are most honourable,' promised Jago Burke.

'I can assure you, your intentions will be on the end of my sword if they're not,' promised Anna. She looked down at Chess. 'If I can get back, I will. OK?'

Chess nodded.

Anna was calmly certain, hair like jet, eyes like jewels. 'You decide what happens. Don't let go of that, Chess. *You* decide.'

'Take a firm hold around my waist,' instructed the Captain. 'And watch out for the bullets.'

Flames lashed from the exhaust as the motorbike screamed out of the back of the house. Before it had cleared the far wall, there was an explosion of hooves and Captain Burke and then the Scythian were galloping after it. By the time the hunters had opened fire, the Sentinels had vanished.

'Oh,' gasped Chess, looking about in the grey dawn light and seeing that Julius and Ragg had disappeared too. 'They've *all* gone.'

'They have their work to do, my love.' Ethel put her crabbed hands on the back of Joachim Breslaw's wheelchair. 'And so do we.' She looked over her shoulder to Captain Riley. 'There will be more than the Plague Breed, Captain. Is the Charitable Operations Executive ready?'

'The COE is always ready.' Captain Riley clicked a fresh magazine into his pistol. 'Coordinated with full military support, courtesy of your meeting with the premiere.'

'Of course it is, dear,' smiled Ethel. 'Everyone has to take a side. This is a battle that no one can avoid. Truth to tell,' she added, as the wheels of the chair turned with a squeak, 'it always has been.'

'The wheels,' observed Professor Breslaw with a tube-quivering shrug. 'Oiling them seems unnecessary, at a time like this.'

The sound of hammer blows resounded down the hallway, from the front door to the kitchen. It was followed by the screech of splintering wood.

'Can you get out?' asked Chess.

'Oh, I dare say we shall.' Ethel pushed her spectacles back up to the bridge of her nose. 'We'll have gone before they can start any fisticuffs with us.'

'Can *we* get out?' asked Crazy Boris in consternation. Chess looked at him. 'OK, OK, silly question.'

Ethel sighed. 'Well, time to go. And I'll be glad to get there. It's taken so long and there's been so much to think about. I feel tireder than ever.'

She set off, pushing Professor Breslaw with Captain Riley alongside her, the wheelchair squeaking as they went. Chess wanted to say something to Captain Riley, to thank him for looking after her, to say that everything would be OK for his family. But she wasn't sure that it would be.

'Keep an eye on Trick,' she called after them.

'A whole cat-skin,' Ethel called back from the hallway, and then there was a silence that could only have been left by their absence.

The silence was ended by something that burst against the upper storey of the house. Chess saw brick and glass plume out and rain down over the small garden.

'Chess?' Pacer was shaking her shoulder as if waking her. 'We have to go. You need to take us out of here. Quickly.'

Chess took a last look at the city, seen through the wreckage of Crazy Boris's house. But from the genteel perspective of Mendoza Row, there wasn't much that was familiar to a street rat.

'Only hours to go to the end of the world. And not even time to prepare a portmanteau,' quavered Lemuel. 'How thrilling. And how reckless.'

Opening the dimensions was like sliding open a pack of cards. Easier, in fact. Chess only had to think of finding a way out, and it was there: a way out of her world and into the vortex. Balthazar, Lemuel, Pacer, Gemma and Crazy Boris went before her. Feeling sick, Chess was the last to leave, and as she did so, she shivered, as if she was being watched. But she ignored that feeling: it was the sort of thing Splinter used to mock her for, and there was no longer room for Splinter, or his memory.

A shrill scream split the dawn as the mortar shell plunged into the kitchen. The detonation sent slivers of shrapnel ripping though the room. The shrapnel lodged in brick, plaster, wood, and passed cleanly through a shape that thickened in the air, thickened into mortal substance: a body, tall and old and thin, wrapped in its own loose folds of skin. The Narrow Man, Bael, his featureless face turned the way that Chess had gone.

You poor, doomed, beautiful creature.

The Narrow Man stooped to touch the floor where Chess had last stood, rubbing the filthy carpet until he had absorbed every last trace of her.

Now, Malbane, now is the time. She travels with a band of fools. Make sure the boy finds her: finds her and brings her to the Core. Finds her and brings her to me.

CHAPTER 7

Splinter was falling.

Falling.

Falling.

Falling forever. That was how it felt. He had stepped into the portable vortex, a small wooden box that should have led him into the part of the vortex that he knew, and then he had realized that he had entered a place he did not know at all. And he had started to fall.

The vortex was the vast emptiness which filled the void in between every time and every place that ever had been and ever would be. Its nothingness was so mind-shatteringly infinite that once something was lost in the vortex it was lost forever.

So he knew that he was lost forever.

The terror of falling had lasted ... Splinter didn't know how long it had lasted. He didn't know for how long he had been falling. In a world of nothing there was no way of tracking the flow of time. Even bodily functions ceased to exist. There was only a mist-filled, fathomless abyss.

There had been no hurry. Splinter's terror had been able

to take its time. He had heard about people who had fallen from mountains, how their screams had seared the snowy wastes before being cut short by the rocks below. They had fallen only for the short time it took for death to smash them. But Splinter's fall would last forever: he had eternity to contemplate a death that might never come.

He hadn't screamed for long.

'I am, above all, a rational creature,' he had confided to one of the many faces he summoned out of the nothingness to talk to. And being a rational creature, it was obvious that shrieking for eternity was a pointless exercise.

But the terror remained: a buried-alive terror that threatened to tear his mind from his body until all that was falling would be a gibbering puppet. So, the thing was to keep thinking. When you were falling forever through nothing at all, the only thing you could hang on to was your mind.

Start with what there is. Remember what there was. Think of what there might yet be. This was the mantra repeated by Splinter and to which he clung like a piece of flotsam.

Start with what there is.

There is the vortex. And in the vortex there are the reachings, the narrow paths which lead to every time and every place. But the reachings are as impossible to see as the rest of the vortex. All you can do is to feel your way along them. But so far, for however long this has lasted, I have felt nothing. If there are reachings in this part of the vortex, I am falling between them. And they are so narrow, so precarious, that I would bounce off any I encounter. I will spin back into eternity before I can ever hang on.

'I am going to fall FOREVER!' screamed Splinter's mind.

'Start with what there is,' he screamed back.

I am dressed in black: trousers and a mandarin-collared jacket and no shoes. All black, but my hands and feet are white and so are my face and my hair.

He touched his hair: rough, long, spiky. And he touched his face, feeling the old scars, running his fingers down to where the skin turned coarse and cracked as old lizard hide. And then he looked at his left hand and forearm, where the skin was also loose as cast-off snakeskin and wrinkled as if by age: the price of life. A measure of his life taken to preserve the remainder. The price exacted by the Codex.

Splinter's fingers were in his jacket pockets, touching marbles, string, lock picks, switchblade and a small triangle of metal: the final plate of the Hermetic Codex, the plate that promised death. The Sages had told Splinter how to use the Codex, and the device had provided him with glimpses of three deaths that lay waiting for him, and with three small triangular plates.

The three glimpses of where death lay waiting: a fan turning; a windblown beach; a narrow man, his knife in Splinter's chest.

But, by drawing his blood with the sharp point of a plate, Splinter was connected momentarily with time, enabling him to see a way of defeating death. And by using two of the plates in this way, Splinter had been able to side-step death on two occasions already. However, use of the Codex came at a price. Using the first two plates had taken its toll on his young body, ageing it. He felt the cracked parchment of his face and neck with the wizened skin of his left hand.

But the Sages had warned him that using the third plate

would deliver him straight to the death it revealed. So, he kept this third plate close, but unused. That way he could keep an eye on death, keep it waiting: death, cheated by Splinter.

He liked that thought so much he wanted to laugh, but Splinter knew better than to start doing *that*. Falling forever was one thing, but to fall forever and be laughing all the way ...

Splinter knew what drawing his blood with the third plate would do, which death it promised: an old man, a narrow man with a crystal knife plunged deep in Splinter's chest. But as long as Splinter kept that third plate in his pocket and so long as he wore the crystal knife given to him by the Inquisitor, Malbane, against the skin of his chest, he felt that he was in control of this death. He could keep this death at bay. And in a world where he was in control of nothing, knowing that he was in control of *something* gave him a little strength.

'I did warn you about getting lost,' said Ethel.

It was irritating when she appeared in his mind like this, but it was also a way of remembering: remembering what there was; what had been.

'I did say that once something is lost in the vortex ...'

'I know, I know,' Splinter huffed back.

Ethel had her hands on her hips and was wearing an old tweed skirt, a sage cardigan and a tatty shawl. The shawl flapped and her grey hair funnelled upwards as she fell with him.

'Did you enjoy being an Inquisitor?' she enquired, leaning over him as if she was standing upright, which enabled

Splinter to calculate that he was falling roughly upside down.

'Technically,' replied Splinter, looking back up at the old lady, 'I don't think I was ever an Inquisitor at all.'

'Well, I am glad you worked that out,' school-mistressed Ethel.

'Actually, I'm *glad* I wasn't,' retorted Splinter.

Ethel squatted down to peer at him closely, her hair streaking up in a cone like a demented pixie's and her skirt billowing out. From where Splinter was falling, this was not a pleasant view. He looked into space, of which there was plenty.

'Glad?' enquired the vision in tweed. '*Glad?*'

'Yes. Very glad.' Splinter was pleased to have flummoxed the old bat, even if it was an old bat of his own imagining. 'The Inquisitors weren't all they were cracked up to be. They were even frightened of *you*! And anyway,' he said, voice trailing away at the thought of his sister, at the thought of how he had betrayed her, 'I'm not sure they brought out the best in me.'

'Well dear, there's not much we can do about *that*, is there?' Ethel stood up and turned to vanish. 'You told me how you used the vortex to track through time's labyrinth. You've *seen* what happens to Chess.'

Splinter had tracked the reachings painstakingly, and found the path that led to the future moment when Chess met her death. And he had witnessed that moment.

Chess dies, I know she dies.

He had seen this.

'So, you see,' concluded Ethel, 'it's a bit late to worry about what brings out the *best* in Splinter Tuesday ... isn't it?'

Splinter realized that this wasn't ridicule, it was a question. Ethel wanted to know if it really was too late.

'It's never too late,' hissed Splinter. '*Never.*'

There would be a way out of this. Always, Splinter's brilliance found a way out. But the old lady had gone and still, he was falling.

Malbane padded through the castle, the hood of his monkish cowl pulled up. The leather soles of his sandals made barely a sound as he passed through the great halls, beneath intricate ceremonial arches of many colours, through the dust-moted silence of clerestories, down corridors of smooth, bulbous stone.

He knew this castle well, its sinuous windings, its endless reaches. Always, it hung with no start and no finish in an infinite azure sky. Usually it was empty as a forgotten sepulchre, the animal-head gargoyles high on the walls, unseen, unblinking: the castle so still that it seemed time itself had forgotten about it. But the castle wasn't empty now. Its occasional occupier was at home and Malbane had come to speak with him.

Saul.

Malbane knew where to look for Saul. He took a spiralling flight of stairs down, as if heading for the kitchens, his black robe sweeping out as he descended. When he was nearly at the bottom he stopped at a portal in the wall of the stairwell: a secret door that would have appeared no different from the rest of the stone wall had it been closed. But it was open.

Malbane pulled back his hood; it was hot in here. His silver hair was neat about his thin, priestly face, which remained pale despite the heat of the passage he had entered. The passage was wide with a low, dipping ceiling of fat-bellied stone. It snaked away from him, broad as a river bed. Hands clasped, Malbane followed its course, walking with measured tread.

It grew hotter as he walked. He came to a room stacked high with glass jars, bottles, spheres, boxes like aquaria, even whole cabinets. No container was the same size as another: each was bigger than the last; every one was made of glass. It was a small room, more like a large closet, and on the wall facing him there was a pair of tall wooden doors. Malbane pushed one of the doors and it sighed open. He stepped into the chamber beyond.

Like the rest of the castle, the walls of this chamber were of smooth-faced stone. They were high, the rock fissured with vents and yawning cavities as if it was a sheet of mucous, tearing as it stretched. Filling the centre of this cavernous chamber was a glass cylinder larger than any in the closet, reaching almost to the ceiling.

Inside the cylinder there was clear liquid and floating within the liquid, a body: naked, wrinkled, gargantuan, fat as a baby. A wretch: a creature that shared the burdens of its master: that fed on them, thereby relieving its master of their weight. This body almost filled the cylinder but there was sufficient space for it to wriggle. It wriggled now, turning upside down so that a face appeared level with Malbane's. The face was spread by the glass, wide as the cylinder. It grinned at the Inquisitor, still upside down, and blew out a stream of bubbles. Then it watched him with eyes peevish as a hag's.

'Your wretch grows bigger by the hour,' observed Malbane, addressing the young man who sat in a wing-backed chair beside the cylinder.

Malbane felt the hot regard of Saul's large, dark eyes and waited for his soft lips to leave the glass from which he had been drinking. Saul set the glass down on the floor beside a bottle of dark, viscous liquor.

'What's the time?' he asked the Inquisitor, eyes smouldering like coals.

Malbane laughed, as if laughing were an effort. 'You know the time.' His face became severe. 'There *is* no more time.'

Saul rested his hard jaw on his palm, elbow on knee. 'So, at last, we have come to the end.'

'There is one more thing,' began Malbane, diffidently.

'I have done enough already.'

'You must go to her, Saul. Now.' The Inquisitor's face acquired a solicitous aspect, and his voice a more persuasive tone. 'We are no more than parts of a machine. This is mechanical. A process has commenced. We can only do what we are meant to do.'

'Words, Malbane. Words are easy,' snapped Saul.

Malbane studied the wretch. He tapped on the glass and the wretch wriggled like an eel: a huge, wrinkled, infantine eel. It bared its gums at him and glared. Malbane looked from the wretch to Saul and back to the wretch again.

'It is becoming difficult to discern who is carrying the pain of the other,' he observed.

Saul stood abruptly, tall in his boots and jeans and white shirt. Taller than Malbane.

Malbane held up a slender hand. 'Save your anger,' he said. He smiled gently. Kindly. 'I have no doubt that for you, Saul, this will be more difficult than it would be for others. There will be conflicts of emotion.'

'What do you know about conflicts of emotion?'

'More than you realize,' answered the Inquisitor.

Saul sighed and turned towards the cylinder, resting his forehead against the glass.

Good, thought the Inquisitor, he is resigned already to what must be done. He patted Saul's shoulder comfortingly. 'She has set out, into the vortex.'

'Alone?'

'No,' replied Malbane. 'There are others.'

'Which others?'

Malbane listed them. 'A boy called Pacer, a girl called Gemma, a man called Boris Sherevsky.'

'Never heard of him,' commented Saul.

'He was,' explained the Inquisitor, 'a popular musician. And there are two more.'

Saul must have detected the quaver in Malbane's voice. 'Go on,' he said, turning round. 'Who are they?'

'Balthazar Broom.' Malbane watched Saul absorb this information. 'And the Traitor.'

'Sprazkin!' Saul's eyes brightened with amazement. 'Mevrad has allowed Lemuel Sprazkin to travel with Chess?'

'Maybe it was not Mevrad's choice.' Malbane sucked in his cheeks, contemplatively. 'Maybe the girl made this choice for herself.'

'And there is no one else with her?' questioned Saul, pacing about the huge cylinder. 'No greater force?'

'Saul, Chess has no need of force.' The Inquisitor watched the tall youth through ancient eyes. 'But it is surprising that she has surrounded herself with such *weakness*. It is, perhaps, helpful.'

Saul came to a halt in front of the Inquisitor. 'If Chess is so powerful, what do the weaknesses of others matter?'

Malbane turned his back on Saul and approached the glass. He put his head on one side as he observed the wretch within. 'The balance is very fine, Saul. Chess is so full of the dark energies, so full of torment that her grasp over herself is . . .' He shrugged and tapped the glass again. The creature frog-kicked to face him and giggled a stream of bubbles. 'Unpredictable. Our task is to ensure that when the time comes, she chooses to end everything, to unleash the energy and destroy time, granting us eternal life.'

'*Our* task?' Saul was at Malbane's shoulder.

Malbane faced the dark gaze. After a hesitation he said quietly, '*Your* task.' He stepped away from the young man's ebony glare and spoke loudly, briskly, displaying his faith in Saul to achieve what was required: his confidence that Saul would do as he was told. 'We require *instability*: Chess's instability. Given her choice of travelling companions, this should not be difficult for you. Broom is a fool and the Traitor is as unpredictable as Chess, in his own way.'

Malbane eked out a smile. 'A warp's appetites can be hidden but they are never extinguished. I am sure that you will be able to find a way of destabilizing this feeble band of travelling companions.' He interlaced his fingers, placidly.

'She is seeking the Core, the heart of the time-space continuum.'

'Seeking?' Saul was intrigued. 'It's a little late in the day only to be *seeking*.'

Malbane nodded with great deliberation. 'It is interesting that Mevrad has not seen fit to direct her to that exact location. It is interesting that she has sent her by way of the Sages.'

'The Sages?' But Saul knew Malbane well enough to read the knowing cast of his eyes. 'You have your own theory as to why Mevrad has allowed this?'

The Inquisitor smiled. 'We conducted an investigation of our own, many years ago. One of our spies discovered that the Sages have a means of transporting Chess to the Core, *but*,' and here Malbane chuckled, 'that means is incomplete; an essential part is missing. We had sent our servant to steal this part but he discovered that it was lost already. Plainly Mevrad doesn't know this. If she did, she would not waste time by allowing Chess to go to the Sages.'

'You know your way to the Core, Saul.' Malbane began to walk to the door by which he had entered. 'Your task is to ensure that when Chess discovers that the Sages cannot help her, when she most needs guidance, you are there to give it. You will ensure that she is in the right place, at the right time, and in the right *state of mind*.'

'I don't like your talk of *tasks*, Malbane.' Saul's voice was raised. 'Don't presume to come here and tell me what my tasks are as if you were ordering one of your grovelling disciples.'

Malbane paused, absorbing this parting display of

belligerence. He sighed. 'These are not my orders, Saul. I am merely the messenger. This is Bael's will. Bael will be there, at the end.'

'And Mevrad?'

Malbane laughed. 'It will be too late. Mevrad's reliance upon the Sages will prove to be a fatal error: for *her*. And you know our master, Saul. You know him better than anyone. Why should he observe the rules when we come to the final gasps of time?' Malbane laughed a little harder. 'Not for the first time, Bael is one step ahead of the Baroness Mevrad Styx. By the time that she realizes he is there to direct Chess in her final decision, it will be too late.'

'And he wants *me* there, too.' Saul's fist knuckled his chest, as if there could have been any doubt about whom he was talking.

'Of course.' Malbane hesitated, choosing with care what he said next. 'You will make sure that she is there, alone and ready to comply with Bael's will. So, for that reason, you *have* to be there.'

Saul shook his head, black locks fringing his face. 'Why me?' he murmured.

Malbane heard the dismay. He turned and smiled his most kindly smile. 'Ah, Saul, we know how difficult this must be. The conflicts …' He shook his head as if it was weighed down with sympathy. 'But now is the time to seize time, and all of us must play our parts. And anyway, my boy, you have been eclipsed for far too long.'

'I am not *your boy*,' hissed Saul, and Malbane smiled to see the malevolence flare back into his eyes. The wretch grimaced and eyeballed Malbane hatefully.

The Inquisitor bowed low. 'You are, of course, your own man. Forgive me.'

Saul approached him. 'And what will you be doing?' he demanded. 'You and the others? What is your ... task?'

'We go here and there, walking up and down upon the faces of the universes,' replied Malbane, modestly, as if he were describing nothing more momentous than a circus trick. 'Armies to command, the final harvest of pain to reap, so on and so forth.'

'You will be there at the end?'

Malbane could not tell whether this was meant to be a command or a question. 'We shall be there at the end,' he replied, coldly. 'It is what we have been living for. But before that, I have one last visit to pay.'

'A visit?' Saul was surprised. 'Now? With so little time left?'

'To the General,' said Malbane and he saw Saul raise a hand to touch his nose, a nose that had been broken by the General's fist. 'We have been concerned about General Saxmun Vane. His loyalty is not beyond reproach. And he has been questioning ours to him.'

This time it was Saul who laughed. 'To *him*?'

'He fears that we have made no provision for his Dog Troopers: for his armies and his colonies.' Malbane looked up, allowing his eyes to rest on the crests and cavities of the smooth rock walls. 'He fears that our eternal, crystal universe was not constructed to provide a haven for his many millions of ... animals.'

'His fears are accurate,' snapped Saul and the wretch beamed, upside down.

'Of course, of course,' agreed Malbane. He toyed with a sleeve of his dark robe. 'We have ensured that his armies will be embroiled in conflict as the universes collapse about them. And, therefore, even if the General wishes to be unhelpful, he will be unable to interfere with our plans. But still,' the Inquisitor shrugged, 'I wish to satisfy myself about one matter.'

'Which is?'

Malbane's voice trailed behind him as he departed. 'We would still like to know what happened to the missing shipments of crystal.'

Sunlight beat upon the terracotta plains, glinted off the maze of metal tubes and finally caught the sheer heights of the black tower on the prison planet PURG-CT483, glancing up its fluted walls like a knife on a sharpening steel.

The tower was solitary, its ascending ramparts ever narrowing until they met at a pinnacle so high above the plain that its shadow reached almost as far as the screams that escaped its basalt walls.

Whenever the maze of steel tubes re-assembled itself, feeding a fresh tube into the tower at its centre, the screaming would begin. There might be a short delay, a matter of seconds, a minute at the most, but always a fresh tube meant fresh prisoners and fresh prisoners meant that the General would feed. And then there would be screaming.

In the slaughter cell, the only sound now was the sound of dragging: three shredded corpses being hauled from the chamber by plastic-gowned orderlies. The remains of murderers: justice combined with nutrition in one bloody act. The General observed a spear of bone retract into his thigh. Sprazkin's failed science had left his body with a tendency to mutate randomly, unless controlled by a treatment prepared for him by the warps. This mutation was inconvenient and sometimes painful. But when he was alone with a prisoner or two, in a locked room, it was fun. The General picked a speck of fresh liver from where it had lodged in his nostril.

Footfalls. Boots. A Dog Trooper. The General didn't have to turn around. He knew this would be a guard. Guards always made a good deal of noise when they approached.

'A visitor, General.'

Although the language they spoke was harsh as a saw on stone, the General detected a tremor in the guard's voice: an attempt to control surprise. A crimson thread of blood dripped from the low ceiling.

'A visitor?' asked the General in a low growl. 'Here?'

He never received visitors in this room. Not unless they had come to feed him. He turned to see the guard looking about the small, barren cell. Its walls and floor were featureless, save for the lavish stains of blood, some wet, some congealing and some as dry as rust.

The trooper was clad in standard issue black combats and body armour. A snub-nosed blaze carbine was slung across his chest. His eyes stopped at the broad red streaks which indicated where the most recently savaged had been dragged from the chamber. Then the trooper saw the General's yellow, carnage-crazed eyes regarding him and he stamped a salute.

'Do my habits offend you?' enquired the General, his tall, rangy form approaching the guard, link-chain jigsaw armour clinking as his iron-shod boots thudded over the floor.

'No, sir!' barked the trooper, unconvincingly.

General Vane raised his left arm. Brass rings encircled it at the wrist and just below the elbow, and between these two rings ran a pair of struts which carried a sharp bolt, currently located over his wrist.

'Perhaps you would like to stay and feed with me?' suggested the General. He inspected his left palm, spotted a remnant of clotted blood and pushing his jackal-sharp muzzle up to it, he lapped loudly, yellow eyes evaluating the trooper throughout. The metal fingers of his skeletal-steel right arm curled and uncurled.

'The visitor has come to speak to you, General.' The guard shifted his feet.

Instinctively, General Saxmun Vane knew the only person who would be likely to be visiting at this hour. Testing the loyalty and the stomach of this soft-furred whelp would have to wait. There was a ripple beneath the fur of the General's left upper arm. The mutations were about to re-commence.

'Doubtless, our visitor is here to ensure that I am not about to do anything that will interfere with his grand scheme.' He eyeballed the Dog Trooper suddenly. 'Do you understand what I am talking about?'

'No, sir.'

The General wolfed out a harsh laugh. 'Of course not. None of our billons of brethren have any idea. But they trust me.' Quietly, he repeated, 'They trust me.'

He noticed the soldier glance at the glistening tongue of

flesh that had just slapped out of the General's neck before thrashing the air and then retracting. With a clench of his left fist, the bolt shot up the apparatus fixed to his arm and buried its sharp nose in his elbow.

'My treatment.' A glass ampoule ejected from the bolt as it slid back to its housing. The ampoule hit the floor with a tinkle and rolled a couple of metres before stopping. 'Don't worry, trooper. My body will behave itself for the time being. Send in the visitor.'

When General Saxmun Vane next looked, the trooper had left and standing in the doorway was Malbane, hands clasped below his waist, face in serene repose.

'You do not look as if the world is about to end,' grunted the General, speaking in Chat rather than his own grating tongue.

'Saxmun.' The Inquisitor's voice was as soft and soothing as the General's was harsh. 'You do not look entirely pleased to see me.'

The commander of the Dog Troopers shrugged. 'I would have thought you would be preparing for the eternal life you have been waiting for, not wasting time checking up on me: wasting what is left of time, that is.' But he understood perfectly well why the Inquisitor had come. He just had to make sure that the Inquisitor didn't realize that he understood this.

Malbane's nostrils flared slightly as he observed the gore splashes that streaked the chamber. 'Your habits are so ...'

'Messy?' growled the General.

'Animal,' came the measured analysis.

The General scowled but under his fur he smiled. This

was the Inquisitors' great miscalculation. 'Why are you here, Malbane?' He watched the Inquisitor through narrow eyes.

'You have been such a loyal ... colleague for so long.' Malbane smiled meekly. 'I wanted to give you my assurance ...'

The splayed silver hand was a sign for silence. 'Don't waste these precious seconds on your assurances.' The General's voice was low and gruff. 'My armies are locked in combat with the X'ath and with the Galen, as they have been for millennia. I expect that when the fifth node comes they will be destroyed, as everything will be destroyed. Apart from you and all your works.'

'Saxmun.' Malbane's voice was velvet. 'We have promised to treat you and your people as you deserve. You have fought for the Symmetry for so long.' A meek smile. 'Anything less would be unthinkable.'

'Coming from someone who specializes in doing the unthinkable, that counts for nothing.' The General knew that in the old, cold eyes of the Inquisitors, his people, billions of them, were already dead. Still, the best way of keeping the management's suspicions at bay was by being disagreeable. Anything less would have been wholly out of character and would provoke lethal suspicion. 'You will do what you will,' he grunted. 'Either way, the Dog Troopers will be occupied fighting your battles until the end.' Which was what the Inquisitors wanted. They could never accommodate the billions of Dog Troopers in their geometrically perfect amarantium universe. And the last thing they wanted was hundreds of millions of the General's troops free to wreak havoc upon their own armies when the universes reached their most critical moments.

'And the girl, Chess? What of her?' The General affected a suitable degree of disinterest.

'She is making her own way to the Core.' Malbane remained standing in the doorway.

'Her *own* way? Without Mevrad?' But the General knew it would be without Mevrad. In the past couple of months, the commander of the Dog Troopers had come to speak to the Baroness Mevrad Styx on more than one occasion. It was not so much an understanding as a truce: for the time being.

'She travels with associates, but without Mevrad.'

'Easy prey for you,' muttered the General. But he had had enough of games now. The Inquisitor was here for more than a conversation about the future, about which there was precious little remaining. It was time to force the issue, or end this conversational dance. 'I am hungry,' he grumbled. 'You interrupted my feeding.'

'Of course,' apologized Malbane. 'I mustn't come between you and your . . .'

'Victims?'

'Food,' smiled the Inquisitor.

Good, thought Vane. Treat me like a fool, Malbane. Treat me like a fool and you will pay the price. But ask me your question. I know why you are here. Ask me the question.

The Inquisitor inclined his head in valediction and turned from the General.

Go on, thought Saxmun Vane. Ask.

On the threshold of the blood-dashed chamber, Malbane paused. His back still faced the General. 'What *did* happen to the missing shipments of crystal, Saxmun?'

When Malbane turned to look back, the General shook his head as if bemused that the Inquisitor should have asked a question like that at a time like this. But the General knew that the fate of an unknown quantity of crystal that had gone missing, the use that could be made of it, had remained a lasting concern of the Inquisitors. There was always the chance that someone else was planning their own surprise with it. The General made sure not to reveal how right the Inquisitors were to be worried.

'The officer responsible was punished,' he explained, and he scratched his lower jaw with his metal, segmented fingers, vacantly. 'Executed. Or sent to the Fleshings. It comes to the same thing.' He shrugged.

'The *crystal*, Saxmun? What happened to the crystal?'

'Ah.' The General pulled his dark lips into a smile. 'It was sold. Sold.' He raised his brows. 'To Rakstran traders. Pirates. As to what they have done with it ...' He raised his hands with a jangle of chain armour and an air of disinterest at such an irrelevance. 'Probably sitting on it still. A pity. It's not as if the market in crystal has much longer to run.'

'We understand that there was a lot of crystal that went missing,' said Malbane, carefully.

Far more than you will ever know, thought the General, but he said, 'I don't know the quantity involved. But the officer responsible confessed under the most extreme torture. Then, I think, he was sent to the Fleshings.'

There had been torture, and the whole bloody business had been recorded should anyone ever wish to check up on this. But the torture hadn't been of the officer involved, merely of some miscreant who had got what he deserved. The officer involved, one Valxata Razool by name, Commodore by rank, deserved a reward. However, it had been vital to sustain the appearance of punishment and so the body of the miscreant had been disposed of and Commodore Razool had been stripped of his command, branded a mutineer and sent to the Fleshings. But he had survived, which was remarkable. And it showed that he was far too valuable an officer to lose. Therefore he had been restored to his high command and, right now, that same officer would be running a system check on the General's personal deep-vortex pilot craft, waiting for the order to scramble.

'A copy disc of the interrogation is available. Please, watch it for yourself,' suggested the General. 'It makes good viewing.' He allowed himself to drool, one long, gluey strand unspooling from the hinge of his jaw. With satisfaction, he saw the Inquisitor stifle a sneer of disgust. '*If* you have the time.'

Malbane shook his head and almost whispered. 'Time has all but gone, Saxmun.'

And then he vanished.

The General waited long enough to be certain he was alone. Then, 'Trooper!' he yelled.

The soft-bristled whelp of a tender-boot half marched, half ran into the room.

'General,' he saluted.

'Send the order for my ship to be made ready.'

'Yes, sir.'

Saxmun Vane put his jackal snout breath-close to the

trooper's face. 'Do you like being on the winning side?' he asked.

The trooper nodded vigorously.

The General's grin was so full of fangs that the trooper leant back, though his feet remained rooted. 'Then watch what happens next.'

CHAPTER 8

Colonel Yalka Erk, Dog Trooper Intelligence Officer Class One, watched the two Krillion interrogators enter the cell and wished that he had taken his pension and retired from military service when he had had the opportunity. Instead, he had volunteered for operations in the sub-Drakner offensive and, given his massive knowledge of the territory, he had been placed in a forward observation position. When that position had been overrun by a Krillion long-range patrol, the other Dog Troopers had been shot. But the Colonel's head was full of information that was useful to the Krillion, so he had been taken alive.

Unfortunately.

The Krillion spread their tools on the desk. From where he was manacled to the stone floor, Colonel Erk caught glimpses of wrenches, pincers, skewers, clamps and syringes. The Krillion were small, barely half his height, but with their ten-fingered hands they possessed a level of dexterity that was perfect for extracting information.

The interrogators' sharp faces were illuminated by the gleam of the steel tools. They barely glanced at the grey-whiskered Colonel as they prepared the equipment. But he knew that once they set to work he would be telling them whatever they wanted to know. And then . . . his knowledge of the whereabouts of Dog Trooper units in the region would seal the troopers' destruction.

Hopelessly, he looked across to the only other occupant of the cell: a skin. The Colonel had no idea what a skin was doing in this territory. He guessed that the human had been unlucky enough to have wandered out of the woods and into the gatehouse of the Krillion compound. The Krillion must have been as puzzled as the Colonel because instead of killing him, they had beaten him, dragged him up here and manacled him to the wall. That had been this morning and, since then, the skin had hung slack on the wall, head down, so that all the Colonel could see of him was his short black hair, and the blood and dirt which streaked his face and torn clothes. He had said nothing in response to Erk's grunts. Erk didn't know much about skins; in his opinion they were a feeble sub-species. This one appeared to be no different.

The Colonel's attention was wrested from the human by the slender probe with the minute rotating disc that one of the Krillion held: the razor-sharp disc that was now approaching his face. It whined like a drill. The Colonel heaved at his chains but was held fast.

'No,' he groaned. But the Krillion were ready to set to work, whatever he said.

What happened next happened very quickly.

Stone erupted from the wall and the skin was free, heavy chains still dangling from his wrists, lumps of rock still encasing the end of each chain. He swung an arm and the chain with its lump of rock *whoomed* through the air, catching the first Krillion under his chin and knocking him off his feet, senseless.

The air hummed and the second weighted chain milled into the other interrogator, the rock flooring him like a mallet. The razor disc landed on the floor, at the same time as his body, and danced about on the flagstones.

The human marched across to Colonel Erk, chain and rock still hanging from his wrists. 'Colonel, we have four minutes before escape will be impossible.'

Colonel Erk nodded dumbly. The skin spoke his tongue perfectly. He dug a set of keys from a Krillion belt and unlocked the Colonel's manacles.

Close up, the Dog Trooper observed the human's hairless skin. It was so soft, so weak. But the eyes of the skin were dark and hard and his hands were strong. One of these hands grabbed the Colonel by the back of his jacket and yanked him to his feet.

'How do we get out?' stammered Erk. They couldn't take the staircase; they'd be caught on it immediately. 'We need a way out.'

'See that wall?' The skin strode across to the black-faced stones he'd indicated and elbowed out a section the size of a window. 'Now it's a way out.'

Erk closed his open mouth and then said, 'But this is a tower.' He hobbled over to the breach in the wall and poked his muzzle through the opening. He pulled back at the sight of the hundred-metre drop. 'We can't jump,' he yelped.

'We don't have to jump.' The human leant out and swung

his left arm. The chain whipped round a power cable that ran from the exterior of the wall down to a massive junction box in the gatehouse yard.

The dark eyes turned to the Colonel. 'Hold on.'

'To what?'

'To me.'

The Colonel put his thin arms over the skin's back, noticing for the first time the neat holes in the back of his shoulders: taps. But he could think of only one kind of soldier which had this kind of strength: which had taps so that armour could be screwed to them bodily. 'Who *are* you?' he asked.

'Captain Box Tuesday,' came the reply. 'Officer commanding Four Cohort, Fourteenth Storm, dreadbolt cavalry.'

'A dreadbolt?' The Colonel grasped for words as he locked his arms around the human's powerful chest. 'I didn't know there were human dreadbolts.'

'Neither do the Krillion. But they're about to.' Box smashed the manacle off his right wrist, then reached out and grabbed the loose end of the other chain. 'Ever been on a death slide, Colonel?'

The Colonel shook his head, speechless.

'You'll love it,' said Box. 'Don't forget to scream.'

Box lifted his feet and with a squeal of metal on metal and a fan of sparks they plummeted, air rushing so fast that Colonel Erk couldn't breathe.

To Box's solarion-reinforced body, the Colonel weighed no more than a light backpack. As they metal-screamed downwards, sparks showering, he assessed what lay ahead.

Krillion all about the compound were pointing up at them and the guards in the gatehouse were preparing to open fire. It was too dangerous to drop there, even if it was the most direct route out. But down in the transport compound, the fleet of Krillion ground scramblers was undisturbed.

According to Box's briefing, the Colonel was an expert in all things Krillion, so he figured that the Colonel should be able to handle one of the bug-shaped, armoured, all-terrain vehicles with their rotating, tri-pronged wheels.

'Ever driven one of those?' Box's voice was snatched away by the buffeting air and the Colonel's reply was cut out by a blaze of machine-gun fire from the Krillion.

They were going faster now and below them was the transport compound. There was a guard hut a little ahead.

'This is where it gets lively,' said Box, in his own tongue. His left hand let go of the chain. Instantly, the iron links unravelled and to the sound of the Colonel's wail, they hurtled down, the chain trailing above them.

Box took the impact, crashing onto the iron roof of the hut hard enough to dent it before reducing the force by rolling onto his side. He heard the Colonel's shoulder break. The old soldier groaned but did his best to keep a grip on Box.

'Hang on, Colonel,' growled Box, pinning both of the snout's wrists in front of his chest as he swung over the edge of the roof and dropped to the ground.

Five Krillion mechanics were waiting: one with a pistol, one with a wrench, one with a blow torch in his ten-fingered hand and two holding nothing. Krillion were as fast as cats, but before any of them advanced, Box had swung the loose chain round the neck of the nearest and lassoed him to belt the next one off his feet.

A blue-white spar of flame hissed towards Box's belly. Box spun away, delivering a reverse roundhouse kick into the Krillion's kidneys and spinning the Colonel from his own body so that his boots swiped the pistol to the ground. As it hit the earth, Box dropped the Colonel, blocked the wrench with his forearm and delivered a crunching knife-hand neck strike.

Only the Krillion who had been holding the pistol was still standing. He hesitated, then ran. Box knelt to break the chain.

'Captain,' gulped the Colonel, pointing. More Krillion than Box could count were pouring into the vehicle yard. 'Can you handle this many?'

Box half-grinned; the old dog was starting to believe he could do anything. 'I'm good,' admitted Box, 'but I'm not *that* good.' Krillion were nasty little runts and there must have been more than thirty. And their numerous fingers and strong hands meant that each Krillion could handle four automatic weapons at once.

'Time to get out of here.' Box ran to the nearest armoured scrambler. It had been parked alongside a row of fuel pumps. As Box drew level with them, he slung the chain round a tall standpipe and used his momentum to swing in a half circle, bringing both feet round to power into one of the fuel units, knocking it to the ground. Then he heaved loose the standpipe. Fuel spurted high into the air and out towards the charging enemy troops.

'Got a match, Colonel?'

Staggering up to Box, Erk shook his grizzled head.

'OK. Here goes.' Box bashed the manacle on his left wrist onto the toppled fuel unit. Amidst a hail of sparks, the manacle cracked open and the fuel ignited. Box threw himself backwards and dragged the Colonel down as the fireball geysered. A moment later, flame spewed out of the sheared standpipe and towards the Krillion horde.

Box wiped his scorched face with his scorched hand and pointed at the scrambler. 'Get in,' he yelled.

Getting in was the easy bit. But the driving unit had been designed for creatures almost half their size, so by the time that he and Erk had squeezed inside, they formed a cramped jigsaw of limbs and bodies.

'For a grey-snout,' panted Box, 'you've got some proper good swearing.' His laughter was punctuated by the clatter of gunfire over the door panel he'd just slammed shut.

The temperature was rising.

In the weak light that penetrated the viewing slits, Box craned his neck to survey the buttons, levers and handles. He puffed out his cheeks. 'OK, Colonel, you've got the knowledge.'

'I've ... got ... the ... fractures,' gasped Erk, in agony.

'Either we get this heap of skak moving, or we roast. Or the little guys fill us full of holes.' Box elbowed a large green button, angrily.

The start-motor whirred and the scrambler coughed into life.

'Hey,' grinned Box, 'I'm even better than I thought.' He ignored the hammering on the doors: the fire must have cut out or been extinguished.

'See that?' The Colonel was using his good arm to indicate a hand-width dial with holes for ten fingers surrounding its face. 'It's called a roamer. Put your hand in. Turn it left or right for direction. Press the internal buttons for wheel action.'

'Wheel action?' Box had no idea what Erk was describing.

'Jump, dig, flip, sprint,' gasped Erk.

'Flip?'

'And don't worry about the weapon systems,' groaned the Colonel. 'Now *drive*.'

'But how?' Box saw a pair of sneaky eyes peer in through the outside of the forward viewing slit.

The Colonel kicked a rod on the roof and the scrambler lurched forwards. 'The further you push that throttle, the faster we go.'

'How do I stop it?' asked Box, worming an arm free from the tangle of bodies.

'Don't worry about that, Captain. Just get going.'

Easy does it, thought Box. But he was off balance and he shoved the throttle hard forwards. The scrambler screamed and leapt and the eyes that had been staring in widened for an instant before vanishing altogether.

They careered ahead drunkenly. Box had seen these machines in action before: seen how the pronged wheels worked like legs, rotating and pulling the vehicle forwards. It meant that the scrambler could handle any terrain, any way up. It also made for a bone-crunching ride.

The scrambler clambered over the stationary vehicles in its path. Box *whoa*'d and the Colonel yelped as it nosed downwards at speed, rolling 360° and flipping them upside down before bouncing belly-down again and scurrying at maximum speed towards the perimeter wall.

'Wall!' cried Colonel Erk and the cab roof thundered as they powered through the concrete.

'OK,' shouted Box as they crashed out of the compound and towards the trees. 'All we have to do now is get to the pick-up point.' But from the juddering, head-banging tumult of the cab, it was impossible to gather anything more than a blur of what was happening outside. Through the narrow viewing slits, the world was a shaking jumble of tall, thin trees and the spaces in between them.

'Watch out!' yelled Box as he saw a trunk coming at them. He stuck his hand over the roamer and turned it clockwise. Instantly, the scrambler cornered right, swerving clear of the tree and putting them head on to the next. It came at them like a battering ram. Box spun his hand anti-clockwise and at the same time heaved down on the throttle. The vehicle braked, rocked sideways and Box's fingers inadvertently pressed down and onto a couple of the deep buttons.

'Whoa!' screamed Box and Colonel Erk in unison as the scrambler rolled, corkscrewing in a wave of earth past the next rank of trees. Through the viewing slits, the world rotated but Box saw enough to see that in their wake there followed a whole file of scramblers. It looked as if the pursuit vehicles were spinning round, but it was Box who felt sick and whose head was smacking about the inside of the cab.

'Tell me about the weapon system,' he shouted as the first incoming cannonade boomed into the exposed base of their scrambler.

They landed the right way up with a spine-snapping thud.

Box punched the throttle forwards and they rocketed ahead. There was a volley of blasts and the back of the vehicle slewed wildly. Box rotated the dial to control the skid but now there was an ominous clanking from the rear and he could feel the traction slipping and jolting. They lurched forwards like a crippled dog.

'We won't outrun them now,' stated the Colonel.

So why aren't they following? thought Box. Through the rear viewing slit he could see the pursuit vehicles drawing to a halt on a ridge behind them. Then he felt the pause and dip as the nose of the scrambler tipped over the ledge of the cliff which split the forest in two.

He had time to appreciate the gentle rush of air as the machine somersaulted through hundreds of metres of space. Dreadbolt or not, he was in no doubt that the bottom impact would pancake them. So, having cursed quietly, he closed his eyes and fixed his mind on the face that he carried in his soul, and the warmth of a kiss that he would carry to his death.

But as the scrambler crashed onto the ground, the warmth and softness were obliterated by a neurone-fast expansion of styrofoam resin. It filled the cab in a moment, suspending him and the Colonel like raisins in a cake.

There was a pause during which Box could hear his pulse pounding. Then he and Colonel Erk were ejected from the resin-packed cab. Amidst a fountain of dry foam they flapped through the air to smack down onto the earth, metres from the wrecked scrambler.

Box burst into laughter, once his lungs had re-inflated. He squinted up at the granite rock face which loomed over them like a gargantuan, petrified waterfall and laughed even harder. He laughed until he heard the sound of the Colonel's groans. Colonel Erk's grey muzzle was caked with blood and one of his feet was twisted at an impossible angle.

'Hang in there, Colonel.' Box cursed himself for wasting time. A fall of rock prompted him to look up: dozens of Krillion were already abseiling down the face of the cliff, machine guns strapped across their backs like clusters of firewood.

Box stopped to think. The pick-up point had been several kilometres east of the compound.

The map. What was on the map he had been shown?

He couldn't recall a cliff on the map, but there had only been woods to the east. There were woods here, so he must have taken a route east. At least he was in the right direction from the compound. Now he had to get them both away from the cliff and hope that help came before the Krillion got to them.

'I can't go anywhere,' gasped Erk.

'Of course you can't. That's what I'm here for.' Box ripped a strip of fabric from his shirt, then bound the Colonel's shins together. The old snout grunted and gritted his fangs against the pain. The first of the Krillion were close to the bottom of the cliff.

'We run,' said Box.

'Until?'

'Until we stop. Or they stop us.' Box hoisted the snout across his shoulders. He filled his lungs with sweet forest air. Behind him, boots thudded onto earth and weapons clattered free.

Box sprinted, hard-targeting into the first belt of trees.

Machine-gun fire crackled, echoing off rock and wood. Box heard the rounds thud into tree trunks or sing past him. He held the Colonel fast with his left arm as his right pumped in time to his thighs. Soft earth kicked up to his right, tracked inwards and then he felt the impact on his right leg.

Flesh would have been pulverized. But metal rang.

My lucky leg, thought Box.

He pumped his legs harder, zigzagging through the narrow trees. He could hear the Krillion in pursuit and now he was running uphill. His thigh muscles felt like they were overheating, whilst his lungs felt like a knife had been stuck between them.

His feet slipped over damp earth and he thumped onto his knees. The Colonel winced but bit back pain. 'Nice,' gasped Box, in his own tongue again. 'Nice and lively ... Never a dull ...' he staggered to his feet, as if he was carrying a plank across his shoulders, ' ... moment.'

And then he was running uphill again, legs ablaze, lungs tearing, teeth gritted. He couldn't keep this up for much longer. The Krillion would be close enough to take him down.

Then he realized that the sound of thunder was not the blood roaring through his ears, the sound of splintering timber not his sinews cracking. On either side of him, hulking riders crashed out of the trees like galloping phantoms. Box stumbled to a halt, eyes half-blind with the beat of his blood. But he caught sight of a snorting bolt, metal teeth bared, a battle hammer hoisted over an armour-clad shoulder, a gun barrel levelled by a pair of silver gauntlets, a banner set in the earth: a dog head snarling.

Box blinked his eyes clear. A dozen dreadbolts had drawn up in a semi-circle with him and Colonel Erk at the centre. A bolt roared and Box felt his heart surge at that brazen, engine-rough cry. Its rider kicked past Box and now the dreadbolts formed a circle round him and the Colonel, weapons drawn. Box could feel the heat of the bio-organs beneath the bolts' metal flanks.

As many as a hundred Krillion had drawn up, only metres away. But they didn't stand a chance. Throwing insults, but nothing else, they withdrew into the trees. Once the last Krillion had disappeared from view, one of the dreadbolts turned about and trotted up to Box who was kneeling by Erk. He had laid the Colonel on the ground. The Colonel was unconscious but alive.

A thin wave of gas rolled down the emblazoned shoulder plates as the dreadbolt released his collar clips and removed his helmet. 'What kept you?' The wolfish face split into a white-fanged grin. Skarl went too far back with Box, had fought too many battles alongside him, to stick to formalities.

'Oh,' Box shrugged, 'just a small army. Really, it was nothing.'

'Nice work, Boss,' nodded one of the riders, wheeling alongside Skarl.

'Are all the skins like this?' Box heard one of his troops whisper.

'If they were, there'd be no fighting for the rest of us,' chuckled another, under his breath.

The bulky form of Raxa thudded across to join them, his

bolt's hooves turning over great clods of tea-dark earth. He led a mount that was riderless.

'Glad you made it, Box.' Raxa pulled off his helmet. His bear-like face was serious. Like Skarl, Raxa had been with Box from the beginning of Box's time amongst the snouts. 'You'd better saddle up.'

Box coughed. His lungs felt like they were smarting. 'The Colonel needs a rest. What's the hurry?'

'There's somebody waiting for you, back at the camp.' Raxa looked over at Skarl.

Skarl's lupine face set bleakly. He gave the order to move out and the dreadbolts formed into two lines.

'What's the matter?' asked Box.

'Any trouble and we'll back you up,' was all that Raxa said.

The camp had been pitched at the northern edge of the forest. The Krillion watchtowers had been taken and now Dog Troopers stood sentry on the ramparts which overlooked the tree tops, their figures black against the vast red sun which melted out of the clouds and into the horizon.

Iron sangars had been constructed around the perimeter area to house the troopers. Their black combats contrasted with the dull silver of the dreadbolt cavalry, and where the dreadbolts wore the black and gold insignia of the Snarling Fourteenth on their shoulders, the troopers wore a silver awlis: the symbol for infinity and the signature of the Symmetry.

The dreadbolts had pitched their tents to one side, dog-head banners set about them. The returning cavalry trotted to their comrades. This was only a small contingent from the thousand-strong cohort which Box commanded, but he was glad to be back amongst them. However, all attention was focused on the matt black pilot ship flanked by two fighters which dominated the centre of the camp.

Box felt his pulse quicken: the whole camp was alive with tension. He dismounted, aware of Skarl and Raxa swinging to the ground close by. Behind them came the hoof-beats and jangling tack of the other dreadbolts.

'Glad you're back, Boss,' said one of the dreadbolts who had been awaiting his return.

'Me too,' said Box, eyes on the ships. He gestured to where the Colonel was slumped in the saddle of Box's bolt, but his eyes remained riveted to the black pilot ship. 'He needs a medic. Broken bones mostly.'

Skarl and Raxa stood alongside him and they all looked at the incongruous craft.

'Take my HV magnum,' muttered Raxa, loosening the straps that held the holstered handgun to his thigh.

Box shook his head. 'I'm meant to be here, by his command. If he wants me dead, I'm dead already. Thanks, Raxa.' Unarmed, he trudged across to the ships.

Troopers had been posted all about the craft and they saluted Box as he approached. Half-heartedly, Box saluted back. He was a street rat and a dreadbolt: the formalities of being an *officer* didn't count for anything. All that mattered was who could fight, and who couldn't.

At the base of the ramp which led up to the pilot ship, he was met by a corporal who pointed up to the open entrance panel. Box climbed the ramp and lowered his head as he entered the loading bay. Inside the ship it was warm and there was a smell of oil. To his left was the cockpit but Box's attention was reserved for the person who was waiting for him in the crew room to his right.

'Where have you been, Captain?' The General's sable cloak hung over his armour and his arms were folded. His yellow eyes gleamed down at Box.

Box had tackled so much since he had last seen General Saxmun Vane, faced off death so many times, that he had almost forgotten what the stab of fear was like. But he remembered it now.

Box saluted. 'Rescuing Colonel Erk,' he replied and, just to be safe, he added a loud, 'Sir!'

'Never heard of him,' sniffed Vane. 'Whose idea was it anyway?'

'Mine, sir. He was attached to us. He fell into enemy hands. I decided . . .'

'Enough.' The General held up a silver hand. 'You should have left the Colonel to the Krillion.'

'Let him die?'

With a clink of chain, the General leant across the small mess table which separated them. 'Yes, Captain: let him die. I have lots of colonels, and many more troopers. But *you* are irreplaceable.'

Box was bound to agree with that.

'Well, you are here now.' The General stroked his long, narrow chin, pin-point pupils regarding Box: calculating.

Under the General's unflinching scrutiny, the crew room shrank until the space between Box's throat and the

General's fangs felt claustrophobically close. Box watched the silver fingers move over the jackal jaw.

'You like my new arm?' came the question.

'Almost as much as my new leg,' Box decided was a safe answer.

'It was a gift,' said the General. 'From your sister.'

Box was perplexed by this but said nothing.

'We have hours left. Do you realize that, Captain?'

'Hours?' The General seemed to be speaking in riddles now.

'Until the fifth node. The spiral horizon.' He waved his silver hand. 'The end of the universes, the end of time, etcetera, etcetera.'

Box couldn't think of a reply so he went for silence again. Silence worked well with the General.

'Tell me, Captain, why are we at war with the X'ath?'

There was no escaping that question, but Box knew the answer. 'To protect the Crystal Mines.' The Twisted Symmetry needed crystal, amarantium, and the Dog Troopers had been fighting for millennia to protect the mines against the X'ath, who wanted the crystal for themselves.

'And why are we at war with the Galen?'

This was a bit more tricky. 'Because,' said Box, hesitantly, 'the Galen allow the X'ath through the deep space shipping lanes which they control . . . which allows the X'ath to attack the Crystal Mines?'

General Vane smiled, long-toothed. 'Very good, Captain. Now, answer me this: what is the best way to free our millions of troopers from this endless combat?'

Box went for as long as he could without scratching his

rough-sheared scalp. But this was such a tough question that scratching was essential. After scratching and thinking, and scratching some more, Box shook his head. 'Don't know, sir.'

The General sniffed contemptuously. 'Why should you, Captain? I didn't choose you for your tactical gifts.'

But Box wasn't here to be sniffed at by anyone. 'I didn't ask to be chosen for anything,' he said. '*Sir!*'

The General's eyes narrowed, but all he said was, 'Like I said, no grasp of tactics.' Then, 'Crystal, crystal, crystal,' he growled. 'The X'ath want crystal because it allows them to regenerate. The Galen want crystal because it gives their physical forms substance. And the Inquisitors want crystal because it has allowed them to build a universe that can survive the collapse of every other universe, even the collapse of time itself.' General Vane leant forwards again, long fangs bared, breath so hot that Box could feel it. 'The answer to everything is *crystal*.'

Before Box could take a step back, the General's savage grin eased into a cunning smile, long toothed but less lethal. 'If the X'ath and the Galen were to be provided with a quantity of crystal sufficient to satisfy their needs, Captain, what then?'

It was obvious that if the X'ath and the Galen could obtain crystal without fighting for it, there would be no Crystal Wars: no need for millions of Dog Troopers to be bound up in eternal conflict, which would leave the Dog Troopers free to do whatever the General chose. But that could only happen if there was enough crystal to pay off the enemy forces. Box thought this through in the time it took him to knit his brow, rub his chin and then stand to attention again. But where could the General obtain so much crystal?

Then, with a dumb opening of his mouth it clicked into place. 'The missing shipments of crystal!'

General Vane's smile deepened. 'Well done, Captain.' He folded his arms and looked down at Box. 'For more than ten years we have been stockpiling the necessary supplies. Waiting for *now*.'

'Now?' Box was doing well but he didn't follow where all of this was going.

'In a few hours' time it is all over.'

'*All* over?' asked Box. He couldn't conceive how there could be nothing: couldn't imagine, *wouldn't* imagine not seeing Anna again. And what about Chess? Where would she be now? How alone was she? Box knew that, ultimately, everything would depend on Chess. And he knew how lost she felt.

The General thumped the table with a metal fist, cracking the plastic table top. 'The Symmetry's forces raise havoc across the universes giving the Inquisitors the final burst of energy they require, and my people are locked in endless combat, waiting for destruction. But,' and now the General raised his fist. Box watched it carefully. '*If* we can break free from our enemies, the Symmetry's enemies, we have a chance to survive.'

'How?'

'It is well for you that you are a good fighter, Captain,' growled the General through gritted fangs. 'Without the X'ath and the Galen to fight, we turn on the Symmetry. Destroy their armies. Allow your sister to destroy *our* masters, uninterrupted. Ensure that if the universes survive, we are ready to obliterate any shred of the Symmetry that remains. Freed of the old conflicts, we will be in a position to run things *our* way.'

Destroy *your* masters, thought Box, but he was thinking so much at once he didn't say anything.

'We have enough crystal to satisfy our old foes for some time, so long as they are agreeable. And a cargo fleet awaits my command, to deliver.'

'Already?'

'It is called advance planning, Captain. I've been planning this for a century: long before the girl was even identified.'

'The girl?'

'Your *sister*,' shouted Vane. He shook his head, hissed out a breath and continued. 'The X'ath already know what is happening. They will receive the first shipment within the hour and then there will be a ceasefire: between us, the X'ath and their Krillion mercenaries.'

'And the Galen?' asked Box.

'That is the problem,' grumbled the General, and he looked at Box in a way that left Box in no doubt that the solution to this problem was going to involve him.

'Communicating with the X'ath high command has been simple enough.' The General pointed to the shadows beneath one of the crew benches and for the first time, Box noticed the spidery, black legs that were nesting there. 'A messenger,' explained the General. 'A rudimentary bio-communication platform enabling secure face-to-face cross-universal contact.'

Box nodded as if that was something more than a heap of

incomprehensible jabber-mash. 'So why haven't you been able to communicate with the Galen?' he asked, cautiously adding, 'And why have you left it so late?'

'If I didn't need you,' growled General Vane, 'I'd ...'

'Kill me?' volunteered Box.

'*Eat* you,' smiled the General. 'Slowly. Apart from your leg.' He sighed. 'The Galen aren't like us or the X'ath.'

'Us? Like the X'ath?' Box didn't think that skins or snouts had much in common with the spikers.

'They are not carbon-based life forms as we are,' explained Saxmun Vane. 'They are ... like gas. Like thoughts. And they don't think as we think. They sense the information that is important to them. Any Dog Trooper who approaches the Galen is just that, a Dog Trooper: enemy.'

'Dead on sight?' suggested Box.

'Dead on thought,' said the General, quietly. 'I need somebody who is not one of my people to negotiate for me.' He looked at Box, keenly. 'You are the best tool I have.'

'How do I negotiate with gas?' Box scratched his head without restraint. This was going from lively to impossible.

'By thinking. You were able to communicate with the stonedrakes, on Surapoor, I believe?'

Box nodded. The General had done his research.

'You are reckless to the point of idiocy.'

Box wasn't sure whether this was intended to be a compliment or not.

'And most importantly, you are not one of *us*. So you will not be killed immediately. That is a start.' The General walked round the table, towards Box, and for a moment, Box recalled the last time he had seen the General: fighting hand to hand against the stonedrake champion, Firebras. Firebras had been brave and kind and a great fighter, but none of that had spared him from the General's blade.

It didn't matter who you were or what you were if it was time to die.

'You are to explain to the Galen that their world is on the edge of destruction.' The General stabbed a finger towards Box with each command that he gave. 'That we shall supply them with all the crystal they need if they withdraw from hostilities forthwith, and that as a gesture of good faith, we bring them crystal *now*.'

Box closed his eyes, driving away the image of Firebras mortally wounded. 'Edge of destruction, ceasefire, give them crystal,' he recited. Anna seemed further away than ever.

'Very good.' The General walked past Box and out of the bay. 'Astonishing that the fate of the universes should rest, in part, upon the contents of your head.'

Box considered telling the General what Splinter used to say about the contents of his head. But then he decided that the commander of the Dog Troopers might not share the joke. And he didn't feel much like joking anyway.

From behind him, the General whispered, 'And we depend upon *you* at so late an hour because all of this has had to be hidden from our masters. By the time that these manoeuvres become clear to them, there must be no time left at all.' Box could feel the General's breath on the back of his neck. '*None!*'

Then he felt the grip of the metal hand on his shoulder. 'You will depart now. And after you have completed this mission, Captain, I will ask you to ride into battle for me one last time.' The General's teeth were a hair from Box's skin. 'You will smash the enemy for me, but this time, there will be a prize for you, I think. A prize that makes your human heart *burn*.'

Box stood still as the General's boots thumped down the ramp, unable to think how the savage snout understood so well how humans felt; not daring to hope that before this was over he might see Anna again.

'How do I get there, sir?' he shouted, eyes hot. 'How do I get to the Galen?'

'You have the use of my ship, Captain,' came the reply. 'And the assistance of the best pilot in the Fourth Navy.' There was a dry rattle of a laugh. 'I think you know him already. His name is . . .'

'Razool!' Box grinned. The limits of what was possible had just moved.

CHAPTER 9

Pacer didn't seem to be worried that his lower legs were trailing into space like a stream of sand. Nor did Crazy Boris. The two of them sat on the reaching, legs dangling in the vortex, and the only thing that concerned them was Pacer's inability to play a chord sequence that Boris was trying to teach him.

'A-B, then E-B.' Crazy Boris positioned his own fingers on an air guitar as he instructed Pacer.

Pacer struck the guitar that rested in his lap.

'It sounds like real music,' said Chess.

Pacer winked at her and struck the chord sequence with aplomb.

Crazy Boris scratched his stubble and turned his dark glasses towards Chess. 'Trouble is,' he observed, 'it's taken him quite a long time to get to this, and the universe might not be around for much longer.'

Pacer slapped out a raucous discord, then glared in the direction of Balthazar who was standing alone, a little further along the reaching from the rest of them. 'What's he *doing*?'

Balthazar had his staff propped against his chest as he turned first one way, then another, squinting into the depths of the vortex. In his badly fitting dinner suit and lace-fronted shirt he looked as if he were suspended in space.

That's the problem with the reachings, thought Chess. They're so thin and you can't even see them. It was like walking along invisible pavements barely one slab wide. And if you walked off them, fell . . . She took a look at how Boris and Pacer's feet dust-devilled into nothingness.

'He's looking for the way,' said Gemma, holding Lemuel's black-nailed hand. 'He used to be a Guide, you know. He told me about it when we went to look for Chess.'

'As I recall,' Lemuel observed delicately, 'on that occasion his guiding was not desperately successful.'

Chess noticed the little squeeze he gave Gemma's hand and she frowned, but Lemuel wasn't looking at her.

'He's not doing much guiding now,' scowled Pacer. 'We've been practically nowhere and it's taken hours.' He whacked another crunching chord.

'Oi!' complained Crazy Boris. 'Respect the equipment. And my ears.'

'Tracking the vortex is not like trotting through the city drains, Pacer.' Lemuel smiled at Pacer. Lemuel had an arsenal of smiles. Chess had learnt them all and she thought that this was one of his most irritating.

He tittered and danced on his toes, mimicking a trotting street rat in a pantomime style. Gemma giggled at the capering warp and Pacer looked as if he was going to smack him over his glass-capped head with the guitar.

'Don't even think of it,' warned Crazy Boris.

The vortex creaked.

That was how it sounded to Chess: how she imagined a wooden galleon might sound before it capsized. Just the one creak: bass; echoing. But one creak in a place of total silence was one creak too many.

The silence which followed was deeper than ever.

'That's not meant to happen, is it?' Pacer scrambled back onto the reaching, guitar neck in hand, legs solid again.

'It doesn't sound healthy.' Crazy Boris knee-creaked his way upright, sunglasses turning one way and then another as he looked about.

'The light ... has changed.' Staring into the cold nothingness of the vortex always made Chess want to blink, as if it dried her eyes out. But now, through the blankness of its eternal space, she thought she could detect colours shifting: pastel blues and greens, luminous red and yellow, out there, almost hidden behind white mist.

'Time is closing in,' trilled Lemuel. 'The substance of the universe is groaning.'

Chess closed her eyes, shut out the bruises of colour. Wondering what lay ahead of her was one thing: she had been wondering what lay ahead of her since the day that the hunters had first come for her and Box and Splinter at the wharf. But now she was actually *here*: here at the time when everything was about to happen. Or about to stop altogether. And now that she *was* here, knowing that something was about to happen and not knowing what it would be, was frightening.

I can do anything. I can find the Eternal. I can destroy the Eternal.

She repeated that thought, grasping at it: grasping at certainty.

But if I get it wrong, if the power won't stop, if I can't stop the destruction, if I can't control *me* . . .

Space yawned again and this time, when Chess opened her eyes, she saw that a line of colossal grey shadows loomed against the dull-hued abyss.

'Brocken spectres,' said Balthazar, returning to them. As he did so, Chess noticed two identical shadows, bigger than the others, approach and add themselves to the line. 'Our shadows, cast against the substance of the vortex by an unseen sun.'

'By *two* unseen suns,' observed Lemuel, and Chess realized that when she moved, so did two of the adjacent spectres.

'Suns? In the vortex?' She waved an arm and two shadows waved back.

'Suns *through* the vortex.' Balthazar leant on his staff.

'Where the twelve suns are one,' recited Gemma.

Lemuel giggled with excitement. 'Ten more to go!' Then he turned his aquiline nose to Gemma and Chess saw his nostrils twitch. 'Sublime,' he murmured.

'Are you alright?' Chess asked him.

Lemuel smiled back, a wild cast to the whites of his eyes. 'Never better,' he whispered. 'Are *you* alright?'

'Course she's alright,' intervened Pacer.

'Are the dark emotions under control, Chess?' probed Lemuel, a hot intensity to his voice now; to his eyes.

'Don't, Lemuel.' Chess looked away. She felt the bending space-fabric clutch at her and she knew that fraction by fraction, Lemuel was slipping too.

'Don't you feel it, Chess?' He laughed, not at all warmly. 'We are so alike, you and I.'

'I hate it when you say that,' snapped Chess.

'Come, come.' Lemuel wagged a metal finger reprovingly. '*I* am a synth, *you* are a synth: made by others, to be used by others.'

In a way he was right. And it was that strange allegiance, built on being different from others, that Chess had taken as a kind of friendship. But out here, as Lemuel began to lose control, it didn't seem like friendship at all.

Pacer reached round Gemma to shove Lemuel in the chest, but the warp's metal hand gripped his wrist quickly, powerfully.

'Dear, dear,' tutted Lemuel. 'Should I twist it a little?' He rotated his hand and with a gasp, Pacer was bent so far back that his upper body teetered beyond the edge of the reaching. Gemma tried to pull away from the flesh hand which kept a tight hold on her arm.

'Stop it, Lemuel.' A tide of anger and fear heaved inside Chess.

'Maybe a little further?'

Pacer was completely off balance. Lemuel had only to release his grip and Pacer would fall.

'Don't, Lemuel,' pleaded Gemma.

'Stop fooling, fella,' warned Crazy Boris, too far away to do anything. 'Cut it out. *Now.*'

But Lemuel only looked at Chess. Always, beneath it all, there was such a lot of sadness.

'Please, Lemuel,' she whispered. 'Please.'

'I need to know.' His voice was shaking. '*I need* to know.'

'It's OK, Lemuel,' said Chess. 'We're friends, remember? Closer than friends. Whatever happens, nothing will change that.'

Lemuel shut his eyes, pulled Pacer back and released him. Pacer rubbed his wrist, glowering. Gemma pulled free of the black-nailed hand and settled against Pacer's black combat jacket, blue eyes glistening with fear, with uncertainty.

'I'll take that.' Crazy Boris retrieved his guitar from Pacer.

'It isn't easy,' mumbled Lemuel, wiping his flesh palm down the side of his silver cross-hatched gown.

'I know.' Chess held him in her eyes, angry and sad at the same time. 'I *know*.' Then she noticed how close Balthazar was to her, so close that out in the nothingness of the vortex, their four shadows were one.

'We must continue,' said Balthazar. 'And you must walk with me, Lemuel. Up at the front. Where I can watch you.' His voice was hard and tense: not the voice she recognized.

Lemuel squeezed past Chess and she didn't feel frightened of him.

'I don't know why . . .' he began to say.

'Sh.' She shook her head.

'Something got into me.' He laughed weakly.

The changes in the vortex are beginning to disrupt *us*, thought Chess. I should have come alone.

Balthazar stepped aside until only his toes were on the reaching. He held the wooden staff high over Lemuel's head as the warp walked to the front.

Maybe that's to keep his balance, thought Chess, or to use as a weapon if he has to. And she knew that had Lemuel pushed him, Balthazar could have dropped the end of the staff to the other edge of the reaching and so checked his fall. And then she noticed that the end of the staff was cased in metal, just like Vladivostok Ragg's. But before now Balthazar's staff had been wooden all the way down.

'You lead,' Balthazar ordered Lemuel. 'I'll tell you where to go.'

'You sure you know the way?' shouted Pacer, who was almost at the back of the line.

'I am sure.' Balthazar's bass voice was smothered by the sound of the vortex creaking.

'I'm glad this isn't a film or a book,' said Crazy Boris. 'Bad stuff always happens to the guy at the back.'

Balthazar kept Lemuel at the front and then came Chess, Gemma, Pacer and finally Boris Sherevsky. As they set off, so did their double shadows, stalking silently across the smudged face of the vortex.

Solitary booms and rumbling groans echoed from the void and behind the whiteness stirred clouds of faint colour.

'Birth pangs,' Balthazar said, as he marched, staff planted beside him in time to his step.

'Sounds more like death throes to me,' muttered Crazy Boris.

But for Chess, every heave of the vortex was a wrench at the roots of her own spirit. For a long time now she had known how close she was to the universe, to the universes, had been able to open space, been able even to step in and out of time, as much as she dared: always warily, fearful of the way she could slide out of control. But never before had this contact with the universes been so physical, so immediate.

These past months she had been hanging on to her *self*, desperate to remain a person: to remain the person she thought she was. But now she realized that the difference between herself and the vortex, herself and the universes, was vanishing. It didn't matter what she clung to. She might as well have been a piece of space trying to hold onto every other piece of space.

'Why did I bring you all?'

She had meant to be thinking, but she must have spoken aloud because Gemma said, 'Because we're your friends, Chess. You didn't bring us, we wanted to come.'

Chess looked round at her. 'But can't you see? It's endless. Out here you're all ... so small. Anything could happen.'

'I get the impression,' drawled Crazy Boris, 'that under the current circumstances, we're pretty small wherever we are. And as for *anything* happening? Chess, *anything*'s been happening since the day you first showed up.'

Chess couldn't help smiling. With the guitar across his back, his lank grizzled locks, his stubbly hang-dog face and the dark shades, Crazy Boris was reassuringly out of place.

'The photograph?' Chess had just noticed the white back of a photograph that poked in a sharp line from the breast pocket of Boris's grey jacket.

'I wouldn't want to be at the end of the world without it,' said Crazy Boris, patting the pocket and then pulling his purple scarf over it as if that might protect its contents.

Chess smiled again and Crazy Boris shook his head. 'Sometimes it's like there's two of you. It's the eyes I think.' He half-laughed. 'Listen to me: the sentimental ramblings of an old man.'

'You're not old,' said Chess. And Crazy Boris *wasn't* old. In fact, since she had met him, he'd livened up a good deal. She turned to follow Balthazar's tall, broad figure and felt a sad ache. Balthazar *was* old, or older, at least. His long hair was three-quarters silver, his door-frame shoulders wrestled by age into a slight stoop, his movements no longer fluid but careful, measured, although that might also have been because of how he was concentrating on the reachings.

'Keep up, old man,' she heard Pacer say to Boris, and she smiled to herself, feeling a warm lightness that not even the endlessness, or the end, of time and space could crush. Then, further along the reaching than she had realized he'd travelled, she saw Lemuel drop to his knees and fall onto all fours.

'What's he doing now?' Pacer was angry and maybe, thought Chess, a little bit frightened. There was something disconcertingly bestial about Lemuel's posture, like an animal about to feed.

Balthazar hurried forwards, staff in hand.

'Lemuel? Lemuel? What are you doing?' he boomed, voice still powerful. 'Get up.'

Chess followed quickly and behind her came the others.

'Get up,' ordered Balthazar again.

Still kneeling, Lemuel shuffled about and pointed at what sat on the reaching immediately ahead of him.

'Look! Look!' he gasped and his face was wild. 'A bowl!' He laughed, a ragged rip of laughter. 'A bowl of blood.'

Chess could see it: a small metal bowl, black against the whiteness of the reaching, and within it there was a dark liquid, its surface gleaming like a mirror. Lemuel dipped in a finger, lifted it out and watched, transfixed, as a fat drop collected on the tip of his nail before dropping onto the reaching beside the bowl.

Everyone stared at the bright scarlet dot.

'How?' Lemuel's voice quavered and his thin tongue worked about his lips like a tail.

'Get back!' Balthazar was facing Chess, facing the rest of them, staff raised. 'Get back!'

'Is he hurt?' asked Gemma.

'He's a freak.' Pacer was seeking a way round the blonde girl, fists clenched. Boris put a hand on his shoulder to keep him back.

'He's a warp,' warned Balthazar. 'Blood drives him crazy. He can't help himself. Just stay back.'

'Lemuel?' Chess didn't retreat, despite Balthazar's warning.

Lemuel's manic eyes locked with hers. 'How?' he gasped, long crescent head shaking. 'How have you done it, Chess?'

'I haven't done anything.'

Lemuel Sprazkin laughed until the creaking of space drowned him out. But when the vortex fell silent again, his eyes were still nailed to Chess. 'And *why*? Why have you done this? Done this to me? You know what will happen.' He began to crawl towards her.

'Get back, Chess,' insisted Balthazar, voice raised.

'I don't know what you're talking about.' The words felt hot in her mouth. She didn't understand what had happened: what she was supposed to have done.

'Oh, yes, you do, you horrid little girl. You nasty little girl.' He cackled as he scrabbled closer. 'But how did you do it?'

'Do what?'

'Oh, all innocent are we?' Lemuel's face contorted and his hands extended like talons. Then he pointed back, back at the bowl of blood. 'It's so . . . so . . . *you.*'

'It's got nothing to do with me.' Chess couldn't stop herself from shouting at Lemuel. The way he was crawling towards her, the way he was leering, frightened her.

'This,' gasped Lemuel, 'has *everything* to do with you.'

It was Gemma who shrieked with shock as Lemuel sprang forwards. Balthazar swung his staff up and it caught the warp right under his long chin. It bowled him backwards and he landed flat on the reaching. As he struggled to get up, his hand caught the bowl and flipped it over. The blood splashed up in a perfect fountain, almost freezing mid-air before splashing across his face and down his front.

The warp began to convulse, eyes rolling, hands beating against the reaching, legs spasming.

'No, no, no.' Chess's nails dug into her palms. She knew that this was too much for Lemuel. She knew how he struggled to contain his appetites. She knew how he was drawn to her like an animal. She knew how incendiary her blood would be to him. But this *couldn't* be her blood.

'Come here, Gemma.' Crazy Boris pulled Gemma to him, turned her face into his chest.

Pacer took the opportunity to squeeze round Gemma and he pushed past Chess, too.

Lemuel was crawling to a kneeling position, his moon-white face speckled red. 'You always knew this would happen.' His voice quavered. 'This is what you wanted, Chess. This is what you wanted.'

'I wanted you here because I thought you were a friend,' Chess hurled back at him. 'Because I thought we understood each other. Because I thought we could help each other.'

'Stay back, Lemuel,' commanded Balthazar.

'You think you can stop me, Broom?' Lemuel tipped his blood-splashed head back and laughed violently. 'You think you can stop me from taking what I made? From taking what should be *mine*?'

'You ain't taking nothing.' Pacer pushed past Balthazar, nearly knocking him off the reaching.

'Pacer, no!' cried Chess.

'I'm ending this now.' Pacer pulled Lemuel to his feet by the chest of his gown.

Lemuel's white face was nose to nose with Pacer's black one. 'Now,' whispered Lemuel, 'both of us know that that was very silly.'

His metal hand moved too quickly for Chess to see, but when her eyes had caught up with it, Pacer's throat was in its grasp. 'Just because I'm very, very clever,' said Lemuel, 'doesn't mean that I can't be strong. That I can't *hurt* you,' and he began to lift Pacer, squeezing at the same time.

'Please, Lemuel, please put him down.' Chess didn't care if she had to beg.

Lemuel's dark tongue slithered out, working at the blood nearest his mouth. He grinned at Chess. 'Nectar.'

Balthazar was frozen, undecided. Behind her, Chess could hear Gemma sobbing into Crazy Boris's jacket.

Pacer was choking, hands digging at the metal hand as it slowly tightened.

'At times like this, I wonder why I spent all those centuries trying to be good.' Lemuel lifted his flesh hand and slid his tongue across the blood stains before adding, 'When *this* is *much* more fun.'

'Please, Lemuel.' Chess spoke as calmly as she could. 'Put him down.'

'Say it three times,' demanded Lemuel, eyes on Chess despite the drumming of Pacer's feet against his shins.

'Put him down . . . put him down.' Chess bit her lip so that she wouldn't cry. She could feel the killing grip on her own throat. 'Put him down.'

Lemuel nodded his head in mock gallantry. 'As your ladyship pleases.'

He swung his arm out so that Pacer was suspended beyond the edge of the reaching.

'Will he scream? Won't he scream?' Lemuel winked at Chess. 'Let's see.' He opened his hand.

Pacer fell.

CHAPTER 10

Chess could have stopped Pacer from falling. She could have held him suspended, even carried him back to the reaching by her will alone. But she did nothing. Shock at what Lemuel had just done clamped her mind, as Lemuel's hand had clamped Pacer's throat.

It was Balthazar who acted first and acted fastest. Even as Pacer had begun to fall, Balthazar swept his staff at the boy's body, and Pacer, with the diehard reflexes of a street rat, reached for it. It caught him beneath his right armpit and he hooked one arm and then the other about it, checking his fall.

Balthazar worked his staff up through both hands, straining against Pacer's weight, powerful shoulders taut. As he did so, Lemuel ran at him, arms raised as if to shove him off the reaching.

'Lemuel, no!' shouted Chess.

Chess didn't know whether the shout had warned Balthazar or whether he had sensed the approach of Lemuel Sprazkin. Whichever it was, he pivoted on his left foot and, keeping hold of the stave with both hands, he drew his right knee up to the lapels of his dinner jacket and then kicked out, a steam train of a side kick, leg parallel to the reaching, foot powering into Lemuel's chest.

The warp flew backwards, crashing onto the reaching on his back before rolling off it. But he didn't fall. His hands snatched at the reaching, metal fingers and black-nailed fingers clutching like bird claws, so that from his chest down his body swung and swirled into space like a pendulum of dust. He heaved himself up, grunting and grumbling, face contorting with rage and the effort of saving himself.

Balthazar remained poised on one foot as he centred his balance. Then, gently, he returned his right foot to the reaching before he finished fishing Pacer from the drop.

Gemma helped Chess to haul Pacer onto the reaching, the double silhouettes replicating their movements against the screen of the vortex like immense shadow puppets.

'Didn't think you . . . cared,' gasped Pacer, wiping the tear tracks from Gemma's face.

'Pacer,' Chess placed her hand against his cheek. 'Pacer, I'm sorry.'

'Sorry?'

'About you being here. About this.'

Pacer looked at her so intensely that Chess had to look away. 'You just don't get it, do you?' he said.

You nearly died, thought Chess. You nearly died and you say *that*? She looked from Pacer to the others and she wished that she had not brought any of them here: had not allowed any of them to come with her.

'Thanks, Balthazar.' Pacer arched his neck left, then right, straightening out the knots, and he rubbed his throat. But he glared at Lemuel.

'It's her fault,' shouted Lemuel, over and over again. He was kneeling, hands clasped, ambergris eyes fixed on Chess. 'You shouldn't have tormented me like this. You shouldn't have done it.' He began to gibber to himself and Chess could see that he was crying: thin white rills down his blood-smeared face.

'I haven't done *anything*,' she said, hoarsely.

Lemuel began to weep more loudly. 'I tried so hard,' he babbled. 'I really tried.'

'Go away, Lemuel.' Balthazar stood between Chess and the warp and he raised his staff.

'But it's her fault,' insisted Lemuel, dragging the sleeve of his gown across his arched nose and smudging the blood across his mouth and cheek in a lurid skid. He staggered to his feet. 'Bad girl,' he said.

Balthazar began to retreat and Chess stepped back with him. 'Leave us,' he boomed.

Chess noticed how Lemuel's eyes fastened on the foot of the staff: on the metal base. He cocked his head to one side, like a bird. 'You switched thumpers,' he said, surprised.

'With Vladivostok Ragg. He is a Guide, as I once was,' stated Balthazar. 'Switching thumpers seemed prudent. Only a staff properly shod will work.' Balthazar sighed. 'Ragg foresaw that there might be problems on the reachings. The fellowship of the BIG Cooperative can overcome even my banishment.' Then his voice hardened. 'I shall count to three, Lemuel, to give you a chance. But I *shall* count to three.'

'But Balthazar,' protested Lemuel Sprazkin, in a high whine. 'I am over the worst now.' The eel-dark tongue that played in the corner of his mouth suggested otherwise. 'I'll be good. I promise. I'll try harder than ever.' A screeching fragment of laughter burst from him.

'One!'

Balthazar raised the staff even higher, its silver foot downmost. His shadows did likewise, gigantic against the void. Space groaned.

'Please don't. Please, please, please,' begged Lemuel.

'Run, Lemuel,' said Chess. She didn't know what would happen but she feared for him.

'Two!'

Lemuel eyed the foot of the staff, wildly. The tip of his tongue was trapped between tight lips.

'Three!'

Lemuel turned and began to lope in the direction they had all been heading before coming across the bowl of blood. He slid his feet in a half trot so as not to lose contact with the reaching. His shoulders were hunched and to start with, Chess could hear him snivelling. By the time a minute had passed he was no bigger than a manikin, hobbling into the lambent glow.

The staff was still held high in Balthazar's hand.

Maybe, Balthazar isn't going to do whatever he was going to do, Chess thought.

Then down slammed the staff. The metal foot hit the reaching with an anvil-clang that sounded the whole vortex through. At once, streaks of electric blue raced out from the foot of the staff and along the reaching in the direction of

Lemuel. The streaks sparked, twining and untwining as if they were racing against one another. In their wake there was a crackling and snapping and against the stained hues of the vortex, Chess could see chunks of whiteness tumbling into oblivion, indistinct as falling glass reflected in a mirror.

The chasing bolts sped away from one another in different directions, revealing cross-paths and turns that plotted the nothingness of the vortex in a sparse grid. Wherever they raced, the reachings collapsed, the debris crumbling into space, visible for a moment before leaving nothing. Then the electric streaks vanished, stopping a little distance short of Lemuel.

Chess watched Lemuel walk back towards them, testing the surface of the reaching as if he were about to dip his toe in water, two goblin shadows mimicking his movements. She could tell when he had found the shattered end because suddenly his foot streamed in a curving, dusty streak as if every particle in it had been caught by a zephyr.

Lemuel pulled his leg back, retreated from the edge. 'Why?' he shouted, his voice flat in the void. 'Why?'

'Balthazar, we can't leave him.' Chess stared out across the abyss. Lemuel looked so small, pathetic, a tiny figure in black suspended in the vastness.

'We have to find another way,' was all that Balthazar said.

'We can't take him with us, Chess.' Crazy Boris was trying to sound reasonable.

'But we can't just leave him,' insisted Chess. She touched the space, touched it with her mind, thought about closing the gaps Balthazar had created in the reachings, thought about bringing Lemuel back. But Lemuel was a danger now, not just to her but to all of them: the work of two hundred years of trying to be good destroyed by a bowl of blood.

Balthazar stood with eyes closed.

'Is he meditating?' asked Gemma.

'He's wrecked the way we were meant to take, and now he's lost,' grumbled Pacer, still massaging the skin where the warp's hand had gripped him.

'Breaking the reachings is sometimes necessary,' Balthazar said to Pacer. 'But a Guide will only do it in an emergency.'

'Please,' wailed Lemuel. 'Please don't leave me here.'

'*Can* you find the way, Balthazar?' enquired Crazy Boris, tentatively.

Balthazar opened his bulging eyes and rubbed his moustache. 'I am not sure,' he admitted.

'Thought so,' muttered Pacer.

'That way!' Balthazar pointed.

Crazy Boris looked where he pointed, surprised. 'What? Back the way we came?'

Balthazar smiled. 'That way is the only way, for the time being. There will be other ways when we have re-traced our steps.'

Crazy Boris shrugged. 'It's a plan,' he said. Then he added, 'Has it struck anyone as a mite odd that somebody should have left a bowl of blood in the vortex?'

Nobody volunteered any further observation on this, but Chess knew that Boris was right. Nothing could have been better calculated to throw their group into chaos than a bowl of blood: particularly a bowl of blood that Lemuel believed to be hers.

Turning her back on Lemuel was horrible. Chess heard

him calling her name until his cries began to sound like a child's. But she didn't look back. Splinter always said you should never look back, and even though it had been a long time since she had listened to Splinter, this time she did. She just kept walking, head down

So much pain.

'We're lost, aren't we?' It was Pacer's accusation that roused Chess from her thoughts. She didn't know for how long they'd been walking but the vortex had deepened to yellow and red, shot with swirls of blue and twists of jade. With every resounding creak of the void she felt her own spirit wrench.

'The Sages eschew unnecessary contact,' explained Balthazar. 'Naturally, their location is difficult to find.'

'That's a "yes".' Pacer scowled at the shadows which were becoming more difficult to see as the vortex bruised more lividly.

'What's that?' Gemma raised an arm, her thin blue dress hanging from it in tatters.

Chess looked to where she was pointing and saw a heap of colour. 'Clothes?' she wondered aloud. She closed her eyes and looked without the hindrance of distance, shrinking the space between her and whatever it was that was draped out on the reaching. Then she opened her eyes with a cold-water gasp.

'Saul!'

Had Chess looked back in time rather than space, she would have seen something very different from the scene now laid out on the reaching. She would have seen Saul, his left forearm wrapped in a blood-soaked bandage and his face bleeding, walking immediately behind two straggle-haired, troll-faced, long-legged, hunch-bodied traders. She would have seen him pull a pistol from the back of his jeans. She would have seen him take a silencer from his pocket and screw it onto the barrel of the gun which then coughed twice at the backs of the traders' heads, felling one and then the other. And then she would have seen Saul select a spot a couple of metres beyond the bodies of the traders, and seen him pull off the blood-soaked bandage and drop it into space before lying down and closing his dark and beautiful eyes.

Chess ran the final metres to where the bodies lay. 'No, no, no,' she kept saying, stepping over the traders who were bowed face-down over the reaching, arms and legs hanging in space. Saul was lying on his side, eyes closed.

It seemed so long ago that she had seen Saul, and yet Chess had never forgotten him: never forgotten the way he had stood up for her; never forgotten his kindness; never forgotten his black hair, his dark eyes, his soft lips. Splinter had mocked her about her feelings for Saul and it had hurt because Splinter always found things that were true enough to hurt. But Splinter wasn't here now, and Chess was able to be near Saul without the needle of Splinter's spite.

At first she just stared down at him, eyes so thirsty for every detail that she drank deeply and silently. And then what she was staring at began to register: the wounds, the blood. The blood had congealed in a strip under his gashed left arm, blackening his grey T-shirt where it had seeped under his ribs, and there was blood splashed across his right cheek. In his right hand, which was folded limply over his side, he held a pistol with the long nose of a silencer attached.

Chess knelt beside him.

'Dead,' she heard Balthazar say. 'Both dead.'

'Hardly surprising, Balthazar,' observed Crazy Boris, 'given the holes in their heads.'

'Who's Saul?' Pacer was standing over Chess, staring down.

Chess removed her fingers from where they had been touching the cut to Saul's cheek. 'A boy, well, a young man really, who we met on Surapoor,' she stumbled.

'Who you *met* on Surapoor?' Pacer eyed the prone figure darkly.

'*Once*.' Why should I have to explain myself? thought Chess, irritably.

Gemma hopped over the ogrish corpses. 'You never mentioned someone called Saul,' she said brightly.

She was right. Chess had never mentioned Saul, not to Ethel, not to Anna, not to anyone. He had been her secret, something she could save for herself out of everything that the Committee wanted from her.

Balthazar knelt by Saul and felt his forehead, his big hand olive-dark on Saul's pale skin.

'Is he alright?' asked Chess.

Saul groaned and opened his eyes, blearily at first and then wide with apparent surprise when he saw Balthazar, Chess and Pacer leaning over him. He pushed himself away from them, gasping as his injured left arm took his weight, and he made to raise the gun.

'Saul, no.' Chess placed her hand over the hand which held the gun, firmly enough to keep it by his side.

Saul looked at her intently and she felt her pulse quicken.

'Chess? You're OK?' His eyes closed and he lay his head back on the reaching. 'Thank goodness.'

'*You* made an impression,' muttered Pacer. 'Not bad going seeing as you only met him *once*.'

Chess frowned at Pacer. 'Is he OK?' she repeated to Balthazar. It looked as if Saul might have lost a lot of blood.

'I'm alright.' Saul smiled weakly, eyes still closed. 'Have you got any water?'

'Have we got any water?' snapped Chess, as if nobody else could have heard what Saul had just asked. She looked about the others. 'Have we got any water?'

'Chess,' said Crazy Boris, 'you know that we haven't any water.'

'He's thirsty,' complained Chess.

'I'll be OK.' Saul propped himself on his elbows and looked around. 'These are just flesh wounds.'

'They're bad,' insisted Chess.

Saul wrinkled his nose, a nose that Chess noted had been broken since she had last seen him. 'They're nothing. You're safe. That's what matters.'

'Forgive the intrusion,' said Crazy Boris, looking over Gemma's shoulder, 'but who are you? Chess seems to have lost the ability to make introductions.'

'I have not,' responded Chess, hotly, and she glared at Crazy Boris who looked at her innocently through his dark glasses. 'His name is Saul and we met on Surapoor, which is where we first met Balthazar when he was living in a tree . . .'

'A tree?' Boris Sherevsky's eyebrows rose above the lenses of his shades. 'Cool, Balthazar. Very cool.'

'Saul helped us when we were being taken to the Twisted

Symmetry's factory,' finished Chess, wishing that she hadn't gabbled like that. She pulled a swathe of chestnut hair away from her face and tucked it behind her ear.

Crazy Boris rubbed his bristly chin. 'You're a young man who plainly gets about a lot.'

'I'm an agent,' said Saul, 'for the Symmetry.'

His words might as well have been quick-set concrete. Nobody moved. Nobody spoke. Chess's thoughts ground to a standstill as she tried to make sense of what she had just heard.

'The Symmetry?' repeated Pacer after a long pause, as if there could have been any doubt about what had just been said.

'It's best to start with the truth,' said Saul, wearily.

'It would be good to continue with it too,' observed Balthazar.

Chess could feel the accusing heat of Pacer's eyes. She tried to ignore it, although her mind was still blank. It was only slowly that Saul's voice began to fill the empty space and she listened to it without thinking, the words writing themselves on the blank page of her mind.

'When I met you, on Surapoor, I had been sent by the Symmetry to make sure that you arrived at the factory. That was my task.' Saul began to unscrew the silencer, which prompted Pacer to step forwards. Balthazar stopped him with a hand on his arm. But Chess didn't fail to notice that Balthazar's bulging eyes didn't move from Saul and that he held his heavy staff like a spear.

At first, Saul seemed oblivious to the bristling watchfulness which surrounded him, but when he noticed how everyone was staring, he dropped the silencer and then the pistol itself over the edge of the reaching and then opened his hands to show how empty they were.

'See? No weapons.' Then he continued. 'I was meant to report on you.'

Chess looked down, avoiding his eyes. But she snatched a glance up, and when she did, the dark eyes were still looking at her.

'I was meant to report on you but I didn't want to. As soon as I met you, Chess, I knew ...' Saul checked himself with a sigh. 'Well, I didn't want to tell the Symmetry about you.' He laughed feebly. 'I wanted to help you. So I said nothing, but a boy called Jerome told the General that I'd helped you.' He shrugged. 'The General nearly had my throat out when I wouldn't tell him about you. He kept me prisoner for months.'

'Prisoner?' Chess couldn't help herself from speaking. 'Because of helping me?'

Saul nodded, face solemn.

'But you're on the same side as the General,' accused Pacer.

'The Symmetry isn't one big happy family,' explained Saul. 'There are different interests, different sides.'

'Which is your side, Saul?' enquired Crazy Boris, but before Saul could reply, Balthazar interrupted.

'You found your way to Surapoor through the vortex?'

Saul nodded and Balthazar continued. 'You navigated your way here?' When Saul nodded again Balthazar announced, 'Then you must be more powerful, more capable than you appear.'

'I don't think so,' replied Saul. 'If I were so powerful, I wouldn't have had the General's fangs practically in my neck.'

'The General did have his fangs on Saul's neck,' agreed Chess.

'And he wouldn't have got away with busting my nose.'

'The General did that?' asked Chess.

'I didn't do it to myself,' laughed Saul.

But now Chess's thoughts had caught up with her. Before they went any further there was something she needed an answer to. 'On Surapoor there was a spook. I saw it. It came for me.'

'What's a spook?' asked Gemma, and she giggled at the silliness of the word.

'A listening thing.' Balthazar fell silent as the vortex creaked and all of them looked at the colours which had stained the vortex, merging into a wash-red backdrop against which their shadows were faint. 'Give a spook even a pinhead of blood and it will listen across eternity for the heart that beat it. And it will find it.'

Saul had said nothing and Chess still wanted an answer. 'The Symmetry must have had my blood. How did they have my blood?' She couldn't bring herself to level the accusation which had played upon her mind for so long.

'They got it from me,' admitted Saul.

Chess clenched her fists, nails sharp into her palms, and she looked down with a fierce unhappiness.

'After I had cleaned the cut on your hand, I kept the rag I'd used. I think I wanted to keep it because it was from you. Jerome had told the General how I'd helped you and they found the blood-stained cloth when they questioned me.'

'So you didn't *give* it to them?' asked Chess watchfully.

'He *says*,' muttered Pacer.

'They took it from me.'

Chess looked up and met Saul's eyes which were bright and . . . honest.

'So why are you here now?' asked Balthazar, but Chess could tell that he wasn't interrogating Saul. He wanted to know what Saul had to say, and she reminded herself that always with Balthazar Broom, curiosity about the Twisted Symmetry trumped caution.

'The General returned me to the Inquisitors months ago,' began Saul.

'*Inquisitors?*' choked Crazy Boris. 'Aren't they the *really* bad guys?'

Saul looked at the dark lenses coolly. 'I said I was going to give you the truth. Do you want the truth?' He gritted his teeth and clenched and unclenched his left hand.

'It hurts?' asked Chess.

Saul nodded. 'I was sent out, this time to watch you. The Inquisitors know you are looking for the Sages and I'm meant to watch what you do, report back to them. But the truth is, I was more than happy just to watch.' Saul smiled and Chess blushed. 'I figured that if the world is about to end, now is the time to be on the right side. To be with the person I want to be with when the end comes.' Chess couldn't even look at him when he said that but her lips wanted to smile.

'Finding you was easy: easier and quicker than expected. I guess that's because we're on the same wavelength.'

Pacer groaned but Chess ignored him and Saul carried on, oblivious. 'I met *them*,' he continued with a jerk of his head at the dead traders, 'by accident. I don't know what they were doing.' He frowned as if trying to capture a memory. 'They said something about blood: a trap?' He looked at the faces which were looking at him. 'It was something to do with you, Chess, and a warp.' He shrugged. 'They were here to cause trouble for you so I killed them.' Saul raised his wounded arm. 'Not without a fight though.'

'You killed them?' echoed Chess, thinking this through, wondering what it meant.

Saul laughed, even though she could see he was in pain. 'Because I like you, Chess. Right away, from when we first met.' He made it sound so natural that this time she didn't feel embarrassed. 'There *are* shades of badness, you know.' He laughed again. 'I've been a Symmetry agent so you'll think badly of me, I know, but I'm not *that* bad. I just want to help you. That's all I've wanted to do from the moment we met. It sounds corny but there it is: it's the truth.' His eyes were like black diamond. 'I wouldn't be here, like this, if I didn't want to help you.'

'Don't take offence, fella, but I can't see how you're going to help us.' Crazy Boris tucked his hands in his jacket pockets as if the background creaking of the vortex was of no significance.

'You want to get to the Sages?' Saul sucked his lower lip for a moment, as if making a difficult decision. 'I know the way.'

'That's good,' said Gemma, 'because we're lost.'

Pacer swore and shook his head. 'Nice one, Gemma.'

'Well, we *are* lost,' insisted Gemma, 'and he can help us.'

'I know what's happening,' said Saul, indicating the shifting face of the vortex with his good arm. 'And I know that you *have* to get to the Sages, Chess. And I know that time is running out. And I'm ready to help.'

'It's a kind offer,' said Crazy Boris, 'but being as how you work for the enemy ...'

'I wouldn't be offering to take you to the Sages if I didn't want to help,' snapped Saul. 'I wouldn't have killed *them*.' Then, coldly, he asked Crazy Boris, 'Do you know how much danger you're in? Do they know, Chess? Do they? I'll be honest, Chess, I can't believe you brought them here.'

Saul's words struck her like a lancet because they were so true. Chess knew that bringing her friends here had been a mistake: already events had taken a near-calamitous turn with Lemuel. The vortex was disintegrating around them and she was about to lead them into the maelstrom. And Saul had understood this at once.

'We don't need you, Saul,' said Pacer, through gritted teeth.

'We're lost, Pacer.' Chess stood between Pacer and Saul. 'We can't hang around forever.' She eyeballed Saul. 'You can take us to the Sages?' Saul nodded solemnly. Chess's fingers found the horse's head in her pocket and they worked as if rubbing it would tell her what to do. She closed her eyes and silently she counted to three. When she opened her eyes, she knew what to say. 'Right. Take us.'

Saul smiled.

The air stung with the reek of smoking carnage as Anna and the Sentinels fought their way through the bowels of the leisure complex. Behind them burnt the carcasses of the plague beasts they had already cut down: great smouldering chunks of putrid flesh, heaped throughout the clubs, the cinemas, the bowling lanes, the corridors, the washrooms. But it was obvious that the Plague Breed had already entered the city in massive numbers: Ethel's prediction of where they would come from was accurate, but her timings were woeful. There may have been hundreds of thousands still waiting to emerge from the wormhole beneath the city, but already there was a tidal wave of pestilence in the streets, ready to rot the city to its core. The Sentinels had arrived too late to stop the breakout.

The city was under attack. Even as Anna had raced here with Jago Burke, she had seen turmoil: government troops on the highways exchanging fire with hunter units; a flare-burst illuminating a street battle between more soldiers and weapon-bearing humanoids she hadn't see before; packs of spindle rippers leaping across the towering rooftops; an artillery shell bursting against a tower block, showering brilliant trails of fire; lines of traffic choking the roads as people sought to leave the city.

But now the Blood Sentinels had hacked and blasted their way down to their target location. Anna stopped to wipe sweat and soot out of her eyes. She knew what was waiting on the other side of the door. Already she was comfortable with her heightened abilities, had adapted to moving faster and manipulating space. Sensing the shapes on the other side of the door came as easily as counting.

Eighty-three plague beasts, and on this side of the door, six Blood Sentinels and Julius. The other Sentinels had been deployed elsewhere in the complex. There had been a lot of killing to do, and far more of the Plague Breed than expected.

Julius rolled up his sleeves, then nodded.

The door was booted open by Jake who pumped a volley of phosphorous shells into the room. Then Julius was in, followed swiftly by Anna. Seren and Étoile remained in the doorway, drew their bows and more quickly than the Plague Marshalls could count, unleashed a storm of arrows that exploded into flame with every treacle-skinned, raw-sored, pus-slimed hulk they hit.

Julius's hands and forearms split open and multi-chambered barrels racked out, tubes springing free to web the area between the barrels and the surrounding air. With an ear-hammering roar, a storm of phosphorous erupted from the Nephilim's fists, smashing the plague beasts to burning chunks.

The Scythian was in the thick of the fighting, eyes wild, mouth savage, axe smashing skulls and breaking limbs and beside him fought Captain Burke, revolvers banging out a hail of flaming bullets.

Anna guarded Julius's back, whirling the Muspell blade to slice one charging creature and then throwing herself at a Plague Marshall as he tried to brain Jago Burke with a skin-tattered morning star. Anne struck in and up, the sword busting free from the Marshall's shoulder in a gout of blood and filth. She spun away before the pestilential eruption could soil her, striking down another beast with a flaming backswing as she did so.

The last arrow burst into fire and the last blast of the shotgun rang in the air as the final plague beast thumped to the floor in a cloak of spitting fire.

'OK, Carl,' Julius's voice was calm and sonorous as ever, 'clear the munitions.' Anna knew that he was talking to the guy who handled the tech for the Blood Sentinels, even though he was located in an operations wagon in a different space-gradient. Julius's arms and hands reconstituted themselves, he rolled down the sleeves of his long black coat, and the last of the tubes withdrew, with serpent flicks, inside his cuffs.

At the centre of the chamber there was a wide shaft. Anna stood where she could look into it. She sheathed the Muspell blade and rested both hands on the pommel, the tip of the scabbard on the floor, as she caught her breath. Across her back was her own sword.

The other Sentinels moved about the room, but still she felt distant from them. They shared only one thing: they were here to fight. Only to fight. But Anna wanted to be elsewhere, to be with Chess and then, when all of this was over, and if they were still alive, to be with Box. It sounded so simple. But the heaps of burning bodies proved that for her, it was far from simple.

Julius stood beside her. He kicked a dismembered hand into the chasm.

'Do we count?' asked Anna.

'Count?' asked Julius.

'Until it hits the bottom.'

'There is no bottom,' said Julius.

Anna sighed. 'Joke,' she said.

From somewhere outside there was an explosion. Dust and grit drifted through the rank air of the subterranean chamber, crackling in the flames that licked over the bodies. Anna brushed fragments of dirt from her razor-sharp fringe and blinked them out of her sapphire eyes.

'Mevrad has made a mistake,' said Julius.

'A mistake?' Anna had heard what he'd said but she didn't like what she had heard.

Julius knelt and peered into the shaft, yellow hair hanging long round his face. 'Mevrad makes mistakes.' He looked across to Anna and she wasn't sure which eye to look back at: the burning red or the icy blue. 'This shouldn't have happened.' She knew he meant the extent of the fighting so far. 'Even after we detonate the bomb down there and close the wormhole, the damage has been done. The Breed has entered the city.'

'Ethel knew about the hole, at least,' said Anna. 'She was mostly right.'

'Mostly right isn't good enough.' Julius stood, tossing a lump of rock in his palm. 'What we get right doesn't matter: the enemy win by the things we get wrong. You think I am unfair? About Mevrad?'

Anna shrugged. 'Nobody's perfect,' she said. She was aware of the other Sentinels cleaning weapons, loading weapons.

'There was a girl, a young woman, called Esme.'

Anna knew about Esme. She knew that a long time ago she had been Crazy Boris's girlfriend. And she knew that something bad had happened to her.

'By Mevrad's calculations, by her researches and

predictions, Esme was special. She was the one who should have been where Chess is now: the one who had the power to save or destroy.' Julius tossed the rock in his hand. 'Mevrad was sure that the best way of hiding Esme from the enemy was by hiding her from herself.'

'Very cryptic, Julius,' said Anna. 'What do you mean?'

'Mevrad decided that the best way of protecting Esme from the Symmetry was by doing nothing.' Julius was speaking more slowly than usual and every word burnt with anger. 'To let her continue with her life in total ignorance of what she was. To leave her alone, unguarded. As if that would save her from the enemy's desire to hunt her down.'

'And?'

'And?' Julius's eyes flared. 'The Symmetry found her, of course. They found her and tore her out of existence because she was the one thing which could tear *them* out of existence. Mevrad's first great mistake.'

Anna was silent.

'Chess's mother, Clarity, was made from the shreds the Symmetry left of Esme. But again, we were caught, unready: this time by Chess's father.' Julius laughed hollowly. 'But this time, Mevrad devised an alternative stratagem. This time, Mevrad decided to gamble. She bargained upon constructing a being as desirable to the enemy as she is to us; as necessary to the enemy's plans as she is to ours.'

'Chess?' asked Anna.

Julius nodded. 'Mevrad gambles upon manoeuvring Chess into the right place at the right time; she gambles upon Chess making the right decision at the right time. And all of this sits well with the enemy, because the gamble may go either way. Mevrad gambles upon Chess destroying the enemy. And the enemy gamble upon Chess destroying everything else.'

Julius opened his palm and out trickled the rock he had crushed. 'The fate of everything depends upon Chess, and there is no more certainty in what she will do than in the roll of a die.'

'Chess won't do what the Symmetry want.'

'You really think so, Anna?' Julius's stare made her look into herself and she found that she had nothing to say.

Julius brushed his hand clean. 'Mevrad has made provision for Chess to get to the Core, the heart of the space-time matrix: the place where she is meant to be for this *gamble* to work. She believes in leaving the final decision to Chess. But the Symmetry do not.

'There is a bond between Chess and me, as there is between the two of us,' and for a moment, Julius's demeanour softened. 'Maybe I sense what Chess can't. The Symmetry will be there at the end, somehow, to drive Chess to their needs.' He folded his arms and looked squarely at Anna. 'We have to pull her out.'

'Pull her out? But the plan ...'

'Look!' Julius swung his arm towards the dead hulks. 'Look here. Look how Mevrad got this wrong. Think what is about to happen to your city. There is no more time for Mevrad's mistakes, Anna, no more time for her gambles. Better for Chess not to be in a position to destroy the enemy, if that means she cannot be used by the enemy to destroy everything else.' He shook his head at the slaughter in the chamber. 'Better the battle than nothing.'

Anna realized why Julius was saying this to her. 'You want me to get her?' Say yes, thought Anna. Please, say yes.

'If Chess isn't at the Core at the *critical moment*, then the battle may rage for eternity but the Symmetry will fail in their desire to end time.' Julius's face was grim. 'You go, Anna. Go with Captain Burke and the Scythian. Bring Chess home.'

Julius was right and Anna loved him for it. Chess didn't have to go through with this, and it had taken someone of Julius's strength to say so. None of them had to go through with this. She could rescue her friend from the abyss that was pulling her apart, which threatened to tear the universes apart. And then, maybe then . . .

'What about Ethel . . . Mevrad?' she asked.

'I shall deal with Mevrad,' said Julius, and Anna thought he looked glad at the prospect. He took the small thermo-nuclear device from his coat pocket and held it in his silver palm. 'We shall close the link. You shall find your friend. Jago Burke can take you to the Sages. Just make sure that you get to Chess before the Symmetry do.'

Jago Burke was already waiting for her and so was the Scythian, his face hard and savage as the gore-spattered battle axe he held in his hand.

'Miss Ledward?' asked Captain Burke, with a slight bow, a swing of his brown hair and a sweep of his gloved hand to where his mount waited in the vortex. 'May I offer you a seat?'

Anna handed the Muspell blade back to Julius and tightened the strap which held her own sword across her back. 'With pleasure,' she said.

CHAPTER 11

'There.' Saul knelt so that Chess could look over his head. 'Through there.' His spectral shadows were cast upon the deepening blue and red of the vortex but his hand indicated a rip in the curtain of vapour before them. Chess peered through the iridescent mist and tried to organize what she could see: a vast complex as big as a city, roughly oval, encompassed by bands that spun and tilted gyroscopically. Sometimes the complex was smooth, so smooth that it had no more definition than mist. At other times, Chess perceived mountainous elevations, precipitous towers burnished by the luminescence of the vortex, walls as polished and lustrous as brass. And sometimes, emerging from the gigantic body, the outside sinking into the inside, the inside drifting out, Chess thought she saw cubical chambers and spiralling thoroughfares and shoulders of the construction's metal skeleton, appearing starkly before disappearing just as suddenly.

It was like an optical illusion, a colossal architectural illusion, always the same but simultaneously changing, full of angles and perspectives that defied possibility but existed right before her.

'It's multi-dimensional.' Saul looked up at her. 'Inside and out, upside and down, past and present and future, all at the same time and the same place. A bit like you.'

'Thanks.' Chess tried to smile but just felt awkward for reasons that she couldn't understand. She wanted to be with Saul, despite Pacer's sullen silence and Crazy Boris's glum face. And whatever the others thought, if they hadn't found Saul they'd be lost still. Saul knew what he was doing out here, which was more than could be said for anyone else. And he was out here because he'd been looking for *her*. She regretted bringing the others here: just look what had happened with Lemuel. But she didn't regret Saul being here.

'Come on.' Saul stood. 'This is CASRA. This is where you'll find the Sages,' and his face switched to a chiselled seriousness as he looked at the vortex, which had darkened to the hue of an angry sunset. Or sunsets. 'Out here, it's increasingly dangerous for your friends.'

Increasingly dangerous for your friends: the words came with a punch that made Chess feel even guiltier, although she knew that Saul hadn't meant her to feel like that.

'What's CASRA?' she heard Gemma ask.

As ever, Balthazar was ready to provide information. 'The Cosmological Agency for Statutes, Records and Artefacts.' He pointed with the staff. 'These are the Antediluvian Halls, where the Time Historians, or the Sages as we've been calling them, monitor the time spiral and do what they can to ensure that the laws of reality are properly observed.'

'Sounds complicated,' said Gemma.

'It is, in truth, impossible,' maintained Balthazar.

'Which explains a good deal,' observed Crazy Boris.

Saul led the way. They passed out of the increasingly livid chasm of the vortex and onto a path that was visible as a band of yellow through the shifting vapours. The bruised hues had gone, but Chess noticed that shadows radiated from her feet like a clock face, although she didn't count how many there were. She looked up and saw no sun, merely a pearl-glow ceiling of foreverness.

Then the Antediluvian Halls seemed to rotate anti-clockwise, very slowly. After what she had witnessed already, Chess could have believed that the multi-dimensional construction was capable of anything, and it took her a little time before she appreciated that the Halls weren't rotating at all. It was she who was rotating, or spiralling, because that was what the path did: it corkscrewed towards the Halls in majestic loops.

Maybe the reachings did this too, thought Chess, but in the vortex there were no points of reference and no sense of which way up you were.

They approached the Antediluvian Halls quickly. Or the Halls grew to fill the space ahead of them quickly. In what seemed like minutes, Chess was standing in front of a colossal wall of orbits and rooms and textures that never stayed the same. She had the feeling that the changes were in how she perceived it rather than in the soaring edifice itself.

'What the hell is it?' Pacer rubbed his eyes.

'There was a time,' commented Crazy Boris, 'when I paid

for stuff that did this to my head.' He took off his shades, swept back his old rocker's locks, looked up, looked down, then put the shades back on. 'It does things to your brain,' he groaned.

'Such a long time since last I stood here,' murmured Balthazar Broom, leaning for a moment on his staff.

'Bet you weren't standing here in a DJ last time you came, hey, Balthazar?' chuckled Crazy Boris.

'I was standing in a cloak of marvellous inversions,' came the reply.

'Yeah, well, ask a stupid question . . .' Crazy Boris scratched his stubble.

'How do we get in?' asked Gemma.

'Just walk,' said Saul, and he vanished into the wall as if he were a ghost.

'Ah, good,' murmured Crazy Boris. 'Business as usual.' He gestured towards the apparent wall. 'After you, Chess.'

'Thanks,' said Chess and she followed Saul.

She emerged into a waiting room: at least it conformed to most waiting rooms she had ever experienced, in atmosphere if not precisely in layout. It was very long with functional steel-framed chairs down either side and at the far end a counter with a brass bell on it, the sort she'd seen when she'd looked through the front doors of cheap hotels. There was a door in the wall behind the counter, and there were double doors in the wall at the end of the counter. There was a sign over the double doors which Crazy Boris read aloud as 'NO ADMITTANCE WITHOUT PRIOR AUTHORITY'. The room emanated a wave of hopelessness.

The chairs were mostly empty although some were occupied by people who looked as if they had been here for a very long time, judging by the mounds of plastic cups about their ankles and the stamp of defeat upon their sallow features. As far as Chess could tell, the occupants of the chairs were human and most of them looked very old.

'You'll not get an appointment,' said one withered gentleman who sat immediately to the left of where Chess was standing.

'They'll keep you waiting until you look like me,' said another a little further along. He pulled out a set of dentures that had been ground down to their pink, plastic gums. 'Got so bored,' he explained, 'I've chewed me teeth away.' He popped the wet appliance back in his mouth and rocked back and forth, chuckling to himself.

'You've got to be joking,' said Pacer under his breath.

'You see before you the perils of attending without an appointment,' explained Balthazar. 'The Sages almost never see anyone they do not want to see. How could they do otherwise? There is a googolplex of beings in the universes. The Sages would never be able to attend to their official business if they attended to every casual enquirer who came calling.'

'Come on,' said Saul. 'We'll let them know you're here.'

'Will they see me?' asked Chess.

Saul looked at her as if she was as crazy as the forgotten callers in the room. 'Of course they'll see you, Chess. You're the most important person in the world.'

It sounded ridiculous and she didn't know what to say.

She laughed awkwardly but she hated it when people said things like that: not that anyone had ever put it that way before. But they said things like how special she was, or how everything depended on her. It wasn't the sort of thing you ever got used to, especially if you'd started out as a street rat, with no more significance than the overspill from a rubbish bin. And as far as Chess was concerned, her specialness only ever caused problems for the people nearest to her. So she followed Saul with her head down, and concentrated on her trainers.

All six of them shambled to a halt at the reception counter. Saul slapped the brass bell and it pinged loudly. A long man, old and in black trousers and tail coat, emerged from the door behind the counter. He approached them slowly, as if he was walking through syrup, and he regarded them down his parrot-beak nose from under heavy-lidded eyes.

When he addressed them it was with a deep and lugubrious, 'Yes?'

'Chess Tuesday,' said Saul, 'to see the Sages.'

'Please take a seat.' The receptionist regarded Chess through mournful eyes and motioned to the nearest chairs with a hand that drooped out of his sleeve as if the fingertips were too heavy for their wrist. 'There may be a little wait.'

'It better be littler than theirs,' warned Pacer, glancing back at the remnants behind them.

Crazy Boris leant towards the counter. 'We've only got until the end of the world,' he explained.

'I shall be as quick as I can,' said the receptionist, face impassive.

'That's what worries me,' sighed Crazy Boris.

The receptionist turned his back on them and plodded through the door behind the counter. The door slapped shut, but before anyone had time to speak, he re-emerged and plodded back to the counter.

'The Sages will see you now.'

'Not bad,' murmured Crazy Boris. 'That's an eleven out of ten for speed of service,' and he winked at Gemma who hiccupped a laugh.

'Where?' asked Chess. 'Where do I go?'

The man pointed and his eyes sighted along his considerable forefinger. 'That way,' he murmured, deep and melancholy.

Chess followed his finger and saw that it was pointing at the double doors.

'Just you, Chess,' said Saul.

'Yeah, I guess that's best,' she agreed. 'You all wait here.' She felt better, knowing that the others were waiting with Saul. Saul knew what to do. She took a long look at Balthazar, Pacer, Crazy Boris and then Gemma. Only Gemma smiled back. Together with Saul's bold confidence, Gemma's smile was the only thing which eased the weight on her heart.

'I don't mind coming with you,' volunteered Pacer.

Chess shook her head. 'You've come far enough already, Pacer.' It sounded stupid but that was what she said and she turned her back on his frown because his frown hurt her and *she* didn't like hurting *him*.

Chess walked through the double doors.

She was in a chamber with metal walls and a metal floor

and an illumination of surgical intensity. She knew that this wasn't really on the other side of the double doors, that she had been transported here as swiftly as thought. And because her mind had absorbed this shift, she knew how to find the way back through the labyrinth dimensions to the waiting room.

The chamber was square, maybe five metres by five, and it reverberated with her footfalls. There were no doors. It was as if she were within a large metal cube. At the centre of the room there was a glass sphere, waist high, containing an arrangement of brass hoops and globes. Chess had seen such a device before, in Lemuel's rooms in Committee HQ. He had called it a pan-dimensional armillary clock. But whereas the twelve brass globes in Lemuel's clock had been scattered on their orbits all about the inside of the sphere, Chess couldn't fail to notice that these brass globes were in near-perfect alignment.

'Hello, Chess,' said one of the two men who were looking at her from the other side of the clock. His hair was white shot with grey and it curled round his face and past his shoulders so that it was difficult to distinguish it from the beard which tumbled almost to his knees. He wore a burgundy brocade dressing gown which was tied about his substantial waist with a gold rope. Chess thought he looked like a wizard, a plump, short wizard, except that she didn't think there was such a thing as magic. The world was weird enough without magic.

'I am Diogenes,' said the man with the beard. He patted the shoulder of the man who sat in the wheelchair beside him. 'And this is Phoenix.'

Chess's heart jolted. She stared at the thin man in his loose, charcoal-grey suit and open-neck shirt, at his gentle hands resting on the arms of the chair, which was neater and smoother than Professor Breslaw's, at his long, kind face with its steel-framed spectacles, at his white hair streaked with black, and at the blue eyes which looked so much younger than the rest of him.

'Uncle Phoenix?' she faltered.

Chess had clung to every detail of what had happened when she had met the memory of her mother in Knott Street, and she had replayed that memory to herself again and again. When she had been imprisoned by the Twisted Symmetry, revisiting the memory of Knott Street had been the only thing that had kept her fragmenting mind close to sanity. And she remembered the things that her mother had said to her.

A really clever person called Lemuel Sprazkin came along and did some unusual science and made Mummy out of Grandma. And he made your Uncle Phoenix, who you don't know.

The man in the wheelchair smiled. His mouth was lopsided, so that his teeth didn't appear to be centred properly, but it was a kind face. Kind and interested.

'Yes, yes, this is your Uncle Phoenix,' said Diogenes, more in keeping with a business meeting than a family reunion.

Chess couldn't think of anything to say and she wasn't sure what to do. She wasn't used to family, not family she didn't already know, and she didn't know about Box and Splinter any more. She didn't want to stare, so she snatched a glance to see whether Phoenix looked anything like her mother, Clarity, and she decided that apart from his hair, which must have once been black, he didn't. So she stared into the pan-dimensional armillary clock and wished that she could think of something significant to say.

'. . . and a third Sage, Old Rumination, was due to be here,' Diogenes was explaining, 'but he is asleep and we thought it best to leave him so. He isn't at his best when first woken, and time is now so short that he's unlikely to get much beyond the stage of first waking.'

'Shades of Clarity,' said Phoenix, brushing his straight hair back with a long hand, 'but you're every bit Esme's granddaughter.'

Chess felt her face redden. And blushing a bit made her blush even more, but she couldn't help it. This was more like being in a family than anything she'd ever known. She took a longer look at Phoenix now. His face was so young and so old at the same time: it was like a badly done ageing-graphic. She decided that he was definitely younger than he looked.

'You are on your own?' enquired Diogenes.

'I've got friends, waiting for me.' Chess pointed at a wall although she realized that in relation to this chamber, her friends could be anywhere. She wondered whether Saul counted as a friend. He was different from other friends: he was different from everyone. So she didn't mention Saul at all. 'I need to know where the twelve suns are one.'

Diogenes hm'd to himself and then tapped the top of the pan-dimensional armillary clock. 'Well, it is nearly three o'clock. Just look.'

Chess looked. 'All I can see are twelve balls in one line.'

'Yes, well, it comes to the same thing.' Diogenes straightened his beard and looked to Phoenix.

'You know what the time spiral is, Chess?' Phoenix asked the question in a much gentler way than clever people normally asked questions. Chess nodded. 'OK. Well, when the time spiral reaches a point that we call the fifth node, it mutates: it enters a phase where there can be massive change. This massive change is possible because so many dimensional planes come into alignment.'

When Chess screwed up her nose he explained what he meant by saying, 'It's as if these dimensions are stacked up in one place, so a lightning bolt can go through the whole lot in one go.'

He pushed a lever and with a whirr of its motor, the wheelchair drew alongside Chess. Then he pointed into the glass sphere. 'So you see, we know when the time spiral has reached the fifth node because the twelve principal suns of these dimensional planes come into line with one another.'

'That's why we had two shadows,' said Chess.

'*Two* shadows?' Diogenes harrumphed.

'In the vortex,' explained Chess. 'I had two shadows. So that must have been from two of the suns.'

'If I were a betting man, which I'm not,' said Diogenes, 'I'd wager that you'd have at least ten shadows by now.'

'What do you want to do, Chess?' asked Phoenix.

He made it sound such an enormous question that Chess had to stop and think carefully before answering, as if there

—[209]—

might have been a real choice to make. But there was only one thing she was going to choose, one thing she had to choose.

Think of a plan and stick to it, Miss Tuesday.

'I want to find the Eternal,' said Chess, poker-faced.

'And then?' asked Diogenes.

'And then I'm going to destroy it.'

Diogenes choked a little and then he fiddled with his beard. 'Yes. Well. That might be difficult.'

Chess shrugged. 'You asked me what I'm going to do. That's what I'm going to do. *If* I can get there in time.' She looked at the Sages, unblinking.

Phoenix looked at Diogenes and said, 'If this is her choice, this is how it has to be. Both of us know that.' When Diogenes scowled, Phoenix said, 'Mevrad saw this. That is why she has made arrangements for it. That is why we are here, in this room.'

Thinking that she was falling in with something that Ethel had planned would once have been enough to drive Chess away from doing it at all. But not now. Her mind was made up. The fact that Ethel might have made her own mind up in the same way was merely coincidental.

'Why *are* we here, in this room?' she asked.

'You have to travel to the focal point of where the twelve suns are one: the heart of the space-time matrix. You have to travel to the Core.' Phoenix wasn't smiling now, and although he was telling her what she wanted to know, Chess could see that it was making him unhappy.

'The Eternal Core Decelerator.' The words bounded from her and when both Phoenix and Diogenes raised their eyebrows in unison she laughed and said, 'Ethel told me that, years ago. She told me it's a weapon. That's what the Eternal is. It's what all the fighting's about. No Eternal: no more fighting. Simple.'

But Phoenix sighed more miserably than before and Diogenes grumbled under his breath, 'Mevrad, Mevrad, Mevrad.'

'Mevrad wanted you to be able to get to the Core without any danger of interference by the Symmetry,' said Phoenix.

'Not that we are taking sides in all of this,' qualified Diogenes. 'CASRA is politically, cosmically and dimensionally neutral.'

Phoenix wasn't protesting about neutrality. Chess realized that he was giving her instructions. 'This whole chamber is a long-range particle grid superimposer.'

'A *what?*' Chess crossed her arms with a creak of her leather jacket.

'A teleporter,' interpreted Diogenes.

'It works by re-mapping all your particles from here to elsewhere: in this case, from here to the Core.' Phoenix directed his chair from Chess's side to one of the four metal walls. His dull reflection moved in tandem beneath him.

Chess walked to where he had stopped. Now she could see that there was a small square defined by hairline cracks: a panel in the wall. 'In here is the key to operate the system. Turn the key and the process will begin, transferring whatever is in here to the Core.'

'Do not turn anything until *we* have gone,' added Diogenes, sternly.

'Have you got a knife?' asked Phoenix, his fingers reaching

up to the panel but not yet pushing. 'A penknife, for example?'

Chess shook her head. Box and Splinter always carried knives but she didn't. 'Why do I need a knife?'

'Blood,' stated Diogenes, as if the word was dripping with it.

'No way,' protested Chess, remembering what Ethel had said about a blood link with the Core.

'For the Core process to work once you get there, your blood will be needed, Chess,' explained Phoenix.

'It need only be a little cut,' added Diogenes.

'You've forgotten that I'm not going there to make any process *work*,' Chess pointed out. 'I'm going to break it. So there's no need for my blood.'

'Perhaps,' said Diogenes to Phoenix, 'we can give her a small knife, before she goes?'

'I am still here, you know,' snapped Chess, who didn't like the way the Sage was talking about knives as if she wasn't there at all. The two men looked at her uncertainly. 'Just show me how this works,' and she pointed at the panel.

Phoenix pushed his palm against the metal and then slid it aside and into the wall. There was an alcove and within the alcove there was a small box and in the front face of the box there was a hole.

'It's gone!' gasped Diogenes. 'Gone!'

Phoenix said nothing but he stared at the hole so hard that Chess thought he was trying to make whatever had vanished reappear by will alone.

'How?' complained Diogenes and he pulled the end of his beard in anguished frustration.

'I have no idea,' said Phoenix, very quietly.

Chess leant towards the panel, lifted one hand to the box within and touched the hole. She put her forefinger inside, feeling the shape, the dimensions and contours within which the key should sit and then turn. And simultaneously, with the fingers of her other hand, she felt the contours and depressions of the horse's head, the chess piece that she had kept in the pocket of her jeans ever since the day she had dug it out from the fireplace in Knott Street.

I know where it is, she realized, I know where the key is. She didn't know why it had been necessary for someone to have removed the key from where it should have been, she knew nothing of the Symmetry's efforts to get to it first, but knowing that the memories of Knott Street were linked to this moment gave her a burst of warmth. She pulled the knight from her pocket and displayed it on her open palm.

'Is this what you're looking for?'

'How?' Diogenes kept saying, eyes like yo-yos.

Phoenix looked up at Chess and brushed the loose hair away from his face, puzzled. 'Have you been here before?'

Chess shook her head. 'It was given to me. By Clarity. By my mother.' Her throat went tight when she said that and she blinked the stinging sensation out of her eyes.

Phoenix laughed and looked at Diogenes. 'Don't ask me!'

'I think,' said Chess, 'that Ethel ... Mevrad ... was involved.'

'Mevrad should *not* be involved,' stated Diogenes, officiously.

'And *you* are meant to be cosmically neutral,' retorted Chess, on Ethel's behalf. There I go, sticking up for Ethel

—[213]—

again, she thought. But as she began to plan what to do next, her thoughts shifted to someone else.

'Time for you to go, Chess,' said Phoenix.

'I know.' But Chess didn't rush to use the key. Her fingers closed on it and squeezed it hard, thinking, thinking, thinking.

'*Time*,' insisted Diogenes, 'is running out.'

Of course time was running out. Chess had only to relax her grip on her mind to sense the stretching apart of the space about her, to feel herself being sucked into the breaking fabric of the dimensions. Now was the time to go to the Core. But even though she knew her friends had already faced too much danger, she didn't want to go on her own. She wasn't sure she could do what she had to do on her own. Alone, she would be overwhelmed, lose herself entirely in the cataclysmic dimensional shift. She needed someone with her to keep her rooted in herself, to remind her of who she was. But she knew that she was meant to go to the Core alone.

'You'll have to leave the room,' she insisted, 'or I'll end up transporting you with me.'

'Yes, yes, of course,' agreed Diogenes. He pointed at Chess's clenched fist and then at the box. 'Just push it in and turn the base. Like …'

'A key?' Chess smiled.

'Are you alright, Chess?' asked Phoenix. Chess could tell that there was more he wanted to say. But maybe he couldn't find the words; maybe there wasn't time. Maybe, if he felt like she did, he had spent all his life wishing that there was somebody to be close to, somebody who was part of his family, and now they were parting almost as soon as they had met.

'Yeah, I'm OK, Uncle Phoenix.' It felt strange to use a name like that: she'd only used a family name once before as far as she could recall, and that had been to a memory. 'I'm fine,' and she laughed abruptly. It was obvious that right now she was anything but fine.

'You don't have to go through with this.' Phoenix spoke tentatively, ignoring the splutter from Diogenes. 'You don't have to do whatever you're planning to do: whatever you think you have to do.'

'I'm going now. Thanks.'

Diogenes burst out with, 'You need something, for the blood.'

'I'm not going to bleed,' replied Chess. 'I'm going to destroy.'

Phoenix closed his eyes. When he opened them he said, 'I wish we had time, Chess. I really wish we had time. But I'm glad we've met, at last,' and he reached out and squeezed her hand, which surprised her. 'Come on, Diogenes,' he said. 'We have to leave her now.'

The two of them turned and crossed the room to the wall opposite, passing the pan-dimensional armillary clock, the hard rubber tyres of the chair running smoothly over the floor. The wall lifted in one sheet like a solid portcullis and the two of them passed into the corridor beyond, saying no more. Once the wall had dropped flush with the floor, Chess was completely alone.

For over a minute she thought this through, chewing her lip and gripping the gaming piece so hard that she might have been trying to wring her decision from it. Ethel had planned for her to make this final stage of the journey alone. She could almost feel Ethel willing her on.

Come on, dear. Don't hang about. Use the key. You're on your own now.

But Ethel couldn't have known how hard this was, how close Chess was to losing her grip on herself altogether.

Trust no one.

Always, Ethel said that. But Ethel wasn't always right. Ethel didn't know what Chess knew. Sometimes you *had* to trust people.

Chess knew that she was frightened: frightened of what was going to happen; frightened that once she was at the Core the forces would tear her from herself. Then anything could happen: the worst things could happen. Chess didn't understand much about how she had been made, didn't really understand all the things that had been done to her, but she did understand that she contained enough energy to destroy everything, if she wanted to: or if she lost the power of choice altogether.

That was why she couldn't do this on her own. That was why she needed someone to come with her. That was why she needed Saul.

The Scythian brought his black stallion to a standstill with a snap of reins. Behind him, Jago Burke halted on his chestnut mare. Looking over Captain Burke's shoulder, her arms on his waist, Anna saw the black stallion rear up. Or maybe it was rearing down. They had just galloped out of a vortex stained black and purple and shot with the colour of clotted blood, and they had ridden onto this corkscrew path. Here, it was difficult to tell what was up and what was down, and the vast edifice ahead of them was so random and in such a state of perpetual flux that it provided no clues.

'Why've we stopped?' asked Anna. 'We've got to get to Chess. Get to her before anything else does.' She scowled at the star of shadows that was cast beneath them by suns that they couldn't see. Or was it above them? 'Your hat is tickling my nose, by the way.'

'Sorry,' said Captain Burke, who sounded more amused than sorry.

The Scythian turned in his saddle, teeth white and vicious against his swarthy face and close black beard, and he spoke to Jago Burke in sharp snatches. Burke replied in the same tongue. The Scythian spurred his horse on, his black cloak billowing in his wake, and behind him followed Anna and the Captain in a spiralling gallop.

'Don't you ever enter by the door?' enquired Anna as they sprang through the wall, following the black rider who had disappeared into it ahead of them.

'Not when I'm on my horse,' replied Jago Burke, as her hooves crashed onto the floor and she skidded to a clattering halt halfway down the waiting room.

Anna looked at the four faces that were turned to her and didn't see Chess's amongst them. 'Where is she?' she demanded, swinging off the horse, her boots hitting the floor with a sharp crack. She strode over to the others, the sword across her back and her leather jacket open. 'Where's Chess?' She looked about, ignoring the several decrepit figures slumped in their chairs. 'Where's Lemuel, for that matter?'

She saw how angry Pacer looked but it was Gemma who said, 'She's gone. With Saul. She appeared here and said that she didn't want to go on alone, and Saul said that maybe one of us should have gone, and I said I'd go, well, all of us said we'd go, but Chess only wanted Saul to go, so she held his hand and they went.'

There were a lot of things Anna felt like saying, but she breathed deeply and slowly and didn't say any of them. Instead, fists on hips, she asked, 'Who is Saul?'

Gemma looked from Pacer to Balthazar and finally at Crazy Boris before saying, 'None of us really know.' Then, as if it might be helpful, she added, 'He used to work for the Twisted Symmetry but he's nice now. They've gone to the place where the twelve suns are one.'

'Brilliant.' Anna looked up at Jago Burke. His gloved hands were folded neatly over the pommel of his saddle. He raised an eyebrow back at her.

'Do *you* know where the twelve suns are one?' she asked.

'Not precisely,' admitted Jago Burke.

'The Sages are here, in this building?' asked Anna.

'They are,' said Balthazar, 'but they are not always ready to receive visitors.'

'Really?' Anna marched across to the counter and thumped the bell. The receptionist entered and approached at a funereal pace.

'We need to see a Sage,' said Anna.

'Really,' croaked the receptionist, looking at Anna down the full length of his nose. 'And is it urgent?'

Before he next blinked, the razor tip of a metre of gleaming steel was resting on his Adam's apple.

'You decide,' said Anna.

CHAPTER 12

'This route is always difficult,' said Razool, buckling the straps across his chest, 'but this time it's going to be dangerous.'

Next to him, Box fastened the straps which would secure him in his own seat. There were only two seats in the cockpit of the pilot ship, and a crammed array of screens, switches, dials and levers. Wires and pipes strung the roof and side panels like arteries.

'Losing your nerve, Zool?' asked Box, looking for the final buckle housing.

Razool turned his sleek, alsatian face to him, baring a row of gleaming fangs in a half grin. 'Just checking you've got a spare set of underclothes, skin. I don't want you messing your only pair. As the senior officer here, it's my job to look after you.'

Box pantomimed a belly laugh and Razool laughed back genuinely, even though, as it happened, he *was* the senior officer. Box knew that a Commodore was only a bit below the General himself.

It was good to be back with Razool. Box hadn't seen him

for months, not since the General had arranged for their collection from Committee HQ after they had returned with Chess. Since then, Razool had been restored to his command as a Commodore in the Fourth Navy, although Box knew that his arm and chest still bore the brands that marked him as a mutineer: false brands, since Razool had been acting on the General's orders when he had diverted the shipments of crystal. And now he and Razool were back in business, seeing through the fate of all that crystal.

'They've been keeping you busy?' Box asked, speaking the rough dog-tongue with ease.

'A little shore leave.' Razool reached up and flicked a row of switches with a hirsute finger. 'Some quality time with Mrs Razool.' He pulled out a unit on a metal arm that wouldn't move until he'd kicked it twice with the heel of his boot. 'Can't believe the General flies this heap of skak.' He looked across at Box, his mane of black hair sweeping down his shoulders. 'Mrs Razool says thank you very much for the taps, by the way.'

Razool stuck out an elbow, indicating the hole above the joint.

'I bet your whelps thought they were cool,' said Box.

'Nope. They just think their father's a robot.' Razool angled a key pad and began to tap in numbers, fingers darting. He wasn't looking at Box, but he asked, 'Seen any more of that human girl, Anna?'

'Nope. And I only see *human* girls,' Box pointed out. 'You know where we're going?' The Fourth Navy navigated the vortex so Razool *would* know where they were going, and Box had flown with him before so he knew what an ace pilot he was, but talking about what they were going to do felt easier than thinking about Anna.

'Of course I know where we're going,' growled Razool. 'But we've got two problems.'

'Only two?' Box whistled through his teeth. 'Easy.'

Razool's head cocked to one side. 'There's a lot of useless things skins can do that I can't, and that noise is one of them.' He blew air, his long tongue pressing up against his fangs. A stream of spittle specked the air and hit Box's cheek.

'Cheers,' said Box, wiping away the spit. With his other hand he scratched the short black hair on his head. 'Go on then: problems?'

'First, the time-space matrix is rupturing.' Razool peered out of one of the small windows. 'It's not obvious out there, but once we're into the vortex, it'll create difficulties. It means we'll have to fly out of the vortex and through the Ice Bucket for the last stretch.'

'Ice Bucket?' asked Box. 'A bucket? With ice?'

Razool laughed and shook his head. 'Box, whenever I see that something as stupid as you can stay alive, it gives me hope.'

'Thanks,' said Box, who decided to treat this as a compliment.

Razool powered up the ship. Behind them and below them, the vortical drives began to whine. 'The Ice Bucket is a giant asteroid field that runs up to the margin of the Galen territory. It's packed with rocks: anything from pebbles to asteroids the size of small moons. Whatever goes in gets smashed to pieces and comes out like dust. Think of a cosmic waste disposal unit and you'll get the idea.'

'Why "ice" though?'

'It's cold. Freezing cold. Ready?'

Box could tell that the ship was about to jump from its current location to the vortex, as near to where they had to go as they could get. After that, Razool would fly them in. 'Always ready,' he replied. 'So, problem one, we get smashed to pieces.'

'Correct,' said Razool. He pressed a red button and sat back, long body in black T-shirt and combat trousers stretching as far as it could in the cramped space of the cockpit.

'And problem number two?' asked Box.

'The Galen hate anything that isn't Galen. I just fly you in, so strictly that's your problem, not mine.'

Box felt the smooth gut-slide of the jump into hyperspace.

'The General told me that the Galen hate Dog Troopers,' he complained.

'The Galen hate Dog Troopers most of all.' Razool shrugged. 'But they don't do friendly with anything.'

Box shrugged. 'I get on with most people.'

'These aren't people, Box. They're thoughts.'

Box looked through the window and whistled low. 'Seen out there, Zool?' Razool raised a hairy brow at the whistle.

Always, the vortex had been a white nothingness, but now it was deep indigo, shot with veins of yellow and green and red, and for the first time since he had become a dreadbolt, Box felt tiny: powerless. It looked as if the menacing turmoil of the vortex could blot him out and carry on without a blip.

'It's the end of the world, Box,' drawled Razool, 'unless your little sister delivers the goods.'

My little sister? Box wasn't sure what Chess was. After he had brought her back from the warp station she had insisted that he wasn't her brother and that Splinter was. If she'd been more normal, that might have hurt more than it did. But Chess had said so little, and when she did speak the things she had said were so slash-dot, that Box had given up trying to make sense of her. And he'd hardly seen anything of her anyway. He'd done everything he could to bring her back home, and then she'd acted like she hardly knew him and then he'd been sent back to war. Not much of a thank you.

Would his little sister deliver the goods? He didn't have a clue. He was here because someone had decided he had a small part to play in saving the world. He was ready to do anything that would help Chess, but it was Anna who was on his mind.

'Speaking of deliveries,' said Box, 'what about the crystal? Isn't that what this is all about?'

Razool pointed up at a vid-screen set in the panel above the front window of the pilot ship. Box had been occupied by what he could see through the window. The view in the screen took him by surprise: a fleet of huge ships, banked up in the wake of the pilot ship like a gargantuan arrow head.

'Whales,' said Razool. 'Deep-vortex cargo ships.'

'How . . .'

'Big are they?' anticipated Razool. Box nodded. 'Having visited your city, I'd say each one is the size of the average street.'

Box whistled through his teeth.

'There you go again,' observed Razool, 'showing off. Each one carries a megaton of amarantium: pure crystal.'

'When the General said that a lot of crystal had been stockpiled, I never guessed he meant this much.'

'You underestimate our leader,' muttered Razool. 'No half-measures. He's been planning this for a very long time. We just have to hope the Galen accept the pay-off. You can close your mouth, by the way.'

'But how did he keep it hidden from the Inquisitors?'

'It's surprisingly easy to hide something that's everywhere at once,' was Razool's reply.

Box scratched his head and asked a question which he hoped would receive a simpler answer. 'So what happens?'

'When we get there?'

Box nodded.

'The fleet remains in the vortex. We enter the Ice Bucket and try not to get smashed. I fly you to the Out Post. You beg for your life. Then you convince the Galen to end a million years of war. We pour the crystal into the Ice Bucket. They lap it up at the other end. You've saved the universe and we fly back to base. Everybody's happy. *Or*,' added Razool, 'you mess this up and everybody dies.'

'No pressure then,' said Box. 'What's the outpost?'

'The Out Post is the only place where carbon life forms can address the Galen.'

'We're carbon life forms, yeah?'

'*I* am,' said Razool. '*You* are difficult to classify.'

Box laughed.

'You couldn't survive in the atmospheres where the Galen

live, beyond the Out Post, and they couldn't survive in the atmospheres in the other direction,' added Razool, 'so the Out Post is the perfect meeting point.'

'It doesn't sound very perfect,' commented Box.

'Right,' muttered Razool through bared teeth. 'Hold on.'

'Hold on?'

'We're there.'

Box looked through the window. He caught the thunderous prospect of the vortex and then it had vanished, replaced by the blackness of space. All about them were rocks, their outlines silvered by the feeble light of a distant sun. Some were craggy, some were smooth as the pilot ship, and some were so huge that they were only visible because of how they appeared as a deeper black against the void.

'At least they're moving slowly,' commented Box.

'Don't count on it,' replied Razool, his voice rising as he snatched the throttle, fired up the boosters and pulled the craft right. Box was thrown hard left and he sensed the *vroom* of something massive hurtling through the after-burn.

He laughed. 'That was close.'

His laugh was cut short by a crunch so loud it sounded as if his teeth had been pulled straight out. His head was flung left, hard enough to dent the coolant cowling. He sensed the ship whirl and was aware, dizzily, of Razool bullying the controls to pull it out of the spin.

Razool shook his head and his dark eyes flashed at Box. 'That was closer.' Then he looked across at the dented cowling. 'Your head's done more damage to the ship than the rock.'

Box would have said something back, but right then his

belly was blasted into his mouth. The ship leapt forwards, diving through a gap in the rocks before pulling a spin away from three colliding boulders.

'OK,' shouted Razool, above the scream of the thrusters. 'You get into the loading bay. Pull on a thermal suit and take some breathing apparatus.'

Box yanked off the straps and climbed over the seats. His powerful hands gripped whatever they could find, leather chair backs, metal pipes, the edge of the entrance panel, to prevent himself being hurled loose by the rollercoastering ship.

'OK,' shouted Razool. 'When we get there, I'll open the hatch. Once you're out, remember to keep hold of the post.'

'There's a post?' Box shouted back.

'Yup. And it's out there, at the end of the Ice Bucket. That's why it's called the Out Post. But it takes a hammering like everything else that's out there, so *hang on*.'

'I've got to save the universes hanging on to a skaking post?' yelled Box.

'Yes you skaking have,' Razool yelled back. 'Mike up and tell me when you're done. I'll pull out to the vortex, but as soon as you call, I'll come in.'

'Great,' muttered Box, stumbling across the loading bay and pulling out one of the thermal suits that was compression-packed behind a cargo net.

'Go in. Hang on,' he chanted to himself, whipping the lightweight suit open. 'Don't get killed. Get them on-side.' The ship was swinging and diving through the asteroid field so crazily that he had to lie on the floor to get into the suit. He lifted his legs to pull on the trousers, then zipped up the chest. 'Close the deal. Call Zool.' He took a throat mike, turned it to the ship's vortical frequency and strapped it on. 'Then get out. Alive.'

The breathing tubes hung by the cargo net. The mask covered nose and mouth in a neat, translucent triangle, and the segmented tube ran to the cylinders which he strapped to his back like aqualungs. Then he pulled tight the hood of the thermal suit.

'Hear me?' he checked.

There was a crackle as Razool adjusted the reception.

'Better?' asked Box.

'Better,' agreed Razool. 'Here goes.'

Box felt the negative *g* of howling deceleration and the pilot ship spun to a stop.

'You know why you're here, Box?' asked Razool, before the airlock slid open.

'Tell me,' said Box, adjusting the fastenings which held the mask in place and waiting with a masked-up smile for the inevitable insult.

'Because you're the only person that can do this. I wouldn't be risking my pelt if I didn't think you could.'

No insult. Box waited just to make sure, then said, 'Thanks Zool,' genuinely surprised.

'Don't thank me,' came the reply, 'just prove me right.'

The overlapping screens of the airlock slid apart. Box saw a plate of rock and several metres onto it, a white post with loose chains attached.

'Whoa!' he yelled, almost before he had time to process the boulder which hurtled in from somewhere left of the ship. It smashed onto the flat rock in an explosion of stone particles and set the rock spinning. The rock came to rest in the same position in which it had started.

'The Out Post is moored to this spatial coordinate,' Razool crackled in Box's earpiece. 'It can't be knocked away. You just have to hang on.'

Box gritted his teeth. He hadn't expected the hanging on to be as desperate as it looked.

'OK, I'm out of here before we take a critical hit,' said Razool.

Box sat on the ledge, then dropped. His boots thudded onto the surface. 'I'm on the rock.' The ship remained above him for a moment and then it had gone. Now he was alone.

He sprang to the post, which was about as high as his chest. He wrapped the chains about his arms until the breathing cylinders were hard against the post. Then he took a look at where he was.

The rock must have been no more than ten metres across, with the post at its centre. Looking ahead, space was black and endless save for the minute speckles of distant stars. However, looking back and to either side and above him, there was a belt of silver-limned rocks which trailed away until his vision ran out. The Out Post really was at the end of the Ice Bucket and, right now, Box was chained to it. Against the vast reach of the asteroid field and the unfathomable blackness of space, he felt miniscule.

'Whoa!' he yelled as an asteroid the size of a house *whoomed* in and artillery-shelled the edge of the Out Post in an eruption of debris. But his yell was checked by the spin which followed, so fast that his eyes couldn't keep up. He shut them tight, pushed himself against the pillar and clung to the chains. When the Out Post slowly came to a stop, he slumped to his knees and heaved a breath in through the breathing apparatus.

'This is worse than PURG-CT483,' he gasped, remembering how he had had to hang on whenever the maze of prison tubes had reassembled.

'Anyone tried to kill you yet?' Razool's voice was comfortingly close in his ear.

'Nope.'

'Then it's not worse.'

'Not yet.' Box blinked because his eyes were swimming with colour, as if he'd been bashed across the back of the head. Had his hands been free, he'd have rubbed his eyes. The colours became more vivid, dizzying, shifting before his eyes with golden haloes and pitch-black centres. He was losing all focus on the kaleidoscopic clouds. He shook his head and screwed shut his eyes to blank out the mesmeric iridescence. When he opened his eyes, the amorphous shapes of colour were still there, denser than before, filling the whole of the space overhead. Then, with a cold dip of fear, Box realized that these weren't phantoms he had conjured out of his splitting head. These morphing, myriad shapes and colours were the Galen.

The next asteroid came in from the side, smashing the Out Post into an eye-busting roundabout spin: colour-rocks-colour-rocks-colour-rocks-colour flashing before him. Box thought he was about to throw up, but he didn't know what to do about the mask that was strapped to the front of his face. He was strong enough to bust an arm free of the chains but the nauseating spin sapped his will, whatever his strength.

He swore desperately as the Out Post came to a stop, rocking gently. He tried to get to his knees but it felt as if all the bone had been pulled from his legs.

What are you?

Step one accomplished, thought Box. I'm a skin, not a snout, so I'm not automatically dead.

What is a skin?

Ah, this is like being with the stonedrakes. I could switch with them: speak in thoughts. Just have to remember speaking like that is instant and there's no hiding nothing.

What are stonedrakes?

Lizards. But I'm a skin. A human being. Not a dog.

No. You are not a dog.

OK. Time for the difficult explanation.

What difficult explanation?

Box shut his eyes and breathed slowly.

The universe is ending. Universes. Might probably end.

Might probably? An interesting concept. Contradictory, almost. Equates with a value of . . .

Box winced. The figure shared with him by the Galen was so mind-numbingly colossal it actually hurt his brain.

The probability of pan-universal destruction is much higher than you state.

'You OK?' growled Razool, who must have heard Box groan.

'Yeah,' gasped Box. 'Big maths, that's all.'

You have a small mind.

Box glared up at the huge sentient clouds. *It's big enough to know you won't survive without our help.*

How can you change the probability of pan-universal destruction?

We can give you crystal. All the crystal you need.

How can crystal change the probability of pan-universal destruction?

Box braced himself for the impact of a rock the size of a petrol station which was spinning out of the asteroid field. But it hummed overhead, not quite grazing the top of the pillar.

How can crystal change the probability of pan-universal destruction?

The question probed Box's mind with a laser intensity and he tried to gather the words to explain. But it was hard to know how to explain things to alien minds when words weren't your weapon of choice and you were under constant threat of an asteroid strike.

If we give you the crystal, you don't have to fight us … the dogs. Then the dogs can be free to stop the destruction. Of the universal pans … pans … pan-universes.

He was sure he hadn't explained it very well, but in the circumstances it was the best he could do.

I just hope they believe me.

Of course we believe you.

Of course they did. It was the same with the stonedrakes. There was no lying, no veiling of the truth, no lack of clarity when you spoke in pure thought.

Box squinted against the intensifying glow of the sentient clouds.

The crystal, he thought, I nearly forgot to tell you of the crystal we . . . I brought.

He pictured the transport fleet in his mind's eye, knowing that the Galen would see what he pictured. He opened his eyes in time to see a small rock hurtling in at him. With both arms bound by the chains his chest was directly in its path. Six months ago this would have slabbed him: but not now. There was time to rip his left arm free of the metal links, then throw himself right and out of the asteroid's path. It hit the pillar in a spray of stone splinters which scattered over Box's back.

'Still with us?' came Razool's steady voice.

'Yeah,' panted Box. 'Having the time of my life.'

'Your thermal's taken a rip,' said Razool, who could monitor the condition of the equipment from the ship.

'Don't worry. I'm keeping warm.' Box's voice rose as he rolled away from the strike of the next flying rock.

What'd you say? thought Box as loudly as he could, realizing that he had just missed something.

Say?

About ending the war. Ending the Crystal Wars.

Captain, they have ended already. Your troops are free to withdraw from our hostilities. Now, give us the crystal you have brought.

Already! thought Box, wondering at the same time how the Galen knew to call him Captain.

A dreadbolt too. You must take care of your thoughts, Captain Box Tuesday.

I'm too busy trying to stay alive to do that.

But this time the Galen were silent and the clouds of

colour began to disperse, as if diluted by the blackness which swam into the spaces which they left.

It was different from all the others, drifted one departing thought. *It survived.*

Box remained kneeling, mind aching as if it had been through a juicer. But the fighting wasn't over yet. He remembered what the General had said: one last battle, a battle for a prize that would make his heart burn.

'OK, Zool,' he said, wearily. 'Get me out of here.'

Can you turn the clock back?

Time was ending but the same question remained.

Can you turn the clock back? Can you turn the clock back?

Splinter was falling and he knew that time was ending. He had fallen from light into darkness: nightfall ruptured by veins of crimson. And the bloodshot gloom was sounded by the groan and boom of space breaking like a mighty ice floe.

Splinter knew that time was ending from what he could see about him and from his researches. Those months with the Omnicon, the Book of All Things, had provided him with a vast knowledge and he had applied that knowledge to what he had heard: the conspiratorial whisperings, the disjointed ramblings of wise men, fools, Inquisitors, kings, and an old lady who wasn't what she seemed.

And he had seen what happened to Chess.

So he knew that time was ending and he knew what would happen at the end of time. And now, as he fell deeper into darkness, he was visited, perhaps for the last time, by faces, by visions, by ghosts.

'How are your scars, Splinter?' asked Oriana Lache.

Oriana Lache, beautiful and cold. But not cold towards him. She had tended his wounds with her own fingers rather than the Inquisitors' power, and had left him with the scars as a bitter memento: scars from wounds written into the history of his body by birds, the murderous metalbacks. He traced the scars even as he fell: the tramlines from his pale forehead to his gaunt right cheek; the long cut down his right shoulder.

'I was a Crystal Priest,' sighed Oriana Lache, 'but I was *your* friend.' Her bright intelligent eyes looked into his, sorrowfully.

Intelligent, but not as intelligent as his.

Splinter closed his intelligent eyes, shutting out the savagery of the metalbacks. But eyes tightly shut were no proof against the gore-streaked ghost of Oriana Lache.

His lips moved, mouthing regrets.

'Idiot,' said Anna. It was the last word he had heard her say to him, and he had continued to hear her say it ever after.

He liked Anna. He shouldn't have been in such a hurry to leave her. But it was easy to realize that *now*, now that time was ending.

'Idiot,' repeated Anna, and Splinter admitted that it would have been easy to realize that *then*. Easy to realize, had he not been dazzled by his own ruthless brilliance. He touched the cadaverous skin of his face with the cadaverous skin of his fingers.

'The price of brilliance,' he whispered.

A price extracted by the Codex.

The three deaths: a fan turning; a windblown beach; a narrow man, his knife in Splinter's chest. But that third death remained in his coat pocket and against his skin, the cold press of the crystal knife in its scabbard.

And written into his own body, the price of escaping those first two deaths.

'A price worth paying?' asked Ethel.

'I might have guessed you'd show up, even at the end of the world.'

'I'm all in your imagination, my love,' Ethel reminded him.

'I know that, but it's your fault you're here in the first place.'

'And was your disposal of Oriana Lache *my* fault? Is it my fault you are aptly described as an idiot? Is it my fault you are here, now?'

Splinter fell in morose silence.

Ethel whispered, 'Is what happens to Chess *my* fault?'

'Yes,' flared Splinter.

'Even if you don't stop it?' Ethel left the question falling with Splinter.

And then, sharing the darkness with him, was the Baroness Mevrad Styx, and she was darkness and light in one.

'You have the power to change this, Splinter,' she told him.

Splinter knew she was right. He knew that there was a way to change this. His brilliance had seen how. And maybe, changing what was going to happen would be a way of changing everything, of making everything better, whatever happened to him.

'It's never too late to make the right choice,' said Mevrad, and despite her frightening beauty, despite her power, Splinter felt as if she was actually saying it to help *him*.

'I don't know ... I don't know,' whispered Splinter.

'No one ever does,' Mevrad whispered back, 'until it's too late.'

And now he was alone again. Absolutely alone.

Can a good thing cancel out a bad thing? Splinter asked himself. Or bad *things*?

Perhaps.

Perhaps there was a way to turn the clock back. It was down to whether he could do it: whether he, Splinter, *would* do it. And if he did do this, if he *chose* to do it, it would, as ever, come down to perfect, immaculate timing.

CHAPTER 13

It was obvious to Trick that Ethel and the man with half a silver face had been arguing.

Trick had just arrived at the forward headquarters with Captain Riley. Their jeep had nearly been hit as Caine had powered it round the fresh shell holes that cratered the wasteland, between the edge of the main city and the Pit. She had stopped counting the number of times she had almost been killed since being called in to act as a liaison runner between the Charitable Operations Executive and the street rats. One minute she had been in the kitchen with Mrs Riley, Oliver and Jasper, listening to the emergency news bulletins that were ordering everyone to leave the city, and the next the jeep had come for her. And then it had begun: the hours of running and hiding; the hunters; the shambling, rotting plague beasts; the marauding whistlers; the packs of spindle rippers; the army of heavy infantry androids clearing the streets with their long-barrelled firearms and manning strangely designed mobile guns which had blasted the city apart, block by block.

She was thirsty and she felt weak, so weak that her limbs

trembled when she stopped using them. But she had to keep going because if she didn't, the city would be overrun. Already, there were skyscrapers that had been demolished by artillery fire, overpasses ripped apart exposing infrastructure like broken twigs; there were hazy columns of traffic choking the ground routes and jacks streaming westwards like refugees. From the ridge above the Pit, the vast northern skyline of the city was a rolling curtain of black smoke drifting skywards in volcanic streamers.

The jeep pulled up on the Pit side of the ridge, out of view of the war zone that the city had become. The forward headquarters consisted of a conglomeration of khaki tents gathered amidst the first rank of the shanty town hovels. The tents were low slung and protected from fire by a shimmering defensive field. The steady hum of the nuclear-powered generators was interrupted by the wham and burst of incoming shells, and the blast of the guns manned by government troops in support of the COE.

Trick followed Captain Riley into a large tent. It smelt of canvas and oil and earth. It was divided into sections, connected by canvas corridors. The Captain was wearing black combats and body armour and his sub-machine gun hung across his back, rattling against his webbing. He led her into a large, central area where there were long trestle tables covered by maps and ring-stained by coffee mugs. There were more maps on huge boards around the canvas walls. Some of these maps looked like street plans and some looked like maps of countries, and Trick thought that some were the sort of charts that astronomers used.

There were banks of VDUs showing moving images or

luminous scrolls of data. Sitting in front of the displays were uniformed operators, some wearing headsets. Over one bank of VDUs there was a digital clock. Trick wasn't very good with writing but she could do numbers, so she knew that the electric-red digits said 2:56:16. It took a few seconds to work out what the clock was doing, but by the time it read 2:56:03, she realized that it was counting down.

Standing at a centrally placed table were Ethel and Julius, staring angrily at one another, and there was a man in army combats. He looked old enough to be important and he wore a pistol holstered on his webbing belt. His hair was cut short and he had a no-nonsense chin and startling blue eyes. Professor Breslaw was sitting there too, and to one side of the tent was the Gun Toting Biker Dwarf, Jake. His darkened bike goggles were still pulled down although he was slouched in a canvas-backed chair, and the faint crash of heavy metal buzzed from the earpieces he wore. In his oily hands he cupped a mug of steaming tea and by his chair was propped a shotgun.

On the centre of the table there was a small glass dome containing an elaborate construction of brass hoops and globes. There were more globes than Trick could be bothered to count and they appeared to be positioned in a perfectly straight line which cut through the space inside the dome.

'Air strikes are out of the question,' the man in the army combats was saying. 'The civilian population is still too widely spread throughout the city. We have to continue engaging on the ground.'

'But the casualties . . .' began Ethel.

'Continue to be horrific, I know.' The soldier's eyes bore down upon the old lady. 'My troops are having to learn how to deal with this enemy incursion as it develops.'

'This has become rather more than an incursion, General,' observed Ethel. 'It is fast becoming a rout.'

'General Phillips,' snapped Captain Riley, saluting. The General returned the salute. All this saluting struck Trick as a bit pointless when the world was about to end.

'How are your troops, Captain?' asked the General.

Captain Riley walked to one of the large, hanging maps which, Trick realized, depicted the city. She could tell this by the broad line of the river which snaked along its bottom.

'Engaging the enemy at sectors eleven, eighteen and thirty-four,' said Riley, briskly. He pointed to the map as he spoke. Trick didn't know exactly what the numbers referred to but she knew that the COE were fighting where the Twisted Symmetry were strongest: in the centre of the city; on the western edge of the Graveyard; in a line cutting across the highways that led west out of the centre of the city and which were packed with fleeing jacks.

'We need more napalm drops on the Plague Breed, here,' Riley continued. He pointed at the city centre.

General Phillips frowned. 'Your units are widely dispersed. How can you move them through the enemy-held areas?'

Trick felt a wave of hot pride when Captain Riley caught her eye before saying to the General, 'Street rats, sir.'

'Street rats!'

'They've set up guiding parties, they're acting as pathfinders, and they are taking my units to where they need to go by routes *underneath* the city.'

—[241]—

'*Underneath* the city?'

'Drains, General. The enemy have superiority of numbers. But they have nothing to match the street rats when it comes to getting about this city.' Captain Riley nodded at Trick and said, 'It's no exaggeration to say that our ability to resist the enemy by constant surprise attacks is due largely to the work of the street rats.'

'Very good, Captain. You know what they say: surprise increases combat effectiveness by a factor of six hundred per cent.' The General hit Trick with a sharp smile and a nod of approval. 'I suppose we have this young fellow to thank, and hundreds like him.'

'I'm not a fellow,' mumbled Trick into her chest, 'and you should thank Hex, 'cos he's the one organizing us. I'm just running messages for Captain Riley.'

The General squatted down in front of Trick. 'There's no "just" about it, young lady. If you've been running the gauntlet all day, you deserve a medal.'

Trick beamed and Captain Riley winked at her. The General walked over to one of the seated screen analysts.

Ethel turned to Julius as if she had been waiting for this opportunity to continue their argument. 'You should never have allowed Anna and the others to go. They're needed here, and in all likelihood, they're in unnecessary danger there.'

'They are *my* Sentinels,' said Julius, unperturbed by Ethel's bellicose outburst. 'I decide how to deploy them.'

'You decide how to deploy them?' rejoined Ethel. 'You and your lack of faith. All you do, all you have *ever* done, is judge me by my mistakes.'

'No, I don't. But we can't afford to get this wrong. Not this time.' Julius folded his arms. 'Pulling Chess out is the only safe option. I am certain of that.'

'You fool,' shouted Ethel with a stamp of her foot. 'This is our one opportunity to defeat the Symmetry. *Forever*.'

'Please, please, please,' came the rasping voice of Professor Breslaw. He held up his hands and Trick was glad because the argument was so nasty, and it was more than a little embarrassing to watch. Even General Phillips and his staff had fallen silent and they were staring at the Committee's commanders in astonishment. Captain Riley adjusted his position and frowned at the floor. Jake's earpieces buzzed and he took a long, slow draught of his tea.

'So, we have a new problem?' The Professor shrugged and a batch of cables that connected his body to the chair jerked in unison. 'Always there are new problems. No plan survives contact with the enemy, you must know that, Mevrad.'

'Yes, I do know that, Joachim. But it is meant to survive contact with our own side,' and she turned a spectacular glare upon Julius.

In the seconds that followed, Trick thought that Ethel's anger really had conjured up the intensifying scream from outside. Then she recognized it as the screech of incoming shells, but before she could throw herself onto the earth, which was the drill she had followed up to now, Captain Riley had grabbed her upper arm firmly but gently.

'It's OK, Trick,' he assured her. 'We're protected by the shields.'

Still, Trick noticed how everyone apart from Ethel and

Julius and Jake winced as the barrage broke on the force fields with a thunderous crash and boom. After the impact, the only sound was the low murmur of the General and Ethel talking. Trick could only catch snatches of what they said:

'Stalwarts out of the Aelvar plane, contacting an abominate grouping ... Havoc Legions in the Fifth and Sixth panhedral sectors ... massive loss of life ... Coronal Ascendant Stormtroops encountering cross-vortical fire from the 805th Havoc Legion ... on every plane, on every front, hopelessly outnumbered.'

The voices blurred into one. All Trick could tell was that things were not going well for the Committee.

'The Symmetry will keep the conflict raging until the end,' she heard Ethel say at last, 'providing every last scrap of pain and destruction for Chess to feed off.'

'Which is why we have to stop her,' insisted Julius. He looked at the digital clock: 2:48:24. 'And we are nearly out of time.' He shook his head.

'All the more reason for you *not* to have engineered a late change of plan,' fired Ethel.

'General?' It was one of the operators, facing a row of VDUs. 'Take a look at this, sir.'

The General stood over him, arms folded, head thrust forwards hawkishly. Trick followed Captain Riley over to General Phillips. There was a row of screens in front of the operator but, unlike the displays that had been monitoring events within the city, these screens displayed gentian moonscapes, brilliant star clusters, psychedelic swirls and shifting patterns.

The operator pointed at a screen at the end of the row, set apart from the others. Trick saw that it was blank save for a line of white across its middle. Every few seconds the line zigzagged sharply, then flattened again.

'Interference?' suggested the General.

'What should it be displaying?' asked Captain Riley.

'This screen monitors the energy profile of HQ itself,' replied the operator. 'It shows input/output and gives an early warning of any security breach. But this doesn't look like a warning.'

'It's not interference, though,' piped up Ethel, who had pushed her way between the two men. 'It's too regular. This is something else.'

Everybody except Jake flinched as static crackled loudly from a speaker in one of the roof corners of the tent. At the same time, the energy profile on the VDU vanished altogether.

Another scrape of static and then, 'Good afternoon ladies and gentlemen. And, may I say, it is a pleasure to be back in the land of the living.' The laughter nearly broke the speaker and most people had to stopper their ears with their fingers. 'Or, should I say, the land of the *virtually* living.'

'Lemuel!' said Ethel.

'The one and only,' said Lemuel.

'But I thought you were back in your body?' Ethel was perplexed.

'I was, but things have gone rather badly, Mevrad.' It was plain that Lemuel relished imparting this news.

'Badly?' Julius's eyes smouldered in Ethel's direction.

'I'm afraid so.'

'How badly, Lemuel?' asked Ethel. She and Julius and the General had gathered in a knot beside Professor Breslaw.

'It seems that the Symmetry were aware of Chess's movements.'

Trick thought that she would have burst into flames had Julius's eyes turned on her the way that they had turned on Ethel.

'There was a trap of sorts,' continued Lemuel, 'laid for me.'

'A trap?' Ethel was incredulous.

'A bowl of blood, to be precise.' An electronic crackle of tittering. 'It quite put me out of my right mind. Or, should I say, it put me back into my wrong one.'

'What have you done, Lemuel?' asked Ethel sternly.

'I haven't *done* anything, Mevrad,' came the equally terse response. 'But the action taken by Broom has separated my body from my fellow travellers: has lost it in fact, in the vortex. *Fortunately*, before I was uploaded after our return from the warp station, I left a copy of myself in cyberspace. It took a little time to arrange things, hence the delay in my cognitive resurrection, but it's just as well that I did. So, now, my mind is marooned in cyberspace whilst my body is marooned in the vortex, and never the twain shall meet. At least not for the time being. And from the way things look out here, time won't be *being* for very much longer.'

'What has happened, to Chess?' Julius's voice was frighteningly quiet.

'Oh, don't worry,' said Lemuel in a way that was bound to make everyone worry. 'Chess has found her own way to the Sages and, even as I speak, she is approaching the Core.'

'With the others?' asked Ethel, and for the first time, Trick detected a sharp strain of anxiety in her voice.

'Not with the others.' Lemuel paused, for dramatic effect, before adding softly, 'But she isn't alone.'

The silence was broken only by a dull crash of cymbals and a distant grind of guitars from Jake's earpieces before Ethel asked, 'Who is Chess with, Lemuel?'

Lemuel said one word and he said it with the breathless anticipation of a pyromaniac igniting a stick of dynamite. 'Saul.'

But if he was expecting an explosion, it didn't come. Ethel's head bent and she sighed, shoulders sloping. Julius closed his eyes and pursed his flesh-silver lips and said nothing.

'Do they know one another?' Ethel muttered to herself, chewing on some loose skin about her thumbnail. 'She never mentioned him to me. Never a word. So how? Of all the people in all the universes, how can she have ended up with *him* now?' When she looked up, Trick could see that her face was drawn and the colour of cold ash. 'I didn't foresee this. I never foresaw *this*.'

Professor Breslaw cleared his crusty throat. 'And the danger that Saul poses? What must we expect?'

'Think of vertigo,' said Ethel. 'You're standing on a cliff, feeling the pull of the drop, and at the crucial moment someone gives you a shove.' Ethel shrugged wanly. 'It's a bit like that.' She clenched her little fists. 'Saul will find a way through the last of her defences. He will find a way that no one else can. You know this, Julius, and you know why.'

'Perhaps, Mevrad, you now see the merits of my decision to send a party to extract her?' Julius allowed himself this, but Trick didn't think he was crowing about being right. He raked his silver fingers through his yellow hair, then addressed the speaker as if Lemuel was actually inside it.

'You know where the Sentinels are that I sent, Lemuel?' he asked. 'Relative to the positions of Chess and Saul?'

2:39:12, said the clock.

'Miss Ledward, you mean?'

'And Jago Burke, and the Scythian,' replied Julius, patiently.

'And Balthazar Broom and Mr Sherevsky and that young vagabond, Pacer,' added Lemuel.

'They are with Anna, too?' lamented Ethel.

'Yes they are. And no, I don't know precisely where they are. I am sorry. Truly, I am.' Lemuel's desperate laughter scoured the speaker. 'Believe me, I wouldn't care to appear like this if I wasn't sorry. I would very much like to help Chess, as some recompense perhaps.'

'Recompense?' Julius frowned. 'Recompense for what?'

'No matter,' said Lemuel. 'Now, doing the best I can, I believe that they must be very near to the Core since all of them, including Miss Ledward and the Sentinels you despatched, have used the teleport system helpfully located with the Sages. By the way, Mevrad, your ruse – employing Samphire to steal the key from the Sages all those years ago, to make sure the Symmetry couldn't steal it first – worked a treat. Very clever.'

Trick could see that Ethel didn't look like she was feeling very clever at the moment.

Lemuel continued. 'However, I fear that the charming Miss Ledward and her friends will need back-up, as the experts put it.' Winsomely, he added, 'We're becoming quite *au fait* with the military jargon, are we not, Mevrad?'

Ethel didn't reply.

'Back-up?' Julius's silver fingers flexed. 'Why back-up?'

'The Symmetry are watching what is happening, Julius. Always they are watching. They wouldn't want your rescue party to spoil the grand *dénouement*.' The virtual warp hummed for a couple of seconds as if considering fresh information. 'Yes . . . by my cyberspatial detections, I believe that three whole Havoc Legions have been despatched to ensure that Miss Ledward and Co don't interfere with the end of the universes.'

'Thirty thousand legionnaires against three Blood Sentinels!' choked Joachim Breslaw.

'Not ideal odds,' acknowledged Lemuel.

Julius fixed Ethel with a baleful stare. 'So this is how it ends, Mevrad? The final mistake. Jake,' he snapped at the GTBD, 'call in Seren and Étoile and find Colonel Greave. The others can stay here. Their skills are not so well suited to open battle with the Legions, but we five must join the others.'

Jake nodded, set down the mug, pulled out the earpieces, picked up the shotgun and stomped from the command area. Trick heard his motorbike fire up outside.

'Julius, if I can help,' began the General.

Julius stopped him with one look. 'General, where we

have to go, what we have to face …' He shook his head. 'Your men are good men. They are needed here.'

'Don't be hasty, dear,' cautioned Ethel. 'I know how angry you must be, how disappointed, but there is still a chance. I know there is. I have considered …'

'You *know* there is?' The contempt in Julius's voice made Trick wince. 'Don't try to tell me this is all part of your plan.' Julius's sonorous voice grew louder. 'Don't tell me you have calculated *this*. Don't pretend that we are facing anything other than annihilation.' Then his voice fell dangerously quiet. 'This has gone wrong, Mevrad. Very badly wrong.'

Ethel rested a small, wrinkled hand on the forearm of Julius's leather coat. 'This can't be stopped now, Julius. You know that. And you will gain nothing by going to fight with the Sentinels.'

Julius lowered his arm, away from Ethel's hand. 'We're not going to fight with them, Mevrad. We're going to *die* with them.'

He marched from the tent.

'It's beautiful,' marvelled Chess. It was beautiful and terrible at the same time.

At some distance from where they stood, and it was impossible to gauge precisely how far, a vast column of shimmering light stretched between the up and the down of this place. The light was full of silver, as scintillating as rushing water caught by sunshine. At its top and at its bottom, the column spread out in every direction so that for as far as she could see, the up and the down were like endless seas of streaming light.

Chess remembered how she used to stand in the shallows of the river, watching the water roll past her bare ankles and, after she had stared at it for long enough, at where her legs met the water, it seemed that the water wasn't running at all but that it was she who was gliding backwards. Now, when she looked up or down at the surging fields of light, she saw that from every direction they were rushing towards the central column. But just like the river water, the effect was to make her feel as if she was rushing backwards, even as she walked forwards.

Chess stopped and knelt down and touched the brilliant ground, if ground it was. The light streamed around her fingers and felt as solid as it did beneath her trainers, but at the same time as she touched it, it was as if a camera had flashed inside her head, and then she saw a weary sun, red as old iron. The image hit her with sufficient force to knock her forwards, and leave her elbow aching as if it had been kicked. Even after she had stopped trying to touch the light, images streamed into her mind as the light streamed around her body: suns flickering in sequence, bright, sepia, cold; a woman loading the magazine of a pistol and laughing, with a little girl at her side; a little boy on a park swing, crying; the clash of two demonic armies on a terracotta dust plain; a hooded monk; an old clock with the hands set at three.

Saul pulled her to her feet. She let him keep hold of her arm. 'Are you alright?'

Chess shook her head. 'All I did was touch it. With my hand.'

'No,' explained Saul, 'you touched it with your mind. You opened your thoughts and it rushed in.'

He was right. She knew now that that was what it felt like: not her touching it, but it reaching into her.

'You've got to be careful, Chess.' Saul looked worried for her, even though she could tell he was trying to make no more of this than he had to. 'All of this,' he looked about at the planes of light, 'is part of all that there is, and all that there has been, and you are part of it. Or it is part of you.' He gave a crooked smile which Chess really liked.

'Is this the Core?' she asked.

He pointed at the towering column of light. 'That's the Core. And all of this is in contact with the Core and everywhere else and every time, and all of it is directly in contact with you. It's like all of this is part of *your* mind.

'For most people, all this pure space-time can take them to times and places where they've already been, or where they're going to go. But you, Chess, you can touch everything, and there's so much.' His dark eyes were trained on her, so close that she could feel their heat. 'So you have to be careful. Open your mind to this and you'll drown in it.'

He was right. She knew this: she had known this for a long time. That was why she had to keep a grip on who she was. But nothing was harder than trying *not* to think about something. Chess knew that Saul was trying to help her, but what he'd said actually made it impossible not to think her way into this massive, pan-dimensional mind. And how could she not when it seemed that it was her mind as well?

That thought alone, and trying to stop it, triggered a blasting wave of images: a sun swiftly sinking against a blasted city skyline; a tree; a family eating together; a snow-crusted moon, forgotten; a crowd at a football match; a square sun seen through a dark hole in the desert sands; the hooded monk, his hand reaching out to her.

'Chess! Chess!'

Saul was shouting at her, pulling her up. Her legs ached from the physical force with which the images and thoughts had struck her and her ears were full of the rush of blood.

'There's too much.' She swallowed air between the words she gasped. 'I can't stop it.'

'You need something to focus on, away from this,' said Saul. And then, before she had time to think of anything, he said, 'What's the first thing you remember?'

'My mother's voice.' It was the one memory of her mother that had always been with her, and idly she sang what she remembered the voice singing as they continued to walk towards the Core.

> *When I was on horseback, wasn't I pretty?*
> *When I was on horseback, wasn't I gay?*
> *Wasn't I pretty . . .*

But then she noticed a sombre cast steal across Saul's face and she asked, 'What's *your* first memory?'

It took him some time to answer. Chess wasn't sure whether this was because he was trying to remember or because he didn't *want* to remember. Eventually he said,

'When I was really little, I used to go to a park on my own. I was always on my own.' He shrugged. 'I don't even have a voice to remember. And I'd go on the swings in this park, and the feeling ... you know that feeling you get, when you're on a swing and it swoops down and then swings back up? That lurch in your stomach?' He looked at Chess, uncertain, and she nodded to encourage him, to keep him speaking. She knew this wasn't easy for him and she realized, with a start, that she had already seen what he was about to tell her.

Saul laughed as if he was really embarrassed. He rubbed his chin, ran the same hand through his thick, black hair. 'It used to make me cry. Lots of unhappiness, I suppose. Out it came.' Apologetically, he added, 'When I was a little boy, I wasn't very happy,' and Chess thought that maybe, inside, he wasn't happy still.

'I know that feeling,' she said, and even though she was frightened about where she was going, and what would happen when she got there, she felt stronger and safer being with someone who understood how she felt.

'What makes *you* unhappy?' Saul's voice had recovered its assured tenor.

Chess began to think of what made her unhappy. There was a delay before any particular memory entered her mind. And then it was like she had pulled the stopper from a high-pressure canister of nightmares. The Symmetry had filled her with so much energy from unhappiness that the memories she could access were as limitless as the souls whose suffering had provided it. The pain and the misery exploded into her. She could barely breathe, and her body dropped and would have hit the streaming floor had Saul not caught her. His arms were about her to hold her up, pulling her body against his.

'It hurts,' whispered Chess. It hurt more than words could describe.

'I'm sorry,' Saul whispered back. 'I should have realized. I'm sorry.'

'Don't be. It's not your fault.' Her body felt as if she'd been so sick she'd sheared every muscle from its bone.

'Maybe you should focus on what you're going to do once you're in there.'

Chess looked at the Core over his shoulder. They had drawn a lot closer and it was more terrifying than beautiful now. It reminded her of a massive waterfall flowing up and down at the same time, smooth and cylindrical.

'It's the heart of space and time,' Saul said softly. 'It's where everything is generated. And where it ends.'

Chess waited until the pain had begun to flow away from her before she whispered in Saul's ear, 'I'm going to destroy the Eternal.'

He stood her away from him, still holding her arms. 'I don't know what that means.' He half smiled. 'All I do know is that there's so much pain and so much suffering, maybe you're here to do something about it.'

'What can I do?' She had seen the pain. She had seen the suffering. And she knew that the universes were full of it. But she didn't want to face the enormity of doing something about it; she couldn't trust herself with that. She couldn't trust herself because she knew that if she had to choose, there was every chance she'd end everything.

She knew that Saul didn't mean it, but he couldn't have set her mind on a worse path.

'The Committee think you can be used to sort everything out,' he observed, neutrally.

His comment must have been well intentioned but its effect was incendiary. 'I don't care what the Committee think,' exploded Chess. To her relief, she found that the anger drove away other thoughts that had been surging into her: drove away pain. The anger was a release.

'OK, OK.' Saul backed away. 'Don't get mad.' He shrugged. 'All I know is that Ethel wanted to use you to run the universes *her* way.' He laughed, as if he didn't realize how angry this made her. 'Maybe she doesn't mind how bad they can be. Maybe she doesn't mind the suffering.'

'She doesn't *know* how bad they are,' flared Chess. 'She hasn't felt it. I have.'

Saul held up his hands, defensively. 'I'll shut up, Chess. I'm trying to help but I'm getting this bit wrong.'

'No, it's my fault.' Chess tried to draw her mind back to herself. But out here it was so difficult to hold it together. And the least thing . . .

'Come on,' said Saul encouragingly. 'Not far to go now.'

They moved across the flowing plane of light and Chess walked beside Saul in a hot silence. It was hard to see how the Symmetry could be wrong if all they desired was an eternity of peace. Surely nothingness wouldn't matter if there was no one there to suffer?

Her efforts to think straight were skewed by the roiling anger she had allowed to bubble up. Yet when she had let it come, the rage had blocked out everything else, which was a relief. In a way it was good. But it allowed thoughts that she had worked hard to lock down to wriggle free. And it made something stir deep inside her: a hot, biting grain of hate. The darkness that was all her own.

When they came to the Core, Chess had to arch her neck to see how it flowed up and down, the silver streams of space and time entwining with one another in constant flux. She wondered at how something so massive could remain in constant motion, but in perfect silence. It was as wide as a couple of tower blocks and above her and beneath her feet, the silver planes coursed into it from every direction.

'It's unreal.' Chess struggled to absorb what she saw, what she felt. 'Everything's unreal.' She turned from the Core to Saul and she searched his face, looking for reassurance. His face was strong and yet so soft at the same time, and just looking at it soothed the anger which pressed on her mind like a detonator.

'We're just standing here, like this.' Chess felt so weak. 'And everything depends on what's about to happen, right? I just feel as jumbled up as I always do.'

Think of a plan and stick to it, Miss Tuesday.

I'm here to destroy the Eternal.

Stick to it.

It was a relief to see Saul smile. 'I'll stay by you, whatever,' he said.

For a moment, Chess thought she could hear her name being shouted, as if from a great distance, and she ignored it: just another distortion in her perception, spun by this extraordinary place.

'Promise? Promise you'll stay by me?' she asked. She didn't know what was waiting for her in the coming seconds. She needed to know that whatever it was, Saul would be there.

'I promise,' said Saul. 'Whatever happens, I'll be with you.'

CHAPTER 14

'Chess!'

Pacer screamed the name a final time before the tiny figures vanished within the pillar of light. His voice was hoarse from shouting and he sank to his haunches with the effort, throat flayed.

'Too late,' said Anna, resting a hand on his shoulder. 'Just too late,' and for the seconds which followed, it felt as if all her strength had been sapped. She stared across the silver plane and the vastness of the space was full of loneliness.

To one side of her stood Jago Burke, gloved fists on hips, and the Scythian, muscle-knotted arms folded. To the other side stood Balthazar, Gemma and Crazy Boris. Crazy Boris had taken off his dark glasses and was squinting at the brilliance, up, down and all about, shading his bleary eyes with his fingers.

'We could not have reached them, Miss Ledward,' said Captain Burke. 'Even had we brought the horses, we could not have reached them.'

They'd had to leave the horses in the waiting room in the Antediluvian Halls. Anna had persuaded the receptionist that their audience with the Sages was a matter of life and death, and a Sage called Phoenix had agreed to let them use the teleport system. But with all of them crammed in, there had been no room in the chamber for the horses and there hadn't been time to debate whether they should travel in separate groups. Their only thought had been to get to Chess as quickly as possible. But they'd failed to reach her.

'What is it?' asked Gemma, looking up at the shimmering sky.

'This is where the dimensions converge,' replied Balthazar. He pointed out, towards the towering pillar of brilliance which merged above and below. 'That is the Core. The heart. The place where the twelve suns are one.'

'I can't see any suns at all,' observed Gemma.

'You can't, but they will be out there, or down there.' Balthazar gestured up, then down with short stabs of his staff. 'This is the place where everything overlaps, everything meets.'

'Which is why the Symmetry want her in there,' said Jago Burke, looking out at the Core. 'Right in the heart of the universes' greatest fault line.'

'Right,' considered Crazy Boris, 'so if Chess loses it in there, lets rip with all this energy the Twisted Symmetry have filled her with, it's the Big Bang all over again?'

'It's more like a Big Shrink, Mr Sherevsky,' said Jago Burke. 'Everything goes into reverse until we're back to nothing at all.'

'Except for the Symmetry,' said Balthazar.

'We need to go,' said Anna. 'Now.' She began to march towards the Core and the others followed.

'All of this, this light, if it is light, it's connected with time, yeah? Connected with the past?' Crazy Boris's voice was wearier than usual.

Balthazar was striding alongside him. 'It isn't light. It is pure dimensional essence: as if mathematics has taken shape. We merely perceive it as light.'

'So is it time, Balthazar?' asked Boris.

'It is connected with all time,' replied Balthazar.

Even as they strode across the silver plane, Anna heard Crazy Boris mutter, 'I guess all you have to do is find a way in.'

Jago Burke marched beside Anna, but he said over his shoulder, 'If the Core starts breaking apart, time will be opening like a trapdoor. It won't so much be a matter of finding a way in as trying not to fall through.'

'It's not a philosophy class,' snapped Anna, and she broke into a jog with Pacer jogging alongside her. Although the surface on which she ran looked no more solid than a molten mirror, her boots hit the light that surged towards the Core as if it was solid ground. Above her, the sky was surging inwards too, as if drawn from all around.

When they had covered what Anna judged to be half the distance to the Core, she became aware of the clumping footfalls behind her slowing and then stopping altogether. Even though she was determined to get to the Core, she stopped too and looked back. Immediately behind her was the Scythian with Jago Burke close by, and behind them were Balthazar and Gemma. Wheezing at the rear and lolloping with a face like a thirsty dog came Crazy Boris. But they hadn't stopped running because of Crazy Boris.

The Scythian stood like a basalt statue in his black cloak and leggings, with the great axe across his back, and he pointed at what Anna would have called the horizon. It was difficult to judge the terrain of these argent planes, but she thought that they were standing a little lower than the horizon, as if the surface had dipped down slightly, towards the Core.

The Scythian spoke sharply, snapping out words from between his teeth, but Anna didn't need to understand his tongue to understand what had stirred him. All along the distant silver rim, a thin dark line had been drawn and, as she watched, this line thickened, extending forwards along the width of the plane. The Scythian's coal eyes were bright, his teeth bared against the black of his thin, sharp beard.

'What is it?' asked Gemma, who looked fragile beside the swarthy barbarian.

Anna could distinguish shapes now. The lines were composed of figures, and the darkness shaded into red of an intense and fiery hue.

'Havoc Legions,' stated Jago Burke, perplexed. 'Two, I'd say.' Then, as the line continued to thicken without showing any sign of clearing the horizon, he said, 'Better make that three.' He swept off his broad hat, brushed a gloved hand through his rich, brown hair and swung the hat back into place. 'This is not good.'

'They look weird,' said Pacer.

We should run, now, thought Anna. But, for a moment, it seemed that the enormity of what was coming towards them had turned their legs to stone.

'The Havoc Legions,' murmured Balthazar, 'are low

density, counter-matter life forms composed of negative energy and sustained by the will of the Inquisitor, Azgor.'

Gemma looked up through her mop of blonde hair and said, 'I didn't really understand that, Balthazar.'

'They're soldiers,' explained Burke automatically, his mind on what was coming towards them. 'They fight by destroying the matter they come into contact with: cancelling it out. But how they appear, and their power, depends upon where in the universes they are. In your world they appear grey, like ghosts, and they destroy instantly, by touch alone. Out here, their density is different: you see them for what they are. They still destroy by touch, but it's slower.'

'Slower?' As far as Pacer was concerned, that sounded worse than instant death.

'It's more like being drained.' Captain Burke's eyes narrowed. 'See how they destroy the air they move through. See the flames?'

Gemma nodded. 'I don't like them,' she said quietly. 'They look like they're from hell.'

She was right. Even from this distance, Anna could see the endless ranks of crimson armour and the fire which streamed from each legionnaire like rags, fluttering. The flaming ranks of the Havoc Legions were reflected by the shimmering planes, so that it seemed a bloody tide was seeping towards them.

The Scythian's hand had dropped to a broad-bladed sword he'd taken from his horse and strapped to his belt before they'd left the Sages. Anna could tell that Captain Burke was gauging the distance to the Core against the rate of the Legions' advance.

'How many?' asked Pacer.

'Ten thousand,' replied Captain Burke.

Pacer groaned. 'Ten thousand!'

'In each Legion,' added Captain Burke.

'They can't be here just for us.' Pacer's voice was hoarse. 'Can they?'

'The Symmetry take no chances,' said Jago Burke. 'They want to stop us. They are here to kill us.'

As Chess passed through the boundary, the pain was intense. It wasn't the same pain that she got from banging her head or from stomach cramp, because it seemed to come from outside as well as inside her body. And with the pain came a myriad of other sensations and images, as if the experiences of a whole universe were forced through her mind in a matter of seconds, and Chess guessed that it was this driving tumult which caused the pain. She staggered, aware of Saul's arms supporting her, and then she was into the Core itself.

Some of what she had felt came with her, the way that bits of spider web stuck after she'd walked through them. But as with strands of web, she brushed them away, mentally, until she was free of them.

'You're OK?' she gasped.

Saul smiled, helping her find her feet. 'I don't have the same link with the universes as you, Chess. I'm OK.'

'I'm glad you're here, Saul,' panted Chess. 'I couldn't do this without you.' Then she looked about. 'I didn't expect it to be so big,' she said, flatly, head aching. She raked the thick chestnut hair from her face.

From the inside, the Core must have been a hundred metres across, which was wider than it had looked from the outside. And, from the inside, the encircling walls glimmered as if light from beyond them was captured by falling water. Chess looked down and then jumped backwards when she saw that she appeared to be standing on nothing.

Saul laughed, kindly.

'I thought I was going to fall.' Chess laughed too, a little wildly, relieved to find that she was grounded firmly on the same level as Saul. Mists of light in different shades peeled off the outer walls and drifted towards her like ink stains underwater. But the laughter stopped when she couldn't see what she was looking for.

'Where is everything?' she asked.

'Everything?' Saul shook his head. 'What do you mean, everything? What were you expecting, Chess? Didn't Mevrad ... Ethel tell you what to expect? She must have done that much?'

'Ethel told me nothing!' snapped Chess and her mood darkened. She turned on the spot, looking all about the inside of the Core. Where was it? Where was the weapon that Ethel had told her about? The weapon that could end the universes and which she alone could control. The weapon that she had come to destroy. Where was the Eternal?

A new brightness lanced her from above and it was joined by piercing spars of light from all around and below. Chess screwed up her eyes and the brilliant light dazzled through her long eyelashes.

Suns. Twelve suns.

'Where the twelve suns are one,' she whispered. The place where she should have found the Eternal.

A tail of light flicked out from the boundary of the Core, lashing round her waist like a whip. It was followed by other narrow tongues of streaming silver. As each of the strands bound itself to her body, about her limbs, Chess felt the vastness of the universes touch her and she struggled to throw them off.

Physically fighting against the break-away streams was useless, but very quickly, Chess found that she could peel them away from her body by will alone: as easily as peeling open the fingers of a small child. But it required a constant effort to keep back the fingers of the Core, and Chess realized that they were seeking her, that they wanted to connect with her. And she realized also that something inside herself was drawing them towards her.

'You're one thing, you see?' said Saul. He pointed at the ethereal wall. 'It wants to be part of you. Or you to be part of it.'

Despite everything that was happening, the grasp of the Core on her mind, the images and experiences that flooded into her with every touch, the pain that they brought, Chess felt the change in Saul's voice. He was watching her with a dark interest.

'You and the universes are one. They want to touch you, Chess. They want to connect with you. They want to get back to you.' He stepped away from her, fascination and fear competing in his face as the strands of light whipped about them.

'I don't like it. I don't want it.' As Saul backed away Chess suddenly felt the fear, and when the next tentacle of light came for her, coiling itself about her left arm, she flung it away with a scream.

Energy pulsed out of her. Chess felt the release as it ripped through the ectoplasm of the Core and she saw the cataclysmic destruction of a distant star field as it erupted brilliantly in her mind's eye.

She gasped with shock, panting, as if she'd dived into freezing water. She was shocked at what she had just done. And, more than that, she was shocked at how good it felt. She felt lighter, freer, as if she had been released from the pain of the dark energy that was stored inside. Then the tearing pressure returned, all the more violently for the momentary release, and she realized that she was on her knees, half blinded by the light of the suns.

'What have you done, Chess?'

She knew that voice. She recognized it. It had come to her in dreams, when waking, from pictures, from reflections, from dead heads, from inside her *own* head.

'You,' accused Chess. The figure was standing directly in front of her. He wore the black robes of a monk with the cowl dropped back and because his outline was blurred by a glimmering light, she knew that he was not actually here, that he was in another place but simultaneously close to her because now every piece of every universe was close to her.

Chess stood.

'Why did it feel so good?' asked the monk.

'Who are you?' asked Chess, although she knew with certainty that this was one of the Inquisitors.

'Chess?' It was Saul, close by although she didn't look at

him. 'Chess, who are you talking to?' He sounded worried.

He can't see what I can see, realized Chess.

'My name,' said the Inquisitor, 'is Malbane.'

'I could destroy you,' warned Chess.

Malbane held up an open palm in a gesture of peace. 'Of course you could, Chess, as you have been keen to remind us, from time to time.'

Chess shielded her eyes as the burning of the suns intensified.

'Where's the Eternal?' she demanded. She felt Saul's arm about her shoulders and the warmth was good, although it was barely a scintilla amidst the infinitude of sensations which clamoured for her. But she was able to think of as many things as she wanted, so she let the comfort of Saul's strong arm sink into her.

'Who are you talking to?' asked Saul.

'An Inquisitor,' said Chess, and when she heard the high, broken tone of her own voice, she laughed. 'His name is Malbane.'

'I can't see him.' Saul spoke quietly, uncertainly, and Chess believed him, not seeing that his eyes looked directly at the figure at which she was looking.

'Where is the Eternal?' repeated Chess.

This time it was Malbane who laughed: a dry, tired laugh like the last breath of winter.

'The Eternal Core Decelerator.' Chess raised her voice, flinging away clutching streams of light. As the dimensional fragments were cast back, so were the worlds they touched: pink cragged mountains; silent planets; laughter; clashing armies; alien towers tearing ragged cloudscapes; a clutch of photographs on a small table: a voice repeating the words, 'we must pass over in silence'. In and out of her mind all of it flashed in a heartbeat: all of it and more, every time the Core touched her.

'Chess?' came Saul's voice. 'What did Ethel say about the Eternal? What did she make you believe?'

'It's a weapon.' Chess spun round to look at Saul and her eyes were hot, her hair wild. 'She said it was a weapon. And only I can control it.'

So much pain. And so much peace. And all within her power.

From behind her there was more laughter and then from her left and right.

Who was laughing? Chess reached into the universes to find the source of the laughter and, reaching back, his spirit stretching through the time and space which connected him to the Core, wherever else he was, was the rag-bound slime of Snargis. And to her left the snake-eyed, red-gowned form of Azgor, and to her right, the slash-featured disdain of Veer.

Four Inquisitors: before her, behind her, on her left, on her right. All connected with the Core, all close to Chess because now, every part of every universe was close to Chess.

'Chess,' murmured Malbane, kinder than she had imagined him capable of being. 'You trusted Mevrad.'

'You trusted her,' repeated Azgor, sibilantly.

'But . . . the Eternal?' Suddenly Chess felt stupid and angry at the same time.

Malbane looked at her with a crushing pity. '*You* are the Eternal, Chess.'

'You are the weapon,' whispered Veer.

'You are the Committee's construction,' hissed Azgor.

'And Mevrad *never* told you.' Malbane shook his head slowly. 'You poor, poor girl.'

Chess bit back a sob, but whether it was a sob of despair or of rage she could no longer tell.

'I can't hear them, Chess.' Saul's voice had risen. Was he panicking? 'I don't know what they're saying, but ignore it. Right?' He had hold of her arms and pulled her round to face him. He shook her hard. 'Whatever they say to you, ignore it.'

Chess nodded but she could feel him slipping away, and all the time, the Core was merging her spirit more completely with itself.

'Listen to me,' insisted Saul. 'If they tell you how good it will feel to end everything, ignore them. If they promise you never-ending peace, ignore them. If they remind you how terrible, how unfair the universes are, don't listen to them.'

He shook her harder, but all Chess registered was the promise of unending peace; an end to everything that hurt. Saul's words served only to illuminate the promises of the Inquisitors. How could words that were so kind, so sincere, turn against her like this?

Chess knew she was losing her grip on her mind.

'I came here to destroy the Eternal,' she laughed. 'I can't destroy myself.'

Saul's dark eyes filled hers. 'I cannot believe how badly Ethel and the Committee have treated you.'

She watched the way his soft lips moved, parting and closing slowly, smoothly, and his voice was gentle and seemed to come from a long way off. She shook her head, unable to speak because she was biting her lips so hard. She closed her eyes and heard herself moaning and she no longer had the will to throw off the fragments of time and space which clutched at her.

Don't give in, Chess. Don't give in.

Was she speaking to herself or was it someone else's voice?

But it was hard not to give in. She wanted to give in: to sink into the arms of the universes, and then tear them out of existence so that there would be peace. Peace for everyone. Just as the Symmetry wanted

'Why didn't you stop me, Ethel?' she choked. 'Why didn't you tell me?'

'Ethel isn't here, Chess,' said Saul. He was kneeling next to her, just as she was now kneeling.

'Mevrad made you for her own purposes,' hissed Azgor on her left.

'Mevrad only ever wanted to *use* you,' spat Veer to her right.

'The Committee *want* a world of pain. A world that they can control,' snorted Snargis from behind her.

'Only we have watched over you, cared for you, wanted what you want, Chess,' Malbane assured her.

'Look, Chess,' whispered Saul, pointing into the space immediately in front of them.

Malbane had lowered an arm, extended a hand and spread open his fingers. Tendrils of light snaked out of the Core boundary and began to knit themselves into a structure of crystal purity, a geometry of harmonious sound and proportion which built itself about Chess and Saul. There was motion and there was stillness and there was a perfect balance. For a moment, Chess was lifted out of her sense-fevered body and released into a numbing tranquillity.

'This is what *we* want.' Malbane's voice was tender, reasonable, compassionate. 'This is what we have created: an amarantium universe of peace unending, every particle of amarantium, of crystal, in touch with every time and every place.'

Lemuel had told her that when she had been made, her body had been infused with amarantium. Now Chess understood why the Committee had instructed him to modify her like this: so that she would make a more effective weapon. A weapon that could touch everything, everywhere.

The Inquisitor's hand shut tight and the vision disappeared. In its place returned a universe of pain, but Lemuel's words remained with her: *you are a girl of many parts: part human, part god, part universe and part wickedness.*

Not even Lemuel had told her what she really was. No one had told her what she really was. The anger coursed through her like magma. The suns were blinding, and now, as the Core reached for her, she let it come, filling her with the universes: their enormity; the cruelty; the suffering; the battles that were raging even now. She drew all this dark energy in, concentrated it and let it tear through her spirit, looking for a way out.

She knew she was sinking. What she was and what she was about to become were separated by a thread. But still she fought against the anger, against the darkness. She couldn't give in because within her own core she knew that destruction was destruction, however much it promised peace. And she wanted to believe that there remained something better than the promises of the Inquisitors. But the pain and the anger made it soul-breaking to hang on.

Saul had his arm about her back and with a voice that was so distraught that it brought her back to the surface of her senses, he said, 'I don't know what I've done, Chess.'

She looked at him and in the seconds which followed she drank betrayal and despair from his eyes, and she didn't understand what had happened.

'Saul?' He was falling away from her, as if the universes were brushing him aside.

'I'm sorry, Chess.'

Out of the searing light of the twelve suns came a man whose naked body was hung with skin as loose as old sacking, as if it had been draped over bone alone. A thin man. An ancient man. A man with no eyes but who exuded the power of seeing everything. A narrow man.

'You!' gasped Chess, still kneeling.

'Obviously,' whispered the Narrow Man.

'Why are you here?'

The Narrow Man cupped her chin in fingers as knuckly, cold and long as a crab's legs. 'I am here to tell you the truth,' he said.

CHAPTER 15

Anna stopped running. There was no point in trying to reach the Core. Thousands of Havoc Legionnaires had spilt across the silver plane like a red riptide, cutting them off. She surveyed the army that encircled them, catching her breath, wondering not what would happen to her but what would happen to Gemma, to Pacer, to Crazy Boris, to Balthazar and to Chess.

On all sides the Legions were drawing in. Now that the closest were no more than a couple of hundred metres away, she could see them clearly enough to make out the spiked and twisted crimson armour, the full-fronted battle helms and the bright, silver sickle-hooks that they carried. They advanced slowly and in disciplined ranks, and about every legionnaire, about the whole army, the air was torn with tongues of flame.

'I don't understand,' panted Anna, 'why we couldn't go faster.' She had just begun to master her abilities as a Blood Sentinel and now she found them slipping from her grasp.

'At the fifth node, the dimensions mutate. Time mutates.' Jago Burke shrugged as if he was apologizing. 'I am sorry to say that in this place at this time, our control over the dimensions is diminished. We are weakened.'

It made sense, but it couldn't have happened at a worse time. Anna looked back towards the Core, where the sea of legionnaires was narrowest.

'Not a chance,' gasped Pacer, knowing what she was calculating. Gemma and Crazy Boris stood shoulder to shoulder with him. Gemma was lily white, almost pale blue with fear. There was nothing that Anna could think of to say to her, but she saw Crazy Boris lower his head and whisper, 'Just close your eyes and think of your favourite person. And I'll stay with you.'

Gemma closed her blue eyes at once and Anna could see her lips working, minutely mouthing the name Chess, over and over again. And she saw Crazy Boris take the photograph from the breast pocket of his jacket and look at it intently.

The Scythian had already un-shouldered his great axe, the leatherbound haft in his sinewy fists, the blood streaked, battle-notched blades waiting to reap their final harvest. He drew back his lips and bellowed at the advancing army.

'At least someone's up for it,' muttered Pacer. 'Hey!' he shouted at the dark warrior. The Scythian turned, no softening in the savage rictus he had displayed to the enemy.

'Yeah,' continued Pacer. 'How's about me using that sword?' He pointed at the short broadsword that hung from the Scythian's belt. When the Scythian frowned, Pacer pulled out his lock knife, held it up and shrugged hopelessly.

The dark brow furrowed further and then the warrior flashed an ivory grin. He pulled the sword free, catching the wide blade with the same hand before tossing it to Pacer. Pacer gripped the plain pommel. The sword was heavy but well balanced and he took a couple of hearty swings to see how it felt. The Scythian nodded with a grin.

'Just try not to kill any of us with it,' observed Anna.

Pacer shot her a glare that reminded her that she wasn't the only person who wanted to help Chess, whatever the cost.

Jago Burke had pulled out his high-explosive flintlock and he held it up to sight along the elaborate barrel. 'Just remember,' he said, concentrating on the firearm, 'the Legions work by weight of numbers. Enough blows from them and they'll drain the life out of you. That's the bad news.'

'And the good news?' asked Pacer, holding the sword as coolly as if he'd never been without it.

'No particular skill is required to fight them. And they can't withstand much impact. So the trick is to batter them out of existence before they do the same to you.' He lowered the flintlock, satisfied with his brief inspection.

'There's a lot of them to batter,' commented Pacer.

'Don't worry,' said Captain Burke. 'Given their obvious numerical advantage, this won't take long.' He looked back at the Core. The vast column that had been silver smooth when they'd first seen it was buckling. Streams of light were flailing out before spinning back into the body or peeling off altogether and then fading out of existence.

'But given whatever's happening in there,' he added, 'nothing is going to last very long now.'

Anna wanted to scream: scream in frustration at having

come so far and so close and failing. 'I'm sorry, Chess,' she said.

'Hey,' said Pacer, trying to smile. 'It's not over yet.'

Anna turned her sapphire eyes to him and saw his determination: not for himself, but for others.

I think it *is* over, she thought. But that didn't sap her will. And seeing that Pacer was ready to stand and fight until he could fight no more, his face set in grim readiness, she remembered back to when they had first met: how she had thought he was just another feral rat. And she had been wrong. Pacer had nothing and he gave everything. And now he was ready to give his last for his friends, for Chess and for the billons who would never know him, who wouldn't have cared.

Just as Box was willing to do.

Anna looked at the small group who stood with her. She saw Gemma, silently repeating Chess's name to herself, saw Balthazar close his eyes as if he was praying, saw Crazy Boris sigh from his soul and tuck the photograph back where it was safe.

Then Anna looked out at the Legions. This *would* be quick.

'Box,' she whispered, thinking of what she had heard Crazy Boris say to Gemma. 'I wish you were with me.'

The mess hall on the troop ship *Stardrake II* was packed. The dreadbolts were eating, drinking, talking. But the whole hall fell silent as Captain Box Tuesday and Commodore Valxata Razool entered. The only sound within the high metal walls was that of boots striking the floor as the two of them strode across the packed hall. Then, as one, the mass of soldiers stood: the battle-scarred stalwarts; the sharp-eyed fresh recruits; the cable-sinewed, metal-flesh cybernetics: an iron force of muscle, fang and fist, built to destroy, always ready to fight, waiting for Box's orders.

As his own boot steps rang in his ears, Box thought of a time, and it seemed a long time ago now, when he had entered the dining hall in Committee HQ to be greeted by the men and women of the Committee's night patrols. He had come from the city's streets and sewers, ragged and dazed, and alongside him had stood Splinter and Chess. Thinking back, the three of them seemed so distant, so small. Now he was an officer in the toughest fighting force in the universes, returning to his troops. But he hadn't forgotten Splinter or Chess or what he had been: what a part of him still was.

'Might have guessed you'd get back in time for slavver, Boss,' said one rough voice.

'Even if he had to save the world first,' said another.

'It was too easy,' growled a third. 'All his bits are still attached.'

But the dreadbolts were proud of this skin who had led them into action so many times already, who had a thirst greater than any of them for battle, who fought with two blades but who ate and drank alongside them as one of their own.

'Silence,' roared Commodore Razool and silence hit the mess hall like an avalanche. As a commodore, Razool outranked everyone in the hall, everyone on board the whole ship in fact. 'Show respect to your officer commanding.'

A thousand arms, metal and flesh, saluted Box: a thousand boots struck the floor like a crack of thunder. Box and Razool saluted back, Box with half a smile at the corner of his mouth, a smile that was returned appreciatively by the troops who saw it.

'That's better,' snapped Razool, whose alsatian muzzle looked ready to rip out the throat of anyone who disagreed with him.

The cohort returned to their eating and drinking and talking, and Box and Razool found the table where Skarl and Raxa sat with a dozen other dreadbolts.

'There's a lot going on,' said Skarl excitedly as soon as Box was sitting beside him. His tongue swept the edge of his snout, wiping away remnants of grease.

'We knew your mission was successful as soon as it happened.' Raxa patted Box on the back before leaning his heavy body back in his chair and folding his arms.

'Troop mobilization?' enquired Razool. Skarl nodded. Razool poured a mug of water for Box and then one for himself. The two of them drank, wiped their faces, refilled and drank again. The mugs banged down on the table in unison and the two of them sighed with satisfaction.

Box hadn't had a drink since he'd departed for the Galen and he'd done a lot of sweating since then. Once Razool had pulled him out of the Ice Bucket, they had flown straight to the *Stardrake II* to rejoin Box's cohort. It had been a short journey because most of it had been swallowed by a vortical jump, but they had heard sufficient over the radio to have learnt that hostilities with the X'ath and the Galen had ceased suddenly. But that didn't mean the fighting was over.

'Everyone's been mobilized,' volunteered a snout with a scrutator in place of his left eye and a right arm whose motors whirred faintly when he moved it.

'Against the *Symmetry*,' added another who, so far as Box could tell, was still in mint condition. One of the new recruits.

Razool reached for an apple and tore off half with one snap of his fangs. Through a mouthful of pulp he said, 'This is what's the General's been waiting for.' The rest of the apple vanished into Razool's mouth but that didn't stop him from talking. 'Before the next couple of hours are out, a skin called Chess will blow the world inside out, or she won't. And if she doesn't, the General wants to make sure the Symmetry are out of the picture for good and we get to run the show. So whilst she takes on the management, we take on everything else.'

'It's not that easy for her,' said Box. He knew how frightened Chess was, how she didn't understand what was happening, how she'd lost her grip on herself.

'I didn't say it was easy,' growled Razool. 'But whilst we wait to see whether the world gets to exist, the Dog Troopers are being despatched to every galaxy, plane and dimension to fight our new enemies.'

'But there's millions of enemy troops.' Skarl scowled.

'Billions,' Raxa corrected him.

Razool took another apple. 'The price of freedom,' he observed, before tearing a chunk from it, noisily.

'And you complain about my manners,' commented Box.

'I like the noise it makes,' crunched Razool.

Box took an apple but didn't eat. For the only time in his

life that he could remember, he wasn't hungry. His stomach was full of something other than food. Not fear. Not excitement. It was full of an emptiness that left no space for anything else.

Razool stopped crunching. 'You OK?'

Box nodded. He didn't want to explain how he felt, how his mind was as full of Anna as his stomach was full of emptiness. How time was on the verge of running out, forever, and he didn't know where she was or what she was doing. How being stuck on this lumbering hulk of metal in a part of the universes he didn't know, and couldn't begin to imagine, made him feel as helpless as the apple that sat in his hand.

The General had made a promise to him, as if he understood what Box most wanted, and now it looked as if that promise was about to come to nothing. Box was angry with himself for believing that the General would keep such a bargain. Why should the commander of the Dog Troopers spare a thought for a skin, now he'd got what he wanted?

Razool must have sensed what he was thinking because his hard eyes drilled into Box's and he said, 'Nothing's over till it's over, Box. Got that?'

Box nodded and took a bite of the apple.

There was a mass scraping of chairs for the second time in ten minutes. The whole mess hall came to its feet. Box looked across to the entrance where there stood a broadly built snout with a Mohican ridge of hair, a sharp grey beard down his chin and a white scar welted across his face.

The dreadbolts saluted and the snout saluted back before heading directly for the table where Box was sitting.

Everyone returned to their seats and Box watched Amun Hak, Commander of the Fourteenth Storm, approach. He was tall and thick-set and in his combat trousers and vest, the old battle marks on his arms and torso were clear to see.

'Commodore,' said Hak, with a nod of his head when he reached the table.

'Commander,' replied Razool, returning the nod and remaining seated.

Formalities satisfied, Commander Hak turned his flint eyes on Box. 'Still in one piece, Captain?'

'So far, sir.'

Hak folded his beef-knotted arms and grimaced. 'Still a mystery to me how a skin can be so hard to kill.' He shook his head but there was a glint of approval at the edge of his stony gaze.

'Stubborn, sir,' said Box.

'If there was time, you'd get a medal for your stubbornness, Captain.'

'Try living with it,' muttered Skarl.

'You got something to say, soldier?' snapped Hak.

'No, sir!' burst from Skarl as he jumped to his feet, knocking over his chair.

'Sit down,' said Hak, wearily. He turned back to Box. 'Trooper forces are engaging enemy forces across the whole territory.'

'Enemy forces?' queried Box.

'Symmetry forces,' clarified Hak. 'The new enemy.' He picked up an apple and put it whole into his mouth, shredding it in seconds. When he had finished, he dug a clawed finger between his molars and screwed up his eyes as if he were digging out ear wax, before liberating a short stalk which he spat onto the floor.

'Thanks to you, Captain, we might all live to fight a little longer.' He re-folded his arms. 'But our troops are stretched; there aren't many dreadbolts to go round.'

Box shrugged. 'Don't know what I can do about that, sir.'

'We've received a message, direct from the General.'

Box felt his heart lurch. The General had promised him a final battle that he would *want* to fight and Box knew what he wanted: to fight for Chess; to fight for Anna. Instinctively, he knew what was coming.

'It seems there's a concentration of Havoc Legions out on the Core.'

'The Core?' asked Box.

'The centre of everything, Captain. The place where the big crash starts. *If* it starts.'

'Chess,' said Box, hoarsely.

Commander Hak raised a shaggy eyebrow and continued. 'There are three Legions.'

'That's thirty thousand ground troops,' stated Razool.

'Thank you, Commodore. We have three Legions preparing to attack seven friendly units.'

'Units?' Box's blood was rising. 'How many in a unit?'

'One.'

'Thirty thousand against seven!' Box's fists were clenched.

'Seven skins,' specified Commander Hak.

'They don't stand a chance.' Box was on his feet, eyes aflame.

'Take it easy, Box,' warned Razool.

'But Anna . . .'

Razool's eyes drove Box back onto his seat. '*Listen.*'

The Commander was puzzled by this outburst. He rubbed his hoary chin but continued anyway. 'We can spare one cohort, Captain.' He nodded at Box. 'Your cohort.'

'A thousand dreadbolts?' Box shook his head.

'I'm sorry it can't be more.' The Commander sucked a fang, his pale pink tongue wrapping itself around the canine before slipping back inside his mouth. 'The rest of the Storm have to group with the Fifth Quake. The General wants us to smash the Symmetry forces out of the Eighth Panhedral before they even know there's been a ceasefire with the X'ath and the Galen. So the rest of the Quake will be heading out that way within minutes. The message was clear, Captain. One cohort, as a personal favour to you.'

Box clenched his jaw. Dreadbolts or not, this was going to be tough. But they had to get going now.

'Believe me, Captain,' said the Commander, 'I've served for longer than a veteran's shore leave and I've never known the General to do a favour for anyone.'

Box stood, flanked by Razool.

The Commander said, 'There's three pod ships waiting, ready to go.'

Box nodded. 'Thank you, sir.'

The Commander fixed him with his steady gaze. 'See you on the other side, Captain.'

'You too, sir.'

Box gave orders swiftly to Skarl and Raxa to ready the dreadbolts, gather them in their packs, mobilize them into the assembly zones. Rapidly, calmly, the orders were passed through the hall and, within the minute, a thousand dreadbolts were moving out.

'Not you, Commodore.' Commander Hak stepped between Razool and Box as they prepared to follow the rest of the cohort.

Razool's eyes narrowed and his jaw set tight. Box turned back.

'No,' said the Commander, definite as granite. 'The General has spared all he can. You have other duties, Commodore. I'm sorry.'

Box stepped forwards but Razool shook his head. 'Lead your troops, Box. Smash the enemy. Back up Chess. And get Anna out of there.'

The Legions advanced like a flaming tide. Maybe it was only a hundred metres to the Core, but the way was blocked by hook and fire. Reaching Chess was impossible: whatever was going on within the churning cylinder of light couldn't be stopped now. And out here, death was coming, slowly and surely.

At this range, Anna could see the detail on the legionnaires' armour: the chest plates marked with the silver loops of the awlis, the symbol of the Twisted Symmetry; the spiny ridges over the shoulder plates, ornate and menacing; the narrow slits that grilled the fronts of the helmets like gills, revealing only darkness within; the rows and rows of bright, silver hooks. And outlining everything, a corona of flame, the sharp tongues of fire cutting the air.

'This is where it gets lively,' muttered Pacer.

'It was looking pretty lively before,' said Anna. But she knew there was no way out of this. She reached behind her shoulder and unsheathed her sword. Strike at the joints. Thrust. Don't kill the blade by biting on metal. Together with Jago Burke, the Scythian, Balthazar Broom and Pacer, they formed a loose circle about Crazy Boris and Gemma. All of them knew that it wasn't a circle that could hold for very long.

There was a flare of light from the Core, followed by another, and then another. In the wake of each flare, there remained a rent in the silver column. The dark rents were appearing throughout the bowing, unfurling walls. The column was breaking apart. Anna looked up and saw that the silver sky was no longer coursing smooth but was swirling, splitting into seams and in between these separate seams, there appeared spaces of blinding whiteness.

'Time breaking,' murmured Balthazar, shifting the staff in his hands.

Crazy Boris looked down. 'It still feels solid enough,' he remarked, but then gasped as a brilliant crack opened even where he was standing. The crack forged a line from where he stood right out across the plane and he jumped away from it. 'The things I just saw! From so long ago.'

'Whatever comes to pass,' rumbled Balthazar, 'nothing shall last now.'

'Unless Chess holds out,' declared Anna, not ready to give up on her friend. She breathed out slowly, closed her eyes, let her spirit sink into the sword she held. 'Unless she remembers who she is,' she whispered. 'Unless she remembers that there are things worth fighting for.'

But the wall of hooks was nearly upon them and then there would be silence. Anna thought, for a moment, of Box, told herself that he *would* come, that nothing could stop him. Then she shut out even that thought and prepared herself for what was about to happen.

Crazy Boris was still muttering to himself. 'Things I'd forgotten I'd forgotten about!' He shook his head in disbelief but Anna barely noticed him. Her natural senses, trained by Kinuq and the swordmaster, Kusanagi, were magnified beyond imagining by the genetic melding, even with the collapse of the dimensions. With her eyes closed, Anna knew where the closest target stood, how many legionnaires she could strike before they struck back, where she would move as they reacted to her light-swift attacks, how many she could cut down before the brutal weight of numbers overwhelmed her. And she knew that defeat was inevitable.

There was a final intensity, as if her mind was experiencing as much as it could before it was cut dead. She heard the rustle of Jago Burke's jacket sleeve against the bandoliers which looped his chest as he raised his revolvers; heard the crack of sinews in the Scythian's powerful arms as he readied his axe; felt the slow tread of the Legions through the breaking plane beneath her boots; felt their heat; opened her eyes and saw death, blazing and bright. And then she sensed something else: something unexpected. Unexpected but not unfamiliar.

'Wait,' she said.

'There's not much time for waiting, Miss Ledward,' observed the Captain. The Scythian uttered a low growl, battle axe aching to swing.

But ahead of Anna, in the narrow gap before the closest of the legionnaires, the air blurred, as if hit by a miasmal heat. And then the blur took form. Five figures: a dwarf with a shotgun, a soldier, two archers in black and a man with a face half of flesh and half of silver.

'Julius,' gasped Gemma, eyes wide open.

'We could of done with another twenty-nine thousand,' muttered Pacer, 'but it's an improvement.'

'Seren, Étoile,' ordered Julius, pulling out the hefty machine pistols from his belt as he assessed the scene in the seconds they had left. 'Put down as much covering fire to our rear as you can. Where their force is heaviest. You, too, Colonel Greave.'

As much covering fire as you can? Anna knew that Julius meant, 'Until you are dead.'

Already the black archers had nocked arrows to their long bows. The man in the combats and the thick belts of ammunition slung over his shoulders swung his multi-barrelled stack of a machine gun outwards and Anna saw how much metal replaced the flesh of his arms, his chest, his legs. His eyes glowed like green lamps and his face was impassive, ready for business.

'Anna, Burke, the Scythian and I will fight to the Core. Their force is weakest that way.'

Anna heard Crazy Boris, mutter, 'None of it looks weak to me.'

Julius strode to Anna, long, black coat sweeping about him. To Anna he said, 'You have to get in there.' He stabbed the nose of a machine pistol towards the Core. 'Get in there and get Chess out.'

'You really think . . .' began Anna.

'I *believe*,' stated Julius.

Anna nodded and turned to face the horde of legionnaires that filled the short distance to the fragmenting Core. They were almost close enough to fight. Her heart beat slow and hard and her muscles prepared to explode into action. She heard Julius say, 'Balthazar, Jake, protect the others.'

'I don't need protecting,' snapped Pacer.

'Good,' said Julius, 'then fight.' He shut his eyes for a moment and whispered, 'I have lived longer than the stars and now there is no time.' Then his eyes opened, blazing, and the machine pistols blasted in a haze of flame and smoke and behind her, Colonel Maximus Greave's machine gun roared out an armour-splintering wall of lead. Beside her, the Scythian's great axe was ready to crack open helms and smash down bodies.

'I *believe*,' whispered Anna. She raised her sword, and the Legions closed in.

CHAPTER 16

'Have you ever wondered why they kept the truth from you?'

Chess remained kneeling, head down, trying not to listen to the voice that was inside her head and outside it at the same time.

There was a slow hiss of dry laughter. 'Perhaps,' volunteered the Narrow Man in answer to his own question, 'because they knew that there would be something *self-fulfilling* about the truth. Too much truth is a bad thing ... for mortals.' Chess felt the cold fingers under her chin again, pulling her face upwards. 'But you are no mortal.'

She closed her eyes because the light was so bright. But she couldn't close her mind to the Narrow Man's voice.

'The first thing you need to know is my name.'

'Bael,' said Chess.

'Good. Good.'

She looked at him now and realized that he held no fear for her, not now she could ...

'... destroy me as easily as thinking?' said Bael. 'See how our minds are alike? Don't tell me I am wrong,' he insisted, a small mouth working in his sag-skinned, featureless face.

'You think there is some fairness in this world that created you? You think that there is anything more than an eternity of misery?'

Bael's face was directly in front of her own. 'You know there isn't,' he whispered, the lipless aperture of his mouth rasping against the skin of her cheek. 'Let go, Chess,' he sighed, reading how she felt. 'Let go.'

It was night in the vortex. It *seemed* like night in the vortex. Perhaps there was a tinge of vermillion to the pitch black. Splinter was falling in darkness, falling through darkness, falling as time and space turned through the fifth node, the point from which the time spiral would continue to turn back out of darkness and into light, or the point at which it would end.

The point at which Chess would die.

Splinter had seen this. He knew Chess would die. He knew how she would die. And if she died, maybe time would turn unmarked. The spiral would revolve, oblivious to what could have been. All the battles, the plans, the great strategies of the Symmetry would come to nothing. But if she lived . . .

Splinter knew that if Chess lived, if she did not bend to the Symmetry's will, if the girl he had always thought of as his little sister did not break on the rack of the Symmetry's malevolence, then maybe, just maybe, she would use her strength, her power, to drive death into the very place that the Symmetry least expected.

Falling now, alone and in eternal darkness, Splinter knew

that Chess could do this. He could admit it to himself: Chess was different; she was special. Ethel had always known this and now Splinter knew that she had planned this moment for so long. Now he understood what Ethel had done. Falling through eternity gave you the time to contemplate these things, so long as time lasted. And he understood, now, that this was Ethel's great gamble: that if Chess lived, that if what Splinter had seen did *not* happen, then when the moment came, she would make the right choice.

But only if she lived.

And now, Splinter realized, he was the one who would decide that. All other choices would depend upon his choice.

It was nearly time.

This was not how Splinter had foreseen his end. There had been a time when his ambitions were limitless, and he had done so much to achieve them. He had done so well. His ruthless brilliance had been devastating and he had ascended the highest pinnacle of power: or maybe it had been the highest pinnacle of his *imagination*. An Inquisitor? The King of Rats?

Reach back. Reach back to what was real, what was true.

Casting away the lavish folly of his imaginings, casting away the grand delusions with which the Inquisitors had sought to poison his mind, Splinter reached back to what he knew was real, what he *had* been, looking for a memory which he could carry with him into the greatest darkness of all ...

Box was crying. Box was crying because his toy soldiers had been taken away from him. Splinter had been crying too when they had first been taken into the cold corridors of the Elms Orphanage. But from the moment that the hard front door had been shut behind them, blotting out the light, he had decided never to cry again, and as far as he could remember, he never had.

Shutting the inside of himself like that door had been shut was what had made him strong; what had made him brilliant. The shutting door had been the start of Splinter: his keystone. Box had spent the rest of his life trying to get back to the light. Chess too. Only Splinter had built himself out of the darkness that he had found inside the Elms.

Out of darkness he had come and in darkness he now fell. But for the first time since that door had been shut, the first time that he could remember, Splinter was ready to reach back to that door and open it.

Can you turn the clock back? Can you turn back time?

Splinter could.

He held that memory, that first memory of the three of them waiting on the doorstep of the Elms Orphanage before this darkness had begun. Then his fingers slipped into his coat pocket and reached for the light.

The dreadbolt war machine moved swiftly, perfectly drilled. One thousand dreadbolts across three close-range transport pods. Box entered pod 014, fastening a coms wire to his neck so that he could maintain communication with his cohort, maintain control. He acted automatically, focused, thinking carefully and coolly, despite the tight heat in his chest.

As he walked on to the run, the deck where the dreadbolts assembled, he received constant updates from the Command

and Dispersal Unit as to enemy troop dispositions, time and distance from touchdown to target, optimal weaponry. Sharply, succinctly, he passed the orders on to his troop commanders.

'Twenty-nine thousand, five hundred and thirty-seven legionnaires,' he relayed, taking his place on the run.

The track lights across the top of the bay were flashing from white to red. All about, the dreadbolts fell into position and then the clamour and crash began as hundreds of runners, young snouts yet to earn their taps, carried in great slabs of armour that had to be drilled into place. The air was riven by the squeal of the torques that the runners used to drive the metal plugs though the holes in the armour and into the taps on the dreadbolts' shoulders, elbows, hips and legs.

Box held out his arms, felt the huge slabs of metal encase his solarion-toughened body, registered their enormous weight, but moved effortlessly. The teams of runners sweated across the run, building the weapon that was the dreadbolts.

Box hadn't forgotten what Captain Strulf had taught him: *bolt and rider are the weapon, son. Bolt and rider are the weapon.*

One thousand dreadbolts against twenty-nine thousand Havoc Legionnaires. Box's hands were now encased in metal gauntlets and he clenched them with a clap of metal. The odds weren't good: this was going to be tough.

'Dropzone one point three kilometres to enemy forces,' relayed Box. 'Enemy front approximately point five kilometres wide.' He thought through the most effective lines of attack, oblivious to the screaming metalwork about him. 'Skarl, your units go left-flanking. Raxa, yours go right-flanking. Contact enemy forces left and right and drive through. Bring your units round in support after me. I'll take the middle and drive through to the Core.'

Through to Anna. Through to Chess.

Skarl and Raxa acknowledged the orders and he heard them repeat the instructions over the net to their pack commanders.

The lights in the bay dropped to a dull red. Two minutes to touchdown.

What I'd give for you to be here, Zool, thought Box. He'd fought his way from the hell-pit of the Fleshings, across half the universe, and every blood-spattered step of the way, Razool had been alongside him: sharp and smart and cooler in the heat of combat than anyone Box had ever known. Odds of twenty-nine to one wouldn't seem so tough with Razool beside him.

Now the hammering of the iron hooves reverberated throughout the run. The bolts were led onto the deck by runners, guiding them by touch alone. The huge black creatures, part beast, part machine, had been designed to respond to the lightest command by the process of neural sculpting: nerves soldered to cybernetics. This meant that the riders' hands were free for what mattered most: destruction.

The bolts snorted and stamped, sparks spraying up from the run in yellow showers. When they shook their black heads and roared, the noise was as loud as engines, and their metal teeth glinted red in the crimson gloom.

—[295]—

Box's mount was brought alongside. Although the creatures had been engineered to kneel, to enable their riders to mount, Box had never required that ritual. He grasped the pommel with his left hand and swung up into the saddle as if he had been wearing jeans and a T-shirt rather than half a ton of armour: armour which would enable him to survive a head-on collision with the enemy at three hundred metres a second.

Bolt and rider are the weapon.

A wall of metal bulldozing into the enemy almost at the speed of sound. The dreadbolts were built to survive the crash. The enemy would be smashed out of existence.

'Enemy forces are energy draining but can't sustain impact,' Box reported. 'On contact, use close combat weapons.'

Havoc Legionnaires could be bludgeoned out of existence but in return, they would seek to draw the life out of their opponents, the negative energy which filled their bodies and their weapons sapping the life force of those who fought them. Box tightened the chains which held the reaper, the long cavalry blade, down the left flank of his bolt: secure but ready to be drawn at the charge. Down the bolt's right flank was chained a long battle hammer. The clatter of weapons and chains filled the run.

Box reached round to the back of his saddle to check that his mace-blades had been secured by the runners. As a rule, dreadbolts didn't use mace-blades: no mace-blade would withstand impact at full charge. But hand-to-hand, face-to-face, Box still preferred to take on the enemy with a blade in each hand. And the dreadbolts knew that no opponent had yet survived his two-fisted lightning strikes.

The troops were all mounted now. A gentle whirring from above and the helmet compression systems descended from the superstructure of the roof. At the same time, the runners brought the heavy battle helms to the warriors. Box reached down, took his helmet and pulled it over his head, locking it into place on his collar with a firm twist. Once the visor was down the helmet interior would be pressurized to enable his senses to operate, his eyes to read the 360° screen display at the sub-sonic speed he'd hit at full tilt.

Less than two minutes to go.

Already, Box could feel the sway of the craft and he knew that together with its sisters, it had been released from the *Stardrake II*. In a little over a minute, they would jump out of the vortex and into the region of the Core. But a minute was a long time when seven were facing twenty-nine thousand.

'Keep fighting, Anna,' Box repeated to himself. 'Keep fighting.'

He took a final look around his troops before pulling down his visor. Each dreadbolt sat in silence, armoured hulks statue-still on their mounts as the compression systems hissed and clinked through their ranks, misty curls of gas rolling over the battle-scarred slabs of armour that were decorated proudly with black snarling dog heads amidst whorls of gold. And amongst the troops were the standard bearers, carrying the battle flags of the Snarling Fourteenth, ready to plant them over the remains of the enemy when the battle was done.

Twenty-nine to one. It could be done. It *had* to be done.

And then Box heard the clock-clock-clock of hoof beats approaching. He looked back down the run to see who this was and out of the pools of gas that drifted through the red gloom came a rider astride his bolt, his sleek black mane not yet hidden by the helmet which he carried under his arm.

'Zool!' Box could have leapt out of his saddle with glee at the sight of the coal-eyed, sharp-faced snout. But he maintained the calm aspect of an officer commanding: just.

Razool drew up alongside him.

'How?' was all Box said, staring ahead coolly.

'I'm a Commodore,' stated Razool, tightening the straps that held the HV magnum in its thigh holster over his armour. He prepared to lock his helmet in place. 'I decide where I fight. And I fight alongside my *friend*.'

Box looked square at Razool, at the battle-wise snout who was his best friend, and he nodded. Suddenly, odds of twenty-nine to one didn't seem so tough. They would smash their way through the enemy until he reached Anna, or until he was smashed out of existence himself.

The lights cut out. The run was in darkness. One minute to go.

It would be a good fight.

The scenes came as a succession of staggering mind-shots to Chess. The Narrow Man had drawn strands of the Core matrix from the rupturing walls and bound them to Chess, merging her thoughts with the times and places of his choice. She had witnessed battles, seen even the explosive destruction of the city, her city, as helicopter gunships slung fire into the urban grids out of which the Symmetry forces replied with vicious and indiscriminate violence. Bael bound her to every shred of pain in the universes and with each journey into the abyss, her will to hold back, to resist the Inquisitors' promises of peace evermore, was eroded. Their voices were relentless.

'End it.'

'End it, Chess.'

'End it now.'

'Forever.'

She felt sick. She felt as if her mind had been pulped. The howling loneliness was desolate. And all the time, before her, behind her, to her left and to her right, there were voices whispering.

'Rest, Chess.'

'Peace.'

'End the suffering.'

'End it *now*.'

Bael was closest of all. Bael was beside her. Numbly, Chess reached for Saul. Where was he? Saul had said he would be here for her but now, instead of his strength, all she sensed was a shrinking, a withdrawing.

'Saul?' she gasped.

'Your betrayal,' Bael's winter lips grazed her ear, 'by the Committee, by Mevrad, started many years ago.'

'I know about Esme,' spat Chess. The anger at what had been allowed to happen to the young woman who had been her grandmother flared inside her and she felt a heat stream from her into the Core. The blast of heat was accompanied by a lightening of her mind, her spirit, for a moment. Then despair returned, more crushing than before after the brief relief she had tasted.

'Good. *Good.*' The Narrow Man's voice encouraged her. 'That's better, Chess. Be honest with yourself. Don't betray yourself the way that others have betrayed you. Be true to what you are. Be *who* you are.'

Chess sensed the energy flowing between her and the Core. The balance between discharge and destruction. Her mind was in touch with the whole plane continuum and with every blast of rage, she felt the moorings of time and space break a little more, and she knew that this was what the Twisted Symmetry wanted: this was the place they were taking her to. And now, after the purgatory she had witnessed, the agony and the misery she had absorbed into her own fibres, this was where she was ready to go. Chess knew that all Bael needed to do was to press the right switch.

I am a weapon. I was made to be a weapon.

But she was more than a weapon. Again, she remembered what Lemuel had told her: that she was part human, part god, part universe. And part wickedness.

I am not *just* a weapon. I am not just what someone else made me to be.

Again, Bael knitted his mind with the Core, drawing it to the time and place he wanted her to see. Chess could no more resist what he showed her than she could stop her own thoughts. But this time a terror had iced her soul.

'Not here,' she begged.

Don't beg. Don't break.

'Please, not here.'

But she had been mistaken: this wasn't the Elms Orphanage, that mausoleum of misery, that place of locked doors and a figure who crept into her room at night. Bael had taken her to a place before the Elms, a place from before her birth, but a place she recognized all the same.

She knew this room: the fireplace, the armchair, the tall lamp. She had seen it via the parallax bangle that Lemuel had made for her and which had taken her here through time. And she had seen it when she had hidden here, day after day, before Splinter betrayed her: before he gave her to the Twisted Symmetry.

This was the place where, for a time at least, her mother, Clarity, had stayed.

'Mummy?' asked a voice that could have been her own. 'Mummy, where are you?' Chess didn't know whether she was speaking or whether she was listening to herself speaking. 'Mummy?'

The tall lamp lay on the floor, illuminating the apartment like an aquarium up-lighter. The armchair had been knocked into its side. The naked bulb in the centre of the ceiling had been smashed and down one section of the wall there were gouged narrow, parallel tracks. Claw marks.

Chess looked at where the claw marks ended. There was a woman curled over, her knees drawn up and her back against the wall. Her black T-shirt was torn open and her trousers were ripped too. Her forearms were clasped about her shins and she was rocking back and forth, and shaking.

'Mummy?' said the voice that was Chess's voice.

Chess recognized the black hair, the strong, slender arms, the woman's face. This was Clarity. This was her mother.

But what had happened?

Clarity moaned, incoherent, face buried against her knees and now Chess saw the black, blood-crusted scoring of tramline wounds which curved round Clarity's white shoulder, from where her back was pressed to the wall, more like burns than gashes. Chess saw more clearly the torn disarray of Clarity's clothing, her nakedness revealed, and with a sickening twist through her stomach, she began to realize what had happened.

That was when Ethel appeared in the entrance to the apartment. The old lady hesitated on the threshold, stopped dead by the expression on Clarity's face as she looked up: a face whose one eye was pink with pain and tears, her mouth cut. Only the black eye patch was as Chess remembered it.

Clarity was shaking, spasms convulsing from her shoulders to her bare heels. But she found the strength to accuse Ethel in a voice that shook with pain and betrayal.

'You promised me I'd be safe,' she shouted. 'You promised that he wouldn't find me.'

The apartment at 11A Knott Street vanished. Chess unravelled the images from her mind, surfacing from what had just been revealed to her as if she was surfacing from freezing water. Time was actually slowing and her thoughts were thudding one upon the other within the mass grave of her soul.

In their dislocated positions, the Inquisitors waited in silent expectation for what would happen next. They waited for their master to speak.

'No more lies, Chess, no more betrayal.' The Narrow Man

cupped her chin with his bony fingers again and this time, Chess noticed how long the nails were. 'Let me tell you who your father is.'

Anna had ceased to sense anything beyond the swing and thrust of her sword, the clash of her steel against the armour and weapons of the Havoc Legions, the sudden release of her blade as she struck down another legionnaire, the heat of burning air and the drawing of strength from her own body as the legionnaires struck back.

A sickle flashed at her face and her sword clanged against it. She kicked back a legionnaire to her left, pulled her sword down and out of the crescent hook and drove it two-handed through the gap between the legionnaire's helmet and gorget. Without pausing, she pulled it free, stuck left, heard the sword smash away an armoured limb and slice through matter that dissolved as she whipped the blade clear, ready for the next assault.

The heat scorched her throat. The world was red: red from the Havoc Legions, red from the burning air, red reflected in the tearing planes above and below. And blinding white where the planes were breaking.

The Core couldn't have been more than thirty metres away. They had hacked and blasted their way through where the Legions were narrowest, smashing the enemy troops out of existence by bullet, axe and blade. But the vast mass had swallowed every round and every explosive the Sentinels had thrown at them and now it was hand-to-hand on every front against an enemy that was limitless.

A hook raked the back of her shoulder and Anna sensed the swell of weakness that accompanied every blow the legionnaires delivered. She staggered aside, but before the hooks could flash from the red wall to her left again, she heard the vroom of the Scythian's great axe as it swung through the hot air, smashing the legionnaires out of existence.

Anna blocked the next attack and risked a glance at the Core. It looked as if the silver walls were unravelling, as if they were melting, running into the planes above and below and leaving darkness behind. She could see figures within the darkness, lit by the silver and red glow of the planes. With her senses sharpened by Julius's blood, she felt the desperation and the rage and the fear of the figure she knew was her friend and she knew that Chess's will was breaking.

'No,' she yelled, driving the sword through a chest plate, flames burning her fingers. She shouldered away a legionnaire, cleaving the red helm of another.

Anna refused to believe that this was over. She refused to believe that they were alone. She refused to believe that Box wouldn't come. Box would come. He *had* to come: and that thought kept her fighting.

Through the crimson haze, Anna saw Balthazar Broom. His heavy staff was blocking and smashing like the arms of a windmill. Behind him and Colonel Maximus Greave were huddled Crazy Boris and Gemma. The guitar was still intact on Crazy Boris's back but his sunglasses were no longer on his face. He was shielding Gemma with his own body, and through the shifting bodies, Anna saw that Pacer and Jake were shielding them both from the mass of legionnaires who were pressing in upon them.

But even amidst the chaos, Anna realized that Julius wasn't with them.

He had fought through the legionnaires and towards the Core on his own, drawing the enemy to himself and away from her. But he had pushed so far ahead that now he was cut off entirely. His machine pistols had been emptied within seconds and out here he was unable to rely upon the cross-dimensional link feeding munitions to his arms, so he was smashing into the enemy with his fists alone, driving them down but losing strength all the time.

'Julius,' yelled Anna to Captain Burke. She hammered her pommel into the face of a helmet, kicked the legionnaire away, speared her sword through the belly of the next. 'Get to Julius.'

His clothes were ripped and he was engulfed by a surging horde of legionnaires but he was fighting still. Together with Captain Burke and the Scythian, Anna hurled herself into the hacking mass. The great axe sang through the air, the cutlass swept into the fiery armour and Anna thrust her sword, aware of a freezing bolt of weakness down her left arm. Her stride faltered.

'Come on,' hollered Pacer, smashing his broadsword with both hands through the thighs of the legionnaire who had been attacking Anna. Together with Jake and Maximus Greave, they bowled forwards, the Colonel's metal arms wielding the multi-barrelled machine gun as a battering ram. Crazy Boris and Gemma came close behind, covered by Balthazar Broom.

It was a desperate push and through it, Anna saw Julius go down. The Scythian roared and sung his axe in a killing arc, smashing the enemy clear of the silver-red plane. She saw Julius struggle up, grappling with the legionnaires whose hooks were raining upon him. And then she was aware of a tall figure striding past her, his black jacket already torn from him, his white shirt brilliant against the ember glow of the Havoc Legions and his long, greying plait trailing behind him as he swung his wooden staff like a claymore.

'Balthazar, stay back,' boomed Julius, his voice clear above the crash of battle.

Brave words. Anna saw Julius fall to his knees.

And then Balthazar was standing over him, his mighty staff staving in helmets, crushing breastplates, breaking limbs and battering the legionnaires out of existence. By wading into the midst of the enemy, Balthazar had won them seconds. Seconds to reach Julius. Seconds to circle him in a defensive shield: to hold back the closest of the Legions.

But there were no seconds left.

'Balthazar,' cried Gemma.

The first sickle took him behind his left shoulder, the second in his right arm. Still he fought but now his white shirt was ribboned scarlet. He elbowed a legionnaire aside, ducked the next scything hook, spun, kicked left and standing over the prone body of Julius, felled two blazing warriors in one humming swing of his staff.

But the blood was flowing and Anna knew that the coldness would be too: the numbness, a weakness deadly as any wound. She fought forwards, shoulder to shoulder with Jago Burke and the Scythian.

'No!' screamed Gemma as a wave of legionnaires broke upon the big man. There were too many hooks, too many blows. The staff swung once more and then Balthazar faltered. The wood slid from his blood-slippy grip and he fell.

They swung and hacked and beat back the legionnaires and reached the bodies of Balthazar and Julius. From the Core there came a great crack, a sound they all heard, a sound they all felt, as if something within each of them had just cracked too. What was left of time was passing quickly, but in the moments that were left, Anna felt as if time had stopped. Even the Legions paused in their assault.

Julius was kneeling. Against him was propped the blood-streaked body of Balthazar Broom, his shirt as red as the legionnaires' armour. The solid, olive-skinned body was motionless, eyes closed. Gemma sobbed and Crazy Boris put an arm about her shoulders, turning her face into his jacket.

'A debt repaid,' murmured Jago Burke. 'Perhaps he wanted this.'

'He didn't want this,' snapped Pacer, angrily. 'No one wants *this*.'

But Anna wasn't so sure. Balthazar's skin was scored with wrinkles, rough, greying, but, despite the wounds, the rips through cloth and skin, there was a softness to his mouth, a trace of a smile, and Anna realized that in those last moments, as the hooks struck home, Balthazar *had* wanted this. For as long as she had known him, five hundred years had been racing to ensnare Balthazar. But now he had settled his life debt *and* cheated time of what it was owed. It was a clever trick and Anna smiled too. In the end, Balthazar

Broom, philosopher and fighter, had beaten time at its own game.

Julius grimaced, resting the lifeless body upon the silver-strung floor, head bowed. His breathing was laboured and beneath the rents in his clothing were the dark wells of deep gashes. Anna could tell that Julius was not so far from where Balthazar now rested.

'Seren,' was all that Jake said as he carried the limp body of the black archer across his arms.

Julius looked up. 'Étoile?'

The GTBD shook his head, then lowered the black-robed archer's body to the silver plane, beside Balthazar. Julius placed a shining hand on Seren's dark brow, closed her eyes, then looked back at Balthazar. 'Not long before we are together again.' He almost laughed. 'It seems that in death, we two are bound.'

'Not much longer before we're *all* bound by death,' said Crazy Boris gravely.

They were surrounded by rank after rank of the Havoc Legions, the faceless helms and bright hooks ready to bear down upon them, waiting to finish this. Why they had paused in the attack was a mystery to Anna. Maybe they were content to block the way to the Core, to ensure that nothing could be done to interrupt what was happening to Chess. Certainly, the final twenty or so metres were packed with enemy troops, haloed in flame, hooks curved like long, bright teeth.

'Anna?' It was Pacer, his voice drifting to her as if from far off. 'Anna, are you OK?'

For the first time since she had been gashed, Anna felt

the throb in her left arm. She looked where Pacer was looking, at the rip in the leather and the treacle-dark blood within. There was a numbness, a loss of sense in her left arm, and she wondered at how Julius, wounded as he was, could carry on.

'I'm OK,' she said, clenching and opening her left fist. Her arm felt cold but she could use it still. But her eyes were hot: hot from the fury of the fight; hot from the fury of the deaths; hot from the fury of what they would be unable to do.

'We came so close,' she whispered through gritted teeth.

She couldn't tell what was happening within the Core. Figures moved and she felt how close they were to Chess. And as the vast plane above cracked loudly, spilling yet more blinding light upon them, and time prepared itself for a new beginning or the end of everything, Anna held the thought of the people she would carry with her until the end.

There was a deep silence. Gemma sobbed without tears and a clump of crushed leaves dropped from her hand.

'So much for hope,' muttered Crazy Boris.

Anna flexed her left arm and swung her sword loosely in her right. 'Never say that,' she growled, the black fringe hanging straight above her bright eyes. 'Hope *never* goes.'

'Hope? How can *we* hope?' Pacer laughed raggedly. 'Come on, Anna. You aren't still expecting Box to show up, are you?' But there was fear in his face too.

Anna stared at him so hard he stopped laughing at once. 'Box *will* come.' He had to come: she had to *believe* he would come. Right now, that belief was the same thing as hope and Anna wasn't prepared to give up on either. She clenched her jaw and quietly she said, 'I know he will.'

The plane shook with a crash of metal as the Legions readied their weapons for the final assault.

'Unless something extraordinary occurs,' sighed Crazy Boris, 'we're out of time.'

Then Jago Burke lowered his cutlass and pointed over the top of the ocean of legionnaires to the far horizon, to where the silver plane curved up to its rim.

'I believe,' he said calmly, 'that something extraordinary is occurring.'

Anna stared through the heat of her eyes as first one, then a second, then a third ship emerged into the haze between the planes. The ships descended slowly, gas blasting from their iron bellies as they touched down. The front drawbridge of the middle ship crashed open in a wave of vapour and even from this distance, Anna could see the first rank of heavy cavalry advance from the gaping mouth. Their armour shone and their weapons were drawn. She closed her eyes, reached across the battlefield and she knew that at the centre of the front rank rode Box.

'I knew you'd come, Box. I *knew* you'd come.'

Two more drawbridges slammed down and the huge, armoured troops poured out. They formed into ordered ranks and now the dreadbolt cavalry began to advance, reapers and battle hammers gleaming, dog-head banners cracking open, iron hooves drumming over the breaking plane, gaining speed, faster and faster until across the silver horizon an armoured wave of destruction was thundering down on the enemy.

Anna's heart pounded.

'Now is the moment,' cried Julius, standing.

Anna readied her sword as the Legions wheeled into action. She would fight until what she wanted was in her arms, or she lay dead.

CHAPTER 17

SPEED: 250 m/s
DISTANCE TO TARGET: 1.1K
TIME TO TARGET: 4.4s
INCOMING: 0

Box read the display on his visor and gave the order to increase speed to the maximum. He felt the bolt's gallop smooth out until it seemed he was flying at the enemy. With the 360° vision the helmet provided, he could see the ranks of his cohort left and right of him and those who were charging in his wake. And he could see the enemy ahead.

SPEED: 300 m/s
DISTANCE TO TARGET: 0.6K
TIME TO TARGET: 2s
INCOMING: 0

There would be no incoming fire from the Havoc Legions. This would be body to body all the way: a question of who smashed who out of existence first.

At this speed it was impossible to read detail. Beneath the bolt's blurred hooves, the ground was silver and the silver was cracking apart to reveal streaks of light of a volcanic intensity. The sky was a perfect mirror of the ground below and some way ahead there towered between ground and sky a huge silver column that appeared to be splitting apart even as he hurtled towards it. Whips of light flicked from the column and into the surrounding space, jumping into the silver streaks that raced across the sky and over the ground. And between the charging dreadbolts and the silver column lay the vast red tide of the enemy.

The Legions had turned to face the dreadbolts. Box knew that deep within them, close to the Core, there would be a knot of humans. He didn't know whether he would find them alive or dead but he knew that he would demolish whatever stood in his path until he found Anna.

TIME TO TARGET: 0.2s

This was the moment. This was the way. Box strengthened the grip on his reaper, lowered his head behind the bolt's metal skull, heard the creature roar, sensed the ramming velocity of the thousand dreadbolts who rode with him and smashed into the enemy.

Bolt and rider are the weapon.

The first hundred metres of legionnaires were flattened in less than a second. Helmets, weapons, breastplates, limbs were crushed, shattered in one pulverizing roar. Box sensed the crash of metal hurtling through metal and caught the tremor and lick of flame. Then the sheer mass of the Havoc

Legions clogged the thundering charge until the dreadbolts were hacking, stamping and hammering their way into the enemy.

Box's bolt reared up, heavy hooves stamping down legionnaires, staving in helmets, snapping through limbs. He pulled it up again, scanning the churning battlefield for any sign of Anna or those she was with. All he saw was fire and the crash of dreadbolt against legionnaire. Skarl and Raxa were already wheeling their troops round to join his central wedge.

'Stay close. Tight formation,' he ordered. Packed together, his cohort could force a way through the enemy towards the Core. If they broke apart it would be far easier for the legionnaires to erode their numbers. And Box wanted to keep as many dreadbolts centred within the cohort as he could so that they could act as a fresh reserve when needed.

'Heavy weapons, flanking fire,' he commanded.

Immediately a new sound blasted over the clash of metal: the blazing staccato rattle of the heavy weapons units, cybernetic arms bearing multiple barrels and close-range explosive munitions. At once, the closest flanking enemy units were shredded to nothing, giving the cavalry space to spread out and drive forwards in a broad wedge.

Left and right, Box hacked, chopped and smashed, wielding the long battle blade two-handed, his mount stamping and biting as he did so, leaping through the enemy in bursts as if wading through a mire. Box was aware of Razool to his left, forcing a way through the enemy troops, shoulder to shoulder with Box's mount. Razool had used his HV magnum until it had run dry and now he hefted the long battle hammer, standing in his stirrups the better to cave in helmets and batter down bodies.

But the strength of the Havoc Legions lay not just in their numbers but in their power to drain energy from other beings by contact alone and the dreadbolts had already taken so much impact that slowly, the life-sapping negative energy of the Legions was seeping through them. Box could sense his troops slowing and was receiving the first reports of dreadbolts down.

A boom cracked across the whole battlefield and, looking towards the Core, he saw the silver cords spinning free of the pillar and darkness swirling up its length. Within the darkness he glimpsed figures, tiny from this distance. And looking in that direction he saw a place where a battle all of its own was raging: a swirl of armour, a flash of silver blades within the fiery mass. There was a minute group of humans, desperately outnumbered. And even from this distance, Box could see one with raven hair and a bright sword fighting the forces of hell as if she were a demon herself.

'Friendly forces at fifty metres. We have to drive through, *now*,' barked Box to Skarl who had ridden up on his left. 'Take the reserve into the Core. I'm cutting right with Raxa and his troop.'

The front of the cohort opened, allowing fresh cavalry to charge out. The legionnaires were not expecting this and in the sudden push their ranks collapsed. In the gap that opened, Box pulled right, towards the knot of resistance which still held out against the red-armoured mass of the Legions. A tight pack of dreadbolts came with him, bulldozing through the enemy.

Across the blazing chaos of the battlefield, Box glimpsed Pacer and a man in black swinging a huge axe, and Crazy Boris and even Gemma. And he saw Anna, moving like light, sword so fast that the only sign of its existence was the damage it wrought. But the surrounding legionnaires seemed to increase their efforts to cut down the humans, as if they were bent on destroying them before help could come.

Box willed his mount on, pulling it up and jumping a wall of legionnaires which had gathered to block his way. He swung the reaper full circle and down as the bolt's forelegs reached through the air. Hissing in a mighty arc, the blade slammed through metal but he felt the sickles rip the underside of his bolt and when the creature landed back on the brilliant plane, he sensed the weakness that caused it to stumble.

The legionnaires were concentrating on the bolts, scything at their legs to bring them down. Before Box was halfway to where he could see the horde battling Anna and the others, his mount was roaring and missing its footing and was becoming increasingly difficult to control.

Blood splashed the visor of his helmet. He knew that it wasn't his blood and at the same time he saw a rider to his right go down in a frenzy of tearing hooks. Box tried to rub the visor clear but his gauntleted fingers succeeded only in smearing whorls and stripes across his vision. Now all he could see was the brightness of the planes and the flame glow of the Legions.

'Stay alive, Anna. Stay alive,' he whispered to himself.

He released the collar clips, pulled off the helmet and flung it away. He flung the reaper too, like a javelin, clean through two legionnaires, then took hold of his two mace-blades.

The bolt was careering headlong, bouldering left then right, drunkenly. Box heaved directly towards Anna even though there were so many enemy troops that he couldn't see her any longer.

'You think you can stop me?' yelled Box. The bolt was going down. '*Nothing* can stop me.' Box drove the bolt into the legionnaires, flattening them as the huge bio-machine crashed to the floor.

But Box wasn't down. In one continuing movement he rolled forwards and onto his feet and then he was running.

Anna was no more than twenty metres away.

Although each slab of armour took two runners to carry, Box's solarion-reinforced body was designed to function under massive stress. Thighs pumping, he lowered his head and shoulder-barged through the first four rows of legionnaires who tried to block his way.

A red figure attacked. Box kicked it so hard that it spun through the air with sufficient force to floor two more. Box's elbows, fists and feet cleared the enemy. Then, with space to wield them, he released the blades, one in each metal-gloved fist. His armour was scored and blackened from the impact of the hooks and in places it had been torn open. There was blood in his eyes, *his* blood, and his lungs heaved in air as his muscles began to ache, but nothing was going to stop him.

Now he fought hand-to-hand, lunging, parrying, slashing, kicking, driving a path forwards. Through the heat and the flames he saw he was not alone. Dismounted, helmets off, dreadbolts were fighting to the left and the right of him and as a gleaming scythe clawed into his face, it was Razool who blocked it with his plated arm before driving the head of his battle hammer up and through the helmet of the assailant.

'What are you waiting for, skin?' roared Razool, fangs bared, black lips ripped back. '*Get her!*'

Gemma was crouching behind Anna and was partly shrouded by Crazy Boris. Box tried to determine who it was that was kneeling by Anna's legs. His long black coat was in tatters and his yellow hair obscured his face and then Box realized it was Julius. The flesh of his face was gored. There were others fighting nearby but it was Anna alone protecting the figures at her feet, surrounded by hacking hooks and tiring even as he watched her.

'On me,' yelled Box, blades in hand. 'Follow me.'

He didn't wait to see where his comrades were. There wasn't time. He ran, felt the blows but didn't stop to fight. He had to get to Anna now, before the hooks tore her apart.

'No!' He drew back a mace-blade, slashed down one legionnaire, then the next, and as the shining points rained down he was there to block them, to take the blows for Anna, to batter down the legionnaires, the blades in his fists clashing and cutting so hard the whole press of the Legion was bowled back.

And the dreadbolts were behind him, *his* dreadbolts, the snarling heads on their armour matched by their own savage faces. Fang and fist, blade and hammer flattened the enemy until there was a ring of armour protecting the tiny band of humans from the blazing mass of the Legions.

No memory had been as bright, no memory as vital. Blades

in one hand, Box pulled Anna to him, embracing her strong body against his. She was so beautiful. And her lips were soft. The flaming legions threw themselves at the dreadbolts, time was breaking but Box and Anna took this one kiss. Then Box slipped his hand free of its gauntlet and he touched her face where the blood flowed.

'I knew,' said Anna, voice hoarse, blue eyes glistening. 'I *always* knew.'

'Me too,' whispered Box.

Razool stomped alongside him, the mighty battle hammer over his armoured shoulder. 'Finished?' he enquired, with an irritating smirk about his muzzle.

'It's nice to see you've brought wolfman with you,' smiled Anna. But Box noticed that her arm remained about his back a little longer and he felt as if no matter what happened now, he couldn't be happier.

But reality returned quickly. His body ached, blood still ran down his face and Julius lay wounded at his feet. And one kiss would change nothing if they didn't get Chess out of the Core.

The man with the axe marched across to where Box and Anna stood and with him came a man in a hat and a leather riding coat, a cutlass swinging in his hand by his side. Behind them walked Pacer and a dwarf with a crowbar. Pacer's dark face was striped with glistening streaks of blood from a gash on his scalp.

'You made it,' he said to Box, warily.

'I hate to miss out,' said Box. He grinned and then Pacer grinned and for a moment it could have been the two of them meeting back at the wharf after a hard day's graft in the city. But only for a moment. Then the crash of battle and the writhing of the Core hurtled in on them.

Razool was kneeling by Julius, a stem pen in his taloned hand, and Raxa stood over them both, his bear-like body resting on his reaper as if it was a staff. Julius pushed Razool away and pointed towards the darkening column that towered between the streaking planes.

'Get her out,' he said to Box. 'Get Chess out of there.'

Although the cohort had demolished a chunk of the enemy, the Havoc Legions still ringed the Core. Looking over the flame-lustred clash of dreadbolts and legionnaires, Box could see that the Core had filled almost entirely with shadow and that at its heart there were three figures. It was impossible to tell them apart. But then he saw the unmistakable thrust of a knife. One of the figures dropped to its knees.

'Chess!' he screamed and he broke out of the shield of dreadbolts and into the battle and, with him, sword in hand, came Anna.

The helicopter gunships cut over the ridge and swung down towards the city like locusts. Spread below them, all the way to the horizon, were the mangled remains of highways, office blocks, blazing skyscrapers and burnt-out traffic.

'So,' sighed Joachim Breslaw, 'there is nothing left to fight over.'

Ethel shrugged. 'That never stops the fighting.'

The two of them were positioned atop the ridge, the Professor in his wheelchair and the old lady standing by his side. Dug in on either side of them and all along the ridge were troops putting down fire on the Symmetry forces that had destroyed the city and which were advancing upon what remained of Committee HQ. The plague beasts, androids, hunters and spindle rippers absorbed as much damage as the Committee and its supporting forces could throw at them, and did not stop. At the foot of the ridge, the remaining agents of the COE were waiting. They had been guided into position by Hex and his street rats, and now they were about to mount a final counter-attack, supported by the gunships that were thumping overhead. But as he readied his men and women, Captain Riley wondered how they could ever hold back an enemy that could pour extra troops through the vortex and whose numbers seemed to be limitless.

The sky was dark: dark even beyond the pall of smoke that rolled across the city. And as the sky darkened, so the sun had become whiter. Sharper.

A mortar round crumped amidst the tentage on the reverse slope of the ridge, shrapnel ripping through the canvas now that the shield was down. But the tents were empty. Every soldier was providing fire from the ridge. There was no one to spare.

The earth kicked up in a thin line of dirt and rounds rang against the frame of Professor Breslaw's wheelchair like tubular bells. From under the travel rug that was tucked about him, he produced a hip flask. He unscrewed the cap, offered the flask to Ethel, who declined, and took a long draught himself.

'Thank you, Joachim, for being here with me. At the end of everything.'

Joachim Breslaw took another deep drink, coughed wheezily, then wiped his lips with the back of his free hand. 'I wouldn't miss it for the world,' he chuckled and the chuckle became a spasm of coughing. Then, gesturing at the sky, hip flask in hand, he croaked, 'Not much longer. Minutes. Maybe seconds.'

Ethel looked up at where the coal sky was striating with pale bolts of light, bolts that seemed to emanate from the brash, white sun. Then, looking out over the city, the whole scene flickered as if a rogue frame had been slipped into a running film and she saw a sky streaked with silver and beneath it a battle rolling, fiery red, and beyond the battle, a pillar of darkness. And then the blazing battlefield had vanished and she was looking out across the devastated city again.

'The spiral has unravelled,' murmured Ethel. 'Time overlaps time and the moment turns into the first arc of a new spiral,' she sighed, 'or into nothing.' She laughed, as if she didn't feel like laughing at all. 'Goodness. It's three o'clock.'

Joachim Breslaw coughed weakly and his breathing was strained. 'Some of us flare and some of us, we merely fade.' He wheezed like a piece of sacking being dragged. 'For me, Mevrad, this moment turns onto nothing.' He fell silent.

And now, beside him, stood the Baroness Mevrad Styx. The soldiers who saw her there, on top of the ridge, thought that the tall, ebony-haired woman, gowned and booted, was an illusion: a vision of a dark angel perhaps, or maybe a sorceress. This was a wild, unnatural moment, and already this day they had seen things that they had never imagined and they knew not to trust their battle-dazed eyes. They held their weapons close, trained them on the abominations below and deadened their minds to the emerging brilliance of the sky and the vision which remained standing on the ridge.

Mevrad said, 'My time is coming to an end too, old friend. And I will give her what strength remains. I and those who have gone before me.' Her keen, dark gaze turned to the racing sky as she lowered her hand and, gently, closed the eye of the figure whose head hung motionless in the wheelchair beside her.

The light spun about them, threads unravelling from the walls of the Core and reaching for Chess, wrapping her in their fragile strands. At the same time, the matrix of the Core swirled outwards as if being sucked into the planes above and below, and as they did so, Chess felt herself reaching out into the universes, and she felt the universes reaching into her.

The Narrow Man's spindly hand had slipped from Chess's chin to the crown of her head, where his long fingers ran through her thick hair as if luxuriating in satin. Chess couldn't stand: couldn't bring herself to stand. She remained kneeling, head bowed, able to see that outside the Core there were shapes, flames, as if the plane had ignited. Noises came to her: sharp, explosive noises and the clash of weapons.

'I don't want this,' she murmured, over and over again, as

if just repeating the words could drive bad thoughts away. 'I don't want to know who I am.'

Box had gone. Splinter had gone. Gemma had gone. Anna had gone. In the darkness that was falling, in a universe of pain, she reached for her mother, for the voice that had always been there. But there was nothing.

'Nothing,' Chess heard herself sob.

The Inquisitors were here. Of course the Inquisitors were here. They had waited for so long that their spirits had extended across what remained of time and space to witness this final act. Before her stood Malbane, hood down, drinking in every sensation with an expression of beatific joy. Behind her, Snargis was wallowing in the death throes of the city. To her right, Veer, with a face of ice. To her left, Azgor, serpent's eyes rolling deliriously with the pain generated by a million Havoc Legions across an eternity of universes.

'This learned weakness,' sighed the Narrow Man, 'it is no good. It is unbecoming. You know what you want, Chess. I know what you want.'

'Nothing.' Chess gritted her teeth, holding back tears.

Don't cry. Please don't cry.

'There is no end to this. Not unless *you* end it.' The Narrow Man squatted beside her, pallid flesh sagging from his emaciated frame, his blank face up close to Chess. He continued to stroke her hair. 'Your mother was strong, but you . . .' His dry lips brushed her ear. 'You are perfect.'

'I don't want to know who I am,' Chess repeated to herself, trying to blot out the Narrow Man's voice. 'I don't want to know who my father is.'

'It is natural to be proud of what we create,' the dry voice whispered in her ear.

Chess shook her head.

'Of course,' the Narrow Man stood, 'Mevrad has sought to pollute you. Did you know that after I had planted you inside your mother's womb, Mevrad had you plucked out?'

'Please,' gasped Chess. The darkness filled her eyes, her ears, her mouth and clawed into her soul. And somewhere, deep inside, it found a darkness all of its own, waiting. *Her* darkness. And when the darkness from without met the darkness within, there was heat. There was power.

'Mevrad mixed your blood, *my blood*, with the Nephilim's. She permeated your body with crystal so that your vast, ineffable spirit could become a weapon for *her* to use against *me*. Was that not wrong of her, Chess? Was that not contrary to every law? To turn the daughter against her father?'

Chess groaned and shook her head.

You are a girl of many parts, Lemuel had told her: *part human, part god, part universe and part wickedness.* The wickedness: her father's part. The dark part. The part that wanted to destroy. The part that was burning its way out of her now.

'Daughter,' hissed Bael.

The darkness inside flared into a scalding ichor, searing her spirit and wracking every joint as it ripped through her body. 'No! No more.'

Malbane smiled to feel the time spiral crack.

'But,' continued Bael, still stroking Chess's head as she knelt at his feet, 'I am patient. I have had eternity to learn the discipline of patience. And I have waited ... *we* have waited, Chess, you and I, for Mevrad's undoing.' He sighed with an ancient weariness. 'She has taught you to hate your father. At every turn she has misled you. And she has used you. And now, Chess, now is the time for her to taste the gall of her own *corruption*.'

Darkness, burning darkness and Chess heard herself cry out, felt the shearing of the time spiral.

'Can you feel it, Chess?' Bael's voice taking her deeper into the void: the void that would end everything. 'The great pain? The grand pointlessness of it all?'

Chess's body swept up and she was standing through no thought of her own. Or maybe there was thought. She couldn't tell. She couldn't tell even whether she was inside herself any more: inside herself looking out, or outside looking in.

'You are *everywhere*, Chess.' The Narrow Man's mouth worked quickly, grasping at the words then spitting them out. 'There must be blood,' rasped his dry lips. 'Blood and the spirit. How else are we to re-shape the universe?'

Other worlds slipped before her eyes: she saw her own city, smashed and smoking, and she gasped. And then she saw Saul. In the maelstrom that was her mind and the universes, Chess had forgotten about Saul: Saul who had said he was helping her, Saul who had said he cared for her, Saul who had led her body and mind into the arms of the Twisted Symmetry.

'You?' Anger choked every other insult she could have screamed at him for his treachery. 'I *trusted* you.'

The Narrow Man had gripped Saul by his head, his thin, stony fingers longer than they had been before. They crabbed round the back of Saul's skull like a cage, and Chess remembered the feeling when Bael had once gripped her like that, his fingers digging deep into her soul.

Saul was on his knees, head down, and Chess realized that this wasn't because Bael had forced Saul's head down, but because Saul didn't want to look at her. It was as if he was ... ashamed.

'Blood and spirit. Blood and spirit,' repeated the Narrow Man, incantatory.

Don't listen. Don't look, said the fraction of Chess's mind where she remained. But she had slid so far into oblivion that now, at last, she was ready to end everything.

'Blood and spirit.'

Fight as she did to look away, there was something mesmeric in the way the withered aperture of a mouth worked in the collapsed featurelessness of Bael's face. And looking as she did, Chess saw that Bael held a knife in his free hand. She recognized the long, solid blade and the simple handle and she drew back instinctively because she knew that a wound from a knife like this was eternal.

There was a faint smile about Malbane's face and Veer licked his lips.

'Not ... my ... blood,' stammered Chess, struggling to form the words.

'Of course not your blood,' snapped the Narrow Man, and he jerked the blade towards Saul. '*His*.'

'*His?*' Dully, Chess recalled Lemuel and the Sages telling her that *her* blood would spill before the work was done.

'You did not walk your world alone.' The Narrow Man chuckled.

Chess struggled to make sense of what he meant. It was difficult because so little of her mind remained her own. Trying to think what the person she had known as Chess thought was like trying to surface from sucking mud.

The Narrow Man was laughing at her now and, all about her, the Inquisitors were laughing too. Their faces switched with the images that flashed through her mind: snapshots from the overlapping planes of the twelve suns; the nuclear glare of the suns themselves; pictures and voices from her past, and a warning from her mother. A warning that Chess realized she had never understood: until now.

You only have one brother, and you mustn't trust him.

'Chess,' said Bael, with a flourish of his knife-bearing hand towards Saul. 'Let me introduce you to your brother.'

CHAPTER 18

Bael pulled back Saul's head so that Saul was looking up at Chess, dark eyes expressionless. Her brother's eyes, staring up at her. Chess took a step back, as if the shock had hit her like a punch. But the shock had hit her with a force more powerful than a punch. Her thoughts had scattered and now her mind went charging after them, trying to scoop them up, trying to recover from the blast of what Bael had just told her. What her father had just revealed to her.

Her brother? Yes, she had no doubt that this hard-jawed, soft-lipped, velvet-eyed boy was her brother. Now that Bael had spoken, she recognized the truth as well as she recognized her own face. And amongst the thoughts that she tried to grasp like water, details surfaced like grit: why the spook on Surapoor had come only for her, not for Box or Splinter; why the bowl of blood on the reachings had driven Lemuel crazy, driven him to accuse *her* of putting it there. It all came down to blood.

Chess looked at the tracks cut into Saul's arm. It was his blood that had flowed into that bowl. His blood that had replicated hers so closely it had driven Lemuel demented. And he had put it there.

'Why?' whispered Chess. '*Why?*'

Saul was silent.

'A family reunion,' snorted Snargis from the dimensions behind her.

'How touching,' sneered Azgor.

'No,' muttered Chess.

'Yes,' hissed the Narrow Man, and he yanked up his arm, dragging Saul to his feet as if Saul weighed nothing. Saul looked at Chess and his eyes continued to bore into her yet say nothing.

'Say something,' shouted Chess. She felt anger surge through her body, blistering hot. 'I trusted you. I ... I ... I thought you were different. How did you ... why? *Why?*' She couldn't find the words for how she felt, but the words she did find she flung at him like stones.

Chess sensed the violence which washed all about the Core and she drew upon it naturally. Reaching out, across the merging planes of time and space, her mind, her spirit drew hungrily upon every shred of dark energy she could find, and drew them into herself where they merged with the power already pumped into her by the Symmetry. And now, driven by the rage, she struck out.

'*Why?*' she shouted.

The matrix of the dissolving Core cracked. The plasmic strands thrashed and the twelve suns flared.

Suddenly, Saul shook himself, to disentangle himself from his father's soul-grasping clasp, but the bony hand only squeezed more tightly and Saul gasped and hung slack, knees buckling.

'Betrayal, Chess,' mouthed Bael. 'Think how you have been betrayed by everyone. By everyone you trusted.'

'No,' roared Chess, trying to hold back the power. But there was no stemming the rush of rage.

'Think how Mevrad has hidden the truth from you, Chess. Mevrad and the others. They never told you about me, your father; they never told you about your brother. Think of their lies, Chess. And feel the pain of all these worlds.'

'Chess ...' gasped Saul, but he was silenced by a jolt of the skeletal hand.

'This creature,' said Bael, jerking Saul's body, 'was sprung from his mother's womb by my blessing in the hope that *he* might stand where you now stand. But his mother was nothing. She was unable even to survive my gift.'

'You killed her.' Saul choked the words out.

'*You* killed her,' snapped the Narrow Man. 'She could not hold my growing strength and live. She didn't have the power of your blood, Chess, of your mother's blood and her mother's before her.' He squeezed Saul's head harder and Saul groaned. 'But this creature, your half-brother, has had his uses. And he has one final use.'

It was too much. Chess knew that she was breaking. She knew that her father was right, that in these universes of pain and suffering she hadn't even been able to trust those closest to her, that she had been betrayed by everyone.

'Good, Chess. Good.' The Narrow Man's mouth, working the words with its shrivelled lips. He held the knife towards her. 'Finish it, Chess. Strike deep. Kill your greatest betrayer. Blood and spirit. Finish our work.'

Our work. The darkness within cried out for release. Her father's darkness. *Her* darkness.

Blood would flow and it wouldn't be her blood. But its essence would be sufficient to seal the link.

The knife was before her. It was in Bael's palm, ready for her to take. One thrust and the blood would flow, and with it would flow enough energy to crash time back to its first beat: to end everything.

'Good,' urged Bael. 'Good.'

Saul was looking at her. He hadn't stopped looking at her. Chess knew that he had never stopped looking at her. But she realized that he was not going to try to speak to her now. He was frightened of her. Frightened of the blazing, thundering thing she had become. Frightened of what she was going to do, not just to him but to everything.

'Such pain, such betrayal,' whispered her father in her ear. And he was right. But now there would be no more.

A calmness entered Chess's mind. She was ready now. Ready to end it. Ready to do whatever the Symmetry wanted because it was the *only* thing to do.

Let the blood flow. Let the end begin. Nothing mattered now. *Nothing.* But she didn't take the knife. She just stared at the facelessness of Bael, waiting, contemplating the long peace ahead.

'No matter,' croaked the Narrow Man, and his fingers worked to reverse the crystal knife in his palm. Now, instead of being tendered towards Chess, the handle was in his grasp in a stabbing grip, the point of the blade towards Saul.

'Blood and spirit,' came the dry voice of her father. 'Blood and spirit,' and he drove the knife into Saul's chest.

The clamour was blinding. Crazy Boris had his arm around Gemma's back. They ran through the battle as if they were escaping a bomb blast. Not far ahead were Anna and Box. Crazy Boris knew where Anna and Box were because there the fighting was wildest. Metal crashed, blood flowed, flames flared, helmets rolled. The Scythian cleared a path in great sweeps of his axe. The dreadbolts spearheaded outwards, driving the legionnaires back. And at the front were Anna and Box, blades whirling.

There was so much: so much noise, so much light. From above and below, the planes spouted helical whips of magnesium intensity, hundreds of metres long. Even with the battle rolling about him, Boris saw that within these brilliant trails there was detail: partial glimpses of faces, bodies, eldritch landscapes, cities, moons, haggard skies. And even with the battle about him, the glimpses revealed by the breaking open of time and space exercised a hypnotic draw. He slipped his shades back on and stopped to stare upwards and then downwards.

Gemma shrieked and then there was a clang as Pacer blocked a hook strike that seemingly came from nowhere.

'Wake up, Boris,' shouted Pacer. He lashed the broadsword side on, striking a legionnaire smack out of existence.

'It's time,' said Crazy Boris vacantly. 'Time for me to go,' and he pointed at the nearest serpentine lash of light which had uncoiled only metres away. But the fighting was so frenzied that those closest to this brilliant burst focused only upon blades and hammers and hooks. Yet, all about, the matrix of the planes was uncoiling in rollercoaster-size arcs and fountains.

'They're nearly there,' shouted Gemma.

Boris heard her voice as if through deep water. It was all so slow now.

I'm not even scared, he realized.

It was like floating, or falling gently. He saw Anna and Box fighting, back to back then shoulder to shoulder, driving forwards, barely a spear throw from the Core, the two combined like one perfect weapon. He felt the heat and quake of the battle.

'Boris, come *on*.' It was Gemma taking responsibility for him now, pulling him forwards, flanked by Pacer and Jake. He stumbled after her, guided by her, his hand in hers. They were close enough to see the shades within the Core. In the darkness two people were kneeling and one was standing.

'Like a priest,' murmured Crazy Boris, and there were memories of peat fires and bare, black lanes and singing. 'When I was on horseback,' he began to hum, but it was no good because Gemma was tugging at him frantically.

He stopped. 'Here,' he said, sliding the guitar off his back.

'We're in the middle of a battle,' shouted Pacer. 'Are you *crazy?*'

'That's what they say,' laughed Boris Sherevsky. He thrust the guitar at Pacer. 'Go on. Take it. You can carry on where I left off.'

Pacer hesitated, then pulled the guitar away before a legionnaire bowled through the space where the guitar had just been, hammered sideways by Jake. Boris had taken the photograph from his jacket pocket. He looked about at the fighting. Pacer would have tried to stop him but he saw Boris's face and he understood: it *was* crazy, but he understood. He just said, 'Thanks Boris.'

'Remember to feel the instrument. Don't overplay it, it'll play itself. You're just helping out.' The old rocker winked at him. 'And *practise*.' Then he was walking towards a tongue of light that uncurled to the height of a tidal wave and then he was gone, vanished into the light with the photograph still in his hand and a sea of dreadbolts and legionnaires clashing in his wake.

Pacer slung the guitar over his shoulder and with Gemma close behind, turned towards the Core. A wall of light broke over him and, gasping, he saw a howling, wraith-rocked place; a giant battle cruiser splitting in two, the two halves sliding into the void of space; saw the city, his city, smashed and burning, and heavily gunned androids and lumbering plague beasts advancing upon a final line of soldiers in the rubble, and, amongst the remnants of the Committee forces, he saw Captain Riley and Hex and Trick.

Pacer saw it all in one widening of the eye. Then he stumbled back, half-blinded, and when he saw again, the time flare had receded and the plane was red and silver and rolling with battle and not far ahead, a figure he recognized as Chess was slumped over a body he realized was Saul's. And over them both there stood a tall, narrow, flesh-melted man with a knife.

Anna and Box had pushed ahead of everyone and had hurled themselves into the legionnaires who were blocking the final metres to the Core. But Pacer knew that there was no way they could reach Chess in the time that was left. He felt the slash of a hook into his back and his shoulders seized up, the strength drained from his legs and he sank to his knees, aware of Jake wielding the crowbar over him like a baseball bat.

Gemma was on her knees by his side.

'It's too late,' Pacer whispered to her. 'It's too late.'

Trick dashed across the rubble-strewn street, hurdling chunks of concrete, panting so hard she could barely hear the cracking blasts of the automata turbo-cannons which powdered the road in her wake. She skidded to a halt behind the corner of what had been a department store but now looked like a demolition site. Brick showered over her from where the final shells from the androids' machine-cannons punched out a segment of the remaining wall. Above her, a helicopter gunship delivered a hissing streak of rockets into the army of androids and plague beasts that were advancing, then slid out of sight before the enemy's heavy weapons could take it down. It was the final gunship. On the other side of the street from where Trick now sheltered lay the wreckage of one of the helicopters that the Symmetry had knocked out of the sky, its fuselage twisted like a broken locust, the rotor blades shattered and splayed like an old picket fence.

Trick slung the cases of machine-gun ammunition to the

gunners who immediately pulled them open and fed the rattling belts into their weapons. Moments later, Hex came galloping in from the other end of the street, two cases of ammunition gripped in each hand. Blood had dried on his cheek and his clothes were ripped and stained with dark patches. But he still managed a mangled grin when he saw Trick.

'Completely surrounded,' he gasped, gulping the smoky air. He pointed towards a high strip of ground less than a kilometre away. 'We've still got units on the ridge but they've no ammo left.' Then he pointed to the open streets that could be seen around them, visible now through the battered shells of the city blocks. 'We've delivered as much ammo as we can.' He sat down and rested his big hands on his knees. 'I've told everyone to go to ground.' He nodded at an exposed road surface below which there would be the city drains. 'The rest of the rats are down there.' Then he hung his head, hair flopping over his face.

Captain Riley rested a hand on the street rat's shoulder. 'You've done a great job, Hex. You and all the gangs. Now we have to hang on with what we have left.' He squinted up at where the sky could be seen through a rip in the smoke. The sun shone white, a perfect circle, and when Trick looked harder, she thought that she could see another, fainter sun behind it, and behind that, another, as if there was a track of suns ending in hers.

An approaching rumble brought her attention back to where she and Hex and the remaining COE agents were preparing to make their final stand.

'Make ready,' commanded Captain Riley. There was a

metallic ripple of weapons being cocked from the agents positioned in shell scrapes, behind walls, behind whatever shelter could be found. Then the enemy swung into this street and all the others in this sector, filling them with the huge, oozing bulk of the plague beasts and the relentless ranks of the gun-heavy androids.

'Fire!' yelled Captain Riley and Trick's world dissolved into gunfire and chaos.

As Saul crumpled, so did Chess. His eyes had been on hers so intensely that despite her anguish and despite her rage, she felt the shock of the blow as if the knife had been driven hilt-deep into her own chest.

Now there was surprise and fear in those eyes, eyes that Chess had thought of so many times, but not like this. But this was what Saul deserved. Her greatest betrayer lay prone, blood pumping out of the hole that the knife had left, his white shirt already stained damson, the pool of bright blood spreading so fast and so wide that the Core seemed to be absorbing it, drinking it. And as the blood flowed out of Saul and into the Core, so the energy quickened through Chess.

Bael had stepped back, bloody knife in hand like a high priest at the ritual slaughter and Chess prepared to stand, prepared to unleash the energy that wanted to flow from her as wantonly as the blood flowed from Saul.

Saul was nothing now. She was nothing. Everything was nothing.

Then she felt a hand tighten on her wrist, the grip stronger, more urgent than she could have imagined.

'Chess.'

That was her name.

'Chess.'

She looked down, looked at Saul, at the eyes that were now searching hers.

'Please, Chess, listen to me.' The grip tightened.

The clash of metal was distant. The glow of flames was distant. The overlaying planes, shearing open, merging, spinning through the Core and through her were distant.

'I'm dying, Chess,' gasped Saul. 'Dying. There is nothing for me now. But I can speak freely, at last. I can speak to you: *really* speak to you.'

Chess remained kneeling by Saul's body.

'Listen to me.' Saul coughed, licked his lips. 'Closer.' He was struggling to speak. Without thinking, Chess lowered her head. She could feel the heat from his mouth as he whispered. 'All my life I have been nothing. And when you came into the world, you were everything. My father ... *our* father ... has thought only of you: your power. What you can do. And I have helped him. Helped *them*.'

Them. The Inquisitors.

Saul blinked, eyes glassy. 'And I have watched you and right from the start, Chess, I didn't want them to hurt you. I was angry with myself. I should have hated you. But I didn't. I wanted to help you.'

Chess found her voice, her own voice. 'Help me? How has any of what *you've* done helped me?'

'On the train, on Surapoor?' Saul licked his dry lips. 'I was there just to watch. I didn't have to step in. But I did. I couldn't bear to see you hurt.'

'But afterwards, with the General, when you were his prisoner?' If what Saul said was true, Chess couldn't understand why the General had been about to savage him, whilst she and Box and Splinter had been hidden, watching.

Saul shook his head weakly. 'A display. To fool you all. To gain your trust in me. Our father has considered many possibilities. That was one of them. It worked better than even he could have imagined, and I have *hated* myself for it.'

'Really?' Chess wanted to sound as if she didn't believe him.

He looked up urgently then. 'Do you have any idea what it's like, being someone like me?' He clenched his jaw. 'This is what I deserve. But all the time, I didn't want them to hurt you.' His hand still held her wrist, not so tight now. 'Remember when *he*, our father, caught you in that club? When you were on your own and Mevrad came?'

Chess remembered. These were *real* memories. All her life she had wanted real memories. She nodded.

'Mevrad came because I told her what *he* was planning.'

And Chess remembered that when she had entered the club, a person had slipped out, hooded. She hadn't seen who it was but she had sensed their presence: recognized it. 'You?' she whispered.

Saul nodded. There was blood at the corner of his mouth and she saw he was trying to swallow it back.

'And when *they* captured you and took you to the warp station.'

'Yes.' Chess bent even further forward to catch Saul's voice which had become very hoarse. Struggling.

'You nearly escaped.'

'Yes,' remembered Chess. 'There was a hole, in the Möbius cell.'

Saul sighed. 'Me. Every day I watched what they did to you and hated them for it. I tried to open the cell for you. I *did* open it.'

Chess's hand had found the back of Saul's head. It was warm and his black hair was as soft as it had always looked.

Saul swallowed as if swallowing hurt. 'I have betrayed you, Chess, sometimes, because there was no other way for me. I'm not strong like you. And all my life I've lived in a world of *hate*. *Their* world. *His* world. But you are different. You're what I couldn't be and you are brave. Really brave.'

Saul coughed and a trickle of blood spilt down his strong chin. 'I've watched you, watched over you. And even when I've done the bad things, I've loved you.' He swallowed slowly. 'Really *loved* you. You were the only good thing. I wanted to tell you that. I wanted . . .'

Chess felt Saul's body relax. His eyes were still open, staring into hers, and his chest rose and fell tremulously. She drew his head onto her lap.

'I'm sorry, Chess,' he whispered. 'I know I'm not what you wanted.'

Chess lowered her head until it was against Saul's chest. She could hear the faint stumbling of his heart and she felt her own body, small and weak, as if she was sinking, inhabiting her mortal frame again. She felt the ache in her own heart, felt it squeeze her chest, felt it intensify every sense in her body. She gasped at this quickening. It was as powerful as the dark energy with which she had been filled, but it was different. It was vital. It was *alive*. It blotted out pain, blotted out suffering. It didn't make them go away but it put her somewhere else, somewhere better, somewhere Chess hadn't known existed. Until now.

'You're *all* I wanted,' whispered Chess, her lips barely moving against Saul's chest. She listened to his heart, listened to it beat slower and slower. Falter.

Silence.

But his body was warm and Chess wanted to stay like that, close to him, for as long as the warmth remained. Her eyes stung although there were no tears. But there was heat: a searing heat that pulsed through her. It scorched her heart, her brain, her spirit. It was so hot that she ceased to feel the fading warmth of Saul's body: it was as if his body was dropping away from her. She stood, suddenly, eyes burning.

'Good. Good,' said her father, standing behind her. 'Feel the rage, Chess. Let it fill you. Remember the betrayal. Betrayed by everyone.'

This time, when the remaining matrix of the Core reached for her, Chess reached back, discovering that she and the universes connected like light and that this sense of light flashed between her and the universes and the brilliance of the suns. And then, in this one crystalline moment, Chess and time and space were one and she saw everything, touched everything, held *everything*. And the energy, the dark energy of a hundred billion tortured souls, howled within her.

'Yes!' cried Bael with hoarse delight. 'Destroy everything, Chess. Destroy it all.'

It would be easy to destroy it all. Now, in this suspended fraction of time, Chess knew how easily she could unleash so much energy that reality would be torn clear of its roots, blasted back to the nothingness from which it had once burst.

Before her, Malbane, eyes closed serenely. To her left, Azgor. To her right, Veer, and behind her, Snargis, grunting and drooling.

'Now, Chess,' urged Bael. 'Now!'

The power ripped through Chess's mind and through her body. She had been built for one thing and that was what she would do. Her father's darkness pulsed deep within, searching for a way out, driving the fury that gripped her spirit. But now there was something else which gripped her spirit, galvanized it, made it explode not with darkness but with brilliance: a brilliance that eclipsed pain, a brilliance that was borne not from hate but from love.

Sometimes the darkness destroys itself, a wise man had once told her. But the darkness was hers, and so was the light.

Chess wasn't frightened of the darkness any more.

'Now!' commanded Bael.

NOW.

The energy blasted from Chess's core so violently that Snargis's eyes bled in the moment before he was obliterated beyond residue. But the destruction didn't cease with his annihilation. Through his vast spirit, Chess drove her own, a roaring coruscation of power, smashing through every pan-dimensional space the Inquisitor occupied, decimating every force he controlled.

In a city, a universe away from the rage of the Core, an army of the Plague Breed suddenly ceased their violence, beasts and automata immobile as statues amidst the great curtains of smoke, and Trick and Hex and Captain Riley shielded their eyes against the nuclear flare of the sun.

'You want destruction,' shouted Chess, turning to face Veer. 'I'll give you destruction. I'll destroy you all.'

And in turning towards Veer, Chess turned her back on Bael, not seeing him lurch forwards, the crystal knife in his sepulchral hand.

Splinter had watched Bael. He had seen what happened: what happened to Chess.

He had seen the crystal knife plunge into her back and he had seen her die.

Chess dies.

He had known this ever since he had searched through time for this final moment and found it on the reachings. Witnessed it.

Chess dies. That was the future. That was the end.

But could you change the future?

Perhaps: if you could change time. If you could turn the clock back. If you were prepared to give up everything. If you were prepared to do anything.

He had created this situation. Splinter, the King of Rats, with his ruthless brilliance had brought the universe to the edge of destruction.

But Splinter Tuesday could change this. Splinter Tuesday could change time.

Chess didn't have to die.

But he did.

Box saw what was happening. After the blast of energy from Chess had boomed through them like a nuclear burst, after the brilliance from inside the darkness of the Core had faded, he saw her turn to face something he couldn't see. And he saw the Narrow Man approach her back, knife raised, ready to strike.

'Chess!' he yelled, but the crash of battle smothered his cry.

He couldn't see everyone: didn't know who was still standing. To his left Julius was staggering forwards, fighting blindly with what strength he still possessed. Close by him were Jake and Pacer. To his right were Captain Burke and the Scythian, deep in a sea of fiery armour, laying waste but unable to advance. Razool, Raxa and Skarl were not far behind, leading a pack of dreadbolts through the legionnaires. And by his side was Anna, matching his blows strike for strike. All of them were close to Chess. But no one was close enough.

Razool battered his way alongside, lungs working like bellows. He swung his hammer, taking the legs from two legionnaires who had come in behind Box. 'Run!' he shouted. But sustained by Azgor's will, the Havoc Legions threw all their weight into the final metres to the Core in a dense and blazing ring.

The heat. The noise. The seconds fading. Anna's sword flashed up, blocking, thrust forwards, impaling. Box's blades swung and struck in a hail of clangs. His armour was scored, torn open, his shoulder plates streaked with his own blood.

'Run!' he heard Razool roar again, hammer whirling, black mane wild.

He had to run: he would never reach Chess by fighting alone. There wasn't time for any parting from Anna. Box lowered his guard and bouldered into the enemy.

There was a blur of flame. The sound of his encased body crashing against armour. The sensation of breaking through coupled with the ebb of strength as the hooks raked him. But he kept running. He lowered his shoulder, taking a legionnaire in the chest, ramming the next one flat, slashing low with a blade, blocking then striking with the other, all the time charging forwards, alone.

He caught a last glimpse of Anna, sword swinging two-handed, teeth gritted as she cut down legionnaire after legionnaire. He saw Julius stumble, then throw himself into the enemy ranks. He saw Razool, Skarl and Raxa surrounded by blazing red, hammer and reapers wheeling high and crashing down; heard Pacer yell as he took a hook in the leg, thrusting his sword at the same time as he pushed Gemma clear.

The Narrow Man raised the knife high.

Metres to go.

'Box. Get her!' yelled Anna

'Stop him!' roared Razool.

Box powered forwards, oblivious to the blows he took. Bodies crashed against his own but he kept going: he *had* to keep going. His muscles were aflame, his lungs exploding, the blades heavy in his hands.

'No,' he gasped. His best wasn't going to be good enough.

'No!' he yelled, hacking down the final legionnaires, hurling himself forwards.

But he hadn't made it.

'*No!*'

The knife came down.

CHAPTER 19

Switch: switch *her* for *me*.

Splinter pushed the tip of the metal plate into his wrist, the third plate of the Codex: the plate that guaranteed death. He felt his skin tear, knew his blood had flowed and let the triangle of cold metal slip from his fingers, but he didn't let go of what he clutched in his left hand. And, with perfect timing, the Codex delivered him out of the vortex and straight to that third death. Splinter stretched wide his arms and took the blow that had been meant for Chess.

Box staggered back when he saw Splinter appear. A trick of time? His mind giving in? But Splinter *was* standing back to back with Chess, arms outstretched, and the Narrow Man's crystal knife was buried to its hilt in his chest.

Only now, after the blow had been struck, did Chess turn round, face aghast at what had nearly happened: at what *had* happened. But Splinter was laughing, triumphal. His long white hair whipped about his gaunt face, the black coat swirled about his body and his eyes were wild and bright.

The Narrow Man bent to pull the dagger free and then Splinter struck. He struck with an embrace, both arms enfolding Bael, and as they did so, his left hand plunged snake-swift into his back, driving the crystal knife that had been a gift from Malbane deep into Bael's body.

'No,' screamed Malbane, howling through the corridors of time.

And Bael screamed, screamed as he felt the amarantium blade cut through time and space, deep into his spirit, wounding him mortally for eternity. His scream cut like the knife. It tore out of the Core and across the broken planes, shrieking through every dimension touched by the twelve suns, driving itself through the terror-stricken souls of all who heard it.

Splinter was laughing and he didn't let go. This was his moment. This was the moment when he wielded the greatest power of all, and wielded it not only for himself but for everyone. He tightened his embrace, pulled Bael closer, knowing that life was seeping from his own body but feeling it run from the Narrow Man's too.

Bael's face contorted, he screamed, he cursed, he shifted his form, but there was no escape from the crystal knife and there was no escape from Splinter.

The battle had stopped. The planes were still bathed in silver and flaming red but the whole moment turned about the tableau at the heart of the Core: the swirling, twisting shadow of Bael, the white-haired demon that was Splinter and the figure of Chess, eyes fiery as the planes, body incandescent with the energy which leapt between her and the churning darkness of the Core.

'No,' screamed Bael, his physical form disintegrating, his spirit drained.

'Yes,' hissed Splinter into the abysmal face and he dug his knife deeper still, embracing his own death more tightly. 'You did not see this,' he laughed. 'You did not see me. This is your end, and the beginning . . . of *everything*.'

Splinter closed his eyes. He knew that these sensations were his last. But nothing frightened him and in a rush of power that carried him beyond every sensation he had ever known, his body died.

The Inquisitors acted in concert, drawing down energy, fusing it, exploding it into the Core. Bael had been destroyed, but together they would kill Chess. They had to kill Chess. The Havoc Legions burst back into motion, Azgor's rage blazing against Box and Anna, Razool and all their comrades. Box saw Chess reach out her arms before the flaming ranks of hook-raking legionnaires turned upon him and he was fighting to stay alive.

The wall of energy hit Chess from every dimension: a roaring power generated by the Inquisitors, sufficient to destroy worlds. But Chess opened her mind and absorbed this force as effortlessly as the universe could merge with itself. Then, eyes blazing, she hurled the power back, magnified by her own spirit and the agonies of a thousand billion souls.

Azgor: Chess knew what was happening out on the broken plane. She knew what Azgor wanted to do to her friends.

The serpent eyes flashed, the taloned fingers crabbed, grasping the fusion blasts of a thousand starfields, clutching nebulae, clawing for survival. Chess hurled the vaults of eternity into the Inquisitor, tearing every field of energy from its orbit, detonating every particle beyond past, present and future, hurricaning through every scintilla of reality she touched: obliterating Azgor and every trace of Azgor.

Anna had fought her way to Box and amidst a swarm of legionnaires they fought together, each ready to be struck down alongside the other: each *wanting* to be struck down alongside the other. Vaguely, numbly, Box was aware of where his comrades fought and he gritted his teeth, fighting to the end and wishing that for all of them this had not been the end they were facing.

And then, suddenly, it was over. The Havoc Legions had vanished abruptly, just as Azgor had vanished, and a screaming wind ripped over the planes as if sucking them clear of every last trace of the Inquisitor. Those who remained staggered blindly into the silent space left by the destruction of the blazing horde.

Box and Anna stumbled forwards together as Captain Burke and the Scythian backed away from the incandescent brilliance with which Chess burnt.

'It's not over yet.' Pacer's voice was shredded.

Box shielded his face with a gauntlet, his un-gloved hand reaching for Anna's, holding it. It was difficult to see what was happening. If Splinter and the Narrow Man were still there, they were lost within the radiance which streamed between Chess and the shadowed boundary of the Core. Then, suddenly, an awful blackness spilt across the whole Core, like ink tipped into water. The blackness engulfed Chess.

'No,' whispered Box, feeling Anna's clasp tighten on his hand. 'Don't give in, Chess. Not now.'

As Malbane and Veer blasted their dark power into Chess, the centre of the Core became a glistering pillar of darkness.

The dreadbolts stood about the battlefield like statues, waiting. Anna turned to Box, embracing him, her lips against his neck, forming words he couldn't hear. Pacer put his arms around Gemma and braced the two of them for whatever was about to happen. Her hand caught the guitar strings in a broken, melancholy discord. Only the solitary figure of Julius remained at the cusp of the darkness, ragged and bloodied but defiant, his yellow hair as tattered as his clothing and his skin.

'We triumph,' he cried but that wasn't how it looked to Box and he saw the dying light in Julius's once-bright eyes.

Veer and Malbane drove their pitch depths of hate and suffering into Chess, into her spirit, with sufficient force to crush universes. But Chess opened her spirit and absorbed their power, just as she had done when she had been the Symmetry's prisoner and they had filled her with their dark energy. They could not hurt her with their hate: they might as well have tried to blot out darkness with darkness. The darkness was hers and so was the light. The more violent the Inquisitors' assault, the stronger Chess became. And now, Chess began to draw their power from them, draining them with a hunger they had never conceived, stripping them of energy faster than they could think, tearing them apart fragment by fragment. There was no way they could hold this back. With the endless reach of the universes, Chess stripped them of everything.

'Look!' Gemma raised a hand and when Box looked where she was pointing, he saw a shattered cityscape as if it had been superimposed over the horizon beyond the Core. Out of this mirage, a figure rose, towering between the planes, spectral with swirling black hair, the flashing eyes of an enchantress and nails that were red as blood.

'I've seen her . . . before,' stuttered Box, rubbing sweat and blood from his eyes, remembering a vision from years ago, when they had been in the detention centre and Ethel had first told him and Chess and Splinter who she really was. And now, behind this vision, another loomed up, filling the horizon beyond the cityscape, vaguer, less substantial than the first. And there were more of these spectral figures rising up from the horizon, one after another until he could no longer see where they ended.

Then light streamed through the vast figures, blistering bright as if together they had cast it from themselves and into the Core, into Chess. Their light spun through her darkness, combined with it, and now Chess was wrapped in darkness and light and she hurled this out in a time-splitting, dimension-cracking storm, seeking every part of the Twisted Symmetry, missing nothing because this is what she had been built to do: because this was what the universes had chosen her to do.

Unstoppable now, Chess drew power from the universes, from the colossal spectres ranged about the Core, from the Inquisitors themselves and from the billions of souls whose agonies she had carried herself. She drew upon it all and released it upon the Inquisitors and all their works.

Spent of his power, Veer's substance was annihilated from

beginning to end with a cosmic agony so great, it crushed his essence from every instant in which he had existed. And across a spirit as deep and timeless as an aeon of nebulae, Malbane clung to his memories for a moment, recalling what it was that had brought him to this. The irony. Then Chess tore him apart, and his final scream, desperate and defeated, echoed through the corridor of eternity as she hurled her energy against every remaining particle of Bael and the Inquisitors, obliterating the Symmetry in a hurricane of power that ended, not with fury, but with the icicle chimes of amarantium falling in crystals over the silver plane from a shattered dimension that was lost forever.

Gemma's laughter was as light as the falling particles of amarantium. 'It's like snow!' Her blue eyes glittered.

'Too fragmented to harm us,' observed Captain Burke, with relief, blinking as he looked up.

Even as the crystal fell, the Core began to change. It drew the streaming planes back into itself and its huge walls of shadow and dark began to gleam again, shot with argent strands. Brilliance swirled through the dark pillar until once more it resembled the colossal column of ever-running silver that Anna had seen when she had first arrived here. And the planes resumed their original aspect, the coursing streams running smooth and flat, the rents of wild light altogether vanished and all trace of the twelve suns gone.

The Core was as it had been.

'The time spiral turns,' murmured Julius slowly, head bowed. 'It turns away from the fifth node and rotates minutely again though the vaults of eternity.' He slumped to his knees.

Box could see the fire and ice in his eyes was dull, glassy, and now the battle had passed, he saw how his body had been shredded by the Legions' hooks. Chess had been hidden by the walls of the Core, but he hesitated to go to her because he knew that Julius was dying.

'Find her,' said Jake, and he tossed the crowbar to the floor where it landed without a sound. 'Leave Julius to us.' He was joined by Captain Burke and the Scythian and they knelt by the figure that lay flat on the floor of streaming silver.

Gemma was the first to run through the outer wall of the Core and behind her came Box and Anna and then Pacer. Box wasn't sure what to expect. What he had experienced had been so massive that he half-expected Chess not to be there at all, as if she had been used up and had merged into the universes entirely. But she was there, kneeling beside two bodies that Box recognized immediately. He slowed his step as he entered the still emptiness of the Core, faltering as he realized that he appeared to be walking on nothing.

Chess's head was bowed, the long, thick chestnut hair screening her face. Splinter's white-haired head lay on her lap and she was stroking his forehead gently. He was dead, as lifeless as the crystal knives which lay scattered about the transparent surface on which Chess knelt: upon which they all walked.

Box made himself look at Splinter's face, anxious as to what he would find there. To his surprise and his relief, Splinter's features were composed. They were tranquil. In fact, Box could have sworn that about Splinter's mouth, there was a shadow of the smile his brother always wore when he had won an argument.

Box braced himself when Chess looked up. After the way she had been before, and after all that had happened here, he expected that her mind would be broken even if her body remained. It would be worse than her not being here at all. But her face was as tranquil as Splinter's, her eyes liquid cool, and she smiled at Box in a way he hadn't seen her smile in years. Box swallowed because, for a moment, he was taken back to a time when he was a little boy who lived in the tunnels at the wharf, and the thought of what lay ahead of that boy seemed too much. Then he felt Anna kiss his cheek lightly and he grinned.

'Why are you so pleased with yourself?' demanded Chess, but there was happiness in her brown eyes.

Box shrugged and laughed because he couldn't say what he felt.

Gemma hugged Chess. Pacer hung back, knowing that he had done all he could, that he had come as far as he could, but that the journey was over. It felt good though, when Chess's eyes made contact with his and she mouthed the words 'Thank you', and it felt absurdly satisfying when the hirsute and powerful grasp of Commodore Valxata Razool clamped his shoulder and the tall, tough snout nodded his head with approval. He growled something that Pacer didn't understand.

'He says, "Not bad, for a skin",' interpreted Box. Razool flashed Pacer half a muzzle of smile that was so full of long white teeth it should have been terrifying.

Box knelt by Chess. 'Are you OK?'

Chess's eyes held his. 'I'm glad it's done.' She saw Box looking at Splinter.

'I should be upset,' said Box. 'Shouldn't I? But I'm not. He looks happier.' Box shrugged his tired, armoured shoulders.

'We'd lost him, but we've got him back now,' said Chess, and Box felt better just to hear her voice, calm again. 'And he was brilliant, Box. I mean, you wouldn't believe ...' Box caught her shoulders as she began to cry. 'He let himself be killed for us, Box. He saved us. Splinter saved us all.'

Anna was with her, too, and Pacer rubbed his eyes which were scorching hot. Only Razool, leaning on his battle hammer, saw the old lady approaching, an expression of hardboiled patience on his worn face.

'Hello, Commodore,' said Ethel in the dog tongue.

Razool nodded politely and said, 'You look transparent, like a ghost.'

'I suppose I am,' admitted Ethel. 'I'm practically not here any longer.'

Chess was the first to see her, after Razool. 'It's over,' she said. 'And thank you,' she added, almost shyly. 'I know you were there, at the end.'

'Me and a number of the others. But we were only helping out. Washed-up relics at a reunion really.' Ethel smiled, very weakly. 'There are so many souls in the universes,' her voice was faint, breathless, 'and none of them will ever know what they owe to you, my love.'

'To all of us,' said Chess and she frowned. 'What's wrong? You've nearly ... gone.' She was still cradling Splinter's head.

'I'm almost done, dear,' explained Ethel. She looked down at Splinter curiously. 'I had my doubts,' she confessed, 'but

I always knew there was something special about Splinter.'

'You should have told him.' Chess smoothed a lock of white hair.

'He wouldn't let me, dear.' Then Ethel looked at where Saul lay by Chess's side. 'I'm sorry about your brother.'

There were many things Chess could have said, about Saul, about her father, about trust, about betrayal. Instead, she said, 'Don't be sorry, Ethel. You should *thank* my brother.' Then, squeezing Box's hand and cupping Splinter's forehead, Chess said, 'As far as I'm concerned, I've got *three* brothers and you should thank them all.'

Ethel clasped her moth wing hands together and inclined her head towards Saul's body. 'Thank you, Saul.' Then, 'Thank you, Splinter.' Finally she turned to Box. 'Thank you, Box.'

Box wracked his brain for an appropriate response, but before he had got beyond mumbling, 'You're welcome,' Anna had drawn in breath sharply and he felt her weight against him. Chess winced too, then groaned.

Ethel remained unbowed but her watery eyes turned to the wall of the Core. 'The last of the Nephilim has passed,' was all she said.

'Julius?' gasped Chess.

'Julius has gone dear. Nobody lasts forever, you know.'

Even with the ache in her core, Chess scowled up at Ethel. Julius had been with her from the start, in spirit and body. They had been part of each other. His death was a death for her, however matter-of-fact Ethel was about it.

'What happens now?' snapped Chess, breathless, eyes darker.

'Arrangements have been made,' was Ethel's mystifying response.

'*Arrangements?*' repeated Anna suspiciously.

Ethel smiled at Anna sharply. 'I am pleased to see you still possess splendid hearing, Anna,' she said. 'Arrangements have been made to place each of you in suitable circumstances.'

'Like witness protection?' suggested Box.

'No, dear, nothing like witness protection. Think of it more like alternative living: apart from you, Commodore. You still have your family waiting for you.'

'You get to go home, Zool,' said Box, in Razool's language.

'Good.' Razool looked at Box carefully, absorbing every last detail. 'And you will be staying? Here?' A wry smile curled a black lip.

'She says that arrangements have been made.' Box shrugged.

Razool nodded. 'I'll get Skarl and Raxa to round up the troops. There aren't many left. Then, yes, at last I go home.'

'Unless the General has other plans,' observed Box.

'The General always has other plans, but I am going home. For good.' Razool clapped Box's arm, and the two of them shook one another by the shoulder.

'Thanks, Zool,' said Box. He couldn't think of anything else to say.

'Friends,' said Razool. In the dog tongue the word sounded as strong, as powerful as its meaning. 'Always friends.'

'Yeah,' said Box. 'Friends.'

Then Razool slung the hammer over his shoulder like a

pick, nodded at the humans and walked away through the shimmering wall of the Core, and although Box thought of him often after that, he never saw him, or Skarl or Raxa, again.

Anna wanted to say that she had family waiting for her, but she knew that she hadn't. She had chosen a different path a long time ago. Life wasn't always the way you'd like to write it, and her family had gone now, or she had gone from them. But she wanted to know what Ethel meant by 'arrangements'.

'What's going to happen to us, Ethel?' she asked. 'What alternative lives will we be living?'

'I don't have time to go into the details,' flustered the old lady, whose transparency was increasing. 'There are so many different universes. We'll slot you all in somewhere nice, for the time being. The Sages know what to do.' She held up a hand, small and see-through. 'You'll all manage very well; you've just saved the universes for goodness sake. You might even be happy,' although she was careful to add, 'for a while, at least,' as if including the small print.

'And *this* is over?' asked Chess, looking about the Core. She wanted this reassurance at least. 'We've finished?'

'You can't ever stop being what you are, my love,' cautioned Ethel, voice diminishing. 'None of you can stop that. But this is over ... for now.' She smiled, more wraith-like than before. The silver walls were visible brightly through her shadowy form.

'For *now*?' protested Chess. Ethel smiled back like a hospital visitor: an almost transparent hospital visitor. 'No. Wait,' insisted Chess. 'You can't just vanish.' There was so much she didn't know. Always, there was so much she didn't know.

'I can. I must,' whispered Ethel. Her little outline was barely visible. 'You could say I'm all used up. My part is ...'

'Wait,' demanded Chess.

'... over,' came the final word, and then, where the old lady had been standing, there was nothing.

CHAPTER 20

The woman in the jade suit looked nearly thirty years old, but if you looked close, you could see that her large hazel eyes were kindled by more than thirty years of living. She was smartly dressed but not ostentatious, and the only piece of jewellery that she wore was a tiny horse's head in jet that hung from a plain silver chain about her neck. There was nothing to show that when she had been much, *much* younger, she had lived in a wharf, by a river, in a city where children like that were called street rats. Nothing, apart from the eyes.

The woman sat at a table in a busy bar with five other men and women: young, *genuinely* young, professional, casual. They spoke quickly, excitedly and they laughed a lot. The woman's hair was long and thick and her chestnut curls were so unruly that when she laughed, she had the habit of brushing them away from her face.

'Hey, Esme, I'm going to the bar. Can I get you a drink?'

The table was already crowded with glasses and bottles and the salvage of cocktails.

She smiled up at the man. 'No thanks, Chris, I have to go.'

'We're going for some food,' said the woman sitting next to her, as if that might tempt her to stay out.

'I'll skip the food tonight,' she said with an easy smile and stood, lifting her jacket from the seat back.

'But it's your birthday,' said the man whose name was Chris.

'I'm saving my energy for the next hundred,' laughed the woman. 'And I've got stuff to do. Work.' She wrinkled her nose at the groans of derision and laughed again. 'It's *late*.'

'We're only just getting started,' said somebody else.

But it was late. It was time to go. And whilst a city like New York would never say it was time for bed, and even though it was a Friday night, she had work lined up for Saturday morning. True, she didn't need much sleep, and she could drink what she liked without ever getting drunk, but her staff needed a break from the boss, even if it was meant to be her birthday. They needed to enjoy themselves without her there. They'd only be young once, and for such a short time.

'Goodnight, Esme.'

Everybody kissed. Everybody said 'Goodnight'. Everybody kissed again. Then she pulled on the jacket, grabbed her bag and moved swiftly through the loud customers before stepping into the street, heels clicking brusquely.

She was no stranger to city streets and she knew the quickest way home through these ones. Taking bin-lined alleys and slipping beneath the fire escapes round the backs of small hotels, she could cut through the city blocks with no need for the expense of a cab, and with far greater speed.

There were hazards of course: thieves, robbers, ugly drunks. A pair of gloved thugs slipped out of a doorway now, homing in on the sharp step of a woman walking these unlit backstreets alone. They homed in close enough to see the horse's head and the bright eyes, close enough to smell the scent she wore.

'Don't,' she said, not slowing her stride, and the men *didn't* because in the moment that they stepped close, they felt their nerves ice and, with the feral sense of the gutter, they knew that here was someone who could damn them a good deal worse than they were damned already.

She emerged from the backstreets and marched through the front atrium of the apartment block where she lived currently. The security guard greeted her with a warm, 'Hi, Esme. How ya doin'?'

She smiled, stopped, spent a little time asking him whether he had recovered from his most recent disaster on the horses, gave him a tip that made him rich for a week and then she took the lift up to her apartment. As she did so, she eyed the woman who stared back at her from the mirror, eyed her with a critical regard, and she subdued the sudden desire to breathe on the glass and write her name.

'Too much lipstick,' she murmured, wondering whether she had ever got over the impact made upon her by Klinky Mallows's lavish use of make-up. 'And messy hair.' Everybody said they loved her hair, but for as long as she could remember, she'd had unruly hair that curled with a determination that made order impossible.

The lift door pinged open. Her tread along the corridor was soft. She entered her apartment, throwing her jacket and bag onto an armchair, then taking a jug of iced water from the fridge and pouring herself a glass. She didn't get drunk but she did get thirsty.

The apartment was spacious, uncluttered save for the few items she had chosen to display: some old leather books; a lotus carved from ivory; a Japanese screen; two ceramic vases boldly faced with Miro designs; an impressionist watercolour on one wall and, on the wall opposite, a huge canvas, modern, with simple geometric shapes and plain tones. The general absence of literature suggested that here lived someone who had never really enjoyed reading. It was plain that what really mattered to the occupant of the apartment were photographs. Framed photographs filled the empty shelves of a solitary bookcase.

They were photographs of Gemma, mostly. A lot of the photographs were of the two of them together: out riding; holidaying; working with the contractors on the first street mission for homeless children; opening the next; the two of them receiving awards; meeting dignitaries; Gemma with her teeth fixed; Gemma growing older, hair drifting from blonde to grey, but always smiling with blue eyes that were so alive, even in those last years.

She didn't switch on the lights. Sometimes the dark was easier, felt softer. She turned up the music and cast an eye towards the bedroom door. Behind that door was the relative comfort of scruffiness. But there were a couple of items to deal with before she could rest. She put the glass on the desk, dropped into the chair and turned on the computer. Then she gazed out of the glass wall, letting the comings and goings of the city traffic carry her mind.

'Happy birthday, Gemma,' she whispered.

Why would she celebrate her *own* birthday? She didn't even know its date and, anyway, she'd spent decades hiding how old she really was. But she made sure always that Gemma's birthday was celebrated, even if she had to pretend it was hers. She'd been pretending it was hers for more than twenty years now. Gemma wouldn't have minded. Gemma would have found it funny.

She closed her eyes and listened to Pacer. He wasn't the best singer that had ever cut an album but Gemma had liked this track most of all so it seemed the right track to listen to tonight. She wasn't sure whether it was blues or rock but it had been popular. Pacer's guitar playing and his voice had made him wealthy and happy and, whenever they used to meet, he'd play his guitar for her and Gemma and sing like that was all they'd ever done. Nobody talked about the time before. He'd played for them until his fingers had become too arthritic to hold a guitar, and even though he'd been dead for years now, for longer than Gemma, the memories they had shared in this world were all happy ones. It had been good to have friends like that.

Her eyes had closed. She was more tired than she realized. But tomorrow morning there would be a meeting with the backers of the next two South American street missions and she had requested that the necessary finance plans be prepared, so she rubbed her eyes and then clicked open her emails.

Two items down there was a message which arrested her breathing: which almost stopped her heart.

FOR THE ATTENTION OF CHESS TUESDAY.

She took a long, slow gulp of iced water. Chess Tuesday. That was a name she hadn't used for over ninety years. But it had been the name given to her in the other place, before the Sages had arranged the alternative living for her and the others, in this place. Before she'd chosen to use her grandmother's name.

She tapped her short fingernails on the top of the desk, then clicked the message open. There was a pause and then a trill of laughter from the speaker. She sat bolt upright, her heart thumping against her ribs.

'Lemuel?' Her voice was older than when she had last used that name. Huskier. But it was *her* voice.

'Chess! How wonderful, and after all this time.' The screen was a blank.

'What are you doing here? What are you doing in there?'

'Questions, questions, always so many questions,' tittered the voice of Lemuel Sprazkin.

'I'm busy, Lemuel,' said Chess, severely.

'You have become *important*,' said Lemuel. 'Not that you weren't, before.'

Chess frowned at the computer. There was a time when Lemuel wrapped her up in his games. Now she could either switch him off or rip whatever passed for his mind out of existence altogether. But neither were necessary at the moment. 'I try to help street children,' she said.

'Ooh, just like me,' rhapsodized Lemuel.

'I'm still waiting to hear what you're doing here.'

'This is where I have been for a very long time. Ever since I was separated from my body, which remains goodness knows where, I have been housed in this world: in cyberspace. Roaming what the people here call the world wide web. Causing all sorts of trouble.' He giggled confidentially. 'People are ever so naughty when they think nobody's watching. Sometimes, I help to get them into trouble.'

'And why are you here now?' But Chess felt uncomfortable because she sensed where this was heading.

'Part of the terms of the new-world arrangement with the Sages was to keep my distance from you, until . . .' and Lemuel hesitated with excessive melodrama.

'Until what, Lemuel?' But with a sense of gravity that dragged her spirit down, she knew what he was about to say.

'Until,' continued Lemuel, and Chess could imagine his flourish of a smile, 'the new spirit has been found. A child.'

Chess sighed, long and slow. In a part of her mind that she had kept as closed as possible, she had known that sooner or later, something like this would happen. And already, she knew what she would do about it. It was as if she had always known what she would do about it and had just been waiting.

'It's all part of the endless, pan-universal cycle . . .'

'Be quiet, Lemuel.' Chess cut him off. Words like that made her mind ache as if they were rubbing deep into old wounds. Lemuel fell silent at once. With some surprise, Chess realized that he no longer dared to tease and cajole her as he once did. That was good, and maybe it was a little bit sad too.

'I'm glad you're OK, Lemuel,' she said after a minute's silent thought. She would have to make arrangements. The

Sanctuary Foundation, the charitable institution set up by Gemma and Chess to run the street missions, would have to be managed by the board without such regular contact with her. But she didn't want to stop working with the missions. She sighed. 'Where is the child?' she asked.

'You sound so much older,' observed Lemuel, before saying, 'In a country called Spain.'

Chess closed her eyes, breathed deeply and let her mind extend in a way it hadn't done in decades. But it was simple to find the child now she had been alerted to her. Or him. The presence was so strong to feel, it was easy to find. That was the problem.

'How did you know?' she began.

'The Sages are meant to be politically neutral,' said Lemuel. 'But the universes look after their own. We can think of this as the universes giving us a head start.'

'There is no Symmetry,' considered Chess.

'No, you disposed of every last trace of them, present company excepted. But,' cautioned Lemuel, 'there will always be dangers rising when the universes settle on a human spirit. The darkness will always find a new way of being. After all, the darkness is as much a part of the universes as *you*.'

'Can you contact the others?' asked Chess, brusquely.

'Yes.' Carefully, Lemuel added, 'It is, if you don't mind my saying so, a little strange how you have kept your distance from one another.'

'It's not strange if you're one of us,' murmured Chess. All of this was resurrecting so much: so much that she had lived without for so long.

'Anna and Box work in the refugee camps, don't they?' Lemuel was saying.

Chess nodded automatically. 'Sub-Saharan crisis management. I find out about them, from time to time. They look after people. Contact them, Lemuel, please. Let them know I need to meet them where the child lives.'

'Splendid! I have become your project manager.'

'Thanks Lemuel.' Chess stood, but before she left the computer she said, 'I'm sorry, about what happened, out on the reachings ...'

'Please do not apologize,' said Lemuel. 'I've been having far too much fun in here for you to feel guilty about me. Are you leaving now?'

'Shortly.' Chess headed towards the bedroom door. 'There's something I have to do first.'

'Ah, yes. Of course. Should have remembered: it was my handiwork after all. Don't forget to send her my love.'

But Chess had already entered the bedroom, shutting the door behind her.

Inside a cabinet by her clothing-strewn bed there was a steel box. It possessed no lid and had no opening, not even a keyhole. It was a box that only Chess could access and she had never felt the need to do so before. But now, for the first time since her Uncle Phoenix had given it to her at the time of her relocation to this world, she put her hand inside. She slipped it through the metal casing with no more difficulty than pushing it through water. She knew what her fingers would find: three crystal knives, two locks of hair, one white and one black, a carved horse's head and a curiously warm bangle. Chess enclosed the bangle in her hand, re-plotted its atomic fields, drew it out of the steel box and reconstituted it back into the bangle.

It was slim and made of a milky-purple glass set about a gold hoop and fastened with a small gold clasp. It was called a parallax bangle. Chess had used one before: Lemuel had made that one, just as it appeared he had made this one. It would contain her blood, taken from a time past, and its operation was simple. By slipping it on and turning the clasp, minute teeth on the inside of the bangle would bite upon her skin, mixing her blood now with the blood of years ago and taking her back for a matter of minutes to the time and the place where that blood had been taken.

'It will take you to Ethel,' Phoenix had explained to her. 'Should you ever wish to see her.' But, until now, Chess had not wanted anything to do with that past. And she had not needed to see Ethel. If she was honest with herself, she hadn't really wanted to see Ethel.

Warily she put the bangle on, turned the gold clasp and the tiny teeth prickled her wrist.

Chess opened her eyes. The room was small and illuminated by the orange glow of the one-bar electric heater. There was a sharp tang of cat and the click of needles knitting industriously. She was lying under a blanket on the cramped confines of a sofa. Box was lying head to toe with her and Splinter was lying on the floor beside them, also under a blanket.

She realized that this was the night when Ethel had first brought them to her flat. She stayed still for a moment because she was so close to Box and Splinter and she had never expected to be so close to them both again. She knew that here, she was eleven and Box and Splinter were both fourteen: they had so much ahead of them and they didn't know any of it yet. Ethel sat in an armchair by the fire, knitting, and her cats, Argus and Sekhmet, were curled around her ankles. Rain clattered against the window.

Chess sat up.

'Oh!' Ethel was startled. She plonked her knitting on her lap. 'You made it.' Then, gathering her composure, she beamed at Chess, 'And how splendid to see that we triumph.'

'It wasn't easy,' said Chess, emphatically.

'It never is, dear. But it is *so* encouraging to meet you like this.' Then Ethel frowned to herself. 'Now I just have to make certain that everything happens the right way round,' and she chewed her lip. 'Your appearing here is like finding the answer to a cryptic crossword, but that isn't the same as me knowing the answers to the clues in the first place.'

Chess inspected her own thin arms. 'It's weird, being eleven again. I feel . . . looser, like I might be about to fall off something.' Then she took the opportunity to stroke Box's cheek, and she leant over the edge of the sofa and kissed Splinter's forehead tenderly enough not to wake him.

'You're only borrowing this moment,' Ethel warned her. 'Be very careful not to disturb *anything*. The you that's sleeping here tonight won't remember any of this when she wakes up properly.' She produced a pin from her lapel and held it for Chess to see. 'May I? I'm going to need a speck of blood for Lemuel to use if this meeting is actually going to happen one day.'

'Wait until I've gone,' said Chess. 'Then, if I wake, I won't know what's happened.'

'Good idea,' agreed Ethel. She sat back into her chair and blinked at Chess. Argus and Sekhmet blinked at her too. 'So, how are you, dear? Or how are you going to be?' She laughed a little nervously, 'I'm not sure which it is.'

'Busy,' said Chess, surprised by her high voice and her filthy hands. 'The Sages re-lifed me in a universe a lot like this one. They made sure I had money. I got some education. I went into business.'

'Business!' Ethel's grey eyebrows rose above her spectacle frames. '*You?*'

'Very successfully,' Chess said airily. 'It wasn't difficult. I went into investment banking. It's easy when you're good at guessing the future.'

'I never found the future all that easy to predict,' confessed Ethel.

Chess inspected the ends of her hair, surprised at the state it was in. It was unsettling how much she had forgotten. She poked a foot out from under the blanket, making sure not to nudge Box. It was a very dirty foot with a sole as tough as shoe leather.

'So have you made a lot of money, dear?' enquired Ethel.

Chess nodded. 'It funds the Sanctuary Foundation. We house street children. Provide healthcare and education. *Internationally*.'

Ethel humphed. 'Don't get all sanctimonious with *me*, dear. It's not as if I spent several millennia doing nothing.'

Chess was hurt. 'I thought you might be a bit proud. That's all. It's not as if I can boast about it to anyone else, is it?'

'I'm sorry, dear. I am. I must be in a state of shock, that's all.' Ethel smiled. 'A happy state of shock.' She eyed Chess thoughtfully. 'I assume you're about to start the work yourself now.'

Chess knew what Ethel meant by 'the work'.

'It's what you're here for.' Ethel scratched her head. 'Or *there* for. This is quite confusing.'

'I've not come to ask about the work,' said Chess. 'I want to know about Box and Splinter.' She yawned. Time was running out already.

'What would you like to know?' asked Ethel, exhibiting little genuine enthusiasm for the making of revelations.

'Who are they?'

'They are brothers. Twin brothers. But I dare say you will have discovered that they're not actually *your* brothers.'

'They're brothers to me,' said Chess proudly, and this time only one of Ethel's eyebrows ventured above the frame of her spectacles. Chess thought that there was the swiftest of glances towards Splinter's silently sleeping form. Box broke the quiet with a rumbustious snore.

'Don't tell me anything of what *will* happen,' Ethel warned Chess.

'I know. I know,' Chess assured her. 'It would give you knowledge that would interfere with what should happen, which would mean that none of it might happen at all.'

'Older *and* wiser,' approved Ethel. 'A combination rarely encountered.'

'Box and Splinter,' Chess reminded her, stifling another yawn.

Ethel fidgeted with her knitting as she spoke. 'When we decided to place you in safety . . .'

'The Elms Orphanage was *safety*?' Chess struggled to contain her derision.

'It was the best we could do in the circumstances. May I continue? Thank you. We knew that we wouldn't be able to watch you all the time, but the Committee needed to ensure that you could survive, whatever happened, wherever you went, even if we lost you, which we did, for a while.'

'Go on,' urged Chess. The time was fast diminishing.

'It was my idea to give you a brother. We searched for a likely candidate: a street child of the right age with the appropriate degree of cunning and courage, of sufficient *survivability*, you might say. Able to take care of you when we couldn't.' The old lady tapped her fingertips together. 'It was impossible to find one such child, but we located twins who, between them, appeared to possess the traits required.' She looked at the sleeping boys with what could have been classified as mild affection. 'What a pair! We wiped their memories, synaptic flushing Lemuel called it, then placed you at the Elms. For which I do offer an overdue apology. Sorry.'

Chess lay down. 'They were good brothers,' she said.

'So it seems,' conceded Ethel, with mild surprise, 'though from what I've seen so far, I wouldn't expect you lot to fight your way out of a quilt cover without making it look like a bag of cats.' Sekhmet flicked her tail. 'Now, as for the work ...'

'No, Ethel.' Chess shook her head. 'This will happen my way now.'

'But the cycles ...'

'No.' Chess fought off sleep. She wanted to let Ethel know

how she felt: she owed her that. 'No more cycles. No more births and re-births. No more spirits carrying the fate of the universes.' She yawned and tried to make herself comfortable on the small space that Box didn't occupy. 'This child is going to have a life. A real life.'

Ethel puffed out her cheeks. 'But all of this has happened before.'

Chess smiled at the old lady. 'Maybe. But if I have my way, Ethel, none of this will happen again.'

Ethel sighed and shook her head. 'It will be your world, dear. I will have passed on.' She held up the pin between waxy, pink fingers. 'It's time for you to wake up. So you'd better go, if you see what I mean.' She smiled at Chess, really smiled. 'I am so looking forward to this little chat, if it happens again.'

Chess put out a small, dirty hand and held Ethel's wrist. 'Don't be too hard on Splinter,' she said, but Ethel stopped her dead with a finger over her lips.

'Sh. Say nothing. I mustn't know *anything* more if this moment is ever to happen. If we are to get this far.'

But there was something else Chess needed to know, had to know. 'My name,' she breathed, sinking fast. 'My real name. What is my real name?'

The old lady bent forwards and whispered in her ear. 'Chess, my love. Your name always was Chess. It's who you are,' and she knelt by the sofa, stroking her hair gently.

Chess felt the force of time drawing her back, pulling her away from the fusty room in the dingy little flat, pulling her away from Box and Splinter, away from Ethel, and for a moment she wanted to stay there, tucked away from everything. And as the past sank back into the past, she wanted desperately to say goodbye to Ethel, wanted to say 'Thank you', though for what she wasn't sure. And when she found herself sitting on her own bed, heavy with a sadness she couldn't place, she knew that beyond time, in another universe, a little girl woke sobbing and not knowing why.

In the foothills of the Alpujarras there are villages built of white stone. Houses sit along the sun-beaten hilltops like worn teeth, overlooking rough meadows of hot grass. Only the brittle clang of church bells cracks the afternoon silence of the narrow streets.

Chess sat in this stillness. The interior of the bar was cool and smelt of coffee. Her own small cup had been drunk hours ago. The monotonous buzz of football commentary from the wall-mounted television disturbed the quiet. Two shepherds in patched jackets sat at a table by the door and said nothing. They regarded Chess from beneath deeply scored brows and from time to time, they smoked.

Outside, the sun blazed the street white.

Even though she hadn't stopped watching the door, it still felt as if she'd been woken abruptly when the man and woman entered the bar. She felt their presence at once: they filled the room far beyond the short reach of their cool, dark shadows.

'Chess!' Box pulled off his sunglasses and grinned at her. His jeans were dusty and he wore a red check shirt with the sleeves rolled up and a loose khaki scarf around his neck.

His hair was still soot black and short and his face was tanned.

Chess hadn't been sure how this would go, but without thinking, she and Box embraced. His strong body felt good.

Anna's solemn beauty hadn't diminished. Like Box, she looked nearer forty than ninety, and her eyes were sapphire blue, her hair raven. She kissed Chess, touched her face and said, 'I knew we'd meet up, when it was time.'

With a scraping of chairs, they sat. The shepherds lit up and watched with blank interest.

'You're ageing well,' said Anna.

'I thought you'd be older,' Chess said to Box.

Box laughed and looked at Anna. 'She donated me some blood,' he said, 'so I could keep up with her.'

'Without Julius, we still age,' said Anna. 'But it's slow, so we get to have our fill of fun.' Chess noticed how they looked at each other a lot. Happy. Really happy. And full of energy.

Box leant down and rapped his lower leg with his knuckles. 'The leg's still as good as new, though.' Chess stole a glimpse under the table and caught the flash of metal.

'You look amazing, Chess,' said Anna. 'I guess that in the immortality stakes, you have the edge.'

Chess wasn't sure what to say. She never was when people told her how good she looked. 'I get my hair cut now,' she said. 'Sometimes.'

'Could have fooled me.' Box rubbed his chin and Chess noticed the shadow of the tap beneath the skin graft over his elbow.

'You've done a brilliant job with Sanctuary.' Anna was serious. All three of them knew how children mattered. And all of them knew that in this world, just like all the others, a lot of them were treated as if they didn't.

'How are the camps?' asked Chess.

'Tough,' said Anna and then she smiled at Box. 'Which is why *we* work there. Isn't that right, honey?'

'We work with the refugees. With displaced populations. There are a lot of warlords who make money out of blocking aid.' Box licked his teeth, which reminded Chess of something she couldn't place immediately. 'When the aid can't get through, or when there's a kidnap, they send us in.' He smiled at Chess. 'We negotiate with the warlords.'

'Yeah' laughed Anna. 'Extreme negotiation.' She turned to Box and they kissed and, as their lips met, Chess saw a circle of Land Rovers, armed gunmen sitting on sacks of grain, heard Anna and Box arguing with them, heard a weapon cocked. Then there were blades. Movement. A flurry of blows. One less warlord and his henchmen. Blood streaking the Land Rovers.

'Starving people shouldn't go hungry,' said Box. 'No excuses. When there's a blockage in the food chain, we clear it.'

There was a long silence before Anna said, 'Lemuel contacted us. I guess it's starting all over?'

Chess shook her head. 'Nothing's starting all over.'

'OK,' said Anna cautiously. 'So is this just a ninety-year reunion?' She glanced about the bar. 'Great venue. A bit low on guests, though.'

'The child's here,' said Chess. 'We need to identify her. Or him.'

'And then?' enquired Anna.

Chess took a deep breath, studied her fingers. 'Then we let her live. I mean, *really* live. Have a life. No wars. No games. No pan-dimensional tricks. Just live.' She looked at Anna and then Box. 'Like we didn't.'

Anna nodded, solemnly. 'I understand. I do.'

'We just leave her?' asked Box. 'Or him?'

Chess shook her head again. A spirit like this couldn't go unguarded: she knew what had happened to Esme. 'We protect her. We watch over her.'

'Or him,' added Box.

'Or him,' continued Chess. 'But we break this never-ending cycle of who saves the universes. We need to break this . . . this prison.'

'You seem to feel pretty strongly about it,' said Box.

'None of this is happening again,' she said.

'I'm all for that,' said Anna with a wry smile.

Chess stood. 'Come on. It's time to find whoever this is.'

They walked out into the glare. Chess took her sunglasses out of the inside pocket of her leather jacket and pushed them on. 'Up there.' She pointed to the church, a little further along the street. 'We can see everything from up there and no one'll notice us. People don't notice what they don't expect to see.'

They found the darkness of a narrow alley, from where they moved to the church roof. It was easy: slip open the space, rearrange it, enter the target point, put it all back together again. But in the move through the dimensions, Chess felt the watching, heard the whispering out of the darkness, and knew that they weren't the only ones interested in this remote village.

—[380]—

'Feel that?' asked Box, as they emerged onto the roof. He had noticed it too.

'That's why we're here,' said Chess. This is what we protect you from, she thought, trying to sense the spirit they were here for. She looked out over the village and the sun glared off every surface.

There was a small square. The perimeter was lined with low benches and a couple of stubby trees. It sat just below the church, hot and flat and speckled with red grit. There was a boy crossing it and behind him came three more. The three shouted to the one, taunting him.

'Is it one of those?' asked Box, leaning over a weathered urn moulding.

Chess shook her head and frowned as she scanned the area. 'But it's near,' she whispered.

A fight broke out. Three against one.

'No,' hissed Anna, pulling Box back. 'They're kids.'

'I was only going to stop them.'

'*There.*' Chess didn't need to point. All of them noticed the child who had come from an alleyway between the houses on the far side of the square.

'It's a boy,' commented Box with pleasure.

'You'd make a lovely midwife,' muttered Anna. 'And girls are easier. Smarter. So this one will take more looking after than we expected.'

'Nice one,' grinned Box as the boy stepped in and broke up the fight. But before the fight was over, he'd taken a punch to his mouth and Chess could see the blood, even from the church roof.

'At least we've found him,' she sighed. She waited until

the other children had left the square. The boy walked to one of the benches and sat down. He licked a finger and investigated the cut.

Chess felt Anna's hand on her shoulder. 'We'll wait here,' said Anna.

'OK.' Chess moved to the alleyway, then crossed the square to where the boy sat. She offered him her handkerchief to wipe his face.

'*Usted es valiente*,' she said. You are brave.

He took the handkerchief and dabbed his mouth. His eyes were dark brown and his hair was as black as Anna's.

'*Cómo te llames?*' What's your name? she asked him. Had she spoken Spanish before? She didn't think she had. But languages came easily when your mind was in touch with so much of the universes at once.

'Miguel.' He squinted up at her and she sat down.

Chess smiled, asked Miguel his age, discovered he was ten years old. He wiped his face in silence and the sun hammered down.

'You are very beautiful,' said the boy. Chess understood him perfectly and she blushed, even though he was only ten. He pointed up to the church. 'You came from up there?'

'You saw me?' He had surprised her.

'Yes. I saw all three of you. I see everything.'

Chess smiled. 'You are a very special boy,' she said.

'Who are you?'

Chess wondered how best to say what she wanted to say. The boy's chocolate eyes were unflinching. She replied, 'I'm your guardian angel.'

'My guardian angel.' He grinned at her then. 'Good. Can I go now?'

Chess felt a tightness in her throat. 'Of course.'

'And you'll look out for me?'

'*Siempre.*' Always.

Miguel walked away. He didn't look back. And although he could see things that other people did not, he never saw Chess again. But he never forgot her. He knew that she was there, particularly at the shadow times of his life. He became a composer with an extraordinary ability to touch minds, to unite them with his music. He had a family and, when he died, he never doubted that he had met his guardian angel in the square of the village where he had been born.

After Miguel, there were others. Together with Box and Anna, Chess watched. They protected: it was what they were there for. And Chess knew that always, the darkness was there too. Waiting, just as she was waiting. The battle was never over: Ethel had been right about that. And the darkness was clever: it brooded, it planned, it took fresh and unexpected forms, pursued novel strategies. But Chess ensured that there was no one to play its games. No grand conflicts. No universal gambles. Maybe the darkness was given space. Maybe there were moments when the darkness triumphed, but that was the price of real life. Of choice. Of freedom. And when time hung heavy on Box and Anna, they didn't wait for it to drag them to dust. They were warriors and they chose a warrior's death, together. Theirs was a fine death.

Chess had always known what it was to be alone, really alone. Alone, she continued her work, *her* way. Life was too precious to be spent playing games with the universes. Nobody asked to be placed at the Core. Nobody wanted eternity to be carried on their shoulders. Chess knew this better than anyone. And as long as her spirit was able, she would never allow it to happen again.

'Have I broken the cycle?' she asked Gemma, sometimes, mulling over their photographs. 'The grand cycle of pan-universal, cross-dimensional conflict? The great cataclysms?'

Of course she had broken the cycle.

'I was once a street rat,' she told one little girl. 'Not that you'll know what one of those is. But I broke the rules.'

'Is it good to break rules?' the little girl asked.

'It's good to break the *bad* ones,' Chess told her. 'However big they are,' and she patted the little girl's hand and then whispered to her, 'Be free to choose. To choose and to love.' Chess had learnt that those were the greatest things, the human things: the things that would always defeat the darkness in the end. Saul had taught her this.

But spirits fade. Some spirits are stronger than others, Professor Breslaw had said. He had been right: but nothing lasts forever. And when Chess found that her own spirit was fading, found that age had wormed its way beyond her decrepit body, found that the task of calculating and predicting and battling had drained her to emptiness, she knew that her time had passed.

There would be others. Always there would be others. But she was over. Did she lie down? She wasn't sure how this ended. So many memories washed back, so many faces: Anna, Saul, Pacer, Gemma, Ethel, Balthazar, Boris, Clarity and the song she sang. But when Chess closed her eyes for the last time, her thoughts were of a fine man called Box, and a boy called Splinter who had proved that nothing is lost forever.

ACKNOWLEDGEMENTS

Nearly everything which happens in the world of the Bad Tuesdays is possible, or it will be. The events in the books are rooted in science: in string theory, parallel universes, black holes, quantum physics, quantum computers, robotics, bio-engineering and of course, that slippery, mind-contorting concept called time. I'm not a scientist but there are scientists who write brilliantly about these things. If you take a look inside Michio Kaku's *Hyperspace* or *Physics of the Impossible*, or David Deutsch's *The Fabric of Reality*, or Stephen Hawking's *A Brief History of Time*, you'll see that what happens in the world of the Bad Tuesdays has its roots in what happens in our world. I'm grateful for the ideas and the excitement given to me by these scientists and others like them.

I'd like to thank Fiona Kennedy and her team at Orion Children's Books for ensuring that the Tuesdays' story could be told, and published. In particular, I want to express my gratitude to my editors, Jon Appleton and Amber Caravéo: to Jon for spotting the Tuesdays in the first place, to Amber for helping them to the end of their journey and to them both for their enthusiastic support and astute guidance.

Before meeting Crazy Boris, I knew nothing about guitars so I'd like to thank Alfie 'Fingers' Chism for explaining the basics. The list of family, friends and my children's friends who have followed the Tuesdays would be very long and inevitably incomplete but their excitement and encouragement has been terrific. My mother and father taught me to love books. Juliet, my wife, has lived with someone who is a busy lawyer *and* from time to time a full-time writer, with love, patience and incredible support. And my own children have been committed guardians of my fictional children for so many years that I know Chess, Box and Splinter would thank them if they could.

Benjamin J. Myers
Cheshire 2012

Don't miss the other books in THE BAD TUESDAYS
sequence . . .

Children everywhere are disappearing.

Orphan, Chess Tuesday, and her brothers, Box and
Splinter, don't want to be next. But they are being tracked by
two powerful enemy organizations, each intent on destroying
the other . . .

Who is good and who is evil? Why do both sides need the
Tuesdays? And can anyone escape the Hunters? Chess, Box
and Splinter are about to embark on a terrifying mission to
find out.

Time is running out.

Chess and her brothers, Box and Splinter, are caught in a bitter struggle between two ruthless organizations.

Now they face a terrifying choice – carry out a dangerous mission for the Committee, or try to outrun the evil Twisted Symmetry alone.

Chess wants to take the mission. But it could prove fatal. And it will lead the Tuesdays into the heart of the very organization that is hunting them ...

Chess Tuesday is on the run . . .

And the deadly Twisted Symmetry are not far behind. They've already hunted down and imprisoned her brothers, Box and Splinter.

In a world where neither friends, enemies nor family are what they seem, trust is not an option. And Chess is about to discover that the truth may be more dangerous than she ever thought possible.

Splinter Tuesday is hungry for power. And he has a daring plan to get it – if he can stay alive!

His brother, Box, is fighting for his life on a distant planet.

His sister, Chess, is learning to walk between the worlds. Only then will she be ready to take on the evil Twisted Symmetry – and win.

But the Twisted Symmetry has plans of its own. Time is running out. Splinter, Box and Chess have never been in more danger.

Chess Tuesday is powerful.

She alone can save the world from destruction – but she has been captured by the evil Twisted Symmetry.

Splinter Tuesday is also in their clutches.

Only Box is free to help his sister, but he is a universe away, in a world where vast armies fight a war that has lasted thousands of years.

And then there's Anna – a girl with spectacular skills of her own.

Can these two fighters find a way to outwit their enemies, save Chess and save the world?